Composers of North America

Series Editors: John Beckwith, Sam Dennison, William C. Loring, Jr., Margery M. Lowens, Martha Furman Schleifer

Henry Holden Huss at about age forty. From *Half Hours with the Best Composers,* ed. Karl Klauser (Boston: J. B. Millet, 1894), pt. 12, p. 574. Courtesy of the Library of Congress.

HENRY HOLDEN HUSS
An American Composer's Life

by
Gary A. Greene

Composers of North America, No. 13

The Scarecrow Press, Inc.
Metuchen, N.J., & London
1995

Based upon the author's doctoral dissertation, *The Life and Music of Henry Holden Huss,* University of Maryland, College Park, 1987.

British Library Cataloguing-in-Publication data available

Library of Congress Cataloging-in-Publication Data

Greene, Gary A., 1952–
    Henry Holden Huss : an American composer's life / Gary A.
Greene.
        p.   cm.—(Composers of North America ; no. 13)
    Revision of the author's doctoral dissertation The Life and music
of Henry Holden Huss.
    Includes bibliographical references and index.
    ISBN 0-8108-2842-1 (acid-free paper)
    1. Huss, Henry Holden, 1862–1953.   2. Composers—United
States—Biography.   I. Title.   II. Series.
ML410.H977G7   1995
780'.92—dc20
[B]   93-46910

Manufactured in the United States of America

Printed on acid-free paper

CONTENTS

FOREWORD

The Series on Composers of North America is designed to focus attention on the development of art music and folk music from colonial times to the present. Few composers of art music before 1975 had their works performed frequently during their lifetime. Many suffered undeserved neglect.

Each volume consists of a substantial essay about the composer and a complete catalog of compositions, published and unpublished. Part I deals with the composer's life and works in the context of the artistic thought and the musical world of his or her time. In Part II the goals of the composer and critical comments by contemporaries are included, as are illustrations and musical examples. Some works which merit performance today are singled out for analysis and discussion. In Part III the catalog of the composer's output has full publication details, and locations of unpublished works are given. We hope that this series will make readers conscious and appreciative of our North American musical heritage.

The books are also intended to help performers and teachers seeking works to use. For them we designed the Part III catalog of the composer's music to allow a quick search for works the author finds of historic or current interest that may be considered for readings and hearings.

Series Editors:
John Beckwith, Sam Dennison, William C. Loring, Jr., Margery M. Lowens, Martha Furman Schleifer

PREFACE

This book is a condensed second look at my doctoral dissertation, *The Life and Music of Henry Holden Huss.* It is important for the reader to know this up front, as there are some underlying assumptions in this book predicated on that fact. The goal in preparing the present manuscript has been to provide a readable introduction to this composer. Consequently most of the obvious trappings of scholarly or academic writing have been removed. One finds, for example, few footnotes. The abbreviated citations in the text are meant to guide the interested reader to the bibliography, while not slowing down the reader unconcerned with such matters. The reader may wish to consult the dissertation when more detailed documentation is required.

Academia also demanded a comprehensiveness not appropriate here. This book is part of a series on composers, so discussions of Huss as a teacher, as a performer, and as a writer on musical matters have been severely circumscribed. Similarly the bibliography has been condensed in order to focus on matters of composition though giving a nod to these other areas of Huss's professional life. I have generally omitted standard reference works (such as *The New Grove Dictionary of Music and Musicians*) or general histories and music bibliographies. Again, the reader should consult the dissertation when more information is desired.

Another change is the result of this being a kind of "second edition." I have continued to look into Huss materials, primary and secondary. Thus one finds some items here that were not known to me at the first writing, and I have made connections the second time around that were missed the first time. Moreover, there are some areas of uncertainty (particularly in the catalog of works) about which I have revised my opinion.

It is vital that a study take full advantage of all the original source material. We are fortunate to have in Huss's case a supply of concert programs, reviews, letters, and other items, present in both quantity and quality, on which to draw. Such a rich trove makes this study of Huss valuable in itself as well as of great significance to scholars in related American music studies.

The primary source is the immense collection of Huss materials in the Performing Arts Research Center at the New York Public Library. Richard Jackson, Head of the Americana Division of the Research Center, told me that the Huss materials came to the Center through the efforts of Barton Cantrell (1930–1985), a musician and collector of musical Americana, who convinced Mrs. Huss to donate them after her husband's death. The gift of "15 music boxes of printed and manuscript musical compositions" to the New York Public Library by Mrs. Huss was acknowledged in a letter of 4 September 1957. The papers and other documents obviously arrived at a later date.

The personal and professional letters, publication contracts and other legal documents, reports from publishers concerning copyright and royalty matters, and personal papers (school records, family records, and the like) are contained in seven storage boxes under the heading "Huss Collection." The Research Center also maintains files of clippings from periodicals concerning musicians and performances, and there is a Huss Clipping File. These clippings appear to have been kept by the Husses themselves and to have been separated from other papers upon the arrival of all the materials at the Center. Similarly, the Center keeps a Huss Program File, also probably initially preserved by the Husses. These first three parts of the holdings are not mutually exclusive; one will find programs in the clipping file, for example.

In addition to these, there are two other Huss collections at the New York Public Library. Photographs of Huss, his wife, friends and students, and the property at his summer home at Lake George, New York, are maintained in a Huss Iconography File. Last, approximately 190 holograph and manuscript scores—some accompanied by sets of parts—are stored in the Huss Manuscript Collection.

Similar materials, though in far fewer numbers, can be found at the Library of Congress and the University of Illinois.

It is important to keep in mind that Huss was fairly successful at getting his music published by major houses and thereby distributed around the country. I always check for his name in card catalogs and, more often than not, find at least one piece in a library holding sheet music. In the catalog of works, therefore, the reader will find location references only to manuscript pieces. Obtaining copies of published items should be possible either through a local library or through inter-library loan.

Other important sources of materials are articles in the periodical literature and Huss's written communications with individuals. When I have quoted a letter or an article, I have tried to maintain the idiosyncrasies of the original, except where what seem to be unmistakable typographical or similar meaningless errors have occurred. Huss and his contemporaries obviously did not expect their private writings to be examined decades later by a stranger; thus the writers were not especially careful about spelling and grammar (or penmanship!) and were wont to use abbreviations and obscure references. Keeping these characteristics in the quotations helps make the individuals involved live before us as human beings rather than pose as specimens for detached scrutiny. Where especially strange items occur in a quotation, I have particularly marked them. Words which would normally appear with accent marks over some of the letters will not have accents at all. This is to preserve the actual content of Huss's words, and should not be taken as an error by the author or publisher.

One challenge in this process of historical investigation is trying to understand the value of the dollar figures one regularly encounters. I have published elsewhere a formula and table for conversion of these numbers into modern values using estimated Consumer Price Indices (CPI) (found in *Historical Statistics of the United States: Colonial Times to 1970,* 1975); in this book, conversions are based on the CPI published in *Monthly Labor Review* (August 1990).

INTRODUCTION

The purpose of this biography is to promote the case of Henry Holden Huss (1862–1953) as an important and respected figure in American music, particularly during the period of his prime, ca. 1885–1925. In a sense, such promotion is not really necessary since the materials presented in this study demonstrate this rather clearly.

But in another sense, some kind of overkill is required as an attention-getting device. Huss is not Salieri competing for historical attention against Mozart in the ocean of European musical tradition and supremacy. He is a currently unknown American musician battling for attention against less unknown Americans in the tiny cove of our own music. Among scholars working in American music, Huss's era is not currently a particularly fecund subject. American music is such a broad area of untouched research interest that scholars may be excused for focusing on other topics (such as tune books, theater companies, and twentieth-century composers). The fact remains, however, that Huss and his contemporaries must seek their place in the face of neglect by those who question the value of pre-1900 American music in the first place and by those who might be supportive but are called to other American fields.

Huss was not a dilettante, not a parlor musician, not a craftsman capable of no more than derivative composition. He was a thoroughly trained composer and an original contributor to the stylistic movements of his time, who produced a respectable, occasionally inspired, body of literature, some of which deserves to take a place in the active performing repertoire once again. We who love music are perfectly comfortable hearing unknown works out of the nineteenth century from a variety of minor European composers. We enjoy these works without reservation, not feeling any need to apologize for their composers not being forgotten Liszts or Mahlers. We can do the same with our American repertoire, and Huss is a prime candidate for such treatment.

This idea raises several issues, and I will take up two here. The most obvious of these is how our culture separates composers into the "major" and "minor" categories. I have not thought about this matter sufficiently to render a fully formed opinion yet, but clearly there are nonaesthetic considerations at work. "Tradition" is a particularly insidious and circular criterion: "Since I have time in my career to perform only the masterpieces of the great composers, I do not play X's music. His music cannot be any good because no one thinks of him as a major composer, and no one ever performs his music." My experience with promoting Huss's music has been that audiences and performers like the pieces when finally given (or force-fed) exposure to them. The gradual appearance of works by his contemporaries on recitals and recordings now suggests that this is generally true of our American romantics.

A related issue is availability. This book and the series to which it belongs (alongside numerous other studies) help answer the questions, Who are some of the neglected composers? What were the kinds of pieces they wrote? And where might one find scores? One is thus left with only a little legwork to obtain copies of music for rehearsal, but this is precisely where the excuses often begin. Now it is patently not so effortless a matter to program the Huss *Piano Concerto* as to do a Brahms piano concerto. On the other hand, pains have been expended in favor of performances of the Beethoven Tenth Symphony and the last two movements of the Schubert "Unfinished." Yet it is obviously easier to resurrect the Beach "Gaelic" Symphony—a work that exists complete—than to go to the trouble of creating (from sketches or less) pieces that never saw the light of day. Our American music establishment lacks only sufficient courage and energy.

With the close of this minisermon, let me point out a further area of consideration in Huss's favor. Beyond his personal significance as a composer, pianist, and teacher, a study of his life has value as well in its ability to increase our understanding of American musical life during the period of about two decades on either side of 1900. This is especially true of musical life in New York City. Moreover, such a study also applies to our understanding of the kind of music heard on the concert circuit Huss traveled, to our knowledge of the ways in which new American works were distributed across the country, to the history of late-nineteenth-century American music organizations, and to the nature of piano pedagogy in America in Huss's time.

Monroe, Louisiana
November 1994

PART I

CHAPTER I

THE STUDENT YEARS

Ancestry

Henry Holden Huss was born in Newark, New Jersey, on 21 June 1862. The family moved to New York City when Huss was two, in which city he died on 17 September 1953. He represents a union of English and German lineages.

On his mother's side, the family has roots in Denmark, Ireland, and medieval England, and in America it can be traced back to Justinian Holden (1613–1691), who arrived in New England in 1634, having left England with his elder brother Richard (ca. 1609–ca. 1695) on 10 April 1634. Oliver Holden (1765–1844), the prolific colonial composer best known for his hymn tune "Coronation," was a descendant of Richard.

The descendants of Justinian included Levi Holden (1754–1823), who was a first lieutenant during the Revolutionary War, serving as one of George Washington's staff officers. Late in life, Huss said that his sister still had in her possession part of a nightcap knitted for Levi Holden by Martha Washington. In Huss's house was a table at which Washington once sat for tea. Huss also claimed that Holden, Massachusetts, was named for one of his maternal ancestors, and perhaps this ancestor was Levi Holden. Levi's granddaughter, Sophie Ruckle Holden (1832–1905), was the mother of our subject.

Huss traced his paternal ancestry back to a Leonard Hus, whom he identified as a brother of the famous Bohemian martyr, Jan. Approximately ten generations separate Leonard from Johann Daniel Huss (1730–1790) of Rittersbach, Germany, who worked as a tailor, schoolteacher, and organist (this is the first known musician in the Huss lineage). By this point in the family history, both a change in name spelling[1] and a new residence in the vicinity of Nürnberg seem

3

Sophie Ruckle Holden Huss at about age twenty. Courtesy of Andrew Schuman.

to be firmly established. Johann Daniel's son Johann Christoph (1756–1810) also worked as schoolteacher and organist.

It was Johann Christoph's grandson George John (1828–1904)—born Johann Georg, but the names were both anglicized and reversed—who emigrated from Roth, Germany, to New Jersey in

George John Huss at about age twenty-four. Courtesy of Andrew Schuman.

1848 in order to escape duty in the Prussian military service. While still in Germany, George had studied piano with his father and organ with an otherwise unknown musician named Lambrecht. In America he worked as an organist. His engagement by the University Place Presbyterian Church in New York City, where he served from 1858 to 1868, precipitated the family's move to that city. He also supported his large family by teaching piano and through a small amount of composition. Apparently, the family lived reasonably well. They had a maid for thirty years, and with money Sophie inherited they purchased two houses on 150th Street in New York and a family summer home on Lake George in upstate New York. Over a decade after his death, George was described as "a beacon light among teachers" of his generation.

From the marriage (1852) of George and Sophie Huss came five children: George Martin (1853–1941), Johanna Dora (1856–1913), Mary Sophie (1858–1931), Henry Holden (1862–1953), and Anna Babetta (1864–1949). Martin Huss made his living as an architect, becoming a senior member of the firm Huss and Buck.

Of the five children, only Martin and Mary in turn had children of their own. Martin's daughter, Gladys (b. 1903), was active as a painter and was interested in musical matters; she was known to be alive in 1967 but is now assumed by the family to have died. She had no children. Henry married Hildegard Hoffmann in 1904, but they had no children. Johanna and Babetta never married.

Mary, by contrast, wed Howard Elmore Parkhurst in a ceremony performed by the Reverend Charles H. Parkhurst (pastor of the Madison Square Church, where the service was held, and the groom's brother) and witnessed by Brazilian Consul-General and Mrs. de Mendonça, Commissioner and Mrs. Rollin M. Squire, General and Mrs. Q. A. Gillmore, Mr. and Mrs. G. Schirmer, and former Commissioner William Laimbeer. Henry Huss wrote a nuptial march for the occasion and served as a groomsman. Parkhurst (1848–1916), among his varied activities, worked as a professional musician. His musical training included work with Josef Rheinberger; he served as organist for thirty years at the Madison Square Church and published two texts on harmony as well as a body of church music.

This union produced five children: Winthrop Elmore (1891–1983), Helen Huss (1887–1959), Gertrude Adelaide (Parkhurst) Lascelles (1889–1986), Malcolm Kingsley (b. 1894), and Dorothy May (Parkhurst) Smith (1896–1967). Malcolm, if he is still living, is Henry Holden Huss's closest living relative.[2] Helen became a noted educator and writer, eventually being awarded the title Professor Emerita in philosophy at Barnard College.

Winthrop was the musician in this Huss generation, though more as a noted writer on musical topics than as a composer. He also worked as an editor for *Newsweek* and for the fourteenth edition of the *Encyclopaedia Britannica,* and he was a stock market analyst for several brokerage houses in New York City.

Early Musical Studies

Huss's first musical composition, from his sixth year, was recorded by a family member along with the circumstances of its creation: "Inspired by seeing the American flag . . . Henry [composed a song] . . . when entering New York harbor . . . returning from a visit to Germany." This little song, consisting of melody and words, was entitled *We'll Anchor in the Harbor* and given a simple accompanying harmony, probably by his father.

This effort may have encouraged his father to begin the child's musical training, as Henry started piano and harmony studies with his father the next year. A biographical essay in the Huss Collection in the New York Public Library offers the following:

> He was nurtured on great musical literature from this time onwards—Bach, especially, was his daily bread—his father taking him regularly to the old Philharmonic and Theodore Thomas concerts, and constantly bringing before him the best music of many times and nations in the home circle.

Huss was interviewed in January 1911 in Birmingham, Alabama, in connection with his tour concert there, by Dolly Dalrymple for the *Age-Herald.* During the interview Huss told this anecdote:

> You see I began to study music almost in the cradle. My father was intent upon my musical education, and I remember a little incident when I was very young of being taken by him to call upon [Anton] Rubinstein [1829–1894]. He knew my father well, and he also knew that I had been set apart for a musical career by him. No question was raised about my talent, Rubinstein giving my father credit for enough acumen not to select a profession demanding genius if I hadn't some spark of it. The great master said to my father: "Bring the boy here and let me feel his back." At which we marveled, but soon understood why it had been done, hearing from the great man how needful a fine, strong physique is to an artist.

Huss later added studies in theory and instrumentation, from 1879 to 1882, with Otis Bardwell Boise in New York City. The following from Louis Elson, writing in his *History of American Music,* illustrates the qualifications of this highly regarded teacher:

> He was born in Oberlin, Ohio (a very active musical town), August 13, 1844. He was educated at the public schools in Cleveland, Ohio, and was an organist at fourteen years of age. In 1861 he studied in Leipsic, under Hauptmann, Richter, Moscheles, and others; and in 1864 there came still further study in Berlin, under Kullak. Then he returned (temporarily) to his native land, and from 1865 to 1870 engaged in teaching, and playing the organ, in Cleveland. From 1870 to 1876 Boise was in New York, as a teacher of composition in the New York Conservatory and organist in the Fifth Avenue Presbyterian Church. He was in Europe again in 1877, composing and studying; and now he won the friendship of Liszt, who helped him in his work and undoubtedly aided him in his recognition abroad. Another attempt in New York followed, from 1878 to 1881, and then came seven years of business affairs instead of music. Finally, in 1888, there began the period of his expatriation, and from that time . . . Boise remained in Berlin. . . . In 1902 he returned to America, taught in Baltimore, and died there, December 2, 1912.

Early on, Huss's studies were known even to distant relatives; in a letter of 21 March 1874, his grandfather Georg Michael Huss wrote about it from Germany to the family.

> Der liebe Heinrich scheint grosse Vorliebe und Anlage zur Musik zu haben. Nun er soll nur recht fleissig Beethovens Werke studieren, vielleicht wird ein zweiter Beethoven aus ihm.

> [Dear Henry appears to have great interest and aptitude for music. Now he should study Beethoven's works only with real diligence—perhaps a second Beethoven will come of him.]

His studies led to the creation of at least three works: a hymn, a string quartet, and a song. The hymn (*How Sweet the Name of Jesus Sounds*) is known to us only by a letter written by Huss to a Mr. Belkman on 11 March 1879, stating that he was dedicating the hymn to Belkman; there appears to be no extant manuscript or print. The Quartet in E (1878) he later described as "a youthful indiscretion written when sixteen years old."

The last of the three, *The Song of Mister Phonograph* (Schirmer, 1878), may be assigned to Huss if one accepts the report, considerably after the fact, that he wrote it under the nom de plume "H. H. H. von OGraph." That report is from an article by one Jim Walsh (*Hobbies,* November/December 1978), who owns an original print of the work "with a picture of Huss affixed to one corner." Walsh furthermore claimed the work to be "the first published musical number concerning Thomas A. Edison's then new invention." Walsh cites no evidence for connecting Huss with this pseudonym; it may be that having a copy of the music with Huss's picture on it was the basis of his claim.

While there is no other evidence connecting Huss with this pseudonym, it is abundantly clear from the work lists that he often wrote under pseudonyms, and perhaps this is the first of a long line. Certainly it has the humor one finds in some of his later choices of pseudonyms. As a work of Huss, it would constitute his first published composition (copyrighted 22 June 1878). One curious feature about the print is that the pseudonym is "H. H. H. von OGraph" on the cover but "H. A. H. von Ograff" on the first page of music.

There are indications of other student works. For example, on 13 May 1882 (a few months before his departure for studies in Munich) a duet for two female voices and piano by Huss (*Now the Golden Morn*) was presented in a recital of the Pleasure and Profit Club at the house of one Miss Donald in New York City. The work was sung by his sister Babetta and a Miss Powell, presumably accompanied by Huss himself. Huss himself played Chopin's Ballade in A-flat and joined with a Miss Merriam in a piano duet.

Studies in Germany

From 1882 to 1885 Huss studied at the Royal Conservatory of Music in Munich. While Huss was there, as he reported in 1935,

> my father bought a Steinway Baby Grand in 1884 (i.e., when Noah built the Ark!). It stands today in my music room and

still has, in a magical degree, beauty of tone and adequate power.

Huss's studies in Munich included work in counterpoint, fugue, instrumentation, piano, organ, and music history. His principal teachers were Josef Giehrl (piano) and Josef Rheinberger (organ, composition). Giehrl (1857–1893) is identified by little else than the phrase "hochgeschätzter Lehrer," courtesy of Hugo Riemann's *Musik-Lexikon* (5th ed.), though Richard Jackson of the New York Public Library has identified him as a pupil of Liszt.

Of Rheinberger (1839–1901), on the other hand, much is known. This German organist, composer, teacher, and conductor studied at the Royal Conservatory in Munich, whose faculty he joined in 1859. His students included Humperdinck, Wolf-Farrari, Furtwängler, and the Americans Horatio Parker, Franz Xavier Arens, Louis Adolphe Coerne, Arthur Whiting, and George Chadwick. As Louis Elson wrote,

> [This] German teacher almost deserves a chapter to himself in an American history of music, for, since 1878–79, when Charles D. Carter, of Pittsburgh, and George W. Chadwick studied with him (they were, we think, the first of the American band), an endless procession, including H. W. Parker, Arthur Whiting, Henry H. Huss, F. F. Bullard, Wallace Goodrich, and others, has passed through Munich and come back to the United States perfected in composition through his influence.
>
> The recent death of Rheinberger will be felt as a distinct loss, since his influence upon American composition has exceeded that of any other European teacher.

Huss later wrote of his experiences with the curriculum and methodology used by Rheinberger:

> The course of study extends over three years. . . . [The] applicants for admission to Rheinberger's classes are given a cantus firmus which is to be worked out in simple counterpoint of the first order with the cantus alternately in soprano, alto, tenor and bass, the voices to be written respectively in the soprano, alto, tenor and bass clefs. In the afternoon of the same day the applicants are all solemnly assembled . . . confronted by a formidable array of professors, each student's exercises being

played. . . . Open fifths and octaves are of course justly considered very atrocious crimes when detected in these exercises, but occurring as great and accidental exceptions are generally graciously forgiven.

The first year's course comprises a review of harmony [and] the study of simple counterpoint. Considering it easier and more practicable Rheinberger starts off with adding three voices to the cantus firmus. . . . The second year's course embraces double counterpoint, fugue, single canon and instrumentation. . . . The third and last year is occupied with double fugue, double canon and the study of form.

The problems are all worked out during the lessons, one student after another being called to the blackboard. . . . Often, when a knotty point is reached, Rheinberger, suddenly seating himself at the piano, will play a few measures which the student at the board is expected to hear with absolute correctness, and to immediately chalk down.

This system of making students compose off hand at the blackboard is pursued throughout the three years' course, and, although generally rather trying at first to the nervous novice, has a beneficial effect in promoting concentration of thought.

As a general thing it was optional whether one did any contrapuntal work at home (except at examination time) or not. On the other hand, those students showing real talent were encouraged to compose in large form at home, the compositions being corrected during the lesson.

It was truly remarkable to observe Rheinberger's versatility in jumping from the critical consideration of perhaps a complicated orchestral score to the blackboard and instantly straightening out the confused tangle into which some student had brought the class exercise.

As an illustration of Rheinberger's wonderful technique in grasping and comprehending the contents of an orchestral score, I remember the case of a new student who had (I believe) just graduated from some North German conservatory. Mr. A (let us call him) submitted to Rheinberger's inspection a ballade for chorus and orchestra (the inevitable "Sängers Fluch" by Uhland). Mr. A stood anxiously awaiting a verdict at Rheinberger's elbow, the latter meanwhile turning over the leaves at about the rate of speed a person would use who wished to see if the pages were correctly numbered. Mr. A lost patience at this apparent dilly-dallying, and as the last page was turned said, with ill-concealed impatience in his tones: "Now, Mr.

Professor, I should like to show you some debatable passages; for instance, in the andante of the second part is the passage effectively scored?" "You mean this place," said Rheinberger, instantly turning to the place; "well, the first horn is rather high, but it will do." A few remarks of like tenor convinced the now astonished and almost dazed student that his new teacher had in the space of a few moments actually grasped all the salient and many of the minor points of the work of fifty-odd pages. Rheinberger is undoubtedly the greatest living teacher of counterpoint and composition. He does not desiccate the imagination and poetic fancy of the young composer by loading him down with multitudes of dry mechanical exercises in counterpoint, but insists that everything, even to the smallest chorale or canon, shall be really musical in its essence.

Two letters also remain to tell us of Huss's first year in Munich. On 15 March 1883 he wrote to his Aunt Anna, saying how much he looked forward to the beginning (on the next day) of the Easter vacation of twelve days, since he had been "working very hard and [was] not sorry to have an opportunity to rest a little, compose a little and write a little." He describes his residence in a building with musicians practicing above and below him as well as his attendance at many concerts and recitals. He is looking forward to the Easter concert at the Court Chapel (conducted by Rheinberger), as it is one of a fine series extending over the winter,

> except for one trifling particular, that is, if you have a reserved seat you are allowed to keep the ticket until about the middle of the concert when a little old man in a blue coat and brass buttons elbows his way in between the seats, and disturbs you perhaps in the most beautiful part by poking you in the back and asking you for your ticket!!

When he wrote to his family on 27 May 1883, he was able to announce (complete with the abbreviations and misspellings common to his informal correspondence) that he had passed his two most important examinations, namely those in piano and fugue.

> Last Mon. at 7 ^{1}/$_2$ a.m. . . . . [All] the Counterpoint students of the Ist, IInd, and IIId classes assembled, . . . made our bow to Prof. R. and Perfall, and set to work to copy our Prüfung [examination] exerc. The first Class had a cantus to copy, which

was to be worked out in Sop. and Tenor. I among the others of the 2nd Class got [a] theme to make a four voiced string fugue on. . . . By dinner time I had finished the first two "Durch-fuhrings" [working drafts] nearly, & by Monday night I had commenced the Engführung [final copy]. Tues., $1/4$ before 11 a.m. it was finished & when I say it was 119 measures you will see I had to go it pretty tough. . . . Wed. 7 $1/2$ a.m. we all assembled again. Rheinberger and Abel played the exercises, . . . R. calling out the name of each student as his example was played. Parkhurst wrote the best fugue of the lot I think, after playing my fugue either Perfall or Rheinberger . . . said "sehr fleissig gemacht" [done very flowingly]. [In the piano examination] when I was called, Giehrl whispered "play the fugue," so I played it [from Bach's C minor Prelude & Fugue] tolerably, (He told me afterwards that I played "sehr ordentlich [very correctly] but seemed very nervous.") That was the extent of my "Clavier Prüfung"!! I am resuming the study of the Concerto and Bülow's Cadenza's for it. . . . My examinations end with the "Musikgeschichte Prüfung" [music history examination] on Thursday. I am going to have my two songs lithographed . . . and sung in the chorus.

From his second year in Munich (1883–1884), several letters survive. In a letter of 28 October 1883 to his family, Huss reports that his sister Mary, who had begun studies in voice in Munich by that time, was singing for Abel. "We" (probably the siblings and some friends) had tickets for a performance of *Israel in Egypt* for 1 November. His studies with Rheinberger had resumed, and the current project in the Saturday class was to "copy in the second hour of the lesson a Beethoven Quartette in order to impress its form on our minds, and R. said I played it 'sehr gut.' " Huss is now studying Brahms's *Scherzo,* Op. 4, with Giehrl. He reports having recently practiced four hours and twenty minutes before a lesson. Plans were being made for a Halloween party, and Parkhurst and Whiting were specifically named as guests. Last, he reports with pride that his "chest is gaining in fullness" owing to an exercise program he has undertaken, but he does not ride horseback partly because of the cost and partly because of fear for his hands.

In his second year of studies, Huss continued attending concerts as an educational diversion and also did some touring to interesting sites near and far. For example, in a letter to his family of 20 January

1884, Huss reports on a trip to Nymphenburg and the beauties of the countryside on the way. We also learn from this letter that Giehrl has given him Rheinberger's Sonata in D-flat, Op. 99, and plans for him to play "the" Beethoven concerto in a concert soon. The concerto he refers to is possibly the G Major Concerto, Op. 58, since Huss did perform that work in 1884 in Munich.

In the spring of 1884 George Huss received a *Semestral Zeugnis* (dated 5 April) on Henry's work at the conservatory over the winter. This report, signed by Giehrl, Rheinberger, and others, offers three evaluations of the boy's work: "Fleiss" (effort), "Fortschritte" (improvement), and "Betragen" (conduct). The report indicated knowledge yet to be learned, rather than knowledge gained (as in the typical American report card). A "1" indicated complete mastery of a subject (nearly equivalent to the knowledge of the teacher himself) and was therefore a mark rarely awarded. In organ and counterpoint, Huss received marks of "2" while in piano his grade was a "1–2." In the other course listed on the report, chorus, Huss received no grade at all, perhaps because this was a required course.

On 18 May 1884 Huss wrote to his family and mentioned another trip to Nymphenburg. He had recently attended a performance by Parkhurst of Liszt's arrangement of Schubert's C Major Fantasie for piano and orchestra. At the rehearsal, Parkhurst's teacher had sat by the piano shouting directions to the orchestra while Abel was conducting. Of more interest here is the following statement:

> I have [been] trying to get a copy of one of the small Munich papers which has an interesting criticism of the concert at which I played. But the newsdealer tells me the ed. are not allowed to sell a copy of [that] particular date as it has been confiscated by the police, and as my barber told me of the critique I shall have to go for his copy!!!

Rheinberger had been coaching Huss in the art of organ improvisation; his latest try was adjudged "recht hübsch" (very beautiful) after following the directive "Preludiren Sie auf dem oberen Manual mit Pedal ³/₄ Takt. D. dur mit actetsbewegung [*sic*]" (Create a prelude on the upper manual with pedal in ³/₄ time. In D Major with moving eighths). At the organ he was working on the F minor Sonata of Mendelssohn, while in his piano lessons he was studying "the 6th Etude of Chopin, the E minor Concerto and the G minor Prelude and

Fugue (2nd Book) [of Bach]." Last, he told of having seen *Le Prophète* recently, a work he characterized as "sometimes melodic, sometimes dramatic, more times vulgar" yet "very cleverly and originally instrumented."

Eight days later, on 26 May, Huss wrote to his brother Martin about the breadth of his conservatory education:

> In addition to what I have gained in piano, composition and contrapuntal studies, I have learned a good deal about organ playing, have had some experience with playing with orchestra, studied the playing of orchestral scores, and have a fair and increasing appreciation of the way to direct an orchestra or chorus.

In this same letter we learn of performances of Huss's music. Giehrl had played a waltz of Huss's at a concert of the *Orchesterverein* and was considering playing the waltz at a concert in Lucerne. One or both of Huss's parents were planning a visit to Munich soon, and Huss was working hard on a "ballade for chorus and orchestra" in order to complete it, with Rheinberger's approval, and have it performed while his parents were there.

During 1884, two important events occurred: Huss made his debut as an orchestral soloist in Beethoven's G Major Concerto, and his *Wald-Idylle* was given its premiere. The *Wald-Idylle,* a tone poem in C Major for small orchestra, has alternated with the *Ballade* published by Schirmer for the designation of "Opus 1" in various work lists; however, in more than one work list in Huss's own hand, he calls it Opus 2. This point is an important one, beyond the designation of this particular work, because it is the first instance of many in which Huss assigned an opus number to an unpublished work. In his mind, he seems to have used the term to denote a work he felt to be of some significance rather than to indicate publishing order. This and other quirks, such as holding a composition back from publication for many years of performance and revision, make the creation of a complete and chronologically accurate work list impossible.

Huss's correspondence home continued during the next (his last) school year. On 28 September 1884 he wrote to his family of his current piano studies. He planned to present at his lesson the next day the first movement of one of the Chopin concertos. He was also at work on a Prelude and Fugue in F-sharp minor of Bach and was reviewing the "first two studies of Chopin."

As for the previous year, a progress report sent to Huss's parents survives. The courses of study listed are the same as those before, and the marks are similar to those of the previous year as well: 2's in "Fortschritte," 1's and 2's in "Fleiss," and 1's in "Betragen." This card is dated 25 March 1885 and is signed by Giehrl, Rheinberger, and others.

On 24 March 1885 Huss joined with some other American students in a benefit recital for the English Church in Munich. Huss accompanied Otto Singer in a violin sonata by Handel. He also played the *Novellette* in E, Op. 21, by Schumann, *Gondoliera* by Liszt, and the *Valse Caprice,* Op. 111, by Raff. Huss's sister Mary sang two of his songs (premieres for both): *Der Trost* and *Das Erste Lied.* Besides the presence of his own music, this 1885 performance is especially interesting because on it Huss presented two solo piano works that were to be mainstays of his repertoire for decades, the pieces by Schumann and Liszt.

On 5 April 1885 Huss writes his family that he plans to go to Venice soon for a visit. His father is planning a visit to Munich, and of this Huss says, "I hope most certainly that he will be here at the time my 'concert stück' [*sic*] and ballade will be performed." The reference to a "ballade" is unclear (perhaps the work for chorus and orchestra referred to in his 26 May 1884 letter home), but the other work was composed as his graduation piece and was performed under the title *Rhapsody* for piano and orchestra, Op. 3. Of the *Rhapsody,* Huss says something of the process of creation, and his excitement causes him some grammatical problems in the telling.

> My concert piece is now nearly done, I suppose you are rather angered that it was performed and laid on the shelf long, long, but you see I have not always been able to work uninterruptedly on it, and then I changed some parts five or more times. . . . The orchestral part is really symphonic in many parts and I think you will be very much pleased Papa to see the careful work I have put in it. The piano part is going to be much more brilliant and "Virtuosenhaft" than I thought at first.

He had recently heard the *Miserere* of Allegri at the Hofkapelle, and he repeats the story of Mozart's encounter with this work at the

Sistine Chapel. He offers this comment: "How strange that composers of the modern Italian school should have so completely lost all of the rare heritage of their forefathers' worth and sublimity of style."

In his letter to his family of 11 May, Huss offers his impressions of his trip to Italy, particularly Verona and Florence. In the latter city he visited the Uffizi Gallery, and he specifically mentions works of Raphael and Dürer. On another topic, Huss reports that Rheinberger is "correcting" the instrumentation and other details in the *Rhapsody*.

On 21 June he reports to his family that the graduation examinations are near. He plans a theme and variations for his counterpoint examination. More important in his mind, however, is the coordination of his father's visit with his performance.

> He *must* arrive in time to hear the last rehearsals of my Concert piece. They will probably commence about July 10th or 12th, the performance being on July 15th. I had my first rehearsal on last Fri. (June 19th). . . . [Some] parts went pretty well, but as it is rather difficult for the orchestra other parts sounded more curious than beautiful!! Whiting remarked he was glad he was not going to play as it sounded very difficult, but I hope I shall pull through all right, and I played it quite surely at the 1st rehearsal.

Huss received his Royal Diploma as one of at least four honor graduates of the conservatory that summer. Besides the performance of the *Rhapsody* as his graduation thesis on 15 July 1885, he later reported that he also had "the rare distinction of being asked to improvise for the entire faculty of the great institution," the first known instance of his use of improvisation. Later in life Huss was known for his skill at improvising on materials provided by his audiences; apparently this talent manifested itself early in his career. Another part of his activities at the graduation ceremonies was his performance of the Sonata in C minor, Op. 111, by Beethoven.

Huss remained in Germany with his father for the summer. On 11 August he wrote to his mother to tell her of some of the sightseeing they had been doing, such as visits to the museums, including the Alte Pinakotek.

CHAPTER II

THE YOUNG PROFESSIONAL

Upon his return to New York City in the fall of 1885, Huss resumed his work as a private teacher (begun at age sixteen), continued his composing, and also began a career as a concert pianist. He apparently achieved some stature among local musicians (perhaps in part a continued reflection of his father's standing) quite early, for soon he was prominently included in professional activities, and like pond ripples, this local reputation also extended to Boston and on to other areas of the country.

One way in which this reputation spread was via performing. By far the most important performance of 1886 was his appearance with the Boston Symphony Orchestra on 30 October and 1 November. His engagement as soloist in his *Rhapsody* was on a program conducted by Wilhelm Gericke in Boston. That Gericke was a respected conductor did not hurt Huss's debut with a major orchestra in an unfamiliar city, and the critics responded well. Louis Maas, writing for the *Musical Courier* of 10 November 1886, offered a report containing praise for the music and an assessment of the performance:

> The young composer set himself no easy task in attempting just
> that kind of a work and may be said to have been quite
> successful. . . . The piano part was well played by the composer,
> and the work received a flattering reception which should serve
> as an encouragement to the talented author.

This was an opinion shared by others. Frank Van der Stucken planned a series of American music concerts for November 1887 in New York City's Chickering Hall. Huss performed the *Rhapsody* in the first concert of the series, on 15 November. The critic from the *New York Times* gave this view of the concert:

18

> The work . . . is founded on intelligent themes, which are
> treated in a vigorous style. The composition suffered severely at
> the hands of its writer. Mr. Huss is a pianist of the somnoles-
> cent school and should hereafter intrust the performance of his
> music to someone with more ability as an executive musician.

Van der Stucken was also connected to Huss's involvement with the Music Teachers' National Association (MTNA). Huss was associated with a number of musical organizations during his career. With the MTNA, Huss was involved at the national level and at several state levels; moreover, while his usual role was as composer-performer, he did serve in some official capacities as well.

Huss's first known association with the MTNA was through the performance of his *Rhapsody* at the 1887 MTNA convention at Indianapolis, given on 5 July by William Sherwood with an orchestra led by Van der Stucken. The conductor had written a letter recommending that the work be programmed in the first place. That Sherwood had formed a favorable impression of the composer is evident in his letter of 9 May 1887 to Huss:

> After the time and interest I have devoted to your admirable
> composition, I trust you will second me in my efforts to bring it
> out in both N.Y. and other cities.

Immediately Huss wished to have another work performed before the MTNA, and he was successful: his *Ave Maria,* Op. 4, was presented to the convention in Chicago by the Theodore Thomas Orchestra and Festival Chorus on 6 July 1888.

The following year, 1889, saw a performance of yet another Huss work before the MTNA. On 5 July 1889, in Philadelphia, the convention heard his *Mottet, "Sanctus"* (so entitled in the program). The examining committee for this convention (the group approving all proposed performances) had been George Chadwick, Van der Stucken, and Johann H. Beck, with Arthur Foote as an alternate.[1] Henry Krehbiel reviewed the performance (*New York Tribune,* 6 July 1889), noting that Huss "has won hearty recognition for the virility and unconventionality of his talent."

Three years elapsed before the next documented connection between Huss and the MTNA. This presentation was of Huss's *Trio* in D minor at the convention in Cleveland on 8 July 1892, and Huss, assisted by Johann H. Beck and Max Broge, performed. At this convention Huss was also appointed to a committee charged with planning a special meeting of the MTNA to be held in Chicago the week of 4 July 1893 in conjunction with the Columbian Exposition there.

Later in this same decade Huss and Van der Stucken were again teamed as performers. Huss appeared as soloist in his concerto in Cincinnati on 22 June 1899 with the Cincinnati Symphony Orchestra under the leadership of Van der Stucken, in connection with the MTNA convention there.

An example of Huss's early involvement in musical affairs in New York City may be seen in an anecdote from the American debut of Josef Hofmann, on 29 November 1887, at the Metropolitan Opera House. Years later Huss told of having attended the series of three recitals; at each the eleven-year-old Hofmann was given a theme upon which to improvise. At the first recital, the theme was provided by Walter Damrosch, at the second by Huss, and at the third by an unnamed musician. Huss's contribution was a "Creole song" given him by the novelist George W. Cable. When Huss went out on stage to play the theme for Hofmann, he later recalled, he saw the wooden blocks on the piano pedals for the child to use. Hofmann asked him to repeat the theme two times, and then "what little Hofmann did with the theme was truly remarkable," reminding Huss of the stories of Mozart as a child.

On 10 April 1889 Huss arranged a concert of his own works at Steinway Hall. Of five reviews extant from this concert, that from the *New York Tribune* speaks both of Huss as a composer and of the problems of young composers in general.

> In one aspect of the case it is rather unfortunate that young composers should ever think it necessary to arrange concerts of their own compositions. [When] von Bülow gives a concert of Beethoven's music there is no lack of people ready to say that two hours even of Beethoven try the patience of music lovers no matter how enthusiastic and sincere in their love they may be. But there is no education either for the public or the ambitious composer like a public performance; in music it is only hearing that is believing. . . .
>
> It was an affair which did not lack the usual drawbacks, but it nevertheless gave testimony to the seriousness and honesty of artistic purpose cherished by the young musician, his learning and his unquestionable, if yet halting and undecided, talent for

composition. In the [piano trio], especially in the first two movements, there were indications of a fancy above the commonplace, a good deal of technical skill and a degree of apprehension of aims and methods which we missed in most of the other music. Simplicity and directness of utterance seem to be the qualities which Mr. Huss needs most.

Apparently Huss wrote a letter thanking Ferdinand Dulcken for his assistance in the program, for there survives a reply of 18 April 1889 to Huss from Dulcken thanking him for his kind words. Dulcken continues:

> Your Rhapsody which I heard at the MTNC [*sic*] played by Mr. Sherwood had already given me the keynote of your talent and ability as an original composer; and I find that your compositions performed at your concert only confirm the high opinion I entertain for you and the great expectations which your 3 styles will in [the] future confirm, and give you a place among the few modern composers who know what they are doing, after having made serious study with an experienced Master.

This statement is unclear in two respects. It is not known what "3 styles" means; perhaps Dulcken is referring to Huss's choral, orchestral, and chamber works. Furthermore one wonders whether Dulcken is suggesting continued study for Huss or simply saying that composers in general only know what they are doing after having studied with a master composer. At any rate, Dulcken offers additional praise for Huss's music and a request that he be shown future works.

To return to the review, one realizes that Huss's standing as a composer meant his standing as an American composer, because native composers often had difficulty achieving recognition simply as composers. Yet this prejudice did not always work as a disadvantage when Huss encountered it, as when his *Romanze and Polonaise* for violin and orchestra was performed at the Paris Exposition by Willis Nowell and an orchestra under the direction of Van der Stucken on 12 July 1889 at the Trocadéro. The works presented at this historic all-American concert in Europe were:

Overture, "Melpomene"   Chadwick
Piano Concerto No. 2   MacDowell

Suite, "The Tempest"	Van der Stucken
Overture, "In the Mountains"	Foote
Romanze and Polonaise for violin and orchestra	Huss
Prelude, "Oedipus Rex"	Paine
Dramatic Overture, "The Star-Spangled Banner"	Buck

One finds numerous references to this concert in contemporary essays on American music, and this suggests that the concert may have been one of the earliest, if not the first, presentations of its kind as well as one of the most extensive exposures at a single sitting of American "serious" music to Europeans. It is also notable that this exposition is more generally known as the occasion of Debussy's famous encounter with gamelan music. A review of the all-American concert was provided by *Figaro* and included the following general observation:

> [It] cannot be denied that the compositions indicate sound and solid study. . . . The American composers oscillate between the French and German Schools; they have, at times, expression, but never originality or color. There is no trace to be found in them of the sentiment which lends a poetic and picturesque character to the melody of the Russians; on the other hand, their construction is superior to that of the Russians.[2]

In the final decade of the nineteenth century, Huss's position in the American musical world outside of New York City began to solidify. In reviews, articles, and the like, one occasionally finds simple references to "Huss." This change implies that his name was familiar enough to make further identification unnecessary. As an example of this solid position, one may cite Frederic Ritter's *Music in America* (1890). In his chapter entitled "Survey of the Present State of Musical Activity," he provides a list of composers, native and immigrant, each of whom represents an "honest promoter of an ideal, pure art-endeavor." Huss is included in the list of forty-eight names as a writer of choral music, songs, piano music, and chamber music. Similarly, the *Musical Courier* ran an article in 1890 entitled "Composers in New York" with the subheading: "Some of the men who make good music for the public—they are not all Germans, though they all studied in German conservatories—several Americans and one Irishman." The purpose of this article was to demonstrate that Boston was not the only center of musical activity, and each musician listed was provided a short biography; Huss was listed as "one of the younger generation of native composers."

As further evidence of this increasing national attention to Huss, one notes the letter of 29 September 1891 from James R. Gilmore: a request for biographical information to be used in *Gilmore's Cyclopedia of American Biography.* Moreover, in this year there was published an essay by Henry Krehbiel on "Music in America" (in *Famous Composers and Their Works,* edited by J. K. Paine, Theodore Thomas, and Karl Klauser) in which Huss is listed as the first of "the younger generation of pianoforte composers who have made their mark." Furthermore, Huss is given credit for having "shown devotion to the larger forms," for "seriousness of purpose and solidity of thought," and for "striving earnestly for original expression in church music." The discussion of Huss is significantly longer than that of all the other younger composers together.

One other sign of this stature, especially among New York City musicians, is found in his meetings with visiting foreign musicians. In late April 1891, Tchaikovsky arrived in New York City to conduct four concerts as a part of the dedication of the new Music Hall (i.e., Carnegie Hall). On 9 May Harry Mawson, treasurer of the Composers' Club, wrote to Huss requesting a contribution toward the expenses of a reception to be given by the Club for the Russian and inviting him to be in the party to meet Tchaikovsky at his hotel. Tchaikovsky's diary entry for 13 May listed Huss as one of his visitors that day. Huss later sketched out in a notebook (with his characteristic curiosities of abbreviation and grammar) an account of Tchaikovsky's American visit.

> In rehearsing [his] suite for strings, Op. 55, [Tchaikovsky] was amazed at the ultra expert powers of reading displayed by the orch. It was difficult for him to believe that the orchestra was reading the suite for the very first time. He went as far as to remark with conviction that "you could not find a European orchestra to do this." He had great charm of manner. A little concert of his smaller works was arranged at this time. I was asked to play the piano part in his great A minor trio, written in memory of a great musician (Nicholas Rubinstein). The affair was arranged very suddenly, one comfort for me as I only had 3 ¹/₂ days to study and rehearse. I had never before played a note

of it. The violinist was Gustav Dannreuter the cellist, Adolf Hertdagen, both sterling artists of great experience.

Tchaikovsky came to the rehearsal and was graciousness itself. His autograph on my copy of the trio is a treasured souvenir. As I remember it after the lapse of 40 years, about his only criticism was that a certain theme might be taken a little slower![3] It was before the days of Taxi cabs [and] horse cabs were difficult to get (it was up in the West 70th Streets) so I was entrusted with the highly responsible task of taking the great man to his hotel. We had to be excessively democratic, and had to put up with the malodorous horse car!!! Among other things he said, "Young composers nowadays improvise too much on paper. It takes me 10 days to write what these youngsters write in 10 minutes!!" "But Monsieur Tchaikovsky," I expostulated, "your music always seems so spontaneous and natural in its beauty." "Ah my friend," he said, "it is as I tell, I compose very slowly. Amongst all the great composers Mozart and St. Saëns were the only composers who thought out the details, contrapuntal niceties of instrumentation, etc. All they had to do was copy those details on paper."

"St. Saëns has great gifts of contrapuntal . . . force, logic, piquant rhythm, mastery of instrumentation, but" (here his voice became absolutely pathetic) "it fails here; in emotional intensity" (tapping his heart). Then he turned to me with "Do you compose?" I had to confess that I had composed since I was 6 years old, and with a gracious generosity which surprised me hugely, he said: "If you would like the opinion of a frank Russian, send me some of your works."

Huss continued in his notebook that he thought this to be only a polite offer and waited before deciding to send some things, only to learn that the Russian had died.

In this decade, Huss's music was again heard in foreign musical circles. In a letter of 26 April 1891 to the *Musical Courier,* Felix Arens reported on his recent American music concerts in Berlin and Hamburg. In this letter he reports a performance in Hamburg of Huss's *Romanze and Polonaise* for violin and orchestra with a Mr. Piening, concertmaster of the Hamburg Orchestra, as soloist. Elson reports that Arens spent the period from 1890 to 1892 in Berlin studying voice and while there introduced orchestral works of various American composers, including Huss, at concerts in Berlin, Leipzig, Hamburg, Sondershausen, Weimar, Dresden, and Vienna. Indeed, the *Musical Courier,* in its 8 July 1891 issue, presented another report from Arens, telling of his intention to lead another performance of the work in Sondershausen, Germany, on 5 July.

Furthermore, there is the suggestion that the first public performance of *Cleopatra's Death* was given by Clémentine Sapio in a concert with Camilla Urso, the violinist, on 8 September 1894 in Sydney, Australia. Knowing that Sapio performed in Australia, that Urso was on tour there in 1894, and that the last sentence in the review quoted below states that the artists were to return to Sydney later supports this conclusion.

> Unquestionably the most prominent feature of the concert under notice was Mme. Sapio's singing of what may be described as a "one song opera," by Henry Holden Huss, an exceedingly clever young American. The composer, who selected Mme. Sapio as his singer . . . while following Wagner in daring and strength of dramatic handling, has produced something which is not only full of fine technical workmanship, but is also glowing with musical fancy and bears on it the stamp of admirable originality. The Shakespeare text is adhered to, and in the thrilling interpretation on Saturday not a word was missed by the audience, so distinctly was each phrase delivered. Working up to a passionate climax, Cleopatra's last cry, "I come, O Antony!" imposes on the singer, a feat successfully accomplished, the D in alt, attacked with the full strength of the voice and dying away to a whisper.

In America, Huss's music often appeared on all-American concerts, though he was opposed to the concept, feeling that American composers should stand on their own in the larger world of music. One of these affairs was announced in one of a series of similar small concert announcements following an extensive article on Huss in the *New York Tribune* of 29 November 1896. This unsigned article, accompanied by a large pencil sketch of the composer, presented a biography of Huss, and it began as follows:

> Among the names which are always mentioned when there is a muster of American composers who have achieved distinction in the serious departments of the art is that of Henry Holden Huss. Mr. Huss . . . devotes himself assiduously to composition and teaching (he belongs to a family of music-teachers).

Huss's local reputation (and from that a certain national fame) was also built upon his work as a teacher. He taught in studios in the Steinway Building in New York City and at his summer home on Lake George. He was also associated with several teaching institutions, the oldest and longest connection of which, lasting some forty years, began in 1895 with the Masters School, a preparatory school for girls in Dobbs Ferry, New York, where he served on the piano faculty. The connection between Huss and this school is largely traced through faculty recitals.

One teaching institution with which Huss tried to become associated was Columbia University. In 1896 Huss was unsuccessful in securing the new music professorship there, losing out to Edward MacDowell. A copy of Huss's letter of application, dated 15 April 1896, has been preserved. Its contents consist essentially of a biography and letters of recommendation. It is interesting to see what he highlighted in his biography, providing a summary of his life up to 1896.

- Piano study with his father
- Studies in composition and counterpoint with Boise
- Studies in counterpoint, fugue, instrumentation, piano, organ, and history at Munich (September 1882 to July 1885), from which he graduated with honors and received a Royal Diploma
- His performance of the first movement of the Concerto in G of Beethoven in Munich
- His performance of his *Rhapsody* with the Boston Symphony Orchestra in November 1886 and with Van der Stucken at Chickering Hall in 1887
- A performance of his *Ave Maria* under the direction of Theodore Thomas in Chicago in 1891
- A projected performance of his Violin Concerto by the New York Philharmonic in the 1896–97 season
- Performances of his *Romanze and Polonaise* for violin and orchestra at the Trocadéro in Paris in 1889 as well as later in Hamburg

One sees in the recommendations accompanying his application what his contemporaries considered to be his qualifications for this teaching position. The three letters (all dated 16 April 1896) were from Anton Seidl, Henry Krehbiel, and Henry T. Finck. Seidl's simply said,

> I consider Mr. Huss a born musician, a born composer, and before all a born teacher. I recommend Mr. Henry Holden Huss with good conscience, very highly, for the position of professor of music in Columbia University.

Krehbiel offered the following:

> I know of no one whose attainments in the science of music, practical views in pedagogies, earnestness of purpose, zeal in behalf of good art and enthusiasm are greater than those of Mr. Henry Holden Huss, and I most earnestly recommend the consideration of his application by the Trustees of Columbia University.

And finally, Finck, then music editor of the *New York Evening Post*, said,

> I take pleasure in recommending Mr. Henry Holden Huss for the position of Professor of Music in Columbia University. He has had the most thorough education obtainable in Germany, and has been a successful teacher of pupils, as well as teachers, in this country. From my personal experiences as a musical critic, I can testify that Mr. Huss is an excellent pianist, and a composer of great merit, his works showing a thorough knowledge of all the higher branches of musical art and science.

As a private teacher Huss believed, in general, that technique should be taught from high-quality literature rather than from exercises, a view that was relatively new in his generation of American teachers. The strength of Huss's convictions in the matter of what materials to use for teaching can be gauged in the vehemence of his statement here and in the quantity of such teaching pieces as he himself wrote. As he wrote in an unpublished lecture on pedagogical subjects ("Idiotic Ancient and Wise Modern Methods of Piano Study," 2 June 1938):

> The good modern way with children is to give them *beautiful* music, not dumb tedious trivial little "time-to-time pieces," which are an agony of mechanical drudgery to the teacher, the pupil, the parents and the entire neighborhood!

He repeated, at this point, his preference for students to create exercises from a technical problem at the moment it is discovered in a musical work. He called this procedure of creating exercises, as needed, the "analytical modern way of practicing."

Unfortunately, virtually no work has been done on the history of piano pedagogy in the United States, so a comparison of Huss's procedures and philosophies with other teachers must wait. Nevertheless, an interest in such pieces created a market for a large-scale project edited by Leopold Godowsky: the *Progressive Series of Lessons, Exercises, Studies and Pieces,* a compendium of graded teaching materials (published by the Art Publication Society) to which Huss contributed at least six pieces.

Huss also published didactic pieces on his own. The public views of his colleagues on some of the teaching pieces are presented in the discussion of the piano music later in this study. However, Huss's set *Happy Days* was commented on twice in private communication to the composer, and these remarks are quoted here. The first is in a 14 March 1925 letter to Huss from Gustave Becker.

> I am glad to have found in your set of piano pieces, "Happy Days," some excellent new material for the younger students of today. The antiquated pieces by Lange, Lishner, Streabog, and others of that type should be sold for old paper and in their stead, much better and more modern compositions, as in your "Happy Days" group, should be brought forward. You offer the growing young musical mind music that is not merely useful for study purposes, but is, above all highly instructing, being both melodious and rich in harmonic coloring. The imaginative element, which you have infused into all of them, gives added charm and attractiveness. I intend to use them and will gladly recommend them to fellow teachers.

The second judgment is found in a 17 November 1932 letter from M. M. Lichtmann, the dean of the Master Institute of the Roerich Museum.

> These compositions are not only of highest musical value because of their beauty of form, harmony and excellent musicianship, but they are especially valuable as teaching material. The educational value of this series is inestimable to piano students of the second and third grades. . . . It is indeed a privilege for every piano teacher to add these compositions to their curriculum, and I shall be very happy to introduce them

broadly in the piano classes, as well as in my own pedagogical
class.

Huss clearly recognized that an advanced student would occasionally need to pay special attention to a particular problem more
intensively than could be done through the performing literature.
Thus, despite his advocacy of using music instead of exercises in
piano study, Huss, in collaboration with his father, produced a set of
exercises, titled *Condensed Piano Technics* (Schirmer, 1904). It is for
these special occasions, rather than for general practice, that the
exercises were written. The "Foreword" presents the authors' purpose.

> These exercises do not constitute a "Method," but aim to strike
> directly and surely at some of the "weak points" and "sore
> points" in the technical development of the average pupil who
> already has a fair amount of proficiency. . . . This work is not for
> beginners or for self-instruction, excepting a few of the simplest
> scale-exercises and arpeggios.

In reviewing the collection for the 19 May 1904 issue of the
Musical Leader and Concert Goer, Emilie Frances Bauer reported the
following incident, thus giving an indication of the views of Huss's
contemporaries on this work.

> In my presence, M. Raoul Pugno threw his arms about Mr.
> Huss and in ecstasy and enthusiasm said, "But, my dear Huss,
> what you have accomplished is of benefit to the entire world;
> you have done things which have been heretofore not only
> unheard of, but unthought of. You are a benefactor to all those
> who study music."

A former pupil, Margaret M. Meachem, offers the following
recollection of Huss as a teacher (of both piano and composition) in
the 1940s:

> In NYC I mostly studied piano with him. I never had a copy of
> [*Condensed Piano Technics*]. . . . H merely used it with me to
> show me how to practice in rhythms for difficult passages of
> early Beethoven Sonatas, etc.
>   As far as composition was concerned he would just deal with
> what I was writing and comment on its adaptability to the
> particular instrument, often the piano. His comments often

had to do with [the] distribution of a chord on the piano to obtain the best sound. His knowledge of the style of the piano masters was extensive. He always said that he thought Beethoven would have used the resources of our modern piano and that we should interpret him thus. He was very particular about pedalling and using a singing tone in melodic passages, with a subservient bass. He always said that learning to practice efficiently and intelligently was of supreme importance. He *did* make exercises of difficult passages in piano literature. . . . He was only interested in teaching music of the highest quality— no commercial teaching material. He had a studio [at Steinway Hall] for years—gratis—with two gorgeous Steinways.

As one might expect, given Huss's involvement in teaching as a career, he was active in a number of music teachers' organizations. The first of these appearing in the surviving Huss-related documents is the Music Teachers' National Association, but he was associated with the beginnings of another American musical organization, the American Guild of Organists. The evidence of his work and skills as an organist is scant. One reference is found in a 27 June 1894 letter to his parents in which he writes that the service of the previous Sunday had gone satisfactorily (though "I had to wear *two* gowns"), and in a letter of 2 July he tells his parents that he is to play at St. Bartholomew's on 1, 8, and 15 July: "Yesterday the service went well, and I did not suffer so much with my two gowns as it was cooler."

In connection with this spate of organ playing, Huss wrote to his parents on 15 July that "I must play on the new organ for you next Fall. Warren says I can play on it whenever I wish." This seems to refer to a new instrument at St. Bartholomew's, where Richard Warren was then organist.

The surviving record must not quite represent his work and perhaps reputation as an organist because Huss was among the group which created the American Guild of Organists in 1896. Huss's role in this enterprise is outlined by the AGO archivist Charles N. Henderson:

> Mr. Huss was one of the 145 founders, however not a "founder in fact"; this distinction was reserved for the original 33 organists whose number was eventually expanded to 145. I cannot find that Mr. Huss took any part in the work or

activities of the AGO. However, his "founder" status is a
permanent distinction. The only reference to him as a member
is in the 1908–1909 year book. . . . The only other reference I
can find is that he resigned from the Guild on May 7, 1910.

Whatever the extent of his work as an organist, as a pianist, Huss
gave numerous solo and chamber recitals, and part of his national
recognition as a composer came from appearances he gave with
orchestras as piano soloist. At first these appearances involved his
graduation piece from Munich, the *Rhapsody* for piano and orchestra.
Later, his piano concerto served as the vehicle for performances with
orchestras in Boston, Cincinnati, New York, Pittsburgh, St. Paul,
and Detroit.

In general the reviews for such performances were mixed, both in
regard to Huss's compositions and to his playing. The response to the
premiere of the piano concerto with the Boston Symphony Orchestra
under Emil Paur at a public rehearsal on 29 December 1894 and at
the formal concert the following night with Huss as soloist is,
perhaps, representative. Some critics noted the inherent disadvantage
to the concerto of placing it between Tchaikovsky's Sixth Symphony
and Berlioz's Overture to *Benvenuto Cellini.* Louis Elson, of the *Boston
Daily Advertiser,* compared these two works to millstones between
which "the piano concerto of Henry H. Huss was ground." The critic
of the *Boston Sunday Globe,* on the other hand, concerned himself with
the inadequacies of Huss as a performer, especially noticeable in
comparison with the skills Bernhard Stavenhagen, a Liszt pupil,
displayed the previous evening. Henry Krehbiel's account (*New York
Tribune*) may serve as a summary:

It is no longer possible to say that it is wrong, even in a
concerto, to make the pianoforte an integral part of the band,
but it must not be asked to yield up all its rights of
predominance. Mr. Huss's concerto did not seem tonight to be
written for the pianoforte with orchestral accompaniment but
for orchestra with pianoforte obligato. To some extent it was
evident enough that this effect was due to the fact that Mr.
Huss's playing of the solo part was not sufficiently assertive. . . .
The [second] movement is the most fluent and ingeniously
conceived one of the three of which the concerto is composed,
and its spirit can be guessed from the paraphrase of its themes
for pianoforte solo, which is printed [in] this issue of The

Tribune. Each movement was respectfully applauded by the audience, and at the close of the whole work the musicians on the platform and in the audience led in a hearty recall of the composer pianist. It was evident, too, that Mr. Paur took a genuine interest in the concerto, for he conducted it with great care and devotion, and had plainly spared no pains in the preparatory rehearsals, though he might have subdued his band more.

In 1895 George Huss had purchased a summer home on Lake George in upstate New York. Henry Huss also spent his summers there, and he eventually inherited the property. At Lake George he rested, taught, and performed. An advertisement for a concert of 1 September 1937 labeled him "the pioneer musician on the shores of Lake George" since 1895. This item also indicated that Huss had been organist at the Community Church at Diamond Point (a part of the Lake George area) for over twenty-five years, so it may be that he had served occasionally as an organist for some time before that regular position began.

> The place at Lake George, which they called "Onelgie," contained over a hundred acres, on the side of a mountain with a view of the Lake, and they had a hundred and fifty apple trees. [George, Sophie and their daughters] used to stay there from May to October, [Martin and Henry] coming later for a shorter stay. They lived in the old farmhouse on the place, where there were also several other small buildings. Henry [later] built a beautiful big studio with a wide piazza on two sides, and he gave concerts there every summer. There was an enormous fireplace at the opposite end from the big Steinway grand piano. [After he married], he built a house for themselves between the old house and the studio, so it became quite a settlement. Water was pumped from their own spring and brook. Besides the apple trees they had a big vegetable garden and fruit bushes, and some years a cow, with a man to look after it all.

Among performances Huss gave at Lake George were numerous benefit concerts, though he also gave these elsewhere. One example is the musicale at the residence of Mrs. A. M. Brereton on 24 August 1896, given for the Hill View and Bolton Road Improvement Society.

The most important event for Huss in 1900 had to have been his long-anticipated performance of his piano concerto with the New York Philharmonic. The orchestra, under Emil Paur, gave the work in a public rehearsal on 21 December and a formal concert the following day. The review in the *Sun,* under the subheading "Tschaikowsky and Huss the Attractions," described the concert this way:

> One-half the programme was devoted to Weber and Beethoven—and was sleep provoking; the other landed its hearers into the very stress and turmoils of the later nineteenth century; no one thought of repose when Tschaikowsky and Henry Holden Huss were being played.
>
> Mr. Huss plays the piano in an extremely polished fashion, but he has not the muscular frame for such a tornadic whirl as this [final] movement. Mr. Huss was recalled several times and consented to play a graceful encore piece, probably something of his own.
>
> The accompaniment to the concerto was sympathetic as far as Mr. Paur's intentions were concerned. But then the Philharmonic Society orchestra is paved with good musical intentions. Ragged is the only word to express the performance of this accompaniment.

In addition to published opinions, Huss received at least two private compliments. On 30 December, Howard Brockway (a composer and fellow Boise student) wrote to wish him a "Happy New Century" and to say

> Your concerto seemed to me immensely effective, and you played with fine aplomb and justness. You gave *me* for one a most delightful surprise, Huss, and that is a sensation one has infrequently to say the least! You must have been highly gratified by your splendid reception, and it gave me (again the "ego") unqualified pleasure.

Huss also was congratulated by the secretary of the Philharmonic, who wrote, on 8 January 1901, to express the gratitude of the Board of Directors for Huss's volunteering to be soloist for his concerto.

> The merits of your Piano Concerto, as well as its spirited interpretation by the composer, were keenly appreciated by our

critical audience, and it affords the undersigned extreme
pleasure to congratulate you upon your well merited and most
encouraging success.

Huss made a return trip to Europe in 1901. The first evidence of
this is a postcard from Richard Strauss. The message on the card,
postmarked 4 July 1901 in Switzerland, consists of only one
sentence:

Sie treffen mich erst vorm 1. September ab in Berlin! [You may
meet me in Berlin only after the first of September.]

Neither the impetus for this note nor whether such a meeting took
place is known. Huss, however, later wrote of the trip.

[I] returned to Nürnberg and met there the director of the
principal orchestra, consisting of 70 men. I showed him my
piano concerto which I had been playing. . . . He said, "Why
not play it here? The orchestra, myself as conductor, three
rehearsals and the concert, will cost five hundred marks."
Today the first violinist would get about this sum.

One other anecdote survives from this trip. In a letter of 16
October 1946 addressed to one Miss Merriman in which Huss
describes some of the anecdotes he planned to include in an
upcoming lecture, he told of meeting conductor Artur Nikisch, "for
whom I whistled (fact!) my piano concerto in his Belgian hotel in
1901." One more meeting between the two is known, for on 3 May
1912 the Bohemians (the New York musical club) gave a farewell
banquet for Artur Nikisch, on the occasion of the end of the tour by
Nikisch and the London Symphony Orchestra in the United States.
Huss, as a member of the club, was present on this occasion and
appears in the photograph of the banquet printed by *Musical America*
on 11 May 1912.

Moreover, this was not the first time Huss had related
such a story to Miss Merriman. In his 16 October 1916 letter to her
are found a few words each on several musical figures; some of these
individuals were persons whom Huss had met or heard perform, and
in these cases the comments relate an appropriate anecdote or
descriptive phrase. Some sample entries:

Henry Holden Huss at about age forty. From *A Portrait Catalogue of American Compositions* (Boston: Arthur P. Schmidt, n.d.), p. 26. Courtesy of Special Collections in Music, The University of Maryland, College Park.

Mahler: Generally the most reserved and taciturn of musicians, [he] opened his heart to me after a monumental New York performance of his great Symphony with the "Hymn to Immortality."

De Pachmann: I wryly refused to be embraced by him because I admired his Mozart playing!

From the next two years there survive some comments by and about Huss, now the famous and respected musician. On 18 February 1902 he responded in a letter to a request from Richard Aldrich for his views about music.

I believe the old Classical forms with slight modifications will still serve in instrumental music for the composer who has anything "individual" to say. If he has *not*, the so-called "new" forms will only serve for a short time to conceal his poverty of thought. The composer who is only original when his music is ugly is not built for immortality.

Music which is so programmatic that it absolutely *requires* an extended programme to elucidate it is only a bastard sort of music. Realism when it enters too far into a musical composition makes of it an inferior sort of phonographic record of outside material things.

In church music I am desirous of doing what little I can to introduce a spirit of reverence. We should lean on the old gregorian spirit even if we clothe it in a somewhat modernized body.

Operatic style diluted and emasculated should be banished

from our church music. Just because our modern life is so
materialistic do we need all the more a spiritualized church
music.

I feel more and more that counterpoint, per se, canon and
fugue, etc. should only be used where they *heighten* the beauty
of a composition. Otherwise they . . . are a vexation and
weariness to the spirit. J. S. Bach in his exalted moods is to me
the most *modern* and profound and the most poetic composer!

I feel the same way in vastly lesser degree about Joh. Brahms.
At times he is seer, a mystical poet, at other times a pedant and
a dry one.

It seems to me that there must be a return to greater
simplicity and naive sincerity in our instrumental music, before
any really great music can be written. A composer if he desires
to write something which will not be ephemeral should only
use primitive folk tunes.

In music drama I believe that in the future "the statue" will
not to the same extent as now be placed in the orchestra, but
that the voices will have more melodic prominence without
losing a tithe of their dramatic freedom of utterance. "Tristan"
is to me the ideal music drama.

This somewhat puzzling last paragraph seems to be a call for
balance between voice and orchestra in opera composition. Obviously
Huss feels the scales have tipped toward the orchestra away from the
balance he perceives in *Tristan.* Unfortunately he did not write an
opera by which his statements could be measured. Moreover, in his
music "simplicity and naive sincerity" are not the qualities that
appear uppermost; a further discussion of Huss's style may be found
later in this study.

In November 1902, Huss's name appeared in an article on
American music in *Theatre.* Here Lawrence Gilman offered his
opinions on "Some Vital Figures in American Music," starting with
a general discussion, then proceeding to biographies of individuals,
all the while tackling the issues of acceptance and aesthetic origins.
He said that Americans have

> adopted a somewhat uncritical attitude toward the American
> composer; we are inclined to accept him *en bloc,* as if the mere
> fact of his Americanism endowed his work with a superior and
> magical virtue—inclined, in the phrase of Philip Hale, "to
> cover mediocrity with a cloak of patriotism." One lacks

somewhat of discrimination, surely, in according the same measure of approbation to Mr. Paine and Mr. Buck, Mr. Foote and Mr. Chadwick, for example, that one accords to Mr. MacDowell, Mr. Parker, and Mr. Huss. Not to perceive the fundamental and incalculable difference between work that is merely unexceptionable [*sic*] and derivative and work that is self-sprung and vital, is to exhibit an unenviable want of critical sensibility. Between the accomplished, conscientious and generally ineffectual work of the Academics and the amiable trifling of certain of the younger men, there is little to choose; but both are equally negligible in comparison with the achievements of such composers as Mr. MacDowell, Mr. Huss, Mr. Parker and Mr. Van der Stucken—musicians of conspicuous individuality and force, who are engrossed in the task of realizing musically, with all possible poignancy and truth, some personal and valid experience of human life—and not [through] the imagined efficacy of an adventitious nationalism.

Huss is described as an "impressionist and a romantic," and like MacDowell,

his art, at its best, is bound over unreservedly to the service of his imagination and his emotions. He holds for himself an ideal whose beauty and nobility he has realized with memorable completeness in such achievements as his fine Scene for soprano and orchestra . . . and his "Home They Brought Her Warrior Dead." I like him less in such music as his piano concerto in B Major and his trio . . . one misses an inevitability of process, a coherence of organism, an instant and perfect felicity. You cannot make so incorrigible a romantic as Mr. Huss has shown himself to be into a wholly satisfactory academic; they are mutually and permanently obstructive, as Mr. Huss, if he has ever reflected upon the matter, must surely know.

In his forty-first year, Huss's role in music was assessed by Edouard Seeligson in an article published by the *Musical Leader and Concert Goer*. Seeligson wrote, in part:

Should one pass verdict on Henry Holden Huss it would be that he is not at variance with music's progress. A man modest enough to constitute a silent yet powerful part in the present controversies about music is to be admired. What Mr. Huss has done differentiates him from others, and with Edward

MacDowell, Edgar Kelley (perhaps a few others), he makes
divisible the line of our own composers. Vigilant and active, he
talks with no supineness or timidity in the cause of future
music.

Some of Huss's contacts with the MTNA have been cited already.
He was also known at various state subdivisions of the organization.
Huss was naturally associated with the New York subdivision, and
the first of the documented connections was a recital he gave on 25
June 1902 at the New York State Music Teachers' Association
convention in Newburgh. The *Musical Courier* of 9 July 1902
described the concert as follows:

> That Mr. Huss and his work in the cause of music were well
> known was evident by the hearty reception he received. After
> the first group of pieces he received warm applause; after the
> second still stronger evidence of appreciation, and at the close a
> singularly spontaneous tribute.

This recital was not Huss's only contact with the conventioneers. The
Musical Courier also reported that Arthur Farwell introduced a
symposium on theory ("Vital Issues in Modern Theory") by reading
"letters from some well-known composers, among them Kelley,
Loomis, Huss, . . . and Gilbert."

Huss's music was also heard at other state subdivisions of the
MTNA, both from his own hand and courtesy of others. One of the
Preludes from Op. 17 was performed in Galesburg, Illinois, on 19
June 1903 in a recital given by Oliver Willard Pierce of Indianapolis
before the convention of the Illinois Music Teachers' Association.
The recital was lauded by Florence French in the *Musical Leader and
Concert Goer* of 25 June 1903 in her assessment of the convention that
"nothing of greater artistic worth" had been presented there, so one
may assume the Huss work was given a suitable performance and
reception.

Huss was invited to give a recital in the summer of 1905 at the
Minnesota State Music Teachers' Association convention in Winona.
This recital took place on 9 June in the First Congregational Church,
and he was joined in it by Mrs. Huss. Tickets for all events to
Association members were $2.00 (approximately $32.73 in May
1994 value), but to attend only the Huss recital required an
expenditure of half that amount. Krehbiel's lecture tickets sold for

fifty cents, as did tickets for the other concerts. A reviewer offered the following among his comments for the *Musical Leader and Concert Goer* of 15 June 1905:

> Both of these artists [the Husses] are so well known and appreciated in the East . . . that it is altogether unnecessary to speak in detail of the well chosen and excellently arranged programme which was so fitting a closing to a splendid meeting. [Huss] has a name to conjure with; as a pianist his technic is without flaw and his authority not to be questioned. As composer he is equally well known, and it was a privilege to hear some of his fine compositions interpreted by the master mind that had conceived them.

One of the most important of the MTNA national conventions with which Huss was associated was that of 1903 in Asheville, North Carolina, where he performed in a concert at the Grand Opera House on 2 July. This is an event of interest for a number of reasons. It shows, for example, his continued association with that organization, especially in light of his election as one of the New York delegates to the "Senate and Council." More important for his private life, one notes that at this convention Hildegard Hoffmann (Huss's future wife) sang on a program the next day. This is the first documented opportunity of the two having spent time together; whether they had known each other previously is unknown.

After the MTNA convention, Huss went to the family home in Lake George. On 13 August 1903 the entire Huss musical establishment participated in a musicale as a benefit for two churches, a Presbyterian and a Methodist Episcopal, at Huss's studio on Lake George. The participants were Huss's father George, sister and brother-in-law Mr. and Mrs. Howard Parkhurst, and siblings Babetta and Martin. Also on the program, in the first known joint performing appearance with Huss, was Hildegard Hoffmann. Appearing after several of Huss's pieces on the program is the phrase "by request," indicating that some works gained a familiarity with audiences so as to be requested at recitals. One finds this phrase on numerous Huss concert programs.

This performance received a review in the local paper, with the opinion that all the performances were of high quality, but we should take note of the comments on Hoffmann, who is a young New York professional and is well known, came especially to sing at this concert and had to leave before the completion of the program in order to fulfill a return oratorio engagement at Ocean Grove, N.J. Her voice is a clear soprano and of pleasing quality, and her rendition of various songs showed a versatile talent which gave much pleasure.

The next year, 1904, was quite important for Huss. The first significant event was his appearance in recital for President and Mrs. Roosevelt and their guests at the White House. At this recital on 22 January (which he later deemed one of his most pleasant memories) he shared the stage with Hildegard Hoffmann and Glenn Hall. A new piano had been placed in the East Room in 1903, an instrument probably used by Huss for this concert.

The event was written up in the social pages of the *Washington Post* and the *Evening Star,* but these accounts were primarily interested in who the guests were and what the guests wore. Huss did receive a letter from Arabella L. Haynes, Mrs. Roosevelt's secretary, thanking him for his performance and conveying thereby from Mrs. Roosevelt "a souvenir [autographed photographs of the Roosevelts] which she trusts you will accept with her best wishes." In the absence of other commentary, it is appropriate to quote from later reminiscences of Huss's 1904 appearance. The first of these is from 1914, recorded by an interviewer.

The East Room was crowded with a distinguished and brilliant audience; the diplomatic corps in its gorgeous uniforms adding color to the sober black and white studies of senators, judges and congressmen. What might have proved a serio-comic incident and came near suggesting Mozart's nose—playing the middle note of a very widespread harmony—occurred during one of Mr. Huss' solos. The floor of the magnificent room was so smoothly polished that it shone with mirror-like brilliancy, and the pianist during a Schumann novellette felt his seat slipping by degrees farther and farther from the piano, until the angle of his arms was anything but legitimate according to rules of modern pianism. With a mighty effort he "saved the day" and the solo by pulling his seat into position during a short fermata. It is needless to say, that a large rug was placed under the pianist before the next group.

Since it is not listed on the program, the Schumann piece was either an internal encore, a substitution, or an incorrect memory.

The second reminiscence appeared in the 17 April 1919 issue of *Musical Courier:*

> After the program was concluded President Roosevelt came up in his characteristically delightful and informal manner and said "No one seems to want to introduce me, so I'll have to do it myself!" He then mentioned as having particularly pleased him two Huss compositions, "The Song of the Sirens" and the "Etude Melodique."

Because of Roosevelt's especial enjoyment of *The Ballade of the Song of the Syrens,* the Husses referred to it thereafter as the "President's Song."

In a later document, this performance is cited, and it is further stated that Huss was invited by President Harding to give a White House recital in the fall of 1923; no evidence survives indicating that recital was ever played. Since Harding died on 2 August of that year, the invitation may not have been renewed by the Coolidge administration.

While the White House recital was a highlight in Huss's professional life, his marriage to Hildegard Hoffmann on 15 June 1904 had an impact upon both his private and professional life. Hildegard Hedwig Adele Hoffmann (20 July 1874–19 April 1969), was the daughter of William Hoffmann, sugar merchant and former American consul general at Matanzas, Cuba. She began her professional studies at sixteen with faculty of the Scharwenka Conservatory (New York) and continued in private studies afterward. Initially her career was as a church soloist, but Hoffmann later became particularly known as an interpreter of song and oratorio. She dated her career from a performance on 25 April 1898, though she had actually been singing professionally before that, and the soprano traveled widely east of the Mississippi to perform. Hoffmann had sung for Governor Roosevelt at a performance of the Albany Oratorio Society; it may have been due to that and her father's diplomatic connections that the invitation to the White House was given.

The engagement was announced in the *New York Herald* on 24 January 1904: the couple had met "a year ago at a musical convention," probably referring to the MTNA convention of the

Wedding party for Henry Holden and Hildegard Hoffmann Huss, June 1904. *Top row, from left,* **Mary Sophie Huss Parkhurst, Sophie Ruckle Holden Huss, unknown, Helen Huss Parkhurst, unknown, unknown, and unknown.** *Middle row, from left,* **Howard Elmore Parkhurst, George John Huss, Gertrude Adelaide Parkhurst, Hildegard Hoffman Huss, Henry Holden Huss, and unknown.** *Bottom row, from left,* **unknown, Dorothy May Parkhurst, Winthrop Elmore Parkhurst, Malcolm Kingsley Parkhurst, and unknown. Courtesy of Andrew Schuman. In an 8 September 1987 letter, Schuman speculates that Mary Parkhurst's face may have received its X from one of her children.**

previous summer in Asheville, North Carolina. Out of respect for Hoffmann's father, who had died less than a year before, the couple had kept the engagement a secret for about two weeks, but the news was becoming known among an ever-widening circle of friends and so was made public after their return from the White House recital. The engagement was further proclaimed by the *Musical Leader and Concert Goer* of 4 February 1904.

One can actually date the Huss-Hoffmann connection somewhat earlier than the Asheville convention since in February 1901 his *Ballade of the Song of the Syrens* was sung by Hoffmann on a recital. Her $15.00 fee (approximately $265.14 in May 1994 value) for two

afternoons of singing arrived in a letter of 27 February 1901 from a
Mrs. Ceballos. Some years afterward Hoffmann wrote some informal
comments about the event on the letter itself; she noted that Ceballos
was the wife of the president of the sugar trust,

> so I got *very* elegant pay for my 2 appearances! I forgot my
> words in Henry H. Huss' (*didn't* know him then) "Song of the
> Sirens" because two fat dames right in front of me wdn't stop
> gabbing—I got back to the text, how? Must have looked pretty
> with gaping mouth as I floundered!!!

From the courtship, there survives only a flower pressed in a note
dated "April 1904, Manchester" and reading "Please send to my
Liebhast all my love and tell her not to forget me!" The wedding took
place at Lake George on 15 June, and the couple planned a joint
concert tour in the fall. Huss's solitary musical life had come to a
close, and a new performing-teaching partnership was being forged.
After the wedding, their musical lives merged: Mrs. Huss essentially
lost her performer's identity except as an interpreter of his songs,
while song production took a dominant position (alongside piano
music) in his compositional output. His performances more often
were joint recitals with her than concerts with orchestras or in
chamber music.

The year was not without its sad moments as well. Huss's father
died on 19 November 1904 (the lack of known performances by Huss
prior to that date suggests that the elder Huss may have died after an
extended illness), and Huss's mother died the following spring, on 6
March, after a fall from which she never completely recovered.

CHAPTER III

RELATIONS WITH OTHER MUSICIANS

As an important musician Huss was, of course, in contact with other musical figures of his time, some regularly and some infrequently. The musicians Huss knew can be grouped into three large categories: fellow composers, fellow performers, and friends and patrons. Since a large part of the value of noting these relations lies in the assumption of equivalent stature on Huss's part to these individuals, it may be helpful first to consider what Huss's perceived relative status was in general at the apex of his career. In the week that Huss performed at the White House, the *Musical Leader and Concert Goer* put his portrait on the cover and proffered a biographical article, which said, in part, that

> when the American composer is spoken of, and indeed, when any modern writer is thought of, the name of Henry Holden Huss naturally presents itself to mind, as he is among the foremost musicians and composers of the day. [When] his works have been played beside the masterpieces of modern and classical music, they have not suffered by comparison.
>
> [As a] pianist he ranks with the best of the day. [In] recitals he holds a unique position, as he interprets Beethoven in a manner that is both educative and genuinely delightful, and he has few equals in the romantic music of Chopin and Schumann. He is perhaps the most superb exponent of Bach in this country. . . .
>
> [Huss] is a teacher of the most exceptional qualities. Indeed it were absolutely futile to look in Europe or in America for his superior.

Some of this must be recognized for the hyperbole that it is: his music did not always escape critical dismissal in relationship to European works, and given the limited repertoire of Beethoven, Chopin,

Schumann, and Bach appearing on his extant program listings, it is difficult to confirm a solid foundation for a reputation as an interpreter of any of these masters.

Similarly, in the *Musical Leader and Concert Goer* of 9 July 1903, Emilie Frances Bauer wrote about American composers and musicians, saying in part,

> The hardest battle that the American has to fight is with his own people, for there are many in respected positions in Europe, and many of the greatest artists and authorities in Europe hold Americans at their real value, which, after all, is all that any one has the right to ask.
>
> I have no desire to measure individuals in Europe against individuals in America, yet I am perfectly willing to mention the names of Joseffy, Huss, MacDowell, Foote, Dr. Mason, Julie Rivé-King, Fannie Bloomfield-Zeisler, Sherwood, J. K. Paine, and [Alexander] Lambert against anybody that Europe holds today for thorough, intelligent, and masterful instruction.

Bauer's argument is somewhat compromised as her list includes persons whose training was either completed in Europe or strongly affected by study there, suggesting (whether or not she intended to) that going to Europe for training was unnecessary because European training had, in a sense, been brought across the Atlantic. However, regarding Huss, this quotation is interesting, for it indicates that his fame is such that his last name (like those of Joseffy and MacDowell) is sufficient identification.

Bauer returned to the subject of American music in the *Musical Leader and Concert Goer* of 23 July 1903, presenting Huss's perspective on American composers.

> Up to the present time it has been the custom of people to speak of composers and American composers. Two of this country's greatest men express intense dislike of the distinction shown. They are Henry Holden Huss and Edward A. MacDowell.
>
> "It is unbearable," says Mr. Huss, "to set aside a space which shall be devoted to American composers, and then, as if they were animals in a circus, the people are requested to step up and see the great curiosity—a real American composer."

This opinion appeared again in an article in the 25 February 1904 issue of the *Musical Leader and Concert Goer,* where it was meant to discourage all-American concerts on the grounds that these foster the view that American music cannot withstand comparison with European music on the same program. The launching point for the article was an all-American concert from which MacDowell had asked a piece of his to be withdrawn.

> When two men of the importance of Mr. MacDowell and Mr. Huss take the same stand, their reasons are worthy of consideration. They would rather lie in obscurity than be represented in the great *omnium gatherum* of American compositions of all classes, for surely America has some of the worst. When people who deal with the American composers know how to discriminate in classifying them, and when the great works that are now in existence will be accepted as great works without reference to the name attached to the score, there will be no objections on the part of these gentlemen to appear upon American programmes.
>
> When we hear such orchestral works as those of MacDowell, Loeffler, Huss, Victor Herbert, Paine, and the oratorios of Horatio W. Parker, the Chamber Music of Arthur Foote, and the fairly innumerable ballads that far surpass anything that Abt and Tosti ever created, it is not difficult to see that the American composer does not need to be patted on the back by those who know nothing about it anyhow.

Huss's name is again mentioned by Emilie Bauer in an essay in the *Musical Leader* of 3 November 1910 on the difficulties experienced by American composers in being treated as equal to Europeans; Huss is quoted as saying "long ago": "Please don't let us be caged as in a circus' side show. I can almost hear the call, 'This way ladies and gentlemen, see the great American composer, next of kin to the bearded lady or the redskins of the woolly west.' " Huss's piano concerto is mentioned as a work that, when performed, is sometimes cited as an orchestra's nod to the American composer.

Other Composers

Huss's earliest contact with a fellow composer (though neither would have been described that way at the time) is preserved in a series of letters exchanged with Edward MacDowell. In the fall of

1876 a mutual friend arranged that Huss should undertake a correspondence with the other young music student, who was then in Paris. Fortunately, Huss made copies of at least some of the letters he sent to MacDowell during the period covered by the correspondence (to the summer of 1877).

In Huss's letter of 12 December to MacDowell, he begins with a discussion of Wagner. He states that "a universal appreciation" of Wagner's operas is a difficult goal due to the considerable orchestral and stagecraft demands of the works as well as the "popular uneducated taste." He further contrasts how "pretty trifling music," as found in Italian operas, can be successfully performed in concert settings while Wagner's music resists performance without staging and scenery. Huss then mentions having heard Madame Annette Essipoff two weeks earlier. He expresses delight in her "delicacy, brilliance and charming accuracy," and he is in wonderment over her memorized repertoire of two hundred works. He closes his letter with a list of his own studies: an idyll of Adolph Jensen, *Feld, Wald und liebes Götter,* Op. 43, No. 2; two Minuets in B-flat of Bach; and the Sonata in D, Op. 10, No. 3, of Beethoven. Furthermore, "Papa" Huss was leading him through Franz Xaver Richter's *Manual of Harmony.*

In his letter of 5 February, Huss bemoans the imminent loss of the Theodore Thomas Orchestra ("the best orchestra in the world") for lack of a suitable concert hall in New York. Because MacDowell has mentioned operas he has seen recently in Paris, Huss tells of having seen *Fidelio* on a family trip to Bavaria in 1873. He, all of eleven at the time, had felt that the performance was done magnificently by the Royal Munich Opera and its leading singers, Mr. and Mrs. Vogel (undoubtedly Heinrich Vogl and his wife Therese). The next evening the family saw the same company in a disastrous *Robert le diable,* particularly marked by failures in the stage machinery. Huss then asks whether MacDowell has heard that the effort to build a "two million dollar opera house" in New York had died for lack of funds and a workable scheme. This topic leads to questions of MacDowell's views on political issues: "Do you believe in hard or soft money, Hayes or Tilden? ('reform or corruption'?) I am a hard money, Hayes advocate." MacDowell concurred in his letter of 27 March: "You asked me about my 'politics' and I am happy to say in this, as in music, I join you most heartily in your opinion as to Hayes and Wheeler . . . by birth and inclination, I am Republican." In response to a question from MacDowell, Huss replies that he is not sure whether he will be going to Europe to study and certainly will not for three or four more years. Huss is also working on the Tausig arrangement of Clementi's *Gradus ad Parnassum* and is making a few tries at composition.

In the last surviving letter from Huss to MacDowell, that of 24 May, Huss reports that music-loving New Yorkers have begun efforts to provide a hall for the Thomas Orchestra. The plan is to build "a monster glass and iron hall, (costing $500,000) on the block . . . now occupied by Gilmore's Garden [i.e., Madison Square Garden]. The underpart of the hall is to be occupied by over 100 little stores." He is now studying the *Rondo* in G, Op. 129, of Beethoven, as edited by von Bülow. Huss is very much amused at the image of Beethoven composing a work on a lost penny. In his theoretical studies, he is at work harmonizing chorales.

In his maturity, one aspect of Huss's relations with his fellow musicians must be seen in his connections with societies of composers and performers. One such group was the Manuscript Society of New York. This organization was founded on 27 August 1889 to provide an opportunity for American composers to hear their works while still in manuscript. It went through a few changes of name, and after the turn of the century it gradually shifted to purely social purposes and died out. New York was not unique in having an organization of this kind; there were Manuscript Societies in Philadelphia (founded 1872), Chicago (founded 1896), and elsewhere. Huss also had ties to these other societies. For example, in 1899 Huss was voted unanimously as an active (composer) member of the Chicago Manuscript Society, the requirement to submit a manuscript work having been waived.

One presentation of a Huss work to the New York group was of his *Trio* in D minor, performed 25 March 1892. A review in the next day's *New York Times* stated that

> the most interesting and musicianly work of the evening was Mr. Huss's trio. The first movement was somewhat reminiscent of Schumann, but the scherzo was really original and exquisite in its treatment. The slow movement was also thoroughly the composer's own work. The last movement was distinguished by the effectiveness of its climax. The trio was much applauded and deserves to be heard again.

Huss's contacts with his colleagues resulted from a number of needs. One example is found in the 13 December 1918 letter from Mrs. H. H. A. Beach, with which she sent six songs "very simple and practical on the whole" to help out his "good work." Huss, from other references in the letter, evidently planned to host a sale of autographed works in order to raise money for some charitable purpose. She also sent a program that must have contained a work by Huss, saying it "will at least serve to show my admiration and affection for <u>one</u> number on the list!"

Besides his contacts through letters with other musicians, Huss also attracted them as audiences for his performances. In a review in the *Musical Courier* of 17 April 1912, for example, the following names appear as invited guests:

Richard Aldrich	Mr. and Mrs. [Herman] Irion (Yolanda Mérö)
Dudley Buck	Modest Altschuler
Rebekah Crawford	William R. Chapman
Mary Knight Wood	Charles H. Ditson
Arthur Whiting	Governor and Mrs. Dix
Mrs. Ethelbert Nevin	Rafael Joseffy

Other Pianists

Huss's contacts among fellow performers included other pianists, violinists, conductors, and singers. A few of these individuals are mentioned here, though some specific contacts are detailed elsewhere in this book, and some individuals are cited only in other contexts.

An undated letter (whose contents suggest that it was written after 24 November 1894) from Huss to his parents implies a friendship between Huss and Rafael Joseffy may have existed before 1897. In this letter Huss relates the following encounter:

> I know you will be delighted when I tell what a perfectly charming time I had with Joseffy on Wed. night. He made me take off my coat and then I fired away! He sat at another piano with [the] orchestral score occasionally putting a clarinet or cello note or two in. I played much better than I had expected to. He thought the concerto very effective and modern but *very*

difficult. He afterwards told Meyer that he was amazed at my piano playing. . . . Meyer was greatly pleased at the whole affair and thought the concerto just *immense.* He is now considering if he can publish it. Joseffy took *me* [to lunch]. . . . Joseffy thinks I would have great success with the concerto in Berlin and Paris and Vienna, etc.

[He] also wishes to play the second piano of the concerto with me sometime. I told Aus der Ohe all about it and she seemed greatly interested. Joseffy suggested that as the climax of the piano part in the end of the first movement was very exciting and effective it would be better to leave out the repetition of it in the orchestra just before the organ point and close; you remember we made the same cut when you and I played it together. Also in the finale at the close to let the piano come in a little sooner before the end of the tutti just before the stretto. Aus der Ohe agreed to both of these suggestions.

A posthumous quotation from Joseffy is contained in the review in *Musical Courier* of 20 April 1916 of a recital the Husses gave in April 1916:

With their gifts they should take the same position in America as that of the Henschels in Europe.

This view from Joseffy is interesting, for in the 27 May 1916 issue of *Musical America* there was published an article on husband-wife musical "teams." The Husses were among those cited, others including Pablo and Susan Metcalfe-Casals, David and Clara Mannes, Ossip and Clara Clemens-Gabrilowitsch, Efrem Zimbalist and Alma Gluck, and Leopold Stokowski and Olga Samaroff.

Raoul Pugno's connection with the Huss story is likewise largely tied to his interest in the piano concerto. He wrote to Huss on 13 December 1897 to request a copy of the score:

After having heard your concerto for piano and orchestra I was so truly interested that I ask you to send me the full score in order to read it at my leisure. I continue to have the same good opinion of your work that I expressed to you at first. It is a work musically of great interest, very personal (i.e. having a decided individuality) and which should produce a powerful effect. I persist in thinking that this work would be an interesting one to make known in France, and I continue to promise you to be the interpreter of it.

Only two days later the *Musical Courier* published Pugno's offer in the context of a larger article on the concerto.

> It is definitely announced that Henry Holden Huss has been engaged to appear as soloist with the Seidl Society this season, when his piano concerto, which is still in manuscript, will be heard. [It] has become very well known to the artists of America and Europe and it has excited both admiration and respect for this talented composer and pianist. The concerto has been received with enthusiasm by all who have had the opportunity to hear it. Joseffy pronounced it one of the most prodigious works in piano literature. Aus der Ohe will play it through Germany before being heard in it here. Pugno has asked the privilege to play it on his return to his own country.

About five years later Huss was still hearing from Pugno about the concerto, for he wrote to his family on 24 October 1902 that

> [Pugno] is really going to play my concerto first in Germany then elsewhere, and in two years return to give a long tour in U.S. when he will play it here. . . .
> [He] has not been able yet to arrange for the performance of his own concertstück. He was much interested in my piano [exercises].

In a letter postmarked 10 January 1904, Pugno wrote to Huss that he regretted having been unable to arrange for a performance of the concerto with the Concerts du Châtelet. However, he has told Edouard Colonne that he wants to play an "oeuvre nouvelle que j'aimais beaucoup." Colonne has responded by suggesting one of Pugno's free dates and turned the concert over to one of his assistants, who wishes to know whether Huss might be present at the performance on 18 December. After Pugno tells an anecdote about a concerto of Saint-Saëns, he concludes by saying that he will also play the Huss work on 16 March in Monte Carlo "avec l'admirable orchestre de Jehin."

This promised performance of the concerto by Pugno and the Colonne Orchestra did materialize. On 17 December 1904 Huss attended a concert by the Philharmonic, and when he went to congratulate Colonne on his successes in America, the Frenchman greeted him with these words, as reported in the *Musical Leader and Concert Goer* of 22 December 1904:

My dear Mr. Huss, what a coincidence, that I meet you here tonight; tomorrow afternoon, at 2 o'clock, Pugno plays your concerto with my orchestra in Paris, and I regret more than I can say that after having conducted the rehearsals I had not the pleasure of presenting an American work of such merit myself, but in the hands of Pierné be assured it is perfectly safe.

Ignaz Paderewski, another extraordinarily popular European pianist, was also a friend of Huss. On 23 October 1915 Paderewski gave a benefit recital in Carnegie Hall for Polish relief. The pianist gave an impassioned address at the commencement of the program but was emotionally overcome and had to retire from the stage. After thirty minutes, some of the audience became unruly. At that point, according to the 24 October 1915 issue of the *World,* Huss rose from his seat and told the audience: "Paderewski must rest, keep quiet!"

Whether Huss had known the Polish virtuoso prior to this event is not documented. However, the two evidently developed a warm relationship later, for Paderewski was a patron of Huss's 10 May 1916 student recital; among the other patrons were David Bispham, Mrs. Charles Steinway, Mrs. Vincent Astor ("a former Huss pupil"), Alma Gluck, and Yolanda Mérö. This recital was a benefit for a charity beloved of Paderewski. On 25 July 1916 Huss sent to Paderewski a check for the $169 raised (approximately $2,283.83 in May 1994 value) and requested three autographed photos for students. Huss received a letter of 27 July 1916 from the Polish Victims Relief Fund thanking him for the donation.

The names of Huss and Paderewski were linked again in 1917, when the Polish musician requested an opportunity to hear some of Huss's students in recital; on 5 June the American obliged him. Present at the recital were also some guests, including Mary Knight Wood ("composer of many charming songs"), Pauline Jennings ("the musical lecturer"), and Ella A. Wrigley ("one of the leading piano teachers of Newark, N.J., and one of Mr. Huss's assistants"), persons who figure occasionally in the Huss biography. (These descriptions are from the review in *Musical America,* 16 June 1917.) Another review of the event, in the *Musical Leader* of 14 June 1917, cites the comments of Paderewski at the close of the recital.

[The] great pianist, in his most gracious and impressive manner, made a short but very complimentary speech to the talented group and their distinguished teacher, saying that they had given him very great pleasure; that he had been greatly interested by the very musical way each one had played; that technically it had been most interesting, and from the interpretative side it had been without reproach. He added that it would embarrass him to try to say which numbers were played the most musically, and laid particular stress upon the phrase that, however great their gifts, however zealous and industrious they might have been, without the safe and artistic guidance of their teacher to lead them through the difficulties of that wonderful world of mystery and beauty—music—their powers would never come to full fruition.[1]

One last keyboard virtuoso may be mentioned here. On 18 October 1934 Isidor Philipp wrote from a New York City hotel to thank Huss for

sending your very interesting pieces and for the very useful Condensed piano technics. I will read all this with more care in Paris, and I hope to see you next year when I am coming back—if I am alive.

Apparently Huss's general performing skills were also maintained into the last years of his life. Huss gave a recital in late June 1946, which was attended by Philipp. The Frenchman wrote in apparent haste on 29 June to offer his congratulations.

Dear friend, I was obliged to leave at 10.15. At the piano you were 48 and not 84, terribly amazing, playing with bravura your difficult and interesting concerto. Miss Haber has played with talent your valse and nocturne and as an intelligent accompanist. The other young lady Miss Field is gifted but her Chopin was distorted. I remember Debussy lecturing a German pianist playing his works: Sir, he told him, play what I have written, or, better, don't play it at all! I hate collaboration.

Violinists

It was only natural that Huss would come to work with violinists. Besides his solo compositions for the instrument, he would have been in contact with concertmasters as a result of his performances with orchestras, and he would have known other fine players because of his compositional and performance interests in chamber music. One of the first of these was Franz Kneisel, whom Huss had probably met when playing with the Boston Symphony. As an example of their collaboration, one notes the premiere of the Violin Sonata, Op. 19, for which Kneisel was the dedicatee, given on a program offered by the Kneisel Quartet on 12 November 1901 in Mendelssohn Hall, New York City.

In addition to his piano concerto, Huss also wrote a violin concerto, dedicated to Maud Powell. There were several contacts between them in 1894. On 29 January Powell wrote that she was prepared to rehearse the work. "Don't you want to try the Concerto some time this week, or have you been too busy with other things to get out the revised edition!"

Powell wrote again on 4 March, but this time her concern was not with Huss's violin concerto. Rather, she wanted his advice on whether her Amati would be able to prevail against the welter of orchestral sound she expected in an upcoming concert in Carnegie Hall with Anton Seidl. "I hope I am not bothering you too much! I shall be very grateful to have you give me your frank opinion."

By 9 July, as indicated in a letter of that date to his parents, Huss had completed the orchestration of the violin concerto, and the first movement had been copied. He had also scheduled a time during the coming week to present the work to Seidl. On the thirteenth he dashed off good news of this audition.

> Seidl took an immense interest in the work and was simply delightful! . . . he thought the "tutti's" were a little too long in the 1st movement. . . . He said any violinist would be glad to learn . . . the 1st 2 movements but the piece was "undankbar," it was a gloomy Scherzo. I'm thinking seriously of writing a new "finale." We spent over an hour and a half with him. Miss Powell thinks I ought to feel very proud.

Huss also came to know Eugène Ysaÿe. In the review in the *Musical Leader and Concert Goer* of 9 July 1903 of Huss's performance at the MTNA Convention in Asheville, North Carolina, the following comment appears:

> Pugno and Ysaÿe are among the greatest admirers of Mr. Huss' composition, and the composer is now writing, in response to a request from [Ysaÿe], a string quartet.

Huss himself later provided the context in which that request came. As noted earlier, in the winter of 1911 the Husses stopped on tour in Birmingham, Alabama, where he was interviewed by Dolly Dalrymple. In the course of the interview, Huss told the following anecdote:

> [Let] me tell you about a visit I once paid to Ysaye, the great violinist. When I arrived at his home by appointment, of course, the famous man had not yet arisen for the day. He implored a few minutes grace in which to make his toilette, and hardly had we gotten down and we were engaged in the examination (on Ysaye's part of some of my compositions), when we were interrupted by an anxious father who had brought a tiny little daughter, some 8 or 9 years old, to play for the great violinist. The father questioned if it would not be well to buy a larger violin as the little hands were growing and the instrument in use was a very small one. Ysaye smiled and shook his head. "No," he said. "Little girl, little fiddle; big man, big fiddle." Then he dismissed them and turned to me and said: "Now, Huss, your music, quick, before we are again interrupted!" Of course, I plunged into the examination with the greatest sort of zest; the result was so dear to my heart, and when the finale was reached the artist turned to me and said: "This is better than good music: it has heart as well as brain. I tell you what, write a string quartet for me."
>
> I promised, although I had rather he had asked me for anything else, for nothing is so difficult as writing a string quartet. In orchestral work one can cover up deficiencies of melodic invention by changes in timbre, but in pure four-part writing there must be the genuine, unadorned beauty or failure. [Asked if he had sent the work, he said] Not yet, for try as I may, I cannot get the last movement to suit me, and until I do I shall never send it!

To close an American tour, Ysaÿe gave a farewell recital, including the Huss Sonata, on 13 April 1913 at Carnegie Hall. That this program was of lasting significance to Huss personally is evidenced by a manuscript biography written shortly before his ninetieth birthday, in which this is the only specific recital date mentioned. Huss recalled, in a document written late in life, that Ysaÿe had first encountered the work "by whistling (with notable coloratura) the violin part, as he had a sore finger" and could not play through the work.

The New York press covered the Ysaÿe recital extensively, and it gave high praise to work, composer, and performer alike. Emilie Frances Bauer, writing in the 14 April 1913 issue of the *Evening Mail,* offered the following assessment:

> Ysaye planned a surprise in his programme yesterday given as a farewell one in which he gave tangible proof of his appreciation of America and what it has given him in affection and support.
>
> He opened with the violin sonata . . . [by Huss], a foremost composer of this country, who sat modestly in the audience as much surprised as any one else.
>
> It is a work of high order, noble of expression, admirable of workmanship and a true poetic vein flows throughout every measure. It is a relief, in a modern work, to get away from the struggle after strange and unmusical effects, to hear pure music instead of marvels of musical carpentry.

The reviewer for *Musical America* of 19 April 1913 informs us that Huss's sonata was a late substitution for one by Gabriel Fauré and praised the work:

> Like the other music of Mr. Huss, who takes rank among the foremost American composers, it is not heard as often as it unquestionably deserves to be.
>
> Mr. Ysaye is said to entertain an especial fondness for this sonata, and he played it as though he did.

The change in program in favor of the Huss work was later explained by A. Walter Kramer in *Musical America* of 24 May 1913:

> By some mistake the Gabriel Fauré Sonata had been announced in the papers and only one Sunday paper contained a corrected notice. Mr. Huss chanced to see this just in time to get to Carnegie Hall, though his wife did not arrive until part of the sonata had been played.

Ysaÿe and the sonata were again linked a few years later. On 20 February 1918 Huss and Arthur Hartmann performed the work in Aeolian Hall. From the review in the *Musical Courier* of 28 February 1918, we learn that the large audience included Ysaÿe and Albert Spiering, both of whom had played the sonata. The *Musical Courier* returned to this program in the 21 March 1918 issue in order to quote from New York's *Evening Post.*

> [Ysaÿe] doubtless wanted to hear how Hartmann would play [the sonata]. He must have been hard to please if he didn't like this performance. The best movement of the sonata is the andante—exquisite in melody and modulation, a piece as charming as the Kreisler gems which all the world adores. Why not issue this andante separately, with some poetic title? Violinists seldom have room in their programs for a whole sonata, but as a short piece this gem could and would be exhibited everywhere. As for the "records" that could be made of it, there's a fortune in it; and Mr. Huss deserves it, for he is one of the best of American composers.

Frank Van der Stucken

A name appearing regularly in Huss's biography is that of fellow New Yorker Frank Van der Stucken. The first connection between the two is found in a letter of 5 April 1886 written by Van der Stucken on Huss's behalf for use with the Music Teachers' National Association. Van der Stucken said he

> takes pleasure in recommending Mr. Holden H. Huss [*sic*], a young American composer, pupil of Joseph Rheinberger. His Fantasie for Pianoforte & Orchestra [i.e., the *Rhapsody*] certainly deserves to be performed at the convention of the MTNA.

As noted earlier, William Sherwood performed the *Rhapsody* with an orchestra led by Van der Stucken. In a review of the performance in the *Indianapolis Journal* of 6 July 1887, W. S. B. Matthews wrote,

> [The] best pieces, those which gave most promise and those which were the cleverest in their actually present condition were those of the purely American writers, Buck and Paine, and the piano-forte rhapsody of the young man Huss, a New York boy, and Van der Stucken, the director.
>
> Mr. Sherwood is entitled to no small credit for bringing forward a new work of this kind. Every such case involves an element of personal sacrifice, for the pianist has to give the go-by to favorite compositions of great masters, such as the

public has already learned to love, and submit himself to the drudgery of learning a new work, which is ungrateful to play just in the proportion that it is original. It is pleasant to record that the splendid work of the composer was duly recognized by the audience.

Etude also had a reviewer present, James Huneker, who wrote the following in the August 1887 issue:

Intensely modern in its effects, the piano is often overweighted by the orchestra, and Mr. Sherwood struggled hard to keep his end up, and succeeded splendidly, as he was in his best form, although not in the best of health, and played with ease a very thankless—that is as far as mere effect goes—piano part.

For the MTNA's Philadelphia convention of 1889, Van der Stucken served on the examining committee that selected Huss's *Mottet, "Sanctus"* for performance, and it was heard at a concert given 5 July 1889. Van der Stucken, however, must not have been in attendance at the convention itself, for on 12 July, he was at the Paris Exposition conducting the American music concert, discussed earlier, at the Trocadéro.

This Parisian concert was repeated in Washington, D.C., on 26 March 1890 at Lincoln Hall. The performance, again under Van der Stucken, included all the works performed in Paris the previous July (except for the substitution of a different MacDowell piece) as well as works by Whiting, Arthur Bird, Frederick Gleason, Arthur Weld, Margaret R. Lang, Wilson G. Smith, and William W. Gilchrist. Huss was present, for he was among those in the receiving line, along with the Van der Stuckens, Paine, Whiting, Weld, Powell (soloist on this occasion in the Huss *Romanze and Polonaise*), and others. The *Musical Courier* account in the 2 April 1890 issue congratulated the "generous Mrs. Thurber" for her efforts, noted that the concert was sponsored by the National Conservatory, and stated that similar concerts were to be given around the nation and would culminate in a "grand music festival" in Omaha on 27, 28, and 29 November. Whether Huss's work or Van der Stucken were associated with any of these fall concerts is not known.

Another interesting connection between the two musicians is documented in a letter to Huss, dated 13 August 1901, from Van der Stucken.

> With this note I send the piano and orchestra scores of your
> Romanza. It took me six full hours to score your piece,
> especially on account of the rhythm, which was too monoto-
> nous and had to be changed here and there. The countermelody
> in the clarinet was also added to vary the rhythm; the effect is a
> very "tranquillo" one, notwithstanding the sixteenth notes. I
> wish you would fix up the piano accompaniment according to
> the orchestra score.

Huss is then instructed to return the orchestra score. Here more
questions are raised than answered, and the most important of these
are, What is the work being discussed? and Why had Huss turned it
over to Van der Stucken to orchestrate? The reference to monotonous
rhythm suggests the *Romance* for violin and piano, but sixteenth notes
are virtually nonexistent in this. Another possibility is the *Romanze*
for cello and piano played by Huss and Bergner on 10 April 1889. It
could be an otherwise unknown work, or it could be a subtitle for
another work where the relationship between work and subtitle is not
known.

The severe tone of the note seems not to have damaged the
friendship between the two men, for Huss contributed much effort to
a testimonial dinner honoring Van der Stucken years later, and the
letters between the two concerning that dinner suggest that the older
man always took a schoolmaster's tone with Huss; perhaps he did
with everyone. The dinner was not to be a surprise, and the surviving
correspondence shows that the planning began months ahead and
that Van der Stucken quickly developed his own ideas about the
occasion. On 19 May 1928 Van der Stucken wrote to Huss asking
that Mrs. Horatio Parker's name be added to the committee planning
the event. He states his intention to contact Walter Damrosch about
the dinner and to be in New York in a few days "to finish the
preliminaries with you." On the twenty-ninth he writes from his
hotel about two works Huss had evidently shown him.

> I read the scores of your "In Memoriam" and your piano
> concerto. The former is an excellent, well-scored composition
> that could not only be used at the coming armistice celebra-
> tions, but should be played by all the orchestras on fitting
> occasions. Why don't you send it to the leading musical
> directors of the country? And especially to Stock who has more
> chances to use it at his numerous concerts . . . as any other of his

colleagues. Does he know your concerto? With the MacDowell
D minor, I consider it to be the best piano concerto written in
the States.

The celebration was set for Van der Stucken's seventieth birthday, 15
October 1928. Plans for the dinner were soon well in hand, for Huss
wrote to Elizabeth Sprague Coolidge on 4 June 1928 with a list of the
committee members:

George Chadwick	Philip Hale
Frederick Converse	William Henderson
E. S. Coolidge	H. H. Huss
Walter Damrosch	Edgar S. Kelley
Arthur Foote	Mrs. MacDowell
Rubin Goldmark	Mrs. Parker
Henry Hadley	Frederick Stock
	Arthur Whiting

On 3 August 1928 Van der Stucken wrote to Huss that he wanted
a tenor to sing some of his songs and that he was contacting Edward
Johnson to see if the singer would be available. Van der Stucken also
had some thoughts on the orchestrated version of *In Memoriam*.

Don't you think you might get one of the numerous prizes to be
awarded for a symphonic composition this year? Or would you
rather have it printed at once? This is a financial proposition to
be considered.

The dinner was held at the Harvard Club under the aegis of the
Bohemians. The program included a presentation by Huss and Arthur
Hartmann of the Sonata for violin and piano in D minor. Van der
Stucken did get his wish for the performance of some of his own songs,
sung by an unnamed tenor. Huss gave a short testimonial speech
praising Van der Stucken for his promotion of American works.

David Bispham

Obviously Huss's professional and personal relationship of longest
duration with a singer was that with his wife, but he had connections

with many other vocalists, among these David Bispham. On 22 April 1898 Huss was assisted by Bispham in a recital at the Waldorf-Astoria Hotel.[2] Bispham is particularly associated with one Huss piece sung on this program, since *All the World's a Stage* (with text by Shakespeare and also known as *The Seven Ages of Man*) was dedicated to him. When the work was finally published in 1928, it bore the following after the name of the dedicatee: "who sang this composition over 400 times in America and England."

It may be that Huss's delay in publishing in this case was to ensure Bispham's exclusive association with the work, though this does not explain the seven-years' delay after the singer's death. As to the singer's interest in this work, a letter from Bispham to Huss of 12 June 1898 states that he tried to get Felix Mottl to put the orchestrated version of the song on a certain program, but there was only time for one work, and Mottl wanted to use a piece by Wagner. "I have, however, your orchestral part with me and shall certainly endeavor to use this most interesting composition at the first opportunity."

The other Huss work sung by Bispham on this 22 April 1898 recital was *Haidenröslein;* this apparent misspelling is commonly encountered in references to the work, and its use may have had some private meaning for Huss. The song was the result of Huss taking Beethoven's sketches for a setting of Goethe's poem and then fleshing these out. In a letter of 16 March 1898 Bispham had requested a copy of the song, although apparently for other circumstances:

> Do send me your little Beethoven song at once, in a key suitable
> for me and a transposed one. I have a chance to use it twice soon.

Despite a lack of documentation, this was obviously the beginning of some kind of personal friendship, for on 22 March 1917 the Husses hosted a musical reception for David Bispham. The guests included the Vincent Astors, Carolyn Beebe, Elizabeth Sprague Coolidge, the Hermann Irions, Hugo Kortschak, Mrs. Ethelbert Nevin, and others. Bispham performed *All the World's a Stage* for the assembly. In its 7 April 1917 issue, *Musical America* reported that Huss was asked to improvise ("a thing which he does fascinatingly"). His student Edwin Stodola suggested "D B" as a theme honoring Bispham: "It was on that that Mr. Huss built his splendid improvisation, which won warm favor from all present."

The Mason Family

It is not known how Huss first came into contact with the Mason family; however, the year after a letter from Van der Stucken had helped achieve a performance of his music before the MTNA, Huss arranged for a letter of introduction to be sent to the Examining Committee of American Composition from William Mason, which letter was sent on 8 March 1888. From this letter is dated Huss's known connection with this remarkable New England musical family.

Huss's principal relationship in the family was with Daniel Gregory Mason (II). On 20 August 1890 Daniel Gregory Mason sent a letter to Huss saying that he and his brother Ned (Edward P. Mason) had often played through Huss's *Romanza*. "I frankly confess that I admire it more than I can express." Mason goes on to inquire about whether Huss's song *Du bist wie eine Blume* has yet been published so that he may obtain a copy of it.

During the second half of 1890, Krehbiel engaged Huss to assist him in lectures on Wagner by performing the musical examples at the piano, with the first lecture to take place on 21 January 1891 in Boston. On 12 December 1890 Mary Mason wrote to invite Huss to a small party on the day following that first lecture. The family hoped to hear his *Othello* (another name for Huss's *Prelude Appassionata*) if he could attend.[3] Huss also heard from an old Munich schoolmate; on 30 December, Whiting wrote,

> And I am glad you are going to give us five chances to find out whether we like him [Wagner] or no. Good! Also, that you have "more than half a mind" to play your trio here. Good![4]

In connection with the January 1891 trip to Boston, Huss did perform his *Trio* in D minor on the twenty-third at Mason and Hamlin Hall with Kneisel and Anton Hekking. An interesting aspect of this performance is that in the second and fourth movements, J. Frank Donahoe played along on the Mason and Hamlin Liszt Organ.[5] Later in the program, Huss's *Prelude Appassionata* and *Reverie* were performed in settings for piano and Liszt Organ, the latter instrument now being played by Edward Mason. Apparently Huss liked the effect of the instrument on his *Trio:* he arranged the second movement as a piano-organ duet (Schmidt, 1890). He also published a solo work for the Liszt Organ, *Idyll Pastorale* (Schmidt, 1890).

Huss evidently planned to spend some time with the Masons in Boston again in the summer of 1891, for on 26 June Edward wrote to say that he looked forward to Huss's arrival on 14 July. Mason added that he was sorry to hear Huss had received neither first nor second place in the "L. O. Library Competition":

> Mrs. Mason and I thought your duo certainly deserved this. I also liked the theme of the solo very much and hope we may publish both pieces. It is very gratifying that you should feel so much interest in the work. I am anxiously waiting to hear more of the [Piano?] Concerto.

The reference here may be to a competition for works composed for the Liszt Organ; if so, the "duo" and "solo" must surely refer to Huss's *Romanze* (from the *Trio* in D minor) for organ and piano and to the *Idyll Pastorale* for Liszt Organ alone, respectively.

On 26 June 1892 D. G. Mason wrote to complain about not having heard from Huss lately; "I had also begun to fear that we should never hear that Piano Concerto of yours; where on earth is it?" He continued:

> Do you know Professor Paine of Harvard? I have been taking Harmony with him. . . . We have very interesting talks with him after lessons on matters musical; and one day he said in passing that he considered you the best of the young generation of American composers. This I think means a good deal, coming from such an able and unbiased judge as he is.

Mason repeats an invitation issued by his mother for Huss to spend some time with the Masons that summer; he has dreams of "musical talks, tricycles, and cold beer." That these "musical talks" were significant to Mason may be gleaned from a comment he made in *Music in My Time* (1938).

> It was through my brothers that I came later to study piano with Ethelbert Nevin, and that I met MacDowell, Loeffler, Chadwick, Foote, and other Boston musicians, as well as Henry Holden Huss of New York, to whose comradely interest my early musical efforts were deeply indebted.

On 12 August D. G. Mason wrote to tell of his pleasure in having had Huss as a guest for two weeks that summer. He adds

> I saw Chadwick yesterday, and showed him my recent compositions. The children's songs are about done now. I may publish them. As the two older ones are already dedicated to you, I shall do the same with "Little John Bottlejohn," if you don't mind?

On 6 December 1892 a letter from Edward to Huss brought a request for Huss's views to be published in a pamphlet entitled "Opinions of Three American Musicians of the Mason and Hamlin Piano-forte." He was asking Sherwood, his uncle William, "and your honored self" for such statements.

Just before returning to Harvard in the fall of 1893, D. G. Mason wrote again. He sent a copy of a song he had written.

> This is very little production to offer in place of the violin sonata, Henry, but it's something. . . . I think your influence is perceptible in the semi-tonal descent of the last stanza.
>
> I don't yet, however, approve of the dissolute old abbé [i.e., Liszt] you rank so high (as I write these words I wink slyly) and I still think Meyerbeer has written some good tunes.
>
> I wish, too, I could hear the [Piano] Concerto. Oh, that _is_ a work! You may well be proud of that, Henry! I can't think of it without beginning to speak in superlatives.

By 30 September Mason was back in school, but he was no less interested in the piano concerto, and he was now curious about the revisions that Huss was making in the work.

> I didn't know there was anything "objectionable" in the first movement of your concerto. Still, I must take your word for it. I hope you haven't altered the cadenza of the 2nd Movement; the place I said called up in my mind such a wild and primeval landscape. That is "dangerously near genius," as one of our Harvard wits says.

A letter from D. G. Mason of 22 December continued this focus by Mason on revisions of the piano concerto.

> My pleasure at getting a letter from you was only exceeded by my pleasure at hearing such a good report of Paur's opinion of

the concerto. But I am very, very sorry you feel it necessary to leave out the "wild birds and desert island" theme, for as you probably remember . . . I had conceived a great admiration for that theme. It is indeed one of the most nobly barbaric things that I know in music, besides being tremendously original. But very possibly the general effect of the whole composition will be enhanced by its omission; I see what you mean in saying that the middle movement should be as restful as possible. Do save the theme and use it somewhere else.

While Paur's opinion on Huss's concerto does not survive, on 21 February 1894 Henry Mason wrote to Huss that he had spoken "today" with Paur on behalf of the piano concerto, so Paur was certainly feeling some pressure from some of Huss's powerful Boston friends:

Mrs. Paur . . . again expressed, for them both, keen appreciation of and admiration for your work; and she assured me that next season they would . . . gladly extend to you invitations to come on and give your concerto.

In addition to visits with the Mason clan, we know that Huss spent some time with his brother-in-law's family at their home in Clinton, Massachusetts. Huss wrote to his parents from the Parkhurst residence on 28 August 1894 that

Mr. Edward Mason insists in sending me a concert grand piano to Clarendon altho I told him I would only be there about 3 weeks. It will be a good opportunity for me to become thoroughly acquainted with the concert grand as of course I only went 2 or 3 times to Boston.

William Mason attended a private presentation of the piano concerto before its true premiere, and he wrote to Huss of his enthusiasm on 21 December 1894:

Your beautiful Concerto gave me a real musical pleasure yesterday afternoon both as regards its composition and its admirable performance, and I congratulate you heartily upon having produced such a fine work. I hold it from beginning to end in very high esteem and what I said about the lack of "jingle" in the last movement you must take as of no account.

> I was sorry afterward that I made that remark, fearing that you might have placed undue stress upon it, and this is one of my reasons for sending you this letter. I shall now look forward to a hearing of the work with orchestra with pleasant anticipation. If you are passing my studio in Steinway Hall within a few days, please come in for a moment as I wish to see you.

The true premiere of the work was given by the Boston Symphony Orchestra under Paur at a public rehearsal on 29 December 1894 and at the formal concert the following night. D. G. Mason contributed encouragement:

> Hurray for you and your Grosse Klavier-Concert! It seems too good to be true that you are really going to play it a week from tomorrow in Music Hall, and that I am going to sit up above [Mason had a box seat above the orchestra] and hear and see you.

Mason also reports he has been studying piano with Whiting, who

> does not approve of some of the things you taught me to do last summer, and I have not yet decided which of you I agree with in these matters. I think on the whole his method is very fine and thoughtful though, but I shall never forget how much good those few weeks of Klavier work [with you] did me, and I shall never cease to be grateful . . . for all the pains you took with me and all the good you did me. . . . I pleased Whiting a good deal by showing him your letter.

The performance was duly reviewed, and there were some comments by the critics that caused Huss to consider revisions in the concerto. In the next letter he received from D. G. Mason he is asked, "Have you made any changes in the Concerto, or are you still mulling it over? I shall be anxious to hear what you do." Some decisions were made quickly, for on 27 January Mason wrote again.

> The first thing to say is that I am glad you cut the Concerto as you describe it in your letter, and I think it will bear the pruning, especially if you sacrifice no more than in that place you showed me. I trust you will also consider simplifying the scoring a little, although I suppose it is pretty hard to bring yourself to that. But consider that in so doing you are but removing some of the complexity which hinders the . . .

> significance and beauty of the thought from standing forth in
> the clear light which it deserves, and would bear without
> discovering any blemishes or imperfections, like a young girl
> who looks most beautiful in frank daylight.

Mason then goes on to new ground by asking about the violin
concerto:

> How is [it] progressing? Have you finished the composition of
> the Finale yet? I wish I could hear it.

In the fall of 1895, Huss contributed further to Mason's musical
education by providing him with a ticket by which Mason could join
him at a concert. The tickets were for a concert of "R.W.," perhaps a
reference to organist Richard Warren or to Richard Wagner. The
next letter from Mason (1 January 1896) suggests Wagner, for he
writes "I hope to see you tomorrow night at <u>Lohengrin</u>."

Four years later, Huss spent part of the summer with the Masons in
Massachusetts again. We know this from a letter of 27 August 1899
from D. G. Mason to Huss thanking him for coming and for the
musical discussions they had during that time.

> Perhaps the best inspiration of all was the noble Pater Noster,
> to which I recur [*sic*] again and again. Its beauty is fundamental
> and abiding, and the thought of it is like the thought of a
> friend. I await impatiently for the day when it is printed and I
> can play it over for myself and learn it.

Three years later Huss's name appeared in an article discussing the
current important names in American music written by D. G. Mason
in the *Outlook* of 15 March 1902. Mason began with a general
discussion of what he thought the essential characteristics of American music were and then presented short biographies of several
composers who he felt displayed those characteristics to advantage. In
his opening he expressed the view that "art" music is founded upon
folk music whether in a conscious or unconscious manner. American
composers, though, did not spring from the folk sources suggested by
Dvořák's work (American Indians or Black slaves), rather from
various European nations. Mason expected an American composer to
reflect being American but also reflect having sprung from a certain
portion of American society. The composer's work would show

> the practical power of the English, the vivacity of the French,
> the moral earnestness of the Germans, and many other transat-
> lantic traits [and] a certain ultimate quality of [its] own, an
> indefinable vigor and effervescence of spirit, a big, crude,
> ardent, democratic enthusiasm.

In his discussion of Huss, Mason includes a summary of Huss's
training and a list of principal works, ending with mention of the
piano concerto ("his finest work").

> It well illustrates his romanticism, which is extreme; though he
> is sometimes turgid in emotion and over-elaborate in harmony,
> his sentiment is so manly and poetic and his style at its best so
> elevated that he is one of the modern romantic school in music.
> One can see that he has studied to advantage not only Bach and
> Beethoven but also Schumann, Liszt, Rubinstein, Tschaikow-
> sky, and Wagner; yet he is entirely original—his half-sensuous,
> half-religious mysticism is characteristic of no one else.

After this, the documentary record for the Mason-Huss friendship
ends except for one incident several years later, reported in the
Musical Courier of 23 September 1914. Huss's summer activities that
year included planning for a tour to the West and South in
November, relaxing in Lake George, taking vacation trips to the
Adirondacks and Berkshires, and guiding three students through
informal recitals in the the Lake George studio. The excursion to the
Berkshires included visits in mid-July to the homes of Elizabeth
Sprague Coolidge and D. G. Mason. In his *Music in My Time,* Mason
described the three-day period, during which the Husses visited, as
"a regular musical festival." On the eighteenth, the Masons held
their "annual studio party" with the Coolidges, the Spragues, the
Ulysse Buhlers, the George Vignetis, the Husses, Miss [Gertrude]
Watson, Alphonse Pelletier ("the horn player"), and Burnet Tuthill.
On the nineteenth,

> we had tea and cake in the garden [at Miss Watson's], and Mrs.
> S—— read some verses, after which Henry Huss begged her to
> allow him to express his thanks by improvising, and led the
> way back to the house, with all of us obediently trailing after,
> quite as if he had been chief undertaker and all the rest of us
> mourners.

Henry Krehbiel

One of the most influential music journalists in America in the late nineteenth century was Henry Krehbiel. Huss was fortunate to impress Krehbiel with his work early in his career, and that favorable impression led to a long friendship. The 1889 performance of Huss's *Mottet* before the MTNA was reviewed by Krehbiel (*New York Tribune*, 6 July 1889), the first known connection between the two men.

> Of the younger American composers, none has been more talked about at this meeting than Mr. Huss. His "Sanctus" received very high classing at the hands of the examiners, and he has won hearty recognition for the virility and unconventionality of his talent. It suggested that his strength lies rather in the handling of harmonies and forms than in the creation of varied and appropriate vocal melody, the solo part conveying the impression that the music had not sprung from the words, but that the two elements had been rather arbitrarily consorted. Nevertheless, the work is heartily deserving of praise, and is pervaded by a genuinely religious spirit. Antiphonal effects between the male and female chorus at the outset on the words, "Holy, holy," and the principal melody of this portion are conceived in a lovely vein, and there is much ingenuity, learning and strength in the fugue which forms the middle part of the work. But the work suffered many indignities at the hands of the chorus and orchestra.

Krehbiel's response to this apparent talent came quickly. It has been noted already that Krehbiel engaged Huss to assist him in lectures on Wagner, beginning in 1891. Early in 1897 Krehbiel engaged Huss to help with another lecture, this time to be held 1 March at Columbia "College" (Krehbiel probably was referring to Columbia University). The subject of the lecture is not certain, but in his letter Krehbiel sent two gospel tunes (*Weeping Mary* and *Baptizing Hymn*) for which he wanted Huss to provide harmonizations ("I know you can make the songs sound well"), so it may be that the topic was American folk music. Possibly, too, these materials were to support a discussion of Dvořák's use of American materials in his symphony. These two melodies, with harmonizations credited to Huss, did appear in Krehbiel's book *Afro-American Folksongs: A Study in Racial and National Music.*

Quite possibly the most important musical event of 1893 in
America was the debut of Dvořák's Symphony in E minor ("From the
New World"). This debut occurred at an open rehearsal of the New
York Philharmonic Society on the afternoon of 15 December with
the presentation at a formal concert occurring the following evening.
Krehbiel organized a lecture-recital on the work at Columbia
University later in December 1893. He requested of Dvořák that the
main themes be written out, and he employed the services of his
colleague Huss, as at previous such lectures, to perform the illustrations at the keyboard. The sheet with the themes in Dvořák's hand
were retained by Huss for rest of his life. After Huss's death, they
became the property of Carl Tollefsen and are now a part of the
Tollefsen Collection housed at Southern Illinois University in Edwardsville.

The story of Huss's *Haidenröslein* also connects the two men. It was
often described in programs and articles as a "reconstruction" of a
melody by Beethoven found in one of his sketchbooks. The sketch
and the Huss reconstruction done in January 1898 (a reproduction of
the already-published Schirmer edition) were offered by Krehbiel to
his readers along with the following explanation in the *New York
Tribune* of both 27 February and 6 March 1898. Krehbiel probably
served as the impetus for the project in the first place.

> Readers of Nottebohm's "Beethoveniana" (which is a classified
> study of a number of the sketchbooks left by Beethoven) were
> prepared for the publication a few weeks ago of a setting by
> Beethoven of Goethe's ballad "The Erlking.". . . The present
> work is a different case. The Beethoven melody for Goethe's
> "Haidenröslein," which Mr. Henry Holden Huss has put
> together from a page of sketches found in the collection of
> autographs made by the late Alexander W. Thayer, is now
> made public for the first time. Herr Nottebohm and the readers
> of the "Zweite Beethoveniana" knew, indeed, that Beethoven
> had contemplated a setting of the poem, for this fact is recorded
> in Chapter LXIII of the book where also may be found a portion
> of a melody which haunted the mind of the composer for a
> considerable space of time . . . [but] is not the one of which Mr.
> Huss made use. . . . [The melody Huss did use] seems never to
> have come under the eyes of a student of Beethoven's sketches.
> Mr. Thayer must, of course, have been familiar with it, but was
> probably waiting to mention it at the time called for by the

chronology in his biography of the master. Mr. Huss's procedure in putting the song together was to follow the sketch, choose from the variant readings noted by Beethoven those which his taste and judgment preferred, and supply harmony and an accompaniment in the spirit of Beethoven's published songs.

Elizabeth Sprague Coolidge

The remaining relationship to be discussed is that between Huss and Elizabeth Sprague Coolidge. Items cited elsewhere indicate that they had a personal friendship and that she was in some way a student of his, but Huss also apparently looked on her as a patron as well.

Huss attended a chamber music festival (sponsored at least in part by Coolidge) in Pittsfield, Massachusetts, on 16, 17, and 18 September 1918. A listing of some of the other persons involved in the event or attending suggests the importance of the festival as well as the heady atmosphere in which Huss found himself: D. G. Mason, Frederick Stock, Kneisel, Gabrilowitsch, Hugo Kortschak, Sonneck, May Mukle, Louise Homer, Susan Metcalf Casals, Lillian Littlehales, and Fritz Kreisler, along with the Berkshire, Flonzaley, and Olive Mead Quartets. The appearance of a quartet by Huss at the 1919 festival can probably be traced to his presence at the 1918 event; it must have encouraged him to look at the genre again after about a decade.

The first performance of Huss's String Quartet in B minor, Op. 31, on 2 July 1919, by the Berkshire String Quartet connects Huss and Coolidge. The Berkshire Quartet evidently appeared under the patronage of Coolidge, for Huss wrote to her on 6 July 1919 to thank her for the performance his work had received. He wrote her again with a more generalized appreciation of her musical sponsorship on 24 November 1919; in the text he also condemned much modern music as "empty glitter" and "meretricious instrumentation."

Coolidge invited Huss to Pittsfield, Massachusetts, for a festival in the late summer of 1921, but Huss sent his regrets on 8 September. In a November letter he explained that the reason he did not accept the invitation was that Mrs. Huss had undergone a serious operation. In this same letter, Huss invited Coolidge to his 30 November recital at Steinway Hall, but she wrote on the eighteenth that she would be unable to attend.

In early September 1922 Huss wrote to Coolidge with the news that he would be attending the "Festival." He said he was looking forward especially to the scheduled Brahms program. "His noble music, so lofty, so full of significant symmetry and unswerving sense of proportion seems especially needed in these transition days of lawlessness and anarchy in music and poetry." He also reported that "Lifschey and Goldstein played my sonatas successfully." On 22 September he wrote again to thank Coolidge for the gift of two tickets to the festival and explained that he and his wife would just barely make it in time by car from Lake George for the afternoon recital.

Huss's summer correspondence the next year included a letter of 8 September 1923 to Coolidge accepting her gift of tickets to the Berkshire Festival. Huss will attend, but his wife has too "large a class of pupils" to attend. Instead, Huss proposes to bring his colleagues Ethel Grow and Jane Cathcart, whom he identifies as an American art song singer, and a piano teacher and founder of a musical club for young students, respectively, and he requests tickets for them. He adds, "It was most kind of you to take my viola sonata with you to Europe. Did anything come out of it and your delightful plan for the composer?" Unfortunately, the answer to Huss's question is still unknown, and the "plan" referred to is also unknown.

In a letter of 26 August 1924 to Coolidge's secretary, Miss Bristol, may be found the explanation for the paucity of Huss performances in 1924: "serious illness" had delayed his writing to her. Who was ill and how seriously is not specified; at this time Huss was sixty-two and his wife fifty. On 9 September he wrote to Bristol again with thanks for an invitation to concerts at the Berkshire Festival and inquired about a ticket for Beatrice Dolan, a student of his.

Huss did attend one more of the festivals at Pittsfield, Massachusetts, for which he kept receiving invitations from Coolidge. He wrote to Miss Bristol on 12 September 1928 to thank her for the efforts to secure additional tickets for a friend and her son. He told her the tickets should be sent to Huss at the residence of Mrs. William Sawyer in Langerfield, New York, since he would be staying there before leaving for the concerts. It is a sign of the nature of past postal service that the next day (the thirteenth) he wrote to Bristol again with the news that the tickets had arrived.

On 1 October 1930 Huss wrote a long letter to Coolidge from which it may be seen that the decline of his stature and the advance of his age had become apparent to him. Ostensibly his purpose was to express thanks with regrets for an invitation to a festival in Chicago. He went on to request that one of his pieces be played at one of the festivals sponsored by Coolidge while he was still "a pilgrim in this vale of tears." He reminded her that she had heard and admired his viola sonata some years earlier. He also reminded her of favorable views on other works held by respected individuals. Coolidge was in a delicate position, and we lack her response to this request.

On 26 March 1931 Huss wrote again to decline an invitation to the festival in Washington (due to "imperative professional engagements") and invited her to hear some students when next she would be in New York. Moreover, he referred her to the 1 October letter, so he was clearly unwilling to let the matter drop, whatever the form her reply, if any, had taken. Coolidge replied on 4 April 1931 to say she was sorry he could not come to the festival and that she could not accept his invitation to his studio; she also made a polite reference to the viola sonata.

Huss tried again, on 19 July 1931, to have Coolidge influence the placement of a work of his on a festival program. Here again he made reference to the viola sonata and Coolidge's favorable reaction to it. According to this letter, she had tried to get Lionel Tertis to perform it. Coolidge replied on 28 July 1931 that she had listened to the viola sonata with "pleasure" and found it "interesting," but that she was leaving the committee in charge of the Washington festivals. Her future plans included the possibility of arranging concerts at schools and in Europe, but these would be made up "almost wholly of ultramodern works which I have generally commissioned to be written."

Two years later he tried again. On 21 March 1933 she replied to a letter of his, stating that she was unable to offer him the assistance (unspecified) he had requested. In reference to his upcoming 4 April recital, she wrote that she hoped he would

> have a successful concert and that affairs will turn for [him] . . .
> in the direction of long awaited improvements.

Huss is known to have turned to her only once more for support. On 14 July 1942 Coolidge wrote again to turn down a request for "a helping hand" and referred him to the Coolidge Foundation in Washington, D.C. She did offer him congratulations on his eightieth birthday, however.

CHAPTER IV

THE MATURE YEARS

The years 1905 to 1909 were a low point in Huss's career, marked by a noticeably diminished level of activity for the first few years of marriage. While his standing as an American composer, pianist, and teacher was firmly established, it may be that the stresses of acclimating to a new spouse and the deaths of his parents in the months following the wedding were the cause of his quietude. By the end of this time, though, he seems to have recovered his former pace, for the period 1910 to 1935 was, in general, an extremely fruitful and productive time for Huss.

Shortly after his wedding, Huss apparently had an opportunity to greet another visiting musician. Camille Saint-Saëns made two trips to the United States, one in 1906 and the other, as a representative of the French government to the Panama Exposition in San Francisco, in 1915. Huss recorded having met Saint-Saëns after a concert, and one assumes this was during the 1906 visit.

> When St. Saëns appeared in New York in the triple role of composer, pianist and conductor, he, in one instance, essayed the impossible, i.e., in playing his own piano concerto (was it the g min. concerto?) and directing part of the time with his head! The effect was not perfectly satisfactory! This half failure, as I afterward found to my cost, nettled him. . . . I begged Franz Kneisel to present me to the master. We found him pacing up and down the greenroom with a frowning countenance. Kneisel presented me and I burst forth with "Oh Monsieur, may I thank you for your magnificent Gothic symphony?" He snapped out "Mais vous me confusez avec Godard! Il a ècrit une symphonie gothique!" Naturally I instantly flushed with resentment. "Mais Monsieur je suis aussi musicien, et je sais bien le difference entre vous, un grand Maitre, et Godard!" but he persisted in repeating his stupid and incredible remark.

How well we all know that Godard was an amiable and sweet young composer who composed amiable and sweet music beloved by school girls 40 years ago! What was there for me to do but to pocket my wrath and politely and firmly bid Monsieur St. Saëns adieu!!

Huss's evident lack of public performance in this first decade of the twentieth century did not affect his professional reputation, for the Husses were honored by their selection as the cover story of the 5 November 1908 issue of the *Musical Leader and Concert Goer.*

Henry Holden Huss is one of the best appreciated of modern writers in this country. . . . Besides the [piano] concerto he has written a number of songs, and is now engaged on a Sonata for 'cello and piano for Alwin Schroeder. Mr. Huss is a pianist of unusual charm, noted for his musical quality and refined style of playing.

[He] maintains a studio, where each available hour has been bespoken for the season, and he gives in conjunction with his wife some delightful recitals. This gifted pair of artists have won a place in the music life of New York which is unassailable.

Huss's reputation as a teacher also continued to grow. For several years, Huss sponsored a student recital with which he rounded out his New York teaching season. Usually these recitals were held in late April or May, and sometimes they were also benefit recitals for various causes. The one given 9 May 1907 is typical: a benefit for the MacDowell Fund (the nature and purpose of this charity are not known). Emilie Frances Bauer, in her review for the *Musical Leader and Concert Goer,* stated:

It is nothing new to say that Mr. Huss is one of the greatest musical forces in this country, basing this especially upon his influence as teacher.

It has often been said and it needs no repetition, that Mr. Huss is an unusual teacher, and his pupils carry a degree of understanding that is not usually found in pupils. He has imparted to all without exception both poetic insight and a beautiful musical touch.

Another student recital was given on 7 May 1908, and one Huss student played the G minor Prelude, Op. 23 (1905), of Rachmaninoff, indicating that Huss kept somewhat abreast of the works of his contemporaries other than fellow Americans and encouraged his students to learn such pieces.

In a letter of 8 May 1928 Henry Fleck of Hunter College wrote to one Mrs. Warren, who had asked his advice on a teacher.

> I would strongly advise you to send your daughter to Mr. Henry Holden Huss. There is no better teacher in this country than Mr. Huss, not only for piano, but also for a thorough training as a composer. He will be a source of inspiration to your daughter.

The names of many of his students can be seen in the performance programs, in the reviews, and in the dedications of some of works. Most of these people seem to have had no discernible impact on the larger musical world, but there are a few names that should be highlighted here: Marion Bauer, Efrem Zimbalist, Katherine Goodson, Winthrop Parkhurst, Florence Beckwith (who became head of the piano department of Trinity College, Texas), Marion Coursen (who became head of the piano department of the Millersville, Pennsylvania, State Normal School), Edwin Stodola (who joined the faculty of the Conservatory of Music in St. Joseph, Missouri), and Elizabeth Sprague Coolidge.[1]

Huss's "teaching" work may also be seen in his lectures. The idea of performing in this way may have come to him from his experiences in working with Krehbiel in the critic's own lectures. Generally Huss offered single appearances, but in 1903 he gave an extended series of lectures—master classes for the students of the "Misses Crawford" of Brooklyn. On these occasions he talked about some aspect of music using musical examples and "pictures thrown upon a screen, illustrative of the lecture and the music given." The events were scheduled for first five months of the year, and in the fall Huss gave a continuation of the series, again for the Crawfords. These lectures included talks on Bach and *Parsifal*. The lectures became so popular that the one on Wagner was held in "the chapter room" of Carnegie Hall; Huss was assisted in the musical illustrations by Babetta Huss and Hildegard Hoffmann. A review in the 10 December 1903 *Musical Leader and Concert Goer* offers this description:

> [Huss] gave in his superbly artistic manner some selections which he also analyzed and brought within the understanding of his audience. In the Bach section of the programme Miss Hildegard Hoffmann sang an aria with a fine appreciation for

the needs of that great master, and her beautiful voice lent itself to enhance the beauty of the song. The "Parsifal" music was made delightfully interesting by Mr. Huss.

That Huss continued to give lectures throughout much of his life is documented. For example, there was a series of four lecture-recitals in February 1935, one each on the operas of Wagner's *Der Ring des Nibelungen*. The prospectus for the series offered the following description.

> Owing to the success of Mr. Huss' Wagner lecture-recitals during the past four years at Hunter College, he has been requested to give a short course on Wagner's "Ring of the Nibelungen" with the unique plan of stressing the melodic beauties of the mighty Tetralogy. There are many melodiously beautiful passages which often escape the listener during the stage performance; sometimes these sections are omitted.

Unfortunately the text of these lectures does not survive, so we are denied both Huss's view of the *Ring* and further information on the performance practice suggested in this last sentence.

His native city and state regularly welcomed him back for concertizing and actively promoted his career. One such visit was heralded by Newark's *Sunday Call* of 29 August 1909, which ran an extended editorial bemoaning the dearth of artists who lived in Newark and thereby introducing an extended (though sometimes naive) discussion of Huss's life and works.

> As a pianist he ranks very high, although he does not consider himself as a virtuoso, preferring to regard the playing of the piano as one of the necessary accomplishments of the educated musician. When he plays in public his object is to interpret the composer and make known the music and not to exploit himself. He has technique sufficient for all demands of modern music, but he uses this technique for its proper purpose only, that of giving the real meaning of the composition he is playing.
>
> As a composer Mr. Huss ranks among the moderns. He does not hesitate to use the most abstruse harmonies if he thinks them necessary to reveal his meaning in his works. [The violin sonata] is an example of this. It has no distinguishing title; it illustrates no program, it mirrors no picture, but it is, nevertheless, purely intellectual music emotionally colored. This sonata

is not for the amateur. [It] flashes a meaning to every auditor capable of perceiving a meaning in music—and Mr. Huss writes for no others—but to the mere lover of momentary pleasure it would be tedious and uninteresting.

We do not know of anything frivolous in his catalogue. Even a simple song contains a real musical thought of permanent worth, and in whatever he has written he has put real musicianship and serious thought. Mr. Huss might write a symphony, a concert overture, a symphonic poem, an oratorio or a cantata, but we can not imagine him writing a comic opera.

With this view of Huss in mind, it comes as no surprise that he would travel to Europe, with his wife, to perform. On 8 July 1910 the couple presented a recital at London's Steinway Hall, but they also spent the summer traveling about in England, France, and Germany. Some of the features of this trip can be discerned from letters home to Huss's sisters Johanna and Babetta.

13 June	Mrs. Huss writes that they have attended services at Westminster Abbey, where Huss tried unsuccessfully to see Frederick Bridge, the organist.
No date	Mrs. Huss writes that Albert Hall "is bad for any music, I'm sure, unless it's 'jam full.' " Huss appends a note: "Yest. at Westminster Abbey . . . the music was beautifully given, the choir giving out real 'pps' as well as 'ffs.' "
18 June	Written from Paris: the London recital date now arranged, with Mukle to play the cello sonata for a $20 fee; "She read it wonderfully yst. and is enthusiastic about it."
25 June	From Paris: the recital is scheduled for the afternoon in order to get critics who will be occupied at night by the two opera companies; Huss has ordered a frock coat ("for the [to us New Yorkers] absurdly low price of $37"); Steinway has provided an upright in their room for practicing.
5 July	From Berlin: they met Boris Hambourg, and "he was very enthusiastic about 'To the Night' and is anxious to hear the cello sonata. I will play it with him on Thurs., and he is coming to our concert. . . . I selected a splendid concert grand today at Steinway's for our

concert. My new coat fits me to Hilda's satisfaction which means something."

No date   From Berlin: "The other day I played my piano concerto to Francesco Berger Sec. of the London Philharmonic Soc. . . . He was <u>most</u> enthusiastic about the concerto and promised to do all he could to get me an engagement with the Soc.!!"

8 July   From London: "Hurrah, hurrah! hurrah!!!! Our concert today was a <u>great great</u> success artistically and socially. The sonata went bully. . . . Mr. Mackey the manager of the Hall tells me that critics of the four big dailies were present: The Times, Standard, Post & Telegraph. The house was <u>well</u> filled but not crowded. [The] net cost of the concert was only about $47.00. We are very happy and thankful. [Hambourg] read over the 'cello sonata with me yest. and wants to play it with me in New York."

26 July   From Paris:[2] "This A.M. I showed Charles W. Clark (the celebrated baritone and teacher here) some of my songs. . . . On Sunday we saw Isadore Luckstone. He was enthusiastic about my songs . . . especially 'Phyllis.' "

5 August   From Kassel: "[We] were invited to an informal musicale. . . . To our great surprise we met Adolf Hertdegen, the former N.Y. cellist. He read my 'cello romanza very artistically." Mrs. Huss performed several songs, including Huss's *Every Day Hath Its Night* and *Ich liebe Dich* as well as the Beethoven-Huss *Heidenröslein.* "[The] company were all very enthusiastic. . . . After I played my 'To the Night,' ["a young spanish-american basso" just engaged at the Hamburg Opera] said it made him proud to be an American, [and] his teacher Herr Hoche was excited about the 'Heidenröslein.' "

10 August   From Kassel: Huss has proposed to play for the Emperor but has received no answer.[3]

16 August   From Kassel: "Today I had an introductory letter to the Opera orchestra Director Herr Dr. Baier. He gives symphony concerts here; liked my piano concerto very much, thought there were many beautiful contrasts in

it." They have recently watched a parade in honor of the heroes of the war of 1870; during the parade, bands played marches by Frederick the Great.

19 August   From Kassel: Huss has requested a small grand from Steinway for his use upon his return to New York as "I want to compose a lot." "In Kassel they are really crazy to have us give a concert the next time we return."

25 August   From Nürnberg: "This A.M. I received a fine letter from Kapellmeister Bruch telling me how much he liked my piano concerto, was sure it would have great success in Germany and would do all in his powers next year to produce [it] with orchestra. He thought it could be done for $100 or $125 which is of course ridiculously cheap."

6 September   On the *Barbarossa,* returning home: "[A piano] teacher in Ziegfield's Chicago Conservatory is going to speak to [Frederick] Stock about my concerto. He is a good friend of Stock's and is very enthusiastic about the concerto." Passengers from St. Louis, Ashland, Nebraska, and Philadelphia expressed interest in having Huss recitals in their cities. The previous afternoon, "I played a few of my pieces." Two piano teachers want to use Huss pieces with their students.

A few months after this one finds evidence of another possible official connection between Huss and the MTNA, an organization not documented in the biography since 1903. This is found in a letter from Huss to A. P. Schmidt written on 28 October 1910. Huss responded to a request from the Executive Committee of the MTNA that he chair the piano conference at their Boston meeting 27–30 December by saying he was not certain he could accept the responsibility but was willing to try.

On 18 September 1911, the Husses offered a recital at Lake George, assisted by his sister Babetta. Huss played the first movement of Beethoven's Sonata, Op. 57 ("Appassionata"), among other works. A review of the performance in *Musical America* offered this assessment:

> Mr. Huss's reading of the . . . Beethoven "Appassionata" gave evidence of a thorough mastery of the noble work. Interpreta-

tion of Beethoven is apt to be academic in these days of
modernity, when performers feel that the masters should be
given in rather strict style to contrast them with the moderns.
Mr. Huss, however, plays it with a wealth of emotional feeling
and brings out every *nuance* with extraordinary ability.

A sample of Huss's stage manner may be seen in reviews quoted by
the *Musical Courier* for the November 1911 concert tour.

In response to an encore Mr. Huss improvised in a wonderful
manner on a theme given him at the beginning of the recital.
Mr. Huss added greatly to the interest and educational worth of
the recital (one of the best in years) by giving a descriptive talk
before some of the numbers.

The Husses often performed on such short tours around the eastern
part of the United States. There were other occasions taking the
Husses away from New York for performances that are worth
mentioning in this context. One was the inaugural concert of the
Philadelphia Center of the American Music Society, held in Wither-
spoon Hall on 6 April 1911, at which Mrs. Huss sang six of her
husband's songs.

The concert tour of 1912 included a stop in St. Paul, Minnesota,
where on 24 November Huss played the first movement of his piano
concerto with the St. Paul Symphony Orchestra at its Third Popular
Concert. This performance was noted favorably in the leading music
journals of the time, and the next day the *St. Paul Pioneer-Press* offered
the following:

Mr. Huss [is] a pianist of excellent ability. [The concerto
movement] was a somewhat grandiloquent composition in a
Wagnerian mood containing, however, some excellent display
of technical effect, evenly rendered with good facility and
admirable finish. The parts with the orchestra were of effective
character and showed unvarying agreement between the latter
and the pianist. In response to an encore Mr. Huss played a
light and boldly fanciful little waltz, his own composition.

The other was on 16 January 1913, when Huss and his wife
performed in the "Artist's Course" at the Masonic Temple in Erie,
Pennsylvania. The prospectus for the "Course" also contained the
following curious item:

[The Husses] have also recently added to their American triumphs a very successful debut at Steinway Hall, London, and return in April to fill other important European engagements.

The couple did not return to Europe in 1913; in fact, there is no evidence suggesting they ever returned. That they had plans to do so is clear from this passage and some of the correspondence associated with the 1910 trip. Very likely a significant factor in their not going was the death of Huss's sister Johanna of cancer on 27 May 1913. It is not unreasonable to assume that her illness precluded Huss's departure for Europe.

On 31 October Huss received legal notice that he was the executor of his sister's estate. Other documents covering this matter extend to 23 June 1914, with the situation complicated because his sister died intestate. Part of her estate included her share of the income from an $11,000 bond, as divided among the children, with their spouses, of George John Huss, with the exception of Mary Huss Parkhurst. The May 1994 value of this bond, using 1913 dollars as the base, is approximately $163,667. This indicates that the total income from the bond was probably significant. It also supports the theory that Huss's father—whose own estate, no doubt, served as the source of the bond—was a financially successful musician.

The last known event in Huss's life in 1913 was a recital he gave with his wife at Aeolian Hall in New York City on 10 December. Richard Aldrich, writing for the *New York Times* the next day, stated:

> Mr. and Mrs. Henry Holden Huss . . . have long been known among New York musicians and amateurs, and a large and friendly audience listened to them.
>
> Mr. Huss is not a virtuoso, and probably would make no claim to be considered more than an artistic and tasteful interpreter of music for its own sake and not for display. In a season when the great pianists are giving the New York public some of the most noteworthy performances of the noblest works in the literature of the piano, his playing . . . cannot be expected to make a deep impression. That [his selections] gave pleasure was indicated by the cordial applause of his listeners.

From Emilie Frances Bauer's review (the *Evening Mail*) of a 1913 recital, we learn that Huss had recently been invited to submit manuscripts to the Library of Congress for its collection, and he reportedly had given a group of published works to the Women's Music Club of Columbus in the spring of 1913 though the records of the Women's Music Club do not mention any gift from Huss. This request by the Library of Congress occupied much of Huss's time during 1914. The Library was creating a special collection of original manuscripts "by prominent American composers." On 12 January Herbert Putnam, the Librarian of Congress, wrote to Huss expressing concern that the manuscripts might have gotten lost in transit, since they had not yet arrived in Washington. Huss replied on the twenty-first that he had not yet had time to select the items. On 4 June 1914 Huss wrote to Oscar Sonneck to apologize for the continued delay in the manuscript matter and to thank him for sending a copy of his opera libretto catalog. On 25 October 1914, Huss again wrote to Sonneck saying that he planned to sort the manuscripts soon; he stated that part of the delay was due to a stressful past year including responsibilities arising from the death of "a beloved sister." At this time he thanked Sonneck for the gift of a flag and offered congratulations to Sonneck on being chosen the editor of *Musical Quarterly* ("a quarterly which is sorely needed by our serious musical public").

On 23 July 1917 Sonneck wrote to Huss (by means of a form letter sent, no doubt, to many composers) to request original manuscripts for deposit in the collection of the Library of Congress. Sonneck wanted to create a collection of "representative compositions of representative American composers." It may be that this was a second attempt, at least in Huss's case, to obtain materials formerly sought in 1913 and 1914.

The last performance by Huss for 1914 was given on 29 December, an all-Huss concert given at the Hotel Schenley in Pittsburgh for the MTNA. A typescript copy of Huss's speech "Observations on a New Era in Piano Study" has on it a notation that he delivered it on this same date to the Piano Conference of the Association, so Huss had a twofold connection with this meeting. This speech and the recital are the last known activities of Huss at a national MTNA convention.

However, Huss's music was heard at least once more at one of these affairs. *La Nuit* appeared in a lecture recital given by Ernest R. Kroeger on "The Emotional and Picturesque in Music." This performance was given on 29 December 1916 at the annual meeting of the MTNA, in Rumford Hall, New York City. Because of the location, it is likely that Huss attended the meeting and the lecture recital.

The review in the *Atlantic City Gazette-Review* of a recital given there on 21 August 1918 by the Husses was quoted in the *Musical Courier's* article on the recital. It presents a view of Huss from the second decade of the century.

> Especial interest was awakened when . . . Mr. Huss appeared as composer. [His] far-famed songs and . . . piano works . . . take rank as among the greatest in the history of American music. His gifts as a song writer are of the highest order. . . . The group of Huss piano compositions form a note worthy contribution to the world's piano literature.

In early April 1919 (the exact date is unknown) Huss entertained a small group with a performance of part of his piano concerto. The *Musical Leader* (10 April 1919) took this as an occasion to speak of American concertos in general. This article offers a possible explanation for the mixed reviews Huss got as a performer, namely, that he may have had inadequate time to prepare sufficiently for some appearances.

> So far as is recalled there are but five [Americans] who have written in large forms and who play or conduct sufficiently well to personally present their works to the public. One of the best known, one indeed of international reputation, is Henry Holden Huss. . . . Huss is so busy with his large class and the extra work he has now undertaken with the Art Publication Society that he has had little time for public performance, but he plays so delightfully he should reappear frequently. As a critic present [at this performance] said, "Such a virtuoso should play his concerto very often in public."
>
> If memory serves aright it was the inimitable James Hun-ecker who said: "Henry Holden Huss has the mien of a puritan pilgrim and composes like a passionate pagan."

With the close of World War I, America's interests and energies turned to social issues at home, and Huss now promoted a new cause, via the *Musical America* of 14 June 1919.

> As good Americans of course we personally will see to it that we obey the national prohibition law; that's one side of the question. But will prohibition prohibit? That's another side.

What effect will the law have on music and musicians? Very little, I think. Personally, I am almost a prohibitionist in practice, but I believe that those musicians who are abnormal and must have (or think they must have) stimulants in order to do their work properly, will probably continue to get their stimulation, if not from liquids, then from drugs. I myself have often found stimulation for the labor of composition in playing a masterpiece of Beethoven or Wagner or Bach.

As an observer of human nature as it is, not necessarily as it should be, I certainly think the workman should be allowed his glass of beer or light wine. Of course, alcohol in excess is a virulent poison, but so are boiled coffee and boiled tea and too much sugar and starch. Magendie, the great French savant, fed dogs on starch for two weeks with the result that they died from diabetes but is that ground for prohibiting the use of white bread, which is mostly starch?

Looking at the questions by and large, I say the thing to do is to relegate strong liquor to the offices of the medical profession and put it under lock and key there, but let those who care for it have, under some sane supervision, their mild beer and light wine; but before my or anybody else's personal conviction is made into law, let the people have a chance to cast a personal ballot on this important question.

The final known performance of a Huss work in 1919 came on 2 July when his third string quartet, in B minor, was performed by the Berkshire Quartet at the convention of the National Federation of Musical Clubs in Peterborough, New Hampshire (this is the first documented connection between Huss and this organization). The work was heard because it had won the NFMC prize of $300 in a competition judged by Adolfo Betti, Franz Kneisel, and Olive Mead. Huss had known of the concert for some time, since he wrote to Elizabeth Sprague Coolidge on 15 May of his delight at the prospect.

The musical journalists commented on the performance and the work in the context of their reports on the convention itself. Walter Kramer described the quartet (for the 12 July 1919 issue of *Musical America*) as "the *pièce de résistance* of the concert of prize-winning works."

The composer and his wife motored over from Lake George, arriving in Peterborough Tuesday evening. I think I have heard and played the big majority of American quartets for strings. I

wish to go on record as considering this work of Mr. Huss's the
best string quartet that I know produced in America; and, what
is more, it is one of his strongest essays in the larger forms. I say
this as a lover of his Piano Concerto, his Violin Sonata, his
songs, choral pieces and piano pieces.

The audience rose to the *Lento* unanimously and made Mr.
Huss rise from his seat and bow after it. At the end of the
quartet he had to bow twice, and then was signaled to make his
way to the stage where in a few exceedingly well-chosen words
he thanked the audience for its reception of his work and paid a
splendid tribute to the National Federation of Musical Clubs.
He returned to his seat in the audience amid hearty applause.[4]

Possibly the last of the great events of his life occurred on 11 April
1920 when Huss presented his piano concerto with the Detroit
Symphony Orchestra under Ossip Gabrilowitsch. The next day the
local newspapers provide similar perspectives on his performances.
The following is from Charlotte M. Tarney writing for the *Detroit
Free Press:*

Mr. Huss demonstrated his ability as a composer much more
forcibly than as a pianist. His concerto is a strong work with
original effects. Mr. Huss plays with precision, with strength
and in rhythmic manner, but the force of individuality which
one would expect from his composition is not evidenced in his
performance of the work.

And there was this from Leonard Lanson Cline in the *Detroit News:*

It was very pleasant to have Mr. Huss at the piano, and the
audience gave him a gratifying reception; but he is not himself
a brilliant pianist, and his work will appear to better advantage
some day when we can hear it under the firm, alert fingers of a
pianist in the manner of Arthur Rubinstein.

Huss later recorded an anecdote connected with this appearance.

In the Autumn [of 1919] we had a 2 piano rehearsal and before
we began Gabrilowitsch said he had   not timed [the concerto]
with a watch, but he guessed it would take about 50 minutes!
I gave him a little mental dig by saying that he was a very good
musician but in this particular case a very poor time estimator,

and that it would [last] just about 29 or 30 minutes, depending on whether the soloist was a very temperamental person or not! With a deliciously humorous, whimsical expression he addressed an imaginary audience in the big empty piano warehouse "Ladies and Gentlemen these composers" (with accent on these) "will [say] any assertion to [advance] their compositions!" My "dander" rose then, and I advised [him] to put his watch on the piano and he would see! I felt very temperamental and [played] the entire work in 28$^{1}/_{2}$ minutes. He apologized humorously and peace reigned once more!

CHAPTER V

THE LAST YEARS AND BEYOND

In the third decade of the century, Huss's standing as performer and composer maintained its high level, as shown by the Detroit performance just cited. His skills as a recitalist as well as a composer were recognized in a recital review in *Musical America* of 10 December 1921 of the "intimate recital" given 30 November 1921. The review also mentioned the recital was followed by a tour of the Steinway warehouses, indicating that Huss was being used as a drawing card for the purpose of promoting piano sales.

> As pianist, Mr. Huss disclosed a style that is characterized by energy, and in moments by combined calmness and strength. Passages in the Schumann number had an almost silken quality, though the artist's playing never lacked precision.
>
> Of the three compositions by Mr. Huss, that most appealing upon a first hearing was the tone poem entitled "To the Night." Here there was a recurrence in various guises of an aptly chosen descriptive theme, consisting of a succession of somber chords ending in a minor cadence.

In the 1920s Huss established new relationships with various musical organizations. He performed some unknown service for the 1923 Song Competition of the MacDowell Society of Cincinnati. Perhaps he served as a judge, for the 18 May 1923 letter thanking him made reference to the "unimpeachable character and high reputation of the judges." In this letter he was also notified of his unanimous election as a nonresident member of the Society, and there is a notation at the foot of the letter that he accepted the honor by a 21 May letter.

In 1924 he received a letter from John C. Freund, president of the Musical Alliance of the United States, welcoming the Husses as members of the Alliance. In joining, the Husses entered an organization whose advisory council included the names of Giulio Gatti-Casazza, Walter Damrosch, Leopold Stokowski, Fanny Bloomfield-Zeisler, Harold Bauer, William Carl, Henry Hadley, E. S. Kelley, Mrs. Beach, and Rubin Goldmark. The Alliance had been founded by Freund in 1917 for the purpose of promoting music in American life and education, of encouraging American composers especially, and of continuing efforts toward the creation of an American National Conservatory of Music. The organization disbanded when Freund died in 1924, so the Husses were among the last new members of the Alliance.

In 1925 the Husses appeared in two important and related performances. On 25 March Mr. and Mrs. Huss, along with Lifschey, gave a recital at the Old Steinway Hall as a benefit for the Huss Scholarship Fund, a means by which the Husses paid for lessons given by them to needy students. The reviewer for the *Musical Courier* offered this assessment:

> Mr. Huss writes with distinct individuality, good melodic line and richness of harmony. His playing too, not only of his own works, but of the others also, is always enjoyable, revealing his thorough musicianship. As an encore he improvised admirably on three notes suggested from the audience.

Late in life Huss said that this performance was the last artist recital given in the Old Steinway Hall and that he had attended concerts in that auditorium since the age of four. The first public concert given in the New Steinway Hall was on 9 November 1925. The *New York Times* had the following to say:

> The name of Huss has been associated with the Steinway studios for more than fifty years, so that it was very appropriate that one of Mr. Huss's own compositions should be played at the first public recital. His [violin] sonata . . . would not be called revolutionary now, it is too distinctly melodious and pleasing for that. The first movement is flowing and rhythmic, the second an andante, played pianissimo, is naturally delightful and graceful and is the best part of the work; the third movement is scarcely worthy to be associated with the first two.

Another review, in the *Musician,* noted that Huss's work was the only American piece on the program.

The program brought forcibly to mind one of the outstanding problems facing the American composer, namely the need of having his music heard more frequently by our public. This means pioneer and in some cases, self-sacrificing effort on the part of concert artists. The rich treasure of creative ability which lies about us represents a shameful waste if there are none to study and bring forth this music where it may be heard and judged. And in this connection Miss Kemper deserves particular commendation for having given a place to the excellent sonata of Mr. Huss, a work which may rightfully hold its own beside the music of any nation or any period. A wealth of melodic ideas and a masterpiece of structure, it fairly electrified its hearers. The graceful slow movement afforded moments of surpassing beauty.

One intriguing feature of the student recital of 25 May 1927 in Aeolian Hall was the only known use of a Duo-Art Reproducing Piano roll of Huss playing his *Prelude in D, Lake Como by Moonlight,* and *The Joy of Autumn.* The significance of the Duo-Art roll, of course, is that this particular kind preserves not only notes, but dynamics, pedaling, and other performance features so that a "recording" of the performance is made. Unfortunately, the roll appears to be lost, and there is no other reference to it in the extant materials. This is also, alas, the only known recording he ever made.

As noted earlier, Huss's teaching work was both private and institutional. In 1927 he took on a new responsibility at a musical institution, for he received a letter, dated 14 October, from May L. Holmes, secretary, on behalf of the Yorkville Music School in New York City, thanking him for joining their Advisory Board.

The Committee feels such deep appreciation of your kindness and your interest in the work of the School, and the honor of having you on our Advisory Board, that I have been asked to express to you our warmest thanks for your willingness to lend your name to our work.

Other names on this board were those of David Mannes, Felix Salmond, and Albert Spalding; Huss was joining an esteemed company. Unfortunately there is no further evidence of his work with this school.

Huss did have another association beginning in this latter period of his career, that with Hunter College in New York City. His first connection there, albeit tenuous, was in his performance in a chamber music series, directed by Henry Fleck. On the 30 April 1930 program Huss and Cornelius Van Vliet presented the cello sonata. In the next year Huss began teaching at Hunter College, a position he maintained until 1938, and he gave other performances there as well.

As a faculty member, Huss gave a chamber concert at Hunter College on 8 March 1933, assisted by G. Porter Smith, violinist. Along with a Mozart sonata, the two played Huss's second sonata in D minor, Op. 33. This concert was broadcast over the radio. A review in *Musical Courier* stated that Huss's work was of more interest to the audience that evening than Mozart's, and quoted Fleck, who introduced Huss's sonata by summarizing Huss's own programmatic descriptions.

> The struggles, joys and sorrows of this life are often interrupted by a heavenly vision of peace and serene joy, but this is silenced by the battle of life. If at the end we welcome it and make it our own, we are crowned at the last with its serene joy and peace.

Other Huss works were heard at the college during the period covered by his teaching there, and an all-Huss program was the composer's last known appearance there. This was given on 18 March 1938, sponsored by Hunter's Music Club, in the form of a lecture-recital. Huss's name did appear on yet one more program: the Hunter College commencement exercises held in January 1939 at Carnegie Hall. On this occasion a new work of Huss's (dedicated to the College Choir) was performed: *The Lord Is My Shepherd.* The work was sung by the choir under the direction of J. Thurston Noé and accompanied by Huss, piano, and G. Raymond Hicks, organ.

As time went by, Huss made fewer trips away from home; whether this was by choice, due to the dictates of age, or because fewer invitations were extended is not known. Among the last of these trips was a series of excursions made to western Maryland. This series was begun by an invitation to participate in the Second Annual Mountain Choir Festival in the resort community of Mountain Lake Park, Maryland. The festival was held 23 June 1935 and was the creation of the Reverend Felix G. Robinson of Keyser, West Virginia. Local promotion in the 13 June 1935 issue of the *Republican* of Garrett County, Maryland, makes it clear that the Husses were considered a drawing card, and Huss wrote an anthem for the occasion: *Lord, Make My Heart a Place Where Angels Sing.* The Husses gave a recital in the afternoon and served as judges in the choir competition. The final event of the day was a performance by massed choir and orchestra, at which the Huss anthem was presented.

The Husses made at least two other trips to this part of Maryland. In 1937, at the Fourth Mountain Choir Festival at Mountain Lake Park, Huss's *Winged Messengers of Peace* received its first known presentation. The work was sung there by the festival choir under Dr. John Finley Williamson. In 1938 summer activities for the Husses included teaching at the "Huss School of Musical Ideals" at Mountain Lake Park in July. The festival program carried the following caption: "This Festival is Dedicated to Mr. and Mrs. Huss because they live dedicated lives to the furtherance of American Art Forms." The school was well attended, and an extra week of classes was added to the planned schedule. The NBC Blue Network broadcast some of the concerts, including unspecified programs wherein Huss played some of his own works.

There are people still living who remember the Husses from the mid-1930s. The following two reminiscences (this first from Lillian Truesdale) are from people who knew him at Lake George.

> Mr. Huss was rather thin, with a small "pod" in front, about five feet 9 or 10, wore glasses and carried a cane, mostly to ward off the dogs that barked at his every appearance—He was usually dressed in grayish trousers, neutral shirt, tie, dark suit coat and a felt or straw hat.
>
> His summer home was about four city blocks up the hill from the corner where the church [St. John's] is situated. Every day he would come walking down the hill flourishing his cane, stopping now and then to contemplate the view or a neighbor's garden or even a neighbor's activities, if that person were doing something outdoors—He was a naturally curious person—He would go to the store, the post office, sometimes to the dock and then wend his way home by way of the path that went through the woods on the south side of the road—this path went behind all the houses and since the woods weren't thick one could see and hear his progress up the hill toward home.
>
> You see, Henry Holden would hoot, whistle, or holler at intervals all the way home and someone up at the house would answer his every call. It must have been interesting and I wish I could remember it more clearly. But I do remember that the natives nicknamed him—"Henry Holden hollerin', hootin', spittin' Huss."

> This was all before World War II and the world was a less
> sophisticated place and summer people were fair game if they
> showed any eccentricities.[1]

And this from Mrs. Richard Beswick:

> I lived in Diamond Point at the time Prof. Henry Holden Huss
> and his wife Hildegard spent their summers at their summer
> house "Mountain Meadows," [a] beautiful spot on the side of a
> mountain. [The] family, Mr. Huss's sister Babetta, she man-
> aged the finances, & sisters of Hildegard's, Matilda and Hesta
> Heuback, made up the house-hold, no children if I remember
> correctly. There was the old farmhouse, where the family lived,
> a large studio for study and teaching, also a house for students.
> Each summer students came to be taught piano by Mr. Huss,
> singing by Mrs. Huss. In the Spring and the Fall the Steinway
> Grand was shipped from N.Y.C. and of course returned. Mr.
> Huss was very near for this operation.
>
> He was an artist, so eccentric to the natives of the Hamlet.
> He was of German [descent]. and when in the mountains, one
> wore sturdy coats, wool trousers, [and] a hat . . . very similar to
> the Alpine drocker. Across from our home was the path, across
> the brook by fast bridge, then up a hill to "Mountain
> Meadows." When Hildegard didn't accompany [him] into the
> Post Office, church practice, etc., he would start yodeling (for
> Hildegard). Then the people had a nickname for him "Hootin,
> Hollerin, Henry Holden Huss"!
>
> When students arrived for the summer pianos were needed
> for practice. I loaned mine to a student; I'm sure I enjoyed his
> time more than he.
>
> Often we went to the Post Office or store for Babetta or Mr.
> Huss, the pay was very little, but the tickets to the recitals,
> having the pleasure of listening to the students perform in
> Church Sunday mornings were worth any chore. This was 1925
> through the 30's Depression years.
>
> To arrive to the feeling this man had [one should] see "The
> Sound of Music." He also gave me a book of his compositions.
> I never did anything with the piano, so Mother later sold it and
> I believe the music book.

A published description from very late in Huss's life in the
International Who Is Who in Music (5th ed.) is probably accurate for the
1930s as well. From it we learn that Huss had "blue eyes, white hair,

[weighed] 140, and [was] 5' 10¹/₂" in height." His principal form of
recreation was given as reading, and he was also described as
"Presbyterian and Republican."

Huss's political convictions were the subject of his letter to the
New York Herald Tribune of 14 August 1952.

> I have been a Republican voter since 1888; my father since
> 1860, when he heard Abraham Lincoln deliver his great Cooper
> Union speech.
>
> The present coming Presidential election has to do not
> merely with the U.S.A., not merely with the Republican party,
> not merely Europe, but with the entire world.
>
> It is going to be difficult enough to win next November; let
> no one who really desires that the right shall win throw even a
> minutely small monkey wrench into the promotion of this
> great issue.
>
> Gen. Eisenhower accomplished the impossible, the incredi-
> ble, when he united France and Germany (enemies for over 900
> years) in an effort to form a defense army.
>
> In electing Gen. Eisenhower we will surely elect the best
> Presidential candidate since Lincoln.

Huss also was known to speak out on local concerns as well, as in
this letter to the *New York Times* of 17 July 1930:

> Would it not be well if our Commissioner of Parks would at
> once take steps to rid—in a measure at least—Bronx Park of
> the ever-increasing scourge of poison ivy? The southeast en-
> trance of the park at 180th Street is lined with this pest. This
> terrible menace should be eradicated at once.

Huss was something of a "joiner," and in addition to organizations
mentioned elsewhere in this study (particularly the Bohemians,[2] the
Music Teachers' National Association, the AGO, and the National
Federation of Music Clubs), he also belonged (at one time or another)
to the Andiron Club, the Young Composers Society, and the
National Association of American Composers and Conductors. He
was also an adjudicator for twenty-five years for the League for Music
Education.

His association with another musical organization begins at about
this time. His performance for the Associated Music Teachers'
League on 10 January 1934 was the opening program for Huss that

year and the first known connection between composer and organization. On this occasion Huss presented a brief explanation of the form and nature of his piano concerto before playing its first movement with the assistance of his student Jeanette Weidman at a second piano.

Huss's financial situation, like that of many others, declined significantly during the Depression years. His own material wealth may have been particularly diminished due to fewer paid performances, fewer published works bringing in royalties, and fewer students. That he had problems is known through various letters and documents. One set of documents details Huss's activities in the Federal Music Project of the Works Progress Administration, the New Deal program designed to aid composers and performers. These activities consisted of performances of Huss's music on various occasions. Once in response to an interviewer's question about the federal government's support for composers through this means, Huss spoke favorably about its value in helping composers as individuals and also helping aid the recognition of American composers in general. Huss's *Elegy* ("Poem for Orchestra") was presented in a concert sponsored by this agency on 31 May 1936 at the Manhattan Theatre. The ensemble for the occasion was the New York Civic Orchestra under the direction of Eugene Plotnikoff.

A program by the Federal Music Project given on 3 June 1936 was an all-Huss concert as part of its "Composers' Forum-Laboratory." The program was arranged by Ashley Pettis and was designed to cover "46 years of a composer's life—1889–1935." The works were arranged in eight groupings, and each was accompanied by short program notes. A review in the *New York World-Telegram* provides a perspective on the evening:

> The right wing of the musical front had its innings . . . last night when [the music of] Henry Holden Huss . . . came up for judgment before the all-hearing ears of the Composer-Forum-Laboratory unit.
>
> Between [pieces in his opening group] Mr. Huss interposed the remark, "I haven't forsaken the major triad, bless me!" Later he reverted to the year 1889 with a piece called "Prelude Appassionata," explaining that at that time "Noah was still building the Ark." Melodic and harmonic conservatism and a certain wistfulness of mood were the keynote of these and subsequent numbers.

When Miss Kemper's music stand slid down with a bang Mr. Huss, accompanying her, said with a smile, "I'm sorry if my music has a depressing effect." While she was tuning up Mr. Huss said to the audience, "I wish we could get rid of all the discords of life just as easily."

There were at least three other concerts linking Huss with this federal agency. On 22 November 1938 the Composers' Forum-Laboratory hosted a concert in Carnegie Chamber Music Hall that included several Huss works. One review was in the *New York Times,* and it is interesting that the article concentrated on the other composer of the day, Morris Mamorsky; nothing is known of Mamorsky.

Another all-Huss concert was given at the WPA Building in Brooklyn on 29 March 1939. The third of the concerts was that of 22 June 1939, when the Composers' Forum-Laboratory of the WPA Federal Music Project in New York City broadcast an all-Huss program over WNYC from the radio station's studios in the New York Building at the World's Fair. The program was presented by Huss, Viola Steimann (student of Mrs. Huss), Jeanette Weidman (Huss student), Carl Tollefsen, and the Federal Forum String Quartet.

Besides the WPA connection, there is other evidence of declining Huss fortunes. On 15 April 1944 Huss received a note from the Douglas L. Elliman Company requesting payment on remaining rent charges for the Huss studios at 109 West 57th Street; the letter stated that no money had been received on this account since December.

By the fall of 1945 Huss was receiving support payments from the Presser Foundation. On 9 November 1945 James Francis Cooke of the Foundation wrote to tell Huss that it was not necessary that the composer send a monthly thank-you note.

I am always glad to hear from you, but we want you to feel in connection with The Presser Foundation that this assistance which we are privileged to give you is something which you have earned through your splendid contributions to music and to musical education.

Huss received this support for the rest of his life. On 17 January 1952 Huss wrote again to Cooke to offer thanks for the monthly stipend check. In this letter he also referred to an unspecified concert earlier in the month: "The Lord gave me the strength to play as I wanted to do, Hildegard says."

Late in life Huss was also receiving money from another foundation. On 5 April 1950 he sent thanks to a Mr. Burrows, and at the same time expressed his characteristic concern for others:

> We send our warmest thanks for the ever helpful generous cheques for $50 from The Musician's Foundation. As time passes we are increasingly grateful for this blessed help. I was very sorry not to be able to attend the April Bohemian's meeting. I was not feeling well. Since my accident of last June I find that work: giving a few lessons, etc. frequently tires me severely. Mrs. Huss and I are much interested in my gifted artist pupil Helen Field. Last week her 70 year old mother had a heart attack and is at present in bed with crippling arthritis. Mrs. Field was threatened by the Nazis at the opening of World War II and they fled from Berlin just in time. Mrs. Field was a Berlin Opera singer. Richard Strauss wrote her a little song. They are now very straitened in their finances and it would be God-send if the Musician's Foundation would give them a little help. We consider them eminently worthy.

The year 1939 saw increasing world tension lead to war, so it is not surprising that "The Huss World Peace Chorus" (*Winged Messengers of Peace*) was heard on a program by a choir under the direction of John Warren Erb at the biennial meeting of the National Federation of Music Clubs on 21 April 1939 at Baltimore.

A few days later Huss's name was again before a federation meeting: the Capitol West Hudson District subgroup. The occasion was a varied program given on 29 April 1939 in Kingston, New York, as part of the first Federation Day festivities. Huss and a Florence Cubberley presented two movements from his first violin sonata, and Huss offered some improvisations.

This was the last documented connection with the federation, but two others should be mentioned. As with the MTNA, Huss obviously had associations with the federation at various levels, though with this organization Huss's known personal involvement was limited to activities inside New York State. In February 1934 the State Federation ran a short article on Huss in its newsletter, the *Empire Record,* to inform the membership that Huss had been selected

Henry Holden and Hildegard Hoffmann Huss in their later years. Reproduced with the permission of the Music Library, University of Illinois at
Urbana-Champaign.

as the second composer in the organization's "gallery of New York State composers."

The State Federation held its 1938 biennial convention at Binghamton on 20–23 April, and the Husses were present. On the morning of the twenty-first, Huss participated in a recital by playing four of his works, and that afternoon Mrs. Huss presented a lecture on "The Psychology of Singing."

A student, Margaret M. Meachem, who knew Huss in the 1940s described him thus:

> He was a very devout Episcopalian. The church on Diamond Point at Lake George (where I spent a summer with the family) was a "summer" church at which the Bishop of Long Island presided. The Homers lived right across the way from the church. His sister Babetta was somewhat of an invalid at that time, and the Husses took care of her with devoted care. They were both, Mr. and Mrs. Huss, very *kind* people. They were . . . nutritionalists and I remember his taking me to the Automat on 57th Street (opposite Steinway Hall) . . . and telling me that I must have their cocoa with a little of their French vanilla ice cream, because it was made of good ingredients. He also had a permanent dish of unsulphered dates which he offered to his students and their mothers (who often accompanied them in those days).
>
> Mr. Huss had a beautiful tone or touch on the piano, and he could extract an enormous sound also. Improvisation was one of his fortes. I went to several concerts where he delighted audiences by calling for notes from the audience, then asking them whether they would like the piece in the style of Chopin, Mozart, etc. His improvisations were masterful. It was very sad to see his "popularity" go down hill. He played very well as long as I knew him.

Huss continued to improvise to the end of his career. In 1945, the slow movement of Huss's first violin sonata enjoyed a performance at the Brooklyn Academy of Music in an all-American program by the Brooklyn Chamber Music Society. The performance was given by Carl Tollefsen and Huss, and after they completed the movement, Huss was requested to improvise a waltz. Furthermore, the 26 October 1952 concert at which Huss was the guest of honor brought forth another improvisation. A description of this incident was offered by Paul Affelder the next day in the *Brooklyn Eagle* and is useful here for its revelation about Huss's stage manner and his improvisatory skills later in life.

> For us, however, the amazing feature was the appearance on the stage of Mr. Huss, who not only told some interesting and lively anecdotes, but also called for three notes at random from the audience and proceeded to improvise a five-minute waltz on them. The improvisation was thoroughly expert, well-planned and beautifully played, with fluency, ease and no wrong notes. It was an astounding exhibition.

Despite the career decline suggested by his financial problems, Huss was still able to generate some curiosity. On 23 August 1946 Nicolas Slonimsky wrote to Huss requesting recent biographical information for a dictionary of American music he was preparing (probably a reference to the 1949 supplement to the dictionary begun by Theodore Baker). Slonimsky was particularly interested in Huss's meeting with Tchaikovsky and in his role as one of the earliest representatives of national American music. Slonimsky also desired Huss's views on modern American music and "whether you favor using American rhythms in music couched in classical forms." Huss replied on 19 September that he was interested in supplying the information requested but wished to wait until his return to New York City, where his papers were.

On 31 October Huss wrote again, now from New York, to invite Slonimsky to his 14 November 1946 recital for the Associated Music Teachers' League at Steinway Hall. On 16 December 1946 Huss wrote to Slonimsky again with apologies for not having sent the information requested. He also sent Christmas greetings and made reference to two recent recitals: that on 14 November and a more recent one on 1 December 1946 at the Westover School in Connecticut. Huss sent one of his musical Christmas cards to Slonimsky later that month and finally sent a list of works and biographical materials on 29 January 1947. In this last letter, he described the December recital as being a lecture-recital covering the topics "Liszt versus Paderewski" and "Gabrilowitsch on the so-called 'Moonlight' Sonata." He also mentioned that Isidor Philipp had been present at the 14 November recital.

On 9 June 1949 the Associated Music Teachers' League offered a program "in honor of two Celebrated Musicians who have just enjoyed Birthdays in their Eighties." The two to be honored were Huss and Gustave Becker; four of Huss's works were presented on this occasion. Isidor Philipp had been invited but was unable to attend because of his imminent departure for France: "[I] shall be unable to hear your Sonata, and I regret it very much."

Huss was a program participant the next spring, when on 9 March, the AMTL held a meeting at which Huss offered "A Few Brief Remarks on the Musical Education of Youth," and Mrs. Huss participated in a panel on voice training. Later in the program various Huss piano works were presented with an eye toward their use as teaching pieces.

The organization thought highly of Huss as evidenced by two posthumous events. After Huss's death there were a few performances of his works, the earliest of these, of course, in the nature of memorials to the composer. On 12 November 1953 there was a memorial service for Huss offered by the AMTL in that day's program. Huss student Gwendolyn Haber played two piano solos, and Carl Tollefsen gave a eulogy. And on 14 April 1955 the AMTL offered a potpourri of American music "by members of the Composers Group of New York" in honor of the tenth anniversary of the founding of that organization. Three songs by Huss were presented by a Sylvia Haskell.

Known performances by the composer in the last few years of Huss's life are few; this may in part be understood by the advancing age of the couple, but another cause may have been the death of his sister Babetta, after a long illness, on 20 March 1949. However, Huss was remembered by his colleagues despite his now quiet life. At the 14 June 1951 meeting of the AMTL, Huss and Gustave Becker were again honored by their colleagues, and three works by Huss were performed. Huss was also honored by a window display set up at the offices of Carl Fischer. Unfortunately, Huss was too ill at the time to go see the display.

Huss's physical health began to decline significantly in 1952. A few extracts, paraphrased or quoted, from Mrs. Huss's diary covering his final months provide a picture of his increasing infirmity, his problems being treated with numerous trips to doctor and dentist.

29 February   Huss fell in the bathroom, necessitating the cancellation of lessons and his confinement to bed with
              penicillin

13 March	"Henry looked badly"
14 March	"Henry's heart; he rested all day, to Dr. evening"
28 April	"Henry canceled dentist—too tired"
6 May	"Henry to dentist (2 extractions)"

Continuing money difficulties were coupled with these medical problems. On 30 April Huss wrote to Herman Irion to request funds.

> Under the Doctor's orders I am doing a little work, and my dear wife is taking wonderful [care] of me. I have had several heart attacks lately, one of them severe. Forgive me if I unfold a tale of woe. The bank which holds the mortgage on our home terrified us lately by demanding an enormous increase in the amortization of the loan. For the last 10 years Hildegard and I have been supporting a group of aged and poverty stricken relatives. In the last 4 years two of them died of cancer. We, as a sacred obligation, have to bear all the expenses. . . . Now we have the 2 remaining relatives [two sisters of Mrs. Huss] on our hands, and we pay for everything. We have received a little help, but not enough. This little has seemed like "Bread cast upon the waters and returning after many days"! Our small reserves are almost all gone! We are very near despair. In spite of relentless economy we are in a pitiable state. Dear friends don't you think the "Musicians Emergency Fund" will help this pair of aged musicians? We have helped and taught absolutely free hundreds of poor students in the last 50 years.

In his letter to Irion, Huss does see some good news in the planned performance by Harvey Shapiro of the *Romance* for cello and piano on Shapiro's 17 June radio recital. This performance was broadcast over WQXR on 24 June, and the pianist for the occasion was Leonid Hambro. A notice of the broadcast in *Musical Courier* contained a notice that Huss's "latest string quartet will be programmed in the 1952–53 chamber music series in the Brooklyn Academy of Music." Another radio broadcast, marking Huss's ninetieth birthday, preceded the Shapiro performance: on 21 June an all-Huss program was presented on WNYC "by request." The program was titled "Reminiscences of Old Times, Henry Holden Huss."

In addition to these honors, Huss was also interviewed by Peter J. McElroy of the *New York Post* (published 15 June 1952). Excerpts from the article point up changes in Huss's external environment during his long life.

When Henry Holden Huss came to his new home in the Bronx it seemed like paradise. The Huss family moved into a stately brownstone at 144 E. 150th St. Trees lined the street. To get to the concert halls which he loved so well, he drove by horse and buggy to the Third Av. El at 143rd St. The quiet of the neighborhood was perfect for his life's work. This was the scene as Huss, a composer, moved to the South Bronx in 1884.

Today Huss and his wife, Hildegard, still live in the same house. The scenery has changed. The trees are gone; factories have sprung up all around and noise from the traffic on the Grand Concourse fills the rooms.

Huss is presently working on a concerto to be performed at the Brooklyn Academy next year. Mrs. Huss, now 75, still teaches voice but spends more time in her backyard garden. When the weather is warm, the couple often go walking in the Bronx Botanical Garden.

A tall, thin man whose sandy hair falls down over his rimless glasses, Huss gets his greatest thrill when he and his wife attend a concert.

The plans for a new work to be presented at the Brooklyn Academy evidently came to naught, for on 26 October 1952 Huss was the guest of honor at a concert there but the only work of his played was his first violin sonata, performed by Carl and Augusta Tollefsen. Paul Affelder's review of this in the *Brooklyn Eagle* was cited earlier in the discussion of Huss as an improviser. In this review Affelder marked his astonishment at Huss's lively stage manner and improvisatory skills, given his age. We may be all the more astounded because of the entry in Mrs. Huss's diary for 22 October: "Henry had bad night, went to Dr. at PM [Presbyterian Memorial Hospital]."

By the spring, Huss seems to have gained strength and more stable health, since Mrs. Huss's diary indicates his visits to his doctor were reduced to one every two weeks. In her entry for 17 May she states that word has just reached her from a friend who had heard *Crossing the Bar* in a broadcast of a service from the Mormon Tabernacle in Salt Lake City.

There were at least two performances that summer marking his ninety-first birthday. On 21 June 1953 the organist at Brooklyn's Fenimore Street Methodist Church honored Huss's ninety-first birthday by playing a Huss work as the prelude to the morning service. On 23 June 1953 Huss gave his final known performance, during a broadcast of WNYC's "Adventure in Music" for that day. Huss played *This Mortal Life* and *Lake Como by Moonlight* and accompanied unnamed soloists in the *Romance* for cello and in two songs, *Shed No Tear* and *Ich liebe Dich.*

Two pieces of good news came that summer. On 24 July 1953 Frances Cohan sent a check for $500 from the Musicians Emergency Fund at Steinway Hall, saying the money was coming to Huss through the fund from an anonymous friend. Apparently another musician broadcast some Huss pieces that summer, for on 26 August Olin Downes wrote to Huss with regret that he had not heard the "broadcast that Newmann made of your music."

Nevertheless, the end of his life was near. As late as 3 September 1953, Mrs. Huss's diary indicates that Huss was getting good reports from his doctor. On the seventh, however, Huss went to the hospital briefly, came home, and returned to the hospital. The next day he felt somewhat better but remained in the hospital. On the ninth he was able to keep down some food.

16 September	In the morning, "Henry no better," "sleeping." In the afternoon, "Gave Henry teaspoonfuls of o-juice several times—he seemed to realize it was I—but didn't see me, and <u>no</u> talk. He got transfusion started before I left at 8 p.m."
17 September	"Located Kensico Deed and Henry's will." "Henry getting oxygen, and breathing really hard. I packed up his things to go to undertaker, intending to come back. While at MacLeans the hsptl. phoned to me that my darling had gone, shortly after noon."

It is notable that Mrs. Huss's diary does not reveal any operation (unless one views the transfusion as such), yet the idea that Huss died after an operation appears in some obituaries.

The memorial and burial rites were immediately forthcoming. Burial was in the family plot in the Kensico Cemetery on the nineteenth. Mrs. Huss noted in her diary that "the sun shone for Henry,—he always had fair weather for his 'events'—how wonderful."

With Huss's death, financial problems for Mrs. Huss became more serious. On 7 October 1953 she received a reply from James Francis Cooke of the Presser Foundation who expressed sorrow for her difficulties and offered $40 per month after she would complete and return an application for such help. Unfortunately, he had to write to her again on 7 December with the news that her application had been turned down on the grounds that she was not so badly off as some other musicians, and he could offer her nothing. That she tried again for funds from the foundation is clear from his 18 August 1955 letter stating that she was still ineligible unless her situation had changed since the 1953 application. That application, dated 15 November 1953, listed the Bronx property as being worth $6000 with an $1800 mortgage, but it was in "very poor repair." Furthermore Mrs. Huss estimated the value of her husband's estate at about $2500. She listed her income for the previous year at $250. Some funds from sale of property eventually did come into the household: the Bronx property was sold in April 1956 for $6500, and the Lake George property was sold for about $900.

On 23 June 1967, it was reported that Mrs. Huss was living in "an over-crowded boarding house for elderly people with a most deplorable environment" in Glen Falls, New York. At this point in her life, she was "failing very rapidly mentally" but still healthy physically. She did not remember moving to the boarding house less than a month before and was unaware of her surroundings. She died on 19 April 1969 at the age of 95, "after having completely lost her mind." An obituary was offered to the *New York Times,* but it was not printed on the grounds that she was not a figure of significant interest.

Huss's status, diminished though it was at the end of his life, still was such that his name was included in a report by Irving Lowens and others on the American Recordings Project, dated 5 April 1960, to the Music Library Association for "Period 6 (1901–1920)." Since there was neither the requisite financial backing nor arrangement with a recording company, however, no recordings were made. Nevertheless, New World Records did include a work by Huss (the *Prelude,* Op. 17, No. 2) on its New World 206, released in 1978, performed by Malcolm Frager.

In addition to the *Prelude,* one other work (*Crossing the Bar,* in an arrangement by Richard Condie) was recorded commercially on Columbia MS 6619, released in 1964, by the Mormon Tabernacle Choir.

PART II

CHAPTER VI

INTRODUCTION TO THE MUSICAL WORKS

This chapter is an introduction to the remaining chapters, in which are found discussions of particular Huss works, and to the Catalog of Music in Part III. It contains a discussion of Huss's compositional work as an arranger and some other aspects of his procedures. Here is also found a discussion of the principal stylistic characteristics to be found in Huss's music.

In each of the following chapters, works were selected for more detailed presentation on the basis of their importance in Huss's performing career. The intent has been to provide a discussion through which a sense of Huss's style could be discerned and by which further interest for performance or study might be stimulated. His music was published by the major houses of the time,[1] such as Schirmer, Schmidt, Ditson, and Fischer, and it was known here in the United States and abroad.

As revealed by the Catalog of Music, Huss composed neither opera nor other large-scale vocal works (such as oratorio), nor did he write multi-movement orchestral works (such as symphonies) other than concerto-type works. His music falls into six categories: songs, choral music, works for piano solo (including didactic pieces), chamber music, music for orchestra (or for soloist and orchestra), and miscellaneous pieces.

Variations in Opus Numbers and Titles

In the introductory matter to the work list, it is noted that Huss has created considerable confusion for the researcher in his perplexing use of titles and opus numbers. This practice appeared early in his career. Discounting for the moment the possible first published work (*The Song of Mister Phonograph,* published under a pseudonym later

109

attributed to Huss), his first certain published work appeared while he was a student in Munich. On 5 February 1884, Huss wrote to his father concerning one of his compositions:

> I received your letter relating to the publication of Mrs. May's piece. . . . I like the title as Martin [Huss's brother] wrote it except that it would be better to call it "Ballade-Fantasie" or if you prefer simply "Ballade."

Furthermore, he says, "I don't want it labeled Op. 1. Would rather stick that on some large work."

The Mrs. May referred to in the letter is the Mrs. Colonel May to whom the *Ballade pour le Piano* (Schirmer, 1885) was dedicated. Contrary to Huss's wish (and justifiably so) it did become Opus 1 on some work lists, since it was the first work published under his own name; nevertheless, this does not help the biographer.

The early history of one of Huss's choral works also illustrates this idiosyncrasy. On 21 April 1889 Huss's *Sanctus* for chorus was performed for the Easter service at St. Bartholomew's Church, New York City. This work embodies an extreme example of Huss's habit of sometimes renaming works, not necessarily after significant revision. There is no direct proof, but this *Sanctus* seems to be the same work as that later called *Festival Sanctus,* which is itself the same work as three others: *Festival Sanctus and Benedictus, Holy! Holy! Holy!,* and *Motette.* As small comfort, it is probably not the same work as the *Festival Anthem.* The connection between *Sanctus* and *Festival Sanctus* is based on the claim in 1904 that the 8 May 1890 performance of the latter was its first performance. Given the possibility of Huss's retitling, it seems more reasonable to believe the 1889 performance was actually the first, rather than that he wrote an entirely new setting of the same text the next year.

Huss did much of his composing at his summer home on Lake George, because his teaching and performing during the winter left him little time for composition. Reports of such work would often surface in music journals, as in this item from *Musical America* of 12 August 1911:

> Six new piano pieces have just been completed and will be published in the near future: they are an "Etude Erotik," dedicated to Paderewski, two "Intermezzi" for Rafael Joseffy,

> an "Impromptu" for Raoul Pugno, an "Albumleaf" and a
> "Polonaise Brillante."

Here is demonstrated the problems Huss sometimes created when he
wrote individual works that later became published as parts of sets.
The modification of the first title given here into *Étude Romantique*
makes this group identical (including dedications) with Huss's *Six
Pieces for the Pianoforte,* Op. 23 (Schirmer, 1912). Moreover, the
oft-performed *Polonaise* certainly was not newly finished, though it
may have been given its final and ultimate shape at this time.

This nomenclatural peccadillo along with his use of pseudonyms
and his haphazard assignment of opus numbers contribute greatly to
the difficulty of clarifying Huss's work list and the performance
history of those works. Huss seems not to have offered any explanation for this. One suspects that he simply titled works as befitted his
mood or the particular performance situation.

The problem of names is similar to that of opus numbers. Since
Huss did not treat "opus" as a publication designation, the term
appears on unpublished music as well. Moreover, he did not always
assign an opus number to what would appear to be an important
work, whether published or not. There seems to be no pattern to his
use of the term.

Opus 25 is one of the especially tangled problems in this regard. A
work list in Huss's hand states that Opus 25 was to consist of five
piano works.

1. Valse Intime
2. Sans Souci
3. The Brooklet
4. Minuet Rococo
5. Impromptu

Of these, only *Sans Souci* ever appeared in print under this designation
(Schirmer, 1915); seeing it as "Opus 25, No. 2" without any other
works in print as a part of the same opus is initially quite confusing.
The *Valse Intime* may have later appeared as the second item in the
Opus 27 set, where a *Valse Intime* dedicated to Harold Bauer is to be
found. The third and fourth titles given here appeared as the first and
last items in Huss's later Opus 26 set. The *Impromptu* is possibly the

same work presented first on the 8 December 1904 recital and
surfacing occasionally since that time, eventually being published in
Opus 23. If this understanding of the history of these individual
pieces and these sets of pieces is correct, then Huss must have planned
Opus 25 before the summer of 1911, when, we were told, he finished
work on the pieces that were published as Opus 23. A repetition of
the list of Opus 25 with some emendations may summarize this
understanding of the final destination of the pieces in question:

1. Valse Intime   to Opus 27
2. Sans Souci
3. The Brooklet   to Opus 26
4. Minuet Rococo   to Opus 26
5. Impromptu   to Opus 23

Besides creating his own music, Huss arranged or transcribed the
work of others. One obvious example of this is the case of *Haidenröslein.*

Apparently, none of his other arrangements survive, so his work in
this area cannot be fully evaluated. Nevertheless, other types of
borrowings and reworkings can be noted. On 18 August 1909, Huss
opened a concert with a transcription of the *Dance of the Seven Veils*
from *Salome* by Strauss and *En Bateau* by Debussy. Huss talked about
the selection from *Salome,* according to the review, saying that "it was
beautiful in spots, but was not sincere music, and that Strauss had
pursued much higher ideals in his earlier compositions." That fall
Huss presented these same transcriptions and another of his arrangements, his paraphrase of two preludes by Chopin.

One final example of this arranger role should be noted. A
program given 18 December 1899 consisted of readings by Virginia
Calhoun from the ancient Hindu play *Sakuntalá,* sponsored by the
local chapter of the DAR. Huss's contribution, as outlined in the
program notes by Krehbiel, was to coordinate music composed by
Karl Goldmark (from his overture to *Sakuntalá*) and excerpts from
four of Wagner's operas (*Tristan und Isolde, Parsifal, Lohengrin,* and
Das Rheingold) into incidental music that he then played at the piano.

Late in life Huss tried to turn this talent for working with the
music of others into an income. On 20 August 1943, Huss wrote to
Carl Engel at Schirmer, stating his interest in doing some editing for
that firm. While Engel's response is not known, that Huss may have

done such work is known since he is among the "Associate and Assistant Editors" on the title page of Louis Elson's *Modern Music and Musicians* (1918).

Principal Style Characteristics

Like any good composer, Huss did not use each of his style traits in every piece, but the following list provides a summary of his principal stylistic characteristics. The discussions of the selected pieces in succeeding chapters refer to these characteristics.

1. Huss had an interest in the cyclic use of materials in multi-movement works. This can take the form of quotation or of theme transformation. This characteristic was sometimes noted by his contemporaries: a review offered by the *New York Times* of the November 1901 Kneisel Quartet concert discussed Huss's use of "community of theme."

2. Huss liked to create musical and dramatic tension by having a developmental section—often involving the sequential repetition of a thematic motive through a series of upward modulations—climaxed with a sudden silence. These silences are generally followed by some important thematic statement, often of the principal theme of a work or movement.

3. Huss had a preference for subdominant harmonies.

4. Especially in the choral music, though not exclusively there, Huss liked to write melodic lines that created a series of appoggiaturas. The effect might be likened to Palestrina filtered through Brahms.

5. Huss developed his material very often in a passage with a sliding tonal center. Key signatures are sometimes changed during these passages, though these changes may have served only to "clear the slate" in the performer's mind of many accidentals rather than marking important structural points in the composition. One occasionally sees passages without a key signature that may be so marked in order to make things easier for the performer rather than indicating C Major or A minor.

6. Alongside this last characteristic should be noted Huss's predilection for blending relative major and minor tonalities. Sometimes his writing in this regard suggests that he thought of a key signature as a set of pitches rather than as a tonal center. This may

explain the comments in a review: among other works on a recital, Huss had presented the first two movements of a new and unfinished work, the *Piano Sonata* in D minor, and regarding this piece A. Walter Kramer wrote in *Musical America* (15 April 1922):

> The work proved to be, like other fine Huss works in the larger forms, a serious essay in the form, a composition replete with vital ideas, which the composer has developed with unerring logic and taste. The themes are characteristic of their composer, and the romantic feeling, which he has shown in his other works, is present here, also. Harmonically he has added a touch of "whole-tonism," but he employs it as a tincture rather than as a base.

7. Several of his etudes, etude-like works, and accompaniment writing in other pieces make use of repeated chords in the piano, in the manner of Schubert's *Der Erlkönig*. Since Huss wrote a number of these pieces with himself in mind as the performer, it may be that he had a particularly gifted way of solving this kind of technical problem; he may simply have liked the percussive effect in the piano.

8. Huss would sometimes set up a tonal center at the beginning of a work, movement, or section and then not go to that key at all. A corollary approach was to have an opening section that has no clear tonal center at all, so the final resolution in the intended key is actually one of a number of possibilities in the listener's ear.

9. Huss's melodic style is extremely variegated; analysis is complicated by his concern for text painting in the vocal music and by his interest in idiomatic writing, especially in the music for his own instrument. In general his melodies tend to be built out of rhythmic motives, sometimes with corollary melodic contour patterns (not strictly melodic motives because Huss does not treat this aspect strictly when he uses it). Usually he adheres to antecedent-consequent phrasing, normally in four-measure lengths. His melodies typically cover slightly more than an octave in range but may reappear in quite different tessituras; the contour often resembles a sine wave pattern centered in the middle of the range, but he also writes arch-type melodies, and less often, "trough-shaped" melodies. Repeated pitches often form a part of his melodies, especially in vocal music, but when leaps appear, these usually are in the context of the harmony; scale patterns, when used, are generally decorated with chromatic tones.

One may look into sources close to Huss for style comments. The following quotation possibly comes from Huss himself writing in the third person:

> Mr. Huss's church compositions all show a strong influence of the strict ecclesiastical style and have many suggestions of the Gregorian modes; his instrumental compositions on the contrary are ultra modern in tendency and very dramatic in style. His aim in his elaborate compositions has always been to use counterpoint and fugues and other artifices of composition only to heighten the interest and beauty of a composition. He has shown little sympathy with the extreme realism of the Programme-music makers of the Liszt–Richard Strauss school.

Other writers also left some keys to his style. It is instructive to consider this subject in light of American composers of his generation in general. There survives a review (in the *Musical Leader*) of a December 1901 rehearsal of Huss's *Pater Noster* given by Richard Warren and his choir during a service at St. Bartholomew's. The reviewer wrote, in part, that

> the composition of Mr. Huss was in no way inferior to those of the very great masters [an organ work of Bach and choral works by Palestrina, Beethoven, and Brahms] in whose company he found himself. To write sacred music of that caliber requires something, in fact, a great deal, besides musicianship, which everyone concedes Mr. Huss to possess, but to write in the spirit of his "Pater Noster" is only possible to one in whom reverence is dominant, in whom a higher life is real as well as ideal, whose soul has not been contaminated by the maelstrom of the world, and one who believes that godliness, purity and sanctity are attributes of the larger portion of mankind. A man is the better for writing such a composition, and people are very much better for the hearing.

Daniel Gregory Mason, writing in the 15 March 1902 issue of the *Outlook,* provided another such general perspective on American composers and an assessment of Huss.

> Our music ought to be cosmopolitan rather than narrowly national. It ought to draw freely from all traditions both of thought and technique, and to derive its unity from pertinence

to individual expression rather than from limitation to a particular racial convention. We should expect it to be more many-sided than perfect, to fall short not so much in versatility of utterance as in clear fusion of style. As a matter of fact, this is what we find to be the case when we turn to the work of our composers. They represent many tendencies: the poetically picturesque and imaginative, the warmly romantic and mystical, the intellectual, the brilliant, the richly colored. They have no one pervasive trait that we can point to as distinctively American, as, for example, we can point to the gloomily passionate as Russian or the pseudo-classically finished as French. Their character is individual rather than racial, their technical resources cosmopolitan rather than national. And it is not to be wondered at that, on the whole, their work lacks clearly crystallized style; drawn from so many sources, it is naturally difficult to stamp with unity.

[Huss's Piano Concerto] well illustrates his romanticism, which is extreme; though he is some times turgid in emotion and over-elaborate in harmony, his sentiment is so manly and poetic and his style at its best so elevated that he is one of the most important American exponents of the modern romantic school in music. One can see that he has studied to advantage not only Bach and Beethoven, but also Schumann, Liszt, Rubinstein, Tschaikowsky, and Wagner; yet he is entirely original—his half-sensuous, half-religious mysticism is characteristic of no one else.

CHAPTER VII

SONGS

As an introduction to Huss's work and reputation as a song composer, one can consider comments by Pauline Jennings, writing in the 15 September 1917 *Musical America.*

> [His] voice . . . as song writer sounds through modern musical art distinct from every other. Song writing is the most frank and personal of arts, and in the Huss songs, with their spontaneous directness in the expression of feeling and their masterly workmanship, we have a self-revelation from the composer.
>
> One of the signs and seals of the Huss compositions is their harmonic unexpectedness, [which] may be called a preeminently distinguishing trait. We are able to rejoice in this music which so seldom says what it might be expected to say, but, by a perennial *surprise* of artistry, reveals strange, new vistas of meaning. [The] exquisitely refined undertones of color are deftly handled, and the richly tinted harmonies appear sometimes as isolated points of color. Color is everywhere in these songs; not crude color, but subtle.
>
> [The] faithfulness to the emotional atmosphere of the poem seems fairly to become part of the lyric, and it penetrates with the plummet of tone beneath the surface of the words; it has also a margin of suggestiveness. And as words in great poetry, beside their center of definite signification, have edges bright with prismatic colors caught from their context, so in these songs many a melodic inflection or well-poised chord derives charm from its relationship.
>
> Seldom have the art of the composer and that of the poet been more closely connected than in the settings given by Mr. Huss to the poems of his cousin, the late Richard Watson Gilder. Among his finest are . . . "After Sorrow's Night" and "Before Sunrise." On these the composer has lavished the

They that sow in Tears.

Sacred Arioso.

HENRY HOLDEN HUSS.

They That Sow in Tears. Schmidt, 1891.

They That Sow in Tears. Schmidt, 1891.

wealth of his art and inspiration. Of beautiful melodic contour, with sustained invention, rhythmic and harmonic power and pulsating emotion, they are mastersongs.

As with his choral music, Huss wrote both secular and sacred songs. One of the earliest of his sacred songs is *They That Sow in Tears,* published by Schmidt in 1891 (see pps. 118–120). This was an extremely successful work commercially: some 3,700 copies were printed and of these only 679 remained to be destroyed for lack of sales.

The piece, on a text from Psalm 126, was intended for use by a contralto or baritone. It is a ternary design: text and tune for "They that sow in tears shall reap in joy" surround a modulatory section on "He that goeth forth and weepeth bearing precious seed shall doubtless come again rejoicing! Bringing his sheaves with him." The musical material for "shall doubtless come again" and "with rejoicing" is treated sequentially, and the tonalities touched upon are closely related to the home key. The piano supports the voice without extensive doubling; in the middle section it especially takes on a life of its own. The work thus falls into the finest lieder tradition of a symbiotic rather than subservient relationship between voice and keyboard.

By contrast, the setting of the Goethe text in *Haidenröslein* (occasionally seen in the correct spelling of "Heidenröslein") differs from the other songs in that it was intended as a Huss contribution to the Beethoven literature more than to his own. The work was published under Beethoven's name by Schirmer in 1898 and provided with the following explanation on the title page: "The Melody arranged from a recently discovered fragmentary Manuscript and the Accompaniment composed by Henry Holden Huss." A reproduction of Beethoven's sketch was included with the publication. The sketch is number 150 in Willy Hess's *Verzeichnis der nicht in der Gesamtausgabe veröffentlichten Werke Ludwig van Beethovens.*

There are two important song sets in the Huss work list. The first of these is titled *Four Songs,* Op. 22, published in 1907 by Schirmer. It may be that the four were not conceived as a unit, given the disunity of key, subject matter, and known dates of composition; certainly this is no song cycle, a format Huss appears never to have used. The entire set was dedicated to Huss's wife.

The available royalty records suggest that these songs were not at

It Was a Lover and His Lass, Op. 22, No. 2. Schirmer, 1907.

It Was a Lover and His Lass, Op. 22, No. 2. Schirmer, 1907.

all successful commercially. No copies of the first song (*Wiegenlied* or *Cradle-Song*) are listed as sold and only ten of the second song (*It Was a Lover and His Lass*), all for low voice in E-flat. Between the two settings of the third song (*Before Sunrise*) in different keys, six copies are listed as sold, and three copies of the final work in the set (*Ich liebe Dich*), the version for high voice, are listed as sold. There is at the New York Public Library an autographed copy of *It Was a Lover and His Lass* upon which a few performance notes have been written by hand, probably by the composer.

Evidently the most performed of the set and the most successful critically was the second song, a setting of Shakespeare's text from *As You Like It* (see pps. 122–124). Not only was the work performed in its original setting, but Huss also made an arrangement of the song for voice and instrumental ensemble and for voice and string quartet; these arrangements were not published. Of this song, William Treat Upton wrote in his *Art-Song in America:*

> To us it is the best song he has written. In it he has caught exactly the right quaint and archaic style, and a very attractive style it is. There is just enough harmonic variety, neither too much nor too little, and the unexpected turn that he gives the winsome melody of his opening bars when it recurs between the verses, is exceedingly whimsical and attractive.

As indicated by Upton, the song comprises three verses interrupted by references to the piano introduction. The musical material for these three verses is not strophic; instead the song is another ternary design with a modulatory middle section surrounded by music firmly in the home key of G Major, though with some chromatic coloration. The tonalities of the middle section center on flat keys, and this probably accounts for the "unexpected turns" to which Upton refers, since Huss must use those quotations to leave and later return to the home key. The vocal line is doubled in the piano though the keyboard sometimes decorates that line or relegates it momentarily to an inner part.

The other important set is *Two Songs with Piano Accompaniment,* Op. 28, published by Schirmer in 1917. Both works in this set (*After Sorrow's Night* and *Music, When Sweet Voices Die*) were also given treatments for voice and instrumental ensemble, but these were not published. Royalty records show sales of twelve and eight copies,

After Sorrow's Night

Poem by
R. W. Gilder

Music by
Henry Holden Huss. Op. 28, No.1

After Sorrow's Night, Op. 28, No. 1. Schirmer, 1917.

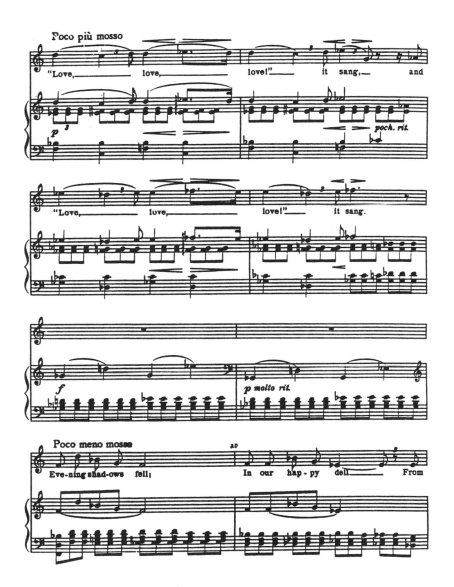

After Sorrow's Night, Op. 28, No. 1. Schirmer, 1917.

After Sorrow's Night, Op. 28, No. 1. Schirmer, 1917.

respectively, of the two songs. The lack of any connection between the two songs in key or date of composition suggests, as with *Four Songs,* Op. 22, that these may not originally have been intended to be linked.

The set was reviewed, in *Musical America* of 31 March 1917, when it first appeared in print.

> It is some time since we have had new songs from the pen of this distinguished composer. Mr. Huss is a busy worker in America's music, but he labors so arduously with his pianoforte teaching in season that little time is left him for composition until the vacation months come around. Those who know his music deplore the fact that he is not able to give himself wholly to creative work. For he is one of the best of all native composers.
>
> A song of modern stripe, in which the piano and voice are treated as complements of each other, ["After Sorrow's Night"] is a mighty and powerful essay. Mr. Huss's harmonization, subtle, rich and colorful, is fascinating. More than that, in addition to all its individual features, it is solid. One feels in it the learning of the composer, not at all in an academic way, however—Mr. Huss's music is never academic, we are happy to add—but one appreciates the value of the years spent by Mr. Huss in Munich. . . . It is dedicated to Oscar Seagle, who has already sung it in his recitals.
>
> Mr. Huss has made the loveliest setting of Shelley's famous lines, "Music, When Soft Voices Die," for a solo voice that we have thus far seen. There seems to be an error in the text as used by Mr. Huss. The adjective is "soft," not "sweet." This is a detail and can easily be adjusted in the next edition. The setting is surprisingly lovely. There is a feeling of "ninths" in it, Mr. Huss having created a peaceful and serene atmosphere with the very materials so often employed for passionate utterances. There are gently swaying triplets in the accompaniment; the voice part murmurs *dolcissimo,* again couched in telling accents.
>
> And Mr. Huss has succeeded in doing something that composers before him have so often failed in; that is, in the repeating of the text. Of course, he does not do so in the first stanza, but the closing lines . . . he restates a number of times and, instead of weakening, heightens his effect. It is a memorable song and one that should be highly prized for recital purposes. It is inscribed to Alma Gluck.

There are more known performances of the first song in the set than of the second, so we will say no more of the Shelley setting other than that the reviewer's interest in correcting a text error remained unsatisfied, as there was no second edition.

The review of the first song is instructive in that the dedication to Seagle is not carried in the printed text (see pps. 126–130). The poem as used here by Huss consists of three short quatrains, each succeeded by a refrain line. The quatrains are set in common meter and the refrain line in the equivalent of $^{12}/_8$ time. The accompaniment, which contains most of the vocal line as well, takes up the characteristic Huss idea of repeated chords during the setting of the first refrain and retains that idea almost invariably to the end of the song. In the second quatrain setting, the melody—and with it the right hand of the piano part—returns to common time. At the close of the second and third quatrains, the repeated chord idea is briefly abandoned altogether. The use of two against three in the keyboard writing in the second quatrain is also used in the third and in the final refrain setting.

The melodic material for each quatrain setting is different, but the material for the refrain, while at different pitch levels, is essentially the same. The work is in A Major/minor, but Huss characteristically begins in another key (here B-flat Major) and then quickly modulates to the home key. The chromatic decoration in the vocal line as well as in the piano writing is extensive. The second quatrain is set in B-flat; the third shifts from G to E-flat. By contrast, the refrain settings do not serve a tonality but rather offer a means of movement from one key to another. A short coda confirms A Major.

CHAPTER VIII

CHORAL MUSIC

Unlike the chamber music, which reflects Huss's German training and orientation toward chromaticism, contrapuntal textures, and theme transformation, the choral music, at least the sacred literature, reflects the realities of church music in the United States, a repertoire much more dependent upon English tradition than German.

Huss wrote both sacred and secular choral music, but even the secular music tends to be written on serious texts emphasizing some moral or patriotic value. Four works are representative of various aspects of Huss's life and career as well as several elements of his choral style: two offer evidence of Huss's revisions—and one of these was among his most commercially successful efforts—the third is a work available in recording, and the fourth is a secular work from rather later in Huss's life.

The first of the revised works is his Opus 4, *Ave Maria,* for female soloists and instrumental ensemble; the two entries in the work list offer more details. Huss apparently had the work published privately in 1888, for no publisher's name appears on the print copy, and the copyright is given there as belonging to Huss. Two years later, however, Huss sold the work to the English firm of Novello, who then published it anew.

Both prints of the work call for soloists, which may reflect a common practice of having paid solo quartets in church, either to replace a full choir or to serve as section leaders in a volunteer choir. On the other hand, the scores of the 1888 and 1890 editions suggest an important conceptual difference: the 1888 score contains a combination organ part and "line score" (the orchestral parts presented as cues in a single staff), such as a person conducting from an organ keyboard might use.

Both versions have the traditional Latin oration to the Virgin as a text and an English text that is not a translation, but rather a text seeming more suitable for use in a Protestant setting. Indeed, the opening words of the English text, "Save Me, O God," appear as a subtitle to the 1888 version. The text underlay makes it clear that the Latin words were the original text. The source of the English text is not given.

There are a number of other differences between the two editions. The 1888 score has passages of a cappella choral writing, while the chorus is never unaccompanied in the 1890 version. Harmonically the versions are identical, and they are the same length. The instrumental introduction is more florid in the later publication; the arpeggiation found there in the piano part is used in much of the accompaniment figuration. The closing "Amen" section is more thickly scored in the 1890 version. One other minor difference is the position of the parts on the page, with the 1888 having chorus at the top, soloists in the middle and accompaniment on the bottom; the 1890 version reverses the order of the chorus and soloists.

In a letter of 4 December 1916 to Huss from the H. W. Gray Company, acting as agents for Novello, Huss received a royalty check of $18.84 for *Ave Maria* on 950 copies of a total of 1450 copies sold between 25 September 1890 and 13 February 1911. (Huss's royalty agreement exempted the first 500 copies.) Extant royalty records show sales of another 160 copies of the Novello version between February 1923 and November 1938.

Among other libraries, copies of *Ave Maria* are in the Tams-Witmark Collection at Westminster Choir College. Catherine B. Malmstrom, Choral Librarian at Westminster, advises that of over 1200 titles, about one-third of are held "in quantity," including two Huss works.

> While we have no record here of the relative popularity of any works in the collection, one might assume that the two Huss works [the other is the *Festival Sanctus*] were chosen for their commercial value over those eight hundred or more works found only in single copy.

The work begins with a theme in D minor but departs from that key and theme in order to present new key areas and materials before returning to the initial idea and tonality. The succeeding keys are D-flat, E-flat (with a change to triple meter here as well), A-flat, and

D minor. At this point there is a return to the common-time meter of the beginning as well as to the opening melody, but that melody is used here to supply a motive upon which Huss builds an extended sequential section; all the performing forces are drawn into this. This section builds dynamically and chromatically to a climactic pause (see pps. 136–139). The motive appears again and leads to a series of closing chords on "Amen." A perusal of the score reveals that Huss has broken up the text by using "Ave [or Sancta] Maria, ora pro nobis" as a refrain. The tonal areas are thus connected with segments of remaining text.

In contrast to the two years between the first and second versions of *Ave Maria,* with the *Festival Sanctus,* for soprano solo, chorus, and orchestra, only a few months were required for the production of a "New Revised Edition." As with the earlier work, Huss himself evidently published the first version, *Holy! Holy! Holy!* or *Motette,* in 1899. The second version was published by the Edward Schuberth Company in the same year. The second version carries the dedication to the Metropolitan Musical Society of New York and William R. Chapman, its director. The work is identified as both Opus 7 and 9 in work lists in Huss's hand.

The differences between the two versions are nearly all either additions of performance directions (metronome, tempo, dynamic, and other similar markings) or changes in the organ accompaniment. For the most part these changes are additions of accompaniment in places where there was none before, although in a few instances, music for the manuals is being added to an already existing pedal part.

The *Festival Sanctus* is a more complicated work than the *Ave Maria.* The work is based upon a careful juxtaposition of various performing forces: accompaniment against chorus, female subchorus against male, chorus against soloist. Connections among most of the various thematic materials are created by having each use an opening rhythmic motive of long-short-short character (usually a quarter note followed by two eighths). Furthermore, the harmonic centers of the work are less readily apparent. For example, the opening section lacks a key signature, and while it does in fact work in the broadest sense through A minor, the section also suggests E-flat, C, B-flat minor, D-flat, and F.

Crossing the Bar, on a text by Tennyson, for chorus and keyboard, does not seem to be a particularly important or significant work

AVE MARIA.

Ave Maria, Op. 4. No publisher, 1888. Pp. 17–20.

AVE MARIA.

Ave Maria, Op. 4. No publisher, 1888. Pp. 17–20.

AVE MARIA.

except that, in an arrangement by Richard Condie, it is one of two works by Huss that have been recorded commercially (see pps. 142–145).

The work was published by Birchard in its anthology for public school music, the *Laurel Song Book*. It was with the 1901 edition of this book that Clarence Birchard founded his Boston publishing house. The book was edited, by William L. Tomlins, with an eye toward musical and textual quality; its emphasis was on the adaptation of art songs and on original compositions of high quality rather than on European folk songs as in other school anthologies of the time. There were eventually a number of "Laurel" music texts, and taken as a group they formed an anthology of music rather than a graded series. Birchard also issued the contents of the *Laurel Song Book* as separate works (the "Laurel Octavo Series") simply by using the same plates.

The Huss work reappeared in the 1908 and 1913 editions of Birchard's anthology (also edited by Tomlins). The arrangement by Richard Condie was published by Fischer in 1964 but is now out of print. Judging from the recordings, doubling of voice parts in places and supplying organ registration are the only changes. This arrangement was recorded by the Mormon Tabernacle Choir under Condie's direction for Columbia ML-6019/MS-6619 (*The Mormon Tabernacle Choir at the World's Fair*) in 1964; the record was withdrawn from Columbia's catalog in 1966, but *Crossing the Bar* reappeared on a later Columbia Masterworks disc (*Sing unto God,* MS 6908), described as "An all-request program of radio and television favorites." This statement suggests a popularity one might not expect in such a minor work, and Birchard royalty records support this idea of popularity: 3100 copies of the work were printed in 1901, and only 669 copies were left unsold and destroyed.

Structurally the work is simplicity itself. Its ternary design parallels the three stanzas of text used, whose opening section in E-flat presents a quiet theme, closing on a deceptive cadence, a middle section of more agitated nature and building to a climactic moment on the dominant. The return to the opening material is supported by an accompaniment suggesting the middle section's *agitato;* having arrived at the same deceptive cadence, Huss then provides a short coda to confirm the home key.

The original publication circumstances of *The Recessional* (or simply *Recessional* in some references to the work), for chorus and keyboard or orchestra with optional organ, were identical to those of *Crossing the Bar* as it also appeared in numerous editions of the *Laurel Song Book* published by Birchard. The text of this work is by Rudyard Kipling. Huss made the setting for chorus and orchestra three years after that for chorus and keyboard.

The problems for the composer working with a text such as this one by Kipling are the need for variety in setting the strophes lest the work turn into a glorified hymn, and the corollary but opposite need for some means of unifying all the variety so created. Perhaps for this reason (and perhaps because of the nature of the singers for whom the work was written), Huss maintained a homorhythmic texture throughout the work in the choral writing. Often the accompaniment joins in this, and this contributes a very solid, majestic quality to the work. There is an instrumental section to open the work and also instrumental interludes between each of the five strophes, except for the first two and the final two, which pairs are separated by a moment of silence. Variety is achieved by utilizing different rhythms, though the poetic meter is constant, and through interesting harmonic coloration and momentary departures from the home key of C minor. Part of the interest of the work is found in Huss's penchant for preparing one key but suddenly going somewhere else.

Winged Messengers of Peace, for chorus and piano, was called, in an advertising leaflet, "The World-Peace Chorus" and described therein as "An Epitome of the World's Aspirations for Peace." The leaflet continued with the following:

> Dr. John Finley Williamson, conductor of the Westminster Choir, endorses this PEACE CHORUS in most enthusiastic terms and says: "It should be sung at all Peace Meetings, large and small."

The work was published by Schirmer in 1937, the year after its completion. The text was written by one Alva Feddé. Royalty records show sales of 708 copies, and Schirmer also made available, on a rental basis, Huss's orchestration. The piano part suggests in some of its features that Huss conceived the work for orchestra from the start. Huss also made an arrangement for male chorus and piano, but there is no record of this arrangement's ever having been performed.

There appear in the work a number of expression marks in the manner of Brahms, and the interweaving of contrapuntal lines in the

CROSSING THE BAR.

Alfred Tennyson.

Henry Holden Huss.

Crossing the Bar. Summy-Birchard, 1901.

CROSSING THE BAR.

CROSSING THE BAR.

Crossing the Bar. Summy-Birchard, 1901.

CROSSING THE BAR.

accompaniment also suggests some Germanic elements in the work's ancestry, rather different from Huss's normal choral style. Another aspect of style is shown in the changes Huss makes in his musical material to fit the changing moods of the text. Toward the beginning, the text is fairly martial (e.g., "Above the crash of flaming shot and shell"), and the accompaniment explodes in fanfare rhythms and motives. Where the text is prayerlike (e.g., "Tell them with love and deepest sympathy"), Huss juxtaposes solo voices with choral sections and uses a more contrapuntal style. Where the text laments fallen soldiers (e.g., "Dry our tears"), a somber, chordal style is adopted with a very simple accompaniment.

The extended length of the work and the changing moods provide Huss with opportunities to change key and meter as well. The associated modulatory sections required for such a variety of tonal centers as well as the chromatic coloration Huss normally utilized add to the harmonic interest of the work.

CHAPTER IX

PIANO MUSIC

The piano music of Huss is a mixture of recital pieces for the mature professional and didactic works for the student. Huss was a firm believer in using music rather than exercises to teach piano students, and he composed works for this purpose. It is difficult to separate the music cleanly into these two categories, however, because Huss would sometimes use what would otherwise seem to be a didactic piece as a recital work.

Many of the works appeared in print in small collections. In the discussion of some of these pieces which follows, our attention will be on selected individual works rather than whole collections.

One of Huss's earliest publications was *Drei Bagatellen für das Pianoforte,* Op. 5, published by A. P. Schmidt in 1889; the German title may reflect Huss's recent studies in Munich. Of the three pieces, there are no known performances of any but the first of the set, *Étude Mélodique* (see pps. 148–151).

The *Étude Mélodique* was a very popular work; Huss included it on recital programs as late as 1938, and it was also played by a number of his students. The original press run produced 600 copies, of which only 10 copies are known to have been destroyed for lack of sales or other reasons. Huss included this composition in his White House recital in January 1904, and it was one of two of his works performed then that especially pleased President Theodore Roosevelt. The work has been recorded non-commercially by John Gillespie in *Nineteenth-Century American Piano Music: A Sampler,* a cassette tape produced by the University of California at Santa Barbara.

The work's didactic value was also recognized. The "Report of the Committee on Piano Curriculum" submitted by Arthur Foote to the 1908 MTNA convention included the *Étude Mélodique* among other works from Huss's pen as recommended. This recommendation came

ETUDE MÉLODIQUE.

HENRY HOLDEN HUSS

A. P. S. 2550

Étude Mélodique, Op. 5, No. 1. Schmidt, 1889.

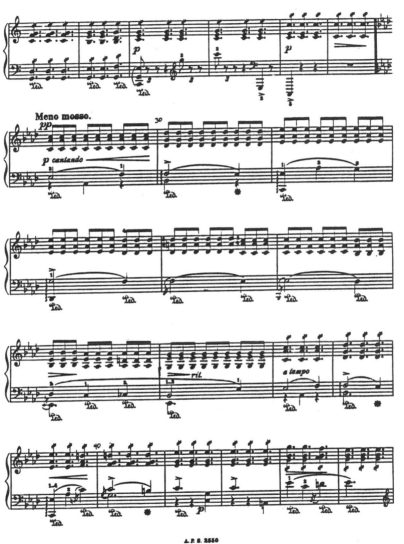

Étude Mélodique, Op. 5, No. 1. Schmidt, 1889.

from piano teachers in several cities who were requested to create a list of "from fifty to a hundred pianoforte pieces and studies important for use in teaching." Other Huss works included in the list were *Condensed Piano Technics,* the *Preludes,* Op. 17, *Menuet,* Op. 18, No. 1, *La Nuit, Etude "The Rivulet,"* and the *Three Pieces for Pianoforte,* Op. 20.

The "etude" aspect of the C Major work is to be found in the rapidly repeated triplet pattern that constitutes the fabric of the work. The design is a clear ternary form in which the middle section pits a sustained lyric line against the triplet pattern while the pattern itself contains melodic interest in the outer sections. The middle section is in A-flat, and this tonal shift provides the only key change in the short piece, although portions of the work do receive some interesting harmonic treatment. The work is simple and straightforward, as one might expect from a young composer writing a work ostensibly for instructional purposes.

The *Prelude Appassionata* and *Etude "The Rivulet"* were apparently not originally intended to appear together in print. The cover page they share does not link the two titles, and it lists separate prices for the two, indicating that the cover page may not have been designed initially for collective use. Furthermore, there is some confusion over copyright dates: the publisher, Schmidt, gives the correct year of 1891 (according to Copyright Office records) on the cover page but incorrectly lists 1890 on the first page of the separate works.

The first of the pair was also known as *Othello* and was dedicated to Huss's friend and colleague Adele aus der Ohe. The second work carries no dedication; moreover, the first page of the music entitles it simply *Etude.* It was occasionally referred to in programs as *The Rivulet Arabesque.* Both works were played repeatedly by Huss into the mid-1930s.

Both works utilize a rhythmic pattern repeated throughout and against which melodic material is contrasted. In the *Prelude* the pattern is a sixteenth rest followed by three sixteenth notes; under the rubric "Allegro molto agitato," this pattern contributes to a sense of perpetual motion. In *Etude "The Rivulet"* the pattern is a chain of triplets whose relationship to the programmatic title is unmistakable. G minor is the key center here, and the "etude" aspect is to be found in difficulty of maintaining the triplet pattern evenly despite its various intervallic transmutations. The Gillespies describe it as a "fine right-hand study piece." The opening four measures in the right hand serve as a recurring motive, but the piece is of free form otherwise.

The piece that has kept Huss's name at all known must be the second of the *Quatre Préludes en forme d'Études,* Op. 17, because this prelude is the only work by Huss that was commercially recorded in its original version and is still available. This recording, released in 1978 by New World Records (NW206), is in an anthology of American piano works entitled *Malcolm Frager plays Adolph Martin Foerster, Henry F. Gilbert, Henry Holden Huss, Ethelbert Nevin, Horatio Parker, Edward MacDowell, John Knowles Paine.*

The Preludes were published by Schirmer in 1901 for sale as individual items. From the royalty records dated 1 January 1928 through 1 July 1951, the following sales can be determined:

Prelude #1 in D-flat	21 copies
Prelude #2 in D	124 copies
Prelude #3 in E	95 copies
Prelude #4 in A-flat	15 copies

The set as a whole was reviewed, together with other works of Huss's (those in Opus 18), at the time of publication in the January 1902 issue of *Music.*

> Mr. Henry Holden Huss, who is favorably known as one of the best American composers, here appears in six compositions from the press of G. Schirmer. The first prelude is in the key of D flat, and the opening form is that of an arpeggio, played quickly by the two hands, the left hand crossing over and completing the affair by means of a superimposed melody note. This is followed by some melody with accompaniment in triplets. The harmonic structure is very modern indeed, and it would be necessary to hear it played very well indeed in order to judge adequately whether inspiration were by chance present in the work to anything like an equal extent with the cleverness of the handling.
>
> The second prelude is in D Major, and the motive is quite like that of one of the Capriccios by Brahms. It is capable of producing a good effect. The third prelude is in the key of E Major and has the wholly unusual form of a prelude for right hand alone, the basses being put in later, the pedal holding the melody. One hesitates to assign a definite value to an idea of

Prelude II.

HENRY HOLDEN HUSS. Op. 17, № 2.

18N41

Prelude in D, Op. 17, No. 2. Schirmer, 1901.

Prelude in D, Op. 17, No. 2. Schirmer, 1901.

this kind, considering that the right hand is almost invariably by far too good for the left hand, which has to accompany it. Prelude four is in A-flat, and affords very pleasing practice for melody with lighter and faster notes around it. The thumbs generally play the chief melodies. All four are clever as work—and perhaps capable of agreeable salon effect.

All the titles of these six pieces are in the French language, from which it will be seen that even our composers do not escape the tendency to polyglottony to which our singers are so dreadfully liable. It is a great thing to encourage the American muse in one of the graceful languages of continental Europe, where all our American work is so highly prized.

The "etude" aspect of the D Major *Prelude* is found in the rapidly repeated pairs of chords in varying guises (see pps. 154–157). The form is simple as well: an opening idea and its repetition, a modulatory section beginning in F minor and sequencing downward chromatically, a repetition of that modulatory section but now beginning in B-flat minor, a transition, the return of the opening material, and a coda.

The A-flat *Prelude,* though selling the fewest copies, was the one most often played by the composer himself. Its structure consists of three melodic ideas presented as a group at the beginning and decorated in such a manner as to suggest an improvisation. This group is then repeated with varied accompanying figuration and harmony, and then the short work closes with an extended coda.

In the same year that Schirmer published the *Four Preludes,* the firm also produced Huss's Opus 18 set: *Menuet et Gavotte Capricieuse.* Royalty records dated June 1905 through 1 January 1941 show that 25 copies of the *Menuet* were sold against only 9 of the *Gavotte;* there is no record of Huss's playing the *Gavotte,* but the *Menuet* appeared frequently on his programs.

In the review quoted above concerning the *Preludes,* comment was also offered about these works.

The Menuet in C Major begins rather sonorously and with promise, but the second measure and fourth are upon a very weak harmonic succession, the net result therefore of the first four measures being at least questionable. This second period is pleasing, and quite along the same line as many bits in Liszt, Liszt having been the first user, and, if anything, a little the

> better, as more to the manner born. The capricieuse Gavotte in
> G minor is capable of pleasing effect.

Despite this unenthusiastic report, the *Menuet* did receive the endorsement of piano teachers, as reported by Arthur Foote to the 1907 MTNA convention.

The year 1904 was a year in which Huss saw several works into print. One of these was his *Poem for the Piano* entitled *La Nuit,* Op. 21, published by Schirmer. The piece had been written by 1903, however, because it was performed in that year.

Royalty records dated June 1905 through 1 July 1945 reveal sales of at least 146 copies, and sales may have been aided by four factors. As with the *Menuet,* Op. 18, No. 1, Foote reported the endorsement by Huss's fellow piano teachers to the 1907 MTNA convention. Huss performed the piece throughout his life, and there is a record of one performance the year after his death. The piece was included (alongside the *Polonaise brillante*) in a sample all-American piano recital program designed by Leslie Hodgson for the June 1925 issue of the *Musician.* The work was orchestrated in the early 1940s by Huss and performed in this arrangement as well.

The piece was often associated with a motto in printed programs:

> Oh Night! how wondrous art thou in thy melancholy, thy
> majesty and thy mystery!

The origin of this motto is unknown. One might expect the work to be arranged into three sections to depict the three characteristics mentioned in the motto, but its ternary design does not echo the affects suggested by the motto.

Another set of works published by Schirmer in 1904 was the *Three Pieces for Pianoforte,* Op. 20. The royalty records dated June 1905 through 1 July 1942 show the following sales:

Valse	325 copies
Nocturne	193 copies
Gavotte	125 copies

Sales of the first piece in relationship to the sales of the other two pieces is not commensurate with the recorded performances. While the *Valse* was frequently included in performances by Huss or his students, the other two works are hardly known to have been played. All of the Opus 20 set were named by Huss's colleagues at the twenty-ninth meeting of the MTNA as suitable teaching pieces. At this same meeting, Kate S. Chittenden, in her "Report of the Piano Conference," commented that Huss's *Valse,* Op. 20, alongside his *A May Morning* (No. 1 in *A Summer Sketch Book*), was viewed as a "lighter composition" of value by one Walter Spry of Chicago in a presentation about his piano school. Chittenden also mentioned Huss's *Bagatelle in C* (the first two works in the set are in that key) as a composition "for the earlier grades that had been found valuable" in her teaching.

A set of works for piano published in 1912 by Schirmer was the *Six Pieces for the Pianoforte,* Op. 23. Royalty records, for copies sold, dated 1 July 1930 through 1 January 1947, exist for only four of the pieces in the set:

1.	Étude Romantique	18 copies
4.	Impromtu	29 copies
5.	Album-leaf	12 copies
6.	Polonaise brillante	4 copies

The set was reviewed at the time of its publication. The following general comments and specific reference to the final work in the set are from a review by A. Walter Kramer for the 8 June 1912 issue of *Musical America.*

> Henry Holden Huss, one of the most individual of contemporary American composers, has once more made an important addition to the literature of his instrument, the piano, in his Six Pieces, Op. 23, which the house of G. Schirmer has just brought forward.
>
> Those who believe that piano music of worth is not being written to-day in America have but to examine this set of compositions to convince themselves at once that they are mistaken.
>
> With bold and massive strokes Mr. Huss has painted his dance in the "Polonaise Brillante," fully Lisztian in its demands on the player and in its effect. The themes are melodic, stirring in character and fitting to the composition. There is every kind of opportunity offered the player, chords, octaves, passage work, thirds and the many other devices of modern pianistic

art, and all is carefully handled with mastery. A thrilling octave passage, five measures long, closes the piece brilliantly.

Let it be recorded here that no American composer has within a considerable time written six pieces for the piano that contain as many solid musical ideas originally set forth, with interesting harmonies, as these of Mr. Huss.

The first four numbers in this set are dedicated to important pianists of the day, the fifth to a critic and writer on musical subjects, and the sixth to a family friend. It is this sixth work that occupies our attention now because of its prominence in Huss's own recitals. This work was played under the titles *Polonaise de Concert* and *Concert Caprice en Forme de Polonaise* before its publication as *Polonaise brillante.* A copy of the score of the *Polonaise* with penciled comments, possibly by Huss himself, is to be found in the New York Public Library; the comments are largely directed toward performance considerations of dynamics and articulation, but there are some alterations of the printed score.

This display piece has the chromatic activity, both decorative and modulatory, native to a work by Huss. The material presented falls neatly into three sections (and corresponding tonal areas) arranged in a rondo form. A short introduction prepares the home key of F-sharp Major used in the A section, where the characteristic polonaise rhythm occurs most prominently. The B section, in the minor subdominant, is more subdued in dynamic and mood. A repetition of some A material leads to the C section, in A Major, in which the polonaise rhythm is used in the accompaniment. This portion of the work is marked to be played somewhat more slowly and also softly. Material from the A section closes the main body of the piece. Here follows a short reference to the C material (now in F Major) and references to the A and B materials (in their original keys); a coda emphasizing interlocking octaves brings the work to an exciting finish (see pps. 162–165).

The last of the piano works to be discussed here is one contained in a set of didactic works but which nevertheless was often played in recital by Huss and by some of his students; this is true to a lesser extent of some of the others in the set. In fact, there is a reference in the program for the 25 May 1927 recital to a Duo-Art piano roll having been made by Huss of *Lake Como by Moonlight,* but the roll was lost or destroyed. The set is known as *Happy Days,* published by Carl

Polonaise Brillante, Op. 23, No. 6. Schirmer, 1912. Measures 110–149.

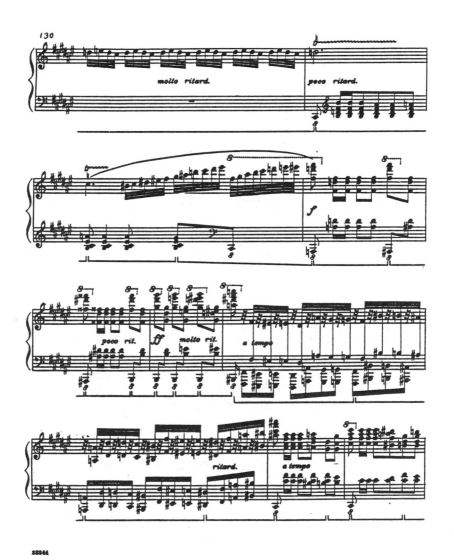

Polonaise Brillante, Op. 23, No. 6. Schirmer, 1912. Measures 110–149.

Fischer in 1923 with the subtitle *Nine Sketches for Piano.* Judging from surviving royalty records, dated 24 January 1924 through 17 April 1963, this set was the most successful commercially of all of Huss's works:

#1	The Fairy Princess	525 copies
#2	March of the Boy Scouts	782 copies
#3	The Peter Pan Baby	574 copies
#4	The Old Duchess at the Court Ball	584 copies
#5	Cherry Blossoms	546 copies
#6	The Sicilian Brigade	402 copies
#7	The Cloud on the Hill Top	851 copies
#8	The Skaters	619 copies
#9	Lake Como by Moonlight	3,078 copies

The grand total of 7,961 copies, it must be remembered, is a minimum total since there are gaps in the royalty records surviving. An advertising leaflet prepared by the publisher offered this description of the series:

> The author of this series of easy teaching pieces has long since gained an enviable reputation as a successful American composer, concert artist and teacher. His works include admirable specimens of practically every form and variety, and he has been particularly successful as a writer of truly worth-while music for instructive purposes.
>
> The present **Happy Days** sketches include easy teaching material of melodic, fanciful and exquisite design, carefully edited for every possible need of young students and proving with unquestionable certainty that instructive principles and pleasing qualifications may be combined with success—if an author only knows how.

The final sentence must have pleased Huss, considering his theories about didactic music; one wonders whether he may have written it himself.

The special interest in this set is the final work, *Lake Como by Moonlight,* described by subtitle as a barcarolle (see p. 167). The advertising leaflet cited above offered this description:

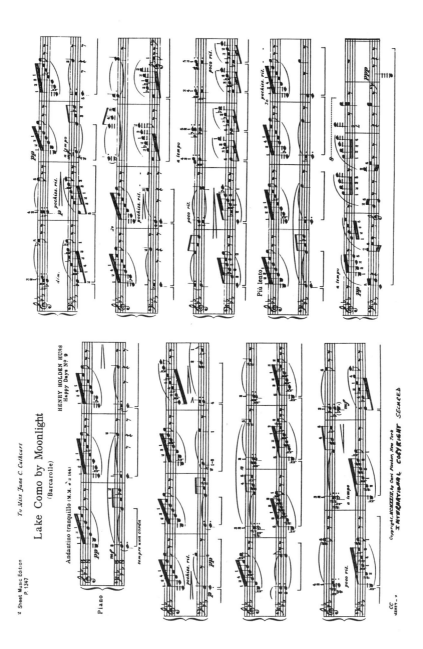

Lake Como by Moonlight ("Happy Days," No. 9). Carl Fischer, 1923.

This concluding number consists of a sustained, expressive left-hand melody, accompanied by dreamy, broken chord passages for the right hand. Later on the process is reversed. [It] demands slightly advanced ability in broken chord passages in flat and sharp keys, and knowledge of how to emphasize the melodic contour of a piece with suitable and proper taste.

The structure of the work is readily apparent: an eight-measure theme is presented in E-flat, repeated in B, and then repeated twice more in E-flat, the second of these statements being a varied statement serving as a coda.

CHAPTER X

CHAMBER MUSIC

Among the chamber works, three pieces may serve to illustrate several of Huss's style characteristics. These works are the *Sonata for Violin and Piano* in G minor, Op. 19, the *Romance* for violin (or violoncello) with piano accompaniment, and the *String Quartet in B minor,* Op. 31.

The *Sonata* is an extended work in three movements ("Allegro con brio," "Andante ma molto sostenuto, Vivace, Andante," and "Finale, Allegro molto"). It was completed by Huss in 1900, according to the holograph score in the New York Public Library, and dedicated to Franz Kneisel who, with Huss, presented the first performance on 12 November 1901 at a concert of the Kneisel Quartet.

The work was published by Schirmer in 1903 and was reprinted in 1920; this second printing of the work involved some cosmetic changes by Huss, and it was labeled "Second edition/Revised by the Composer." According to the surviving royalty reports to Huss from Schirmer, forty copies of the sonata were sold between 1905 and 1963, and eleven copies of the second movement, as a separate publication, were sold during the same period. Given that reports for some years are missing, it is reasonable to assume that more copies of both publications were actually sold.

This interest in the second movement, also known as *A Northern Melody* and as *Romance for Violin and Piano,* is borne out in the literature commenting on the work, as in this view from Arthur Shepherd (writing in the second edition of *Cobbett's Cyclopedic Survey of Chamber Music*).

> The hand of a skilled musician is clear throughout the sonata, and it is distinguished by its personal charm. This is particularly noticeable in the second movement, a blend of minuet and scherzo, which is almost Ravelian in its self-restraint and clarity.

169

To Mr. Franz Kneisel.

Sonata.

Henry Holden Huss. Op. 19.

Sonata for Violin and Piano, Op. 19. Schirmer, 1903. Movement I, measures 1–106.

The popularity of this composition is demonstrated by the large number of performances it received. It is noteworthy that Huss transcribed one movement for piano solo and used it as an encore on his 10 December 1913 recital in Aeolian Hall, New York City.

The opening theme of the first movement is to some extent a study in displaced accent (see pps. 170–171). The piano plays a harp-like accompaniment figure in alla breve time against which the violin plays a melodic figure whose accents precede those in the piano by the distance of a quarter note. A transition through the submediant leads to the second theme in B-flat, presented first in the piano. The development begins by presenting the opening motive of the first theme under the new key signatures of A Major and E-flat minor; then Huss abandons key signatures altogether for a section of rapidly changing key areas. The motive is also developed by changing its melodic intervals slightly beyond that required by a shift from minor to major, and by writing it in augmentation. The unchanging characteristic throughout the development of this idea is the ac-cented pick-up note that served to create rhythmic/metric tension between violin and piano at the outset of the movement. Huss compresses the recapitulation by presenting the two themes in invertible counterpoint between the two performers. The transition material reappears to lead to the coda in the parallel major. The coda introduces a new theme in F Major before returning to the home key and the principal theme, with which the movement is brought to a close.

The second movement is a ternary design in C Major. An important aspect of the movement is the interest created in timbre; various pedaling and bowing effects abound, and the violin is played *con sordino* at times. In a Brahmsian manner, many subtle changes of dynamics and tempo are also indicated. Shepherd's characterization of the movement as a minuet and scherzo is easily seen, for the opening idea strongly suggests, in rhythm and phrasing, a stately dance, while the middle portion is much lighter. Leaping to G minor without benefit of a transitional modulation, Huss opens the "Vivace" section of this movement with a transformed version of the principal theme of the first movement (see pps. 174–175). This section is itself a ternary design, with the middle portion being quasi-developmental and emphasizing B-flat Major. A long pedal point prepares the return to C Major and the "Andante"; this pedal point, however, is underneath harmonies centered around B-flat, thus tying the two related tonal centers of G and B-flat together in an interesting fashion.

The third movement begins in a strange fashion by preparing the listener, through two piano chords, for F Major/minor but then actually commencing in G minor (see pps. 176–179). The movement is a rondo with a short introduction and coda. The A section material (rondo theme) appears first in G minor, second in E minor, and third back in G minor. The first B section is a ternary design; a second B section is a binary design on the same material. An interesting feature of both B sections is that their second subject is derived from the coda theme from the first movement. In its ternary form, the B section opens in B-flat Major, shifts to F Major, and returns to B-flat Major. In its binary form it opens in G Major and shifts to D Major. A new idea is used as closing material in the coda. A reviewer for the *Violin World* (15 October 1911?) offered this comment:

> After a rather exhaustive search, or research, into the publications of our prominent music houses, a number of concertos and sonatas have revealed themselves. In the opinion of the present writer, the finest sonata by an American is that of Henry Holden Huss, Op. 19, published by the Schirmer Press; it is a *real* sonata, big in conception and written by one who has something of import to say and knows how to say it, all fashioned with a firm and powerful hand. From the opening measures, which have in them a note of desire to attain a set goal, from the second subject, harmonized as only Mr. Huss can, to the subtle harmonies of the poetic slow movement and the elfin-like scherzo, there is always present a central idea, from which the subordinate bits emanate. The last movement is brusque, noble, majestic, and is a true finale in every sense of the word.

The *Romance* in E for violin and piano was issued simultaneously in a transcription by the composer for violoncello and piano; both works were published by Schirmer in 1907 (see pps. 182–185). The dedication to Maud Powell appears in both editions, and it is this dedication to a violinist that engenders the assumption that the violin version, rather than that for cello, is the original. Because Huss used the title "Romance" (and its equivalents in other languages) rather freely in connection with solo works for violin and piano, it is difficult to know exactly how old this work is or how many times the

Sonata for Violin and Piano, Op. 19. Schirmer, 1903. Movement II, measures 24–77.

Sonata for Violin and Piano, Op. 19. Schirmer, 1903. Movement III, measures 1–115.

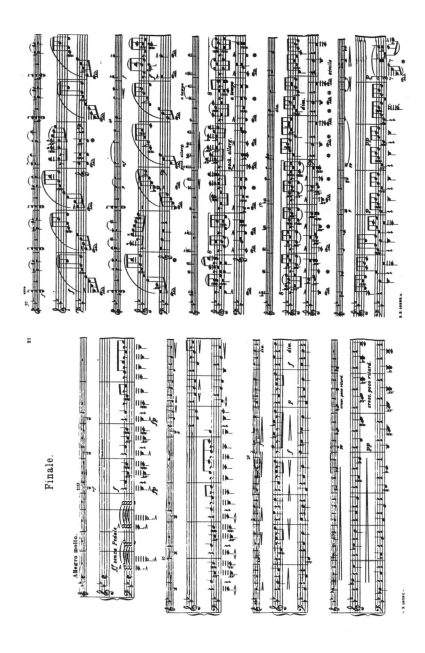

Sonata for Violin and Piano, Op. 19. Schirmer, 1903. Movement III, measures 1–115.

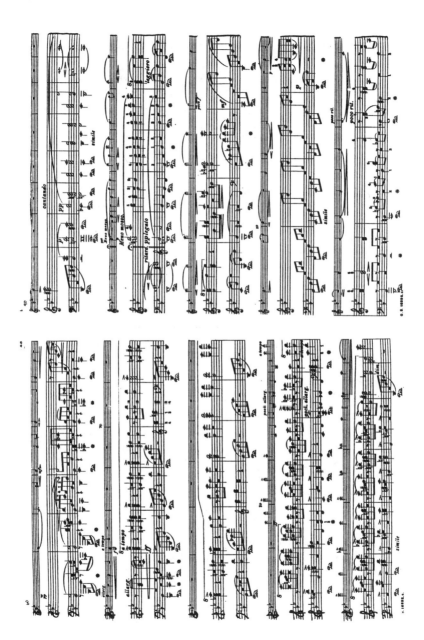

work was performed; it may even be the cello *Romanze* performed by
Huss and Frederick Bergner in a recital given in Steinway Hall, New
York City, on 10 April 1889.

It has been suggested earlier that this may have been the work
orchestrated in 1901 by Frank Van der Stucken, since he referred to
the monotonous quality of the accompaniment part and his attempts
to bring interest there. What became of that orchestration is not
known. Assuming the two works are the same, how many of Van der
Stucken's modifications became a part of the printed work is
indeterminable.

The violin and cello versions of the piece are not exactly the same.
The work is a ternary design, and on the return to the original
material, Huss marks the cello *con sordino* but not the violin. At the
end of the work, the violin part closes with a sustained E for the last
four measures whereas the cello part has the E treated with an
expressive octave drop in the middle of the four measures. Otherwise,
the cello part is the violin part played an octave lower.

The structure of the work is simple: a ternary design, as stated
earlier, that suggests an interest in harmonic exploration in the
middle section reminiscent of a sonata form. This middle section
builds sequentially to a climactic moment, following which the
soloist descends in free time by arpeggio to a pedal A. An abbreviated
statement of the original material closes the work.

In his book *Tune In, America,* Daniel Gregory Mason suggested
that two Huss works belonged in his list of

> chamber music compositions outstanding for beauty, original-
> ity, and feasibility for professional and amateur groups of
> ordinary technical skills.

These works were the *Sonata for Violin and Piano,* Op. 19, and the
String Quartet in B minor, Op. 31.

The *Quartet* had received such recognition previously, for it had
won the unanimous endorsement of the judges for a $300 prize from
the National Federation of Musical Clubs, and it was one of two
works (the other by Leo Sowerby) selected from a field of twenty-
three for publication by the Society for the Publication of American
Music. The prize carried with it a performance of the work by the
Berkshire Quartet at the NFMC meeting in 1919. The publication

selection was based on a private performance of the work by a quartet including Hugo Kortschak, a violinist in the Berkshire Quartet.

The *Quartet,* completed in 1918, was published by Schirmer in 1921 on behalf of the Society for the Publication of American Music. The published version was edited by Kortschak, and a manuscript score with his markings on it can be found in the Library of Congress. The work was dedicated to Elizabeth Sprague Coolidge.

The work was made available for purchase as a score and as a set of parts. Copies of one or both of these are widely distributed. Curiously, a copy of the work, probably just the score, is also in the British Library, put there for copyright purposes; this is the only Huss work known to be in a foreign collection.

As to the musical content of the piece, one may turn again to Arthur Shepherd in *Cobbett's Cyclopedic Survey of Chamber Music.*

> As an expression of the composer's ripe maturity, this work gives clear evidence that the hazardous methods of modernist experimentation hold no allurements for him. The harmonic weavings of Franck may have left their impression here and there, but the energy and charm of the first movement bear clear token of an artistic personality capable of filling articulate expression. The work is of excellent proportions; there is no striving after effect; no faltering in the handling of the medium. A work of direct and warm appeal, sincerity of purpose and sureness of effect.

The *Quartet in B minor* is in four movements: "Allegro ma non troppo, ed energico," "Scherzo," "Andante con molta espressione," and "Finale, Allegro vivace." The first movement opens with a series of arresting chords before presenting the first theme, a nervous, syncopated idea. The second theme, a lyric effusion, appears in the unexpected key of B-flat, though this second theme section also includes statements of the second theme in D and the first theme in B-flat (see pps. 186–187). This is followed by a third thematic section, now in F-sharp Major and preparatory to the return of the first subject in B minor. This reappearance is an abbreviated version of its original form, and it is followed by a statement of the second theme in B Major. Only at this point is the composer's use of sonata procedures made clear. Motives from the second and third themes are used during a short modulatory section leading back to the principal

Romance

Henry Holden Huss

Romance. Schirmer, 1907.

Romance. Schirmer, 1907.

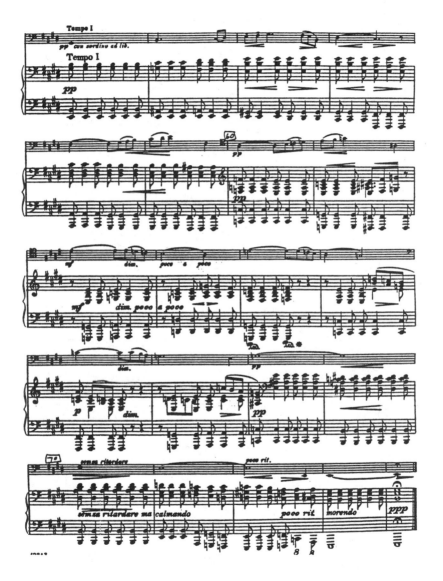

Quartet for Strings, Op. 31, in B minor. Schirmer (for the Society for the Publication of American Music), 1921. Movement I, measures 57–95.

rit. - al - - -

83 Tempo I° *(ma un poco più mosso)*

f risoluto

II

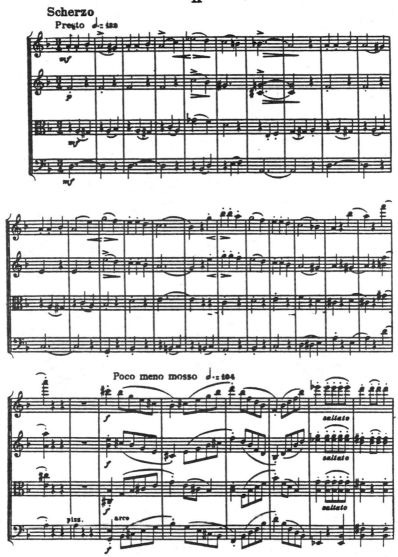

Quartet for Strings, Op. 31, in B minor. Schirmer (for the Society for the Publication of American Music), 1921. Movement II, measures 1–146.

Quartet for Strings, Op. 31, in B minor. Schirmer (for the Society for the Publication of American Music), 1921. Movement II, measures 1–146.

125 Poco meno mosso

137 Tempo I°

Quartet for Strings, Op. 31, in B minor. Schirmer (for the Society for the Publication of American Music), 1921. Movement III, measures 18–51.

IV

Quartet for Strings, Op. 31, in B minor. Schirmer (for the Society for the Publication of American Music), 1921. Movement IV, measures 1–34.

theme, again in B minor. One final quotation of the second theme, in B minor and *con sordino,* and the movement is brought to a close.

The Scherzo movement opens in D minor (see pps. 188–191). This movement is in the traditional dance-and-trio-da-capo format of minuets and scherzi from the eighteenth and nineteenth centuries, but the internal form of each of these large sections is anything but the expected. The scherzo section of the movement involves three themes heard in a rondo arrangement. The A material is very stable harmonically, while the B and C segments provide periods of harmonic instability. The Trio begins in F Major with the instruments marked *con sordino.* Its thematic segments may be labeled D E F D E F D, where the E material begins in A-flat and the F material begins in E Major. The term "begins" is used advisedly for all segments in the Trio, for each is quite short, and to get to the next key center requires fairly rapid departure from the center heard at the beginning of each theme. In this way, just as the B and C material contrasted in instability with the A material of the Scherzo, so also does the general instability of the Trio contrast with the greater stability of the Scherzo. In the da capo presentation of the Scherzo, the second A segment is omitted, and the *con sordino* color obtained in the Trio is maintained throughout the da capo, but otherwise the da capo offers only slight variations on the original material, usually in the form of changed orchestration or slight deviation in rhythm. For some curious reason, Huss retained in the da capo the three-measure rest closing the scherzo before the Trio section; this means that the movement actually ends with a three-measure rest.

A return to B minor marks the beginning of the slow movement. This short movement is in a ternary design clearly demarcated by a tempo change, to "Allegro con brio," and a key change, to D minor (see pps. 192–193). The middle section also involves thematic material of an entirely different character than that in the opening section, one important difference being Huss's use of contrapuntal textures in the slower outer sections. At the return of the opening idea, Huss marks the strings *con sordino.*

The Finale of this quartet begins in a manner similar to, though more condensed than, the manner of the opening movement: a series of arresting harmonies not apparently related to the tonality of the movement itself. The movement proper begins in B Major, but then there is a shift in mode to the home key of the quartet (see pp. 194–195). The musical materials are collected into two large "theme groups," an A group and a B group. After the initial presentation of each group, only portions of each group are then used at any given moment; the alternation of these portions provides the structure of the movement. In general the A material appears in either mode of the B tonality, while the B material appears in other keys (for example, D Major, F Major, and F-sharp minor) before a final presentation, closing the work, in B Major.

There are thematic connections among the various movements of the quartet. In the broadest sense, the thematic material appearing throughout makes considerable use of alternation between a principal note and neighbor tones at the remove of a minor second. More specifically, the principal theme of the first movement is the direct model for the first theme in the Scherzo. The second theme of the first movement is related, by the presence of the same beginning motive, to the D theme of the second movement (i.e., the opening theme of the Trio section) and to the opening and middle themes of the slow movement as well as to the opening idea of the Finale. The Trio theme is the source of the B theme in the Finale. This interconnectedness of material provides the quartet with a unity not directly dependent upon the idea of theme transformation but certainly upon a manner of treatment similar to that procedure.

CHAPTER XI

ORCHESTRAL MUSIC

Of the works for orchestra, only one is important enough to be discussed here: the Concerto in B, Op. 10, for piano and orchestra. Possible exceptions to this might be the *Rhapsody* for piano and orchestra and the *Violin Concerto,* both of which are the same kind of piece as the *Piano Concerto.* However, only the *Piano Concerto,* particularly the first movement, had a regular presence in Huss performances. Moreover, it is this piece that is most likely to be revived from among his large-scale compositions. Furthermore, the known revisions given it by the composer are of interest sui generis.

The work appeared in print twice, the orchestral part in piano reduction, both times by Schirmer and both times in a two-piano format. Schirmer brought out the first version of the original in 1898, four years after the concerto's completion. Performances after that date led to changes by the composer, and a revised version was published in 1910. Both versions carry a dedication to Adele aus der Ohe.

Schirmer also served as the rental agency for the orchestra score and parts, neither of which were ever published, but were rented in manuscript. The materials for the first version appear to be lost. The materials for the second version were returned by Schirmer to Mrs. Huss in 1956, and they are now housed in the New York Public Library.

A comparison of the two versions of the concerto in their published forms reveals few changes beyond the addition of rehearsal letters and such expression marks and other directions that a composer-pianist would offer to other interpreters in order to clarify his intentions. There is one significant exception to this characterization in the final movement. Here one finds that approximately the last half of the movement has been changed to a considerable extent. The overall length of the work is about the same. Thus a close approximation of

198

the work can be gained, insofar as the first two movements are concerned, from the earlier edition, but one must see the later edition to have Huss's clarified view of the Finale.

The Gillespies' *Bibliography of Nineteenth-Century American Piano Music* describes this concerto as an "extremely difficult, lushly romantic composition." One also may read contemporary reviews of both versions of the concerto. A review of the first version, in the *Musical Courier* of 20 June 1894, provides an excellent description of the work:

> After a questioning introduction given out by the brass over a sulky organ point, sustained by the tympani and contra bassi, the piano jumps into the arena with a bold, downward, octave sweep, and at once . . . we get the first subject, march-like and thunderingly triumphant. It is very modern in color and feeling. Mr. Huss has knelt at Bayreuth, he has also had Polish dreams. . . . [A] lovely second subject appears, and is one of the best things in the movement. It is a very difficult movement, and will tax the endurance of any virtuoso, but . . . Huss never writes for effects of virtuosity. His octave and chordal passages are Lisztian, to be sure, but then the Weimar master set the pace for us; we cannot go back to the prehistoric nakedness of the Mozart concerto.
>
> The composer has placed his cadenza near the middle of the movement. In the regular working out section we get again the new quality in Mr. Huss' work. It is positively exuberant and to a genuinely profound scholarship there is an additional freedom and mastery. . . . The coda is ingenious, but not too long spun out.
>
> [After] listening to the last movement I reached the conclusion that in two opposing whirls there must be a centre where absolute rest obtains. It is the doctrine of Kenetic stability, and the dreamy melody in E-flat [in the second movement] with its tentative gropings after that divine repose . . . is very soothing. But the swirl of the last allegro, with its heaven-storming forefront and agitated swing and brio drags us once more into the impassioned Hercules' vein of the first movement. Without any pretension at organic unity, but rather as a thought sequence, the opening theme peeps forth thunderously and then a genuine "Wilde Jagd" until the close.
>
> I could detail for you many delightful things in this concerto. For instance, what could be more charming than the second subject of the first movement, with its transition from G

Concerto in B, Op. 10. Schirmer, 1910. Movement I, pages 3–4.

> minor to D minor, and the Magyar lilt to A minor? Nothing
> new, you cry; but mark how unexpectedly it greets you! The
> complete concerto abounds in harmonic surprises, yet gives one
> the impression of a whole and not a series of detached sketches.

As a preparation for Huss's performance of the piano concerto
with the New York Philharmonic Society six days later, the *New York
Tribune* ran an article (on 16 December 1900) describing the plan of
the concerto and providing some of the important themes. Obviously
this essay applies to the 1898 edition, yet it can be instructive for
anyone desiring a summary discussion of the work. Of additional
interest is the reviewer's closing observation that this "is a concerto
for pianoforte and orchestra, not for pianoforte with orchestral
accompaniment."

The first movement, "Allegro maestoso," is a sonata-form design.
The orchestra provides a short introduction, after which the soloist
offers a short section of technical display, somewhat reminiscent in
scheme to the opening of the E-flat concerto of Beethoven (see pps.
200–201). Two different melodies make up the first theme group,
but it is the first of these (the march-like theme mentioned in the
review above) that reappears most often as the movement unfolds.
These two melodies are traded between soloist and orchestra. A
modulatory transition sets up the key of A-flat, in which key the
second theme is presented in the orchestra. A closing subject, in
D-flat but with suggestions of B-flat minor, leads to the development. Huss then removes his key signature. While the first material
presented is the martial tune in A minor, one suspects that here is not
an A minor key signature but an attempt to simplify matters for the
performers in light of the chromaticism to follow. The development
relies generally on the second theme for its material. A long cadenza
followed by the martial air and the closing subject (now in B) lead to
the recapitulation, wherein first and second themes are presented
again, all in the home key. A short cadenza and another presentation
of the march-like melody (in B) are followed by the closing subject,
here beginning in E but modulating back to the home key.

As suggested in the *Musical Courier* review, the ternary-design
middle movement, "Andante con sentimento," is quite restrained in
mood. For the most part, thematic material is presented in the
orchestra with arabesques above in the piano part. The first section is
in E-flat although Huss presents in the short orchestral introduction

one of his harmonically misleading openings, here in A-flat (see pps. 204–205). The meter alternates gently between common time and $^{12}/_8$. The middle section changes key (to B-flat), mood (to "Grazioso") and meter (to $^4/_8$). A short closing melody, related to the military air in the first movement, prepares for the varied repetition of the initial material. A brief reference to the middle section allows for another return to the opening theme and tonality, with which the movement closes.

The Finale, "Allegro vivace," is a combination of rondo and sonata elements. The rondo format can be seen in the abundance of themes alternating and contrasting with the initial theme and its key. The sonata aspect is found in the middle portion of the movement: a tonally unstable, quasi-developmental section in which the rondo theme does not appear in its native key, though the alternation of themes continues. This native key is B minor, despite the movement's orchestral introduction commencing in E-flat, but at the movement's close a shift of mode puts this theme into the home key of the concerto. A coda beginning with a modified quotation of both parts of the first theme group of the first movement, along with a last reference to the rondo theme in B, brings the work to a close (see pps. 206–209). The coda, after these quotations, consists of an extended acceleration to the end of the piece. No thematic material is present here, so the listener's attention is focused on the virtuosic display and the corollary ensemble difficulties. No doubt this is the "Wilde Jagd" idea the reviewer had in mind.

Walter Kramer's 22 July 1911 review in *Musical America* of the 1910 version provided a virtually measure-by-measure commentary. Kramer began by mentioning the paucity of American piano concertos in print. He then offered a summary of the performances of Huss's work up to that time, including word that the concerto had been approved "by the Chicago Musical College as a work for examination." After the analytic discussion, the author closed with this assessment:

> To one who has heard the concertos for the pianoforte by modern European composers, such as the works of Saint-Saëns, Busoni, Reger, Hofmann and Sauer, this American work takes a very high place with even the most minute comparison. Henry Holden Huss stands today in the front rank of American creative minds, and though this work has been before the

II.

Concerto in B, Op. 10. Schirmer, 1910. Movement II, pages 31–32.

Concerto in B, Op. 10. Schirmer, 1910. Movement III, pages 59–62.

Ritmo de quattro battute

Maestoso.

Concerto in B, Op. 10. Schirmer, 1910. Movement III, pages 59–62.

22290

public a number of years and has brought him much praise from critics everywhere, it is essential that the work be better known. Virtuosi of the present day are eager, we learn, to take up new works of merit. The American pianist is now coming before the public more than ever before, and it is his duty to bring out the works of his fellow countrymen when they show themselves deserving of performance. In this concerto Mr. Huss has written with a master hand; he has said many beautiful things marked by great individuality, gifts melodic and harmonic, and a sense of rhythmic effects deserving of the highest praise.

CHAPTER XII

MISCELLANEOUS PIECES

The miscellaneous pieces consist of a number of works not belonging to other categories. Here one finds the sketchbooks, the organ pieces, the duos for Mason and Hamlin Liszt Organ and piano, the musical greeting cards, and various other individual works. Works mentioned only in reviews and announcements are also included in this grouping because their intangible nature prevents their inclusion in any of the other categories. Future research may discover information to justify removal of some of these items to other categories.

Two subgroupings of pieces in this category, constituting the largest aggregates of pieces among the miscellaneous works, deserve particular mention. Perhaps the most interesting of the works here from a performer's point of view are the works involving organ. Here are found a number of wedding marches, for example, though there are also wedding pieces to be found among the solo piano works. These appear to have been composed at the request of his students. There are also the works for the Mason and Hamlin Liszt Organ, discussed earlier in the text.

Of especial interest among these organ works are two pieces that may be useful as service music to church musicians. They are the two works included by Dudley Buck in his 1896 *Vox Organi* collection; thus they also have a historical interest, being published alongside organ works by American composers who were Huss's contemporaries. These compositions also recall references made earlier in the text to Huss's work as an organist and to his connection with the founding of the American Guild of Organists.

As a manifestation of his personal charm, the musical greeting cards for Christmas, New Year's Day, and Easter attract some attention (see pps. 212 and 213). There are dozens of these extant from a wide span of years, both in manuscript and printed on card stock. The ones in the sketchbooks often have associated name lists

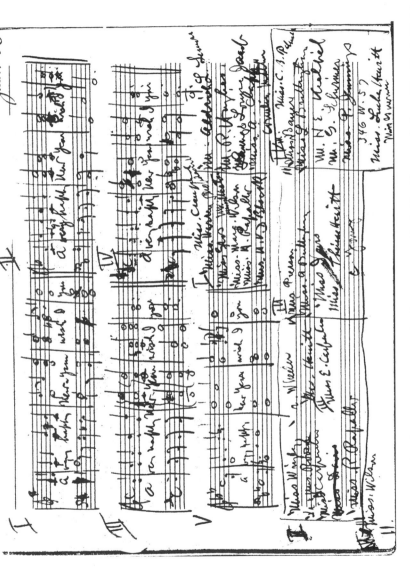

Henry Holden Huss, sketch for the New Year's Greeting for 1 January 1903. Used by permission of the Music Division, the New York Public Library for the Performing Arts, Astor, Lenox and Tilden Foundations. Each of the five greetings has a different mailing list, including such names in Huss's biography as Marion Bauer, Henry Krehbiel, Gustav Schirmer, and Pauline Jennings.

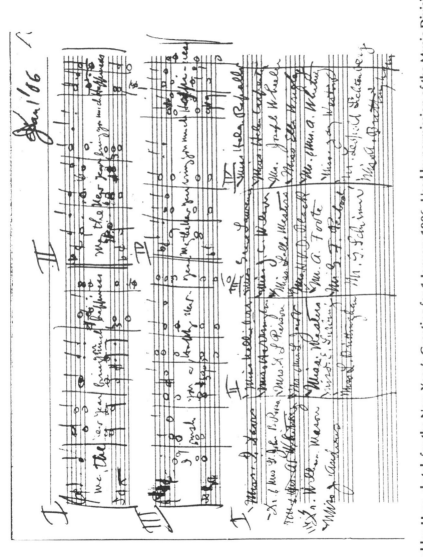

Henry Holden Huss, sketch for the New Year's Greeting for 1 January 1906. Used by permission of the Music Division, the New York Public Library for the Performing Arts, Astor, Lenox and Tilden Foundations. Each of the four greetings has its own mailing list, including such names as the Arthur Whitings, William Mason, Arthur Foote, and Gustav Schirmer.

on the same page indicating who received them, and the work list in Part III includes some of those whose names appear on the lists. The name lists obviously give some idea of the range of Huss's personal and professional friendships.

The musical settings of the greetings also constitute a microcosm of his harmonic language and his ingenuity in treating the same few texts year after year. The performing medium, if any is really intended, is dubious: solo keyboard, keyboard with solo voice, and chorus are all suggested at times. Moreover, the settings are quite short. Assuming these pieces were really meant for any kind of performance, each would last perhaps ten seconds.

One other item among the miscellaneous pieces is a definite curiosity: *Glimmering Star,* a transcription by Neal Ramsay for alto saxophone and piano, published in 1978. This transcription came to my attention only through the most serendipitous circumstances in 1989, and I wrote to Ramsay for further information. Unfortunately, it had been too long since he did this transcription, and he was unable to recall any information about it. How odd it would be if Huss's name were to live on in connection with a contest piece in a medium for which he himself never composed.

PART III

CATALOG OF MUSIC

The works are listed here in chronological order of composition (as best that may be determined) within each of several categories of works: songs, choral works, piano works, chamber music, orchestral music, and miscellaneous works. The reader is reminded that there is a discussion of each category in Part II. The works listed here are the published pieces, complete unpublished pieces, and those incomplete pieces that are known from documentation outside of the music manuscripts; the completeness of a manuscript work is not always clear, and future assessments may change this view of the contents of the manuscripts somewhat.

A system of markings is provided to assist performers in finding suitable literature in this catalog:

*   *   pieces with a significant history of performance
*   p   pieces especially recommended to performers with an advanced level of skill
*   s   pieces especially recommended for students or those of more modest skills

Program references are to performances known through announcements, reviews, and printed programs found in periodicals and in collections of Huss materials in the Library of Congress and the University of Illinois. The largest single source of such programs is the Huss Program File in the Music Division of the New York Public Library.

Manuscripts of the pieces may be found in various collections as can information about some pieces. When referring to these collections, I have created a system of abbreviations, based on the sigla used in the *Répertoire International des Sources Musicales:*

U-HF	The University of Illinois's Huss file
NYp-HC	Huss Collection of papers and documents in the Music Division, the New York Public Library
NYp-HCF	Huss Clipping File in the Music Division, the New York Public Library
NYp-HMC	Huss Manuscript Collection in the Music Division, the New York Public Library
Wc	Music Division, Library of Congress

For published works some additional information is provided. Approximate performance times are given. Publishers are noted by means of the following abbreviations, and these abbreviations are followed by the copyright date. Works are assumed to have been copyrighted by the publisher except where noted.

AP	Art Publication Society
CF	Carl Fischer, Inc.
CP	The Composer's Press, Inc.
DI	Oliver Ditson, Inc.
DS	Dirk van der Stucken
GR	H. W. Gray, Inc.
GS	G. Schirmer, Inc.
MI	Millet, Inc.
NP	No publisher given
NV	Novello, Inc.
NY	New York Tribune Association
SB	Silver, Burdett, Inc.
SH	Shawnee Press, Inc.
SM	Schmidt, Inc.
ST	Ed. Schuberth and Co.
SU	Summy-Birchard, Inc.
TP	Theodore Presser, Inc.

Creating a catalog of works by Huss is subject to a number of problems. He was quite cavalier about titles, opus numbering, completion dates, foreign orthography, and many other details. (Chapter VI has a detailed discussion of this issue.) Consequently, some titles in the catalog are doubtful: they may be secondary titles for another work, they may be new titles for re-workings of another piece, they may represent pieces actually composed by someone else, or they may be titles for works planned but never composed. Some of these options are suggested in this list. This list represents the best understanding of his works and their relationships to date.

To assist the reader in using this catalog, a summary of the categories and the work numbers comprising them is provided here.

Songs

All the songs are assumed to be for solo voice accompanied by piano except as noted; when the piano part is an orchestra reduction, this is so noted. Text sources not identified are unknown.

1. *We'll Anchor in the Harbor;* written by Huss at age five (ca. 1867); manuscript in Rebekah Crawford Collection in Wc

2. *Ode to the Minstrel;* text by Mary Huss; holograph score (dated 20 March 1877) in NYp-HMC

3. *The Song of Mister Phonograph;* GS/1878; timing 2:45; probably composed by Huss (under pseudonym of H. H. H. von Ograph)

4. *Das erste Lied;* written by 24 March 1885 program; apparently lost

5. *Der Trost;* written by 24 March 1885 program; apparently lost

6. *My Songs Are All of Thee;* text by R. W. Gilder (from "The New Day"); holograph score (dated 22 July 1886 and bearing the dedication "especially composed for my dear brother Martin") and part (dated July 1886) in NYp-HMC

7. *Über allen Gipfeln ist Ruh;* subtitled "Abendlied"; written by 10 April 1889 program; text by Goethe; apparently lost

     8. *Mondnacht;* written by 10 April 1889 program; text by
       J. Eichendorff; apparently lost

     9. *There Is Sweet Music Here;* written by 10 April 1889
       program; text by Tennyson; apparently lost

*p 10. *The Ballade of the Song of the Syrens;* SM/1891; timing 2:20;
       written by 1889; text by C. J. Lee; dedicated to Mrs.
       Theodore Toedt; cf. Nos. 141 and 375

*p 11. *Songs from the German;* SM/1891; timing of set 3:00; all
       written by 10 April 1889 program

         #1   "Der Jasminenstrauch"; timing 1:00; text trans-
             lated by "Mrs. C"; dedicated to Alice Durfee

         #2   "Du bist wie eine Blume"; timing 1:00; text by
             Heine and translated by "Mrs. C"; dedicated to Mrs.
             Charles Tyler Dutton; two holograph scores (one
             dated July 1947; the other with dedication to his
             wife; both with German text only) in NYp-HMC;
             fragment of untitled piano work with reference to
             this text as holograph score (dated 4 July 1947) in
             NYp-HMC

         #3   "Der Lenz"; timing 1:00; text translated by "Mrs.
             C"; dedicated to "My Dear Sister Mary"

*p 12. *Home They Brought Her Warrior Dead;* GS/1902; timing
       2:45; written by 10 April 1889 program; text by Ten-
       nyson; German translation by Mrs. Josef Rheinberger;
       dedicated to "My Sister Mary"; three holograph scores
       and two copyist's scores (one signed by Huss and in-
       scribed to David Bispham) in NYp-HMC (one score has
       German text different from that in published song); two
       holograph scores and set of parts of arrangement for alto
       and orchestra in NYp-HMC; cf. No. 206

    13. *On the Wild Rose Tree;* text by R. W. Gilder; two
       holograph scores (one in D Major, and one dated 1889
       and in E-flat Major) in NYp-HMC; with these scores is a
       reference to D Major as the key for a soprano and C Major
       for an alto

 s 14. *The King and the Pope;* ST/1889; timing 3:30; text by C. H.
       Webb

 p 15. *They That Sow in Tears;* SM/1891; timing 2:30; text from
       Psalm 126; dedicated to Mrs. Walter Cutting

*p 16. *All the World's a Stage, Op. 16 for Basso-Baritone and*

Orchestra (or Piano); DS/1928; timing 7:00; written by early April 1898 program; text by Shakespeare; dedicated to David Bispham "who sang this composition over 400 times in America and England"; also known as "The Seven Ages of Man"; one holograph and four manuscript scores in NYp-HMC (with accompaniment arranged for piano with orchestral score); cf. No. 378

p 17. *Haidenröslein;* GS/1898; timing 1:00; text by Goethe; "The Melody arranged from a recently discovered fragmentary Manuscript [of Beethoven] and the Accompaniment composed by Henry Holden Huss"

18. *Well He Slumbers;* mentioned in letter from D. G. Mason of 27 August 1899 to Huss in NYp-HC; apparently lost

19. *Carol for Christmas;* text by N. Tate; dedicated "To my dearest father and mother"; holograph score (dated December 1901) in NYp-HMC

*p 20. *My Jean;* GS/1904; timing 1:30; text by R. Burns; dedicated to Mrs. William Bunker; holograph score (with title "Of a' the Airts the Wind Can Blow") and sketches (dated 19 December 1901) in NYp-HMC

21. *Give the Kiss I Gave to Thee;* written by 25 June 1902 program; text from unidentified Spanish source and translated by J. E. T. Dowe; dedicated to Miss Louise Hamilton; two holograph scores in NYp-HMC

22. *Plymouth Hymnal 165;* text by N. Tate; dedicated "To my dearest father and mother"; holograph score (dated December 1902) in NYp-HMC; different from Nos. 98, 120, 153, and 175

23. *Traüme;* mentioned in Huss letter of 5 February 1904 to unspecified person in NYp-HC but may not have been written by Huss; if by Huss, apparently lost

24. *Je ne veux pas avoir peur;* mentioned in Huss letter of 5 February 1904 to unspecified person in NYp-HC but may not have been written by Huss; if by Huss, apparently lost

25. *In Verdure Clad;* mentioned in Huss letter of 5 February 1904 to unspecified person in NYp-HC but may not have been written by Huss; if by Huss, apparently lost

26. *My Mother Bids Me Bind My Hair;* mentioned in Huss letter of 5 February 1904 to unspecified person in

NYp-HC but may not have been written by Huss; if by Huss, apparently lost

*p 27. *My World;* DI/1904; timing 1:00; text by K. Trask; manuscript score in NYp-HMC

*p 28. *Four Songs, Op. 22;* GS/1907; set dedicated to "My Wife"

    #1 "Wiegenlied" ("Cradle-Song"); timing 1:30; text by Hejduk; translated by Philip Mosenthal; dedication is "For my Liebheart [*sic*] Hildegard"; holograph score (dated 24 December 1904 with text in German only, but an incomplete score has English text only) in NYp-HMC

    #2 "It Was a Lover and His Lass"; timing 1:30; text by Shakespeare; two holograph scores in NYp-HMC; cf. Nos. 350 and 366

    #3 "Before Sunrise"; timing 2:30; text by R. W. Gilder; dedicated "To my darling Hildegard; holograph score (dated December 1905) in NYp-HMC; cf. No. 350

    #4 "Ich liebe Dich"; timing 1:30; text by Rückert

  29. *The Fool's Prayer;* text by E. R. Sill; two holograph scores (one dated 1905) and solo vocal part (no piano) in NYp-HMC; arrangement of choral work version for solo and piano, with dedication to David Bispham; cf. No. 156

p 30. *The Night Dance;* text by T. Moore; holograph score (dated 20 July 1908) and dedicated to his wife; cf. No. 166

  31. *Phyllis;* written by 11 September 1908 program; apparently lost

  32. *Once Only;* text by R. W. Gilder; three holograph scores (one incomplete and dedicated "To Mr. George Fergusson"; another dated 16 December 1908 and dedicated "To my Hildegard"; another dated Xmas 1908) in NYp-HMC

*p 33. *Ev'ry Day Hath Its Night;* text by Tennyson; four holograph scores (versions labeled for high voice [dated 21 December 1909], for mezzo [dated 1 September 1937], for alto, and "too high") and two incomplete holograph scores in NYp-HMC; four of these scores are in D Major, one in E Major, and one in E-flat Major; one score has dedication "To Miss Christine Miller"

34. *The Year's at the Spring;* written by 9 May 1910 program; may be alternative title for another work; apparently lost

*p 35. *While Larks with Little Wing;* GS/1910; timing 2:00; text by R. Burns; dedicated to Marcella Sembrich

*p 36. *The Birds Were Singing ("A Song of Despair");* text by R. W. Gilder; two holograph scores (one dated December 1910 and dedicated to his wife; other score's cover has NYp note that this is from the Eva Gauthier Collection and has her autograph above title) in NYp-HMC; cf. Nos. 350 and 352

s 37. *The Moon;* SB/1915; timing 1:00; text by G. MacDonald; score in possession of publisher marked "Paid $12.50 6/17/13"; published in *Progressive Music Series,* Book 4

s 38. *Baptizing Hymn;* GS/1914; timing 0:45; published in Krehbiel's *Afro-American Folksongs: A Study in Racial and National Music;* harmonized by Huss from folk-tune provided by Krehbiel in 23 February 1897 letter to Huss

s 39. *Weeping Mary;* GS/1914; timing 1:00; song published in Krehbiel's *Afro-American Folksongs: A Study in Racial and National Music;* harmonized by Huss from folk-tune provided by Krehbiel in 23 February 1897 letter to Huss

*p 40. *Suppose;* GS/1916; timing 1:40; text by E. Field; dedicated to "Mme. Buckhout"; holograph score (dated 25 December 1910) in NYp-HMC

p 41. *My Luv' Is Like a Red, Red Rose;* text by R. Burns; dedicated to his wife; holograph score (dated 18 July 1911) in NYp-HMC; cf. No. 160

*p 42. *Two Songs with Piano Accompaniment, Op. 28;* GS/1917
   #1 "After Sorrow's Night"; timing 2:00; text by R. W. Gilder; may have been intended to be dedicated to Oscar Seagle; four holograph scores (one dated 22 December 1911) in NYp-HMC; unfinished manuscript score of arrangement for low voice in NYp-HMC; cf. Nos. 347 and 350
   #2 "Music, When Sweet Voices Die"; timing 1:30; text by Shelley; dedicated to Alma Gluck; two holograph scores (one dated "July 18, 1915 Lake George") in NYp-HMC; cf. Nos. 163, 349, and 386

43. *A Song to the Lute in Musicke;* text by R. Edwardes ("Master of the Children of the Royal Chapel in Queen Elizabeth's

Reign"); two holograph scores (one dated 18 December 1912, and the other dated December 1912) in NYp-HMC

44. *Carpe Diem;* also titled "Carpe Diem/O Mistress Mine"; text by Shakespeare; dedicated "To my darling Hildegard on her birthday"; two holograph scores (one, incomplete, dated 17 July 1913 and the other dated "for" 20 July 1913) in NYp-HMC

*p 45. *A Summer Night;* GS/1914; timing 2:30; text by M. Schaffy; translated by Huss; dedicated to Louise Homer; holograph score (dated 22–24 December 1913 with English text below German; entitled "Sommernacht/Lied für Sopran"; "begun in subway") in NYp-HMC

46. *Journey's End in Lovers' Meeting;* written in summer 1913 (known from the *Musical Leader* of 26 March 1914); apparently lost

*p 47. *The Happy Heart;* text by T. Dekker; dedicated to his wife; holograph score (dated Xmas 1914) in NYp-HMC

48. *Dead Mountain Flowers;* text by Tennyson; dedicated "To Miss Marjorie Meyer"; two holograph scores and sketches (one dated 18 December 1914) in NYp-HMC

*p 49. *When I Was wi' My Dearie;* dedicated to his wife; three holograph scores (one dated 11 December 1915; one for low [in E minor] and one for medium [in A minor] voice, the other in B minor) in NYp-HMC; "Absence" appears as subtitle and as only title on these scores

*p 50. *The Very Speech Love Learnt in Paradise;* text by J. Thompson; dedicated "To my own Hildegard"; holograph score (dated December 1916) and parts for violin (obbligato for this song; no mention of this on pianovocal score) and soprano (no piano or violin notes given) and miscellaneous sketches in NYp-HMC; often performed without the violin part; cf. No. 351

51. *Tsain Dour Ov Zo Vag;* Armenian patriotic song harmonized by Huss; holograph score (dated May 1916) in NYp-HMC

52. *Cherry Ripe;* text by T. Campion; dedicated to his wife; holograph score (dated July 1916) and sketches in NYp-HMC

53. *Three Armenian National Songs;* written by 1918; "Harmo-

nized and the Accompaniment composed by Henry Holden Huss"; holograph score, part, and sketches (references to "p. 53," "p. 57," and "p. 71") in NYp-HMC

#1   "Vanetzi More Yerke" ("The Song of the Mother")

#2   "Menk Angeglozt Zinror Yenk" ("We Are Sincere Soldiers")

#3   "Harachank" ("A Lament")

54. *Go Lovely Rose;* text by E. Waller; dedicated to his wife; holograph score (dated July 1919) in NYp-HMC

*p 55. *The Smile of Her I Love;* text by R. W. Gilder; dedicated to his wife; three holograph scores (two dated Christmas 1919; two in A Major and one in G minor) in NYp-HMC

*p 56. *Pack, Clouds Away;* written by 14 March 1920 program; text by T. Heywood; dedicated to his wife; six holograph scores and one copyist's score (in various keys) in NYp-HMC; cf. No. 360

57. *A Shepherdess;* text by A. C. T. Meynell; dedicated to his wife; holograph score (dated July 1920) in NYp-HMC

58. *Shepherd with Thy Tenderest Care;* dedicated to his wife; two holograph scores (one dated December 1920) in NYp-HMC; one score has title "Shepherd with Thy Tenderest Love"

59. *From "The Sound of the Heart's Desire";* text by Yeats; holograph score (dated "February 15 1921") in NYp-HMC

60. *Still, Still with Thee;* text by H. B. Stowe; dedicated to his wife; three holograph scores (one dated 1921; one incomplete) in NYp-HMC; one score has "For the Etude Prize Contest"

61. *Blest Are the Pure in Heart;* text by J. Keble; dedicated to his wife; two holograph scores (one dated 18 July 1921 and one dated 20 July 1921) and one other score in NYp-HMC

*p 62. *The Daffodils;* text by Wordsworth; dedicated to his wife; two holograph scores in NYp-HMC (one dated July 1922)

63. *Softly Fades the Twilight Ray;* text by S. F. Smith; dedicated to his wife; two holograph scores (one dated December 1922) in NYp-HMC; first page of one score has "Evening Hymn" as title and "Softly Fades the Twilight Ray" as a subtitle

64. *Summum Bonum;* text by R. Browning; dedicated to his wife; holograph score (dated 1923) in NYp-HMC

*p   65. *A Book of Verses;* text by O. Khayyam; dedicated to his wife; four holograph scores (two dated 19 December 1923; other two have 1923 only) in NYp-HMC

66. *Home;* text by N. B. Turner; holograph score (dated 18 July 1924) in NYp-HMC

67. *0 Lamb of God;* text by J. G. Deck [?]; dedicated to his wife; two holograph scores (one dated Christmas 1924; the other dated December 1924 and with title "O Lamb of God Still Keep Me") and a third score (dated 1924 and specifying organ as accompaniment on title page) in NYp-HMC

68. *Jesus, Thou Source of Calm Repose;* text by C. Wesley; dedicated to his wife; holograph score (dated December 1925) in NYp-HMC

69. *In Love, If Love Be Love,* mezzo voice, viola obbligato, and piano (often performed without viola); subtitled "Vivian's Song for Mezzo Voice with viola obbligato and accompaniment of pianoforte"; text by Tennyson; dedicated to Miss Ethel Grow; holograph score in NYp-HMC (dated 1926 twice in the score); cf. No. 359

*p   70. *Pan;* text by S. Alexander; dedicated to his wife; two holograph scores (one dated both 14 July 1926 and 20 July 1926) in NYp-HMC; cf. No. 361

71. *The Moon Like a Pale Bird;* text by J. S. Wise; four holograph scores (one dated 1926 and one dated 13 December 1926 and with a different ending from the other scores) and one copyist's score (versions for medium and high voice) in NYp-HMC; three scores have "The Moon Like a Bird" as a title

72. *America the Beautiful;* text by K. L. Bates; holograph score (dated 29 January 1927) in NYp-HMC

*p   73. *The Spring of Love;* text by S. Brooke; six holograph scores (one dated 19 July 1927; for various voice ranges) in NYp-HMC; some scores carry dedication to his wife

*p   74. *I Dare Not Ask a Kiss;* text by R. Herrick; three holograph scores (one dated December 1927, and one dated 15 December 1927; one for medium voice and the other for high voice) in NYp-HMC; one carries descriptor "Canzonet for Medium Voice"; two scores have "Elektra" or "Electra" as subtitle, but the word is crossed out each time; two scores carry dedication to his wife; cf. No. 169

75. *Daphne ("Midas 1593");* text by J. Lyly; dedicated to his wife; holograph score (dated 18 July 1928) with second score and sketches in NYp-HMC

76. *Sunrise Song for Dobb's {?} Play;* holograph score (dated 6 February 1929) in NYp-HMC

77. *Chinese Lullaby;* holograph score (dated 6 February 1929) and part and additional piano part in lower key in NYp-HMC

*p 78. *Irish Faery Song;* text by Yeats; this title appears on a 25 May [1929?] program, but work definitely existed by 22 March 1935 program; holograph score in NYp-HMC; for "voice and piano or harp"; not the same as No. 96

79. *The Leaves Are Dark;* text by R. W. Gilder; dedicated to his wife; holograph score (dated 14 June 1929) in NYp-HMC

80. *Into a Ship Dreaming;* text by de la Mare; dedicated to his wife; two holograph scores (one dated July 1929, the other incomplete) in NYp-HMC

81. *The Sunday Pirate;* text by W. Holbrook; three holograph scores (one dated 15 December 1929 and titled "Siesta"; another has "Siesta" on it but that is crossed out) in NYp-HMC; one score has dedication to his wife

82. *For unto You Is Born This Day;* text from Luke 2; dedicated to his wife; holograph score (dated 23 December 1929) in NYp-HMC

83. *Fear Not, Fear Not;* text from Luke 2; dedicated to his wife; score (dated Xmas 1929) in NYp-HMC

84. *{The Sun and Moon and Stars Are Mine};* dedicated to his wife; holograph score (dated July 1930) in NYp-HMC

s 85. *The Lion Who Sleeps with His Mouth Open;* text by H. E. Slezinger; written by 17 January 1931 program; holograph score (dated 2 December 1930) and sketches in NYp-HMC

86. *I Will Bless the Lord at All Times;* text from Psalm 34; dedicated to his wife; two holograph scores (one dated

December 1930, one dated 12 December 1930, and one dated Xmas 1930) in NYp-HMC; one score has organ manual indications

87. *Sandman;* music is "Lake Como by Moonlight" (cf. No. 246); written by 17 January 1931 program; apparently lost

88. *Yet, Ah, That Spring Should Vanish with the Rose;* text by O. Khayyam; translated by E. Fitzgerald; holograph score (dated July 1931) in NYp-HMC

89. *Auld Lang Syne;* traditional text and tune; dedicated to Marion Sexton; holograph score (dated 15 December 1931) in NYp-HMC

90. *Advice to Lovers;* more often known as "If You Would Love and Loved Be"; text by J. Dunbar; dedicated to his wife; holograph score (dated Christmas 1931) in NYp-HMC

91. *Sonnet XCVIII;* text by Shakespeare; dedicated to his wife; two holograph scores (one dated July 1932, and the other dated 19 July 1932) in NYp-HMC

92. *If Music Be the Food of Love, Play On;* text by Shakespeare; dedicated to his wife; holograph score (dated Xmas 1932) in NYp-HMC

93. *Christmas Song;* text by M. E. Sexton; holograph score (dated 1933) in NYp-HMC

94. *Light in Dark;* text by J. P. Peabody; dedicated to his wife; holograph score (dated July 1933) in NYp-HMC

95. *As the Hart Panteth After the Water Brooks;* text from Psalms 42 and 43; dedicated to his wife; holograph score (dated 15 June 1934) in NYp-HMC

*p   96. *Shed No Tear ("Faery Song");* CP/1949; timing 2:45; text by Keats; dedicated to his wife; five holograph scores (one dated July 1934; one titled "Faery Song Rhapsody" dated 12 July 1936) in NYp-HMC (in various voice ranges); most of the holographs have "Faery Song" as the sole title; subtitled "Rhapsody for Voice and Piano" in one holograph; one score composed "By Peace Will Come"; "This Song Won First Place in the 1948 Contest sponsored by the Composers Press, Inc."; not the same as No. 78

*p   97. *A Little Serenade;* GS/1944; timing 2:30; text by R. Bloomfield; dedicated to Dr. and Mrs. Maximilian Bloomfield; various titles on manuscripts are "Eine

Kleine Nacht Musik," "Eine Kleine Nachtmusik," "Eine Kleine Nachtmusik/Serenade," "Eine Kleine Nacht Musik/Lullaby-Serenade," and "Eine Kleine Nachtmusik/Lullaby-Serenade"; nine holograph scores and one copyist's score (one dated December 1934, and one untitled ["Sleep you sweet, then sleep you now"] but dated 14 December 1934; four different keys represented) in NYp-HMC

98. *Xmas Carol;* text by N. Tate; dedicated to "my dear pupil Katherine and her dear children"; score (dated December 1934) in NYp-HMC; different from Nos. 22, 120, 153, and 175

99. [*Bless the Lord, O My Soul*]; text from Psalm 103; dedicated to his wife; holograph score (dated Xmas 1934) in NYp-HMC; different from Nos. 115 and 119

100. *Help Us to Help Each Other Lord;* text by C. Wesley; holograph score (dated July 1935) in NYp-HMC

101. *I Will Sing of the Mercies of the Lord;* text from Psalm 89; dedicated to his wife; two holograph scores (one untitled but dated 3 July 1935) in NYp-HMC

102. *Song in Rococo Style;* text by N. Grimald; dedicated to his wife; two holograph scores (both dated December 1935) and sketches in NYp-HMC; one score also has title "A True Love"

103. *I Will Love Thee, O Lord;* text from Psalm 18; dedicated to his wife; two holograph scores (dated July 1936) in NYp-HMC

p 104. *When You Love Her, Adore Her;* also known as "If You Love Her, Adore Her"; dedicated to his wife; three holograph scores (both dated Xmas 1936; one with additional material and dated 1940) in NYp-HMC; in various keys

105. *Interval;* text by F. Thayer II; dedicated to his wife; two holograph scores (one dated July 1938) in NYp-HMC

106. *With Pipe and Flute;* text by A. Dobson; dedicated to his wife; holograph score (dated Christmas 1938) in NYp-HMC

107. *I Look to Thee;* text by Longfellow; dedicated to his wife; holograph score (dated 1939) in NYp-HMC

108. *Jerusalem the Golden;* text by Bernard of Cluny; dedicated to his wife; holograph score (dated July 1939) in NYp-HMC

109. *Interlude;* written by 20 September 1939 program; may be a new title for another song; if not an alternative title, apparently lost

110. *The Magic of Thy Beauty;* text by Byron; dedicated to his wife; two holograph scores (dated December 1940 and dated 1941) in NYp-HMC; one score has "There Be None of Beauty's Daughters" as a title

111. *A Christmas Thought;* "To Marion"; score (dated 18 December 1940) in NYp-HMC; with 1941 score of "The Magic of Thy Beauty"

112. *The Magnificat;* text from Luke 1; dedicated to his wife; holograph score (dated July 1940) in NYp-HMC

113. *I Will Extol Thee;* text from Psalm 31; dedicated to his wife; holograph score (dated July 1940) in NYp-HMC

114. *The Right Will Win;* text probably by Huss; holograph score (dated March 1941) and sketches (one dated April 1941) in NYp-HMC; "A Pledge from the U.S. to the British Empire"; one sketch has title "The Right Will Win—Uncle Sam to John Bull" and next to first music system with text "Sent *without* text only as a piano piece"; text is very dark—may have been put in lightly as a guide during composition of piano work, then darkened to make a solo song; another sketch titled "Aid to Britain"; "To Marion"; cf. No. 178

115. *Bless the Lord, O My Soul;* text from Psalm 103; dedicated to his wife; holograph score (dated July 1941) in NYp-HMC; different from Nos. 99 and 119

116. *Carol for Katherine Clark Morris;* setting of "God Rest Ye, Merry Gentlemen"; score (dated December 1941) in NYp-HMC

117. *Jesus, Thy Boundless Love;* dedicated to his wife; holograph score (dated 8 December 1941) and one other score (dated Xmas 1941) in NYp-HMC

118. *Solfèges;* textless pieces for voice and keyboard; all dedicated to, and apparently composed as Christmas, birthday, or wedding anniversary gifts for his wife, except for that dated January 1950, which is dedicated "To my dear friend Carl Dies with affectionate good wishes"; holograph scores (dated July 1942 [second copy of this later in collection and dated "circa 1947"], December 1942, 13

December 1942, July 1943, Xmas 1943 [with subtitle "Une Pace D'Amour" (*sic*)], June 1944, July 1944, December 1944, 1 December 1944 [untitled but the same genre in all other respects], 16 June 1945 [untitled but the same genre in all other respects], [17 June 1945], 20 July 1945/8 July 1945, December 1945, April 1946, June 1946, December 1946 [with descriptor "Barcarolle"], December 1947, June 1948, July 1948 [subtitled "Menuetto Classique"], 20 July 1949 [titled "Birthday Prelude" rather than "Solfège" but the same genre in all other respects], July 1949, [January 1950], June 1950 [titled "Solfège Prelude"], July 1950 [titled "Solfège Intermezzo"], December 1950, June 1951, July 1951 [titled "Sunshine of Happiness"], December 1952 [subtitled "Cradle Song for the Christ Child"], 15 June 1953 [incomplete?]) in NYp-HMC

119. *Bless the Lord, O My Soul;* text from Psalm 103; dedicated to his wife; holograph score (dated December 1948) in NYp-HMC; different from Nos. 99 and 115

120. *Hymn for Christmas;* text by N. Tate; dedicated to his wife; holograph score (dated 20 December 1951) in NYp-HMC; different from Nos. 22, 98, 153, and 175

121. *Dobbs 1952;* text from Ecclesiastes 9; holograph score in NYp-HMC

122. *A Child's Bedtime Prayer;* "Dedicated to the Little Wonder"; three holograph scores (one dated 1952, and one dated 31 January 1952) in NYp-HMC

123. *Christ Is Risen;* dedicated to his wife; holograph score (dated April 1953) in NYp-HMC; not the same as No. 142

UNDATABLE SONGS
(IN ALPHABETICAL ORDER)

124. *Chanson;* text by A. de Musset; dedicated to Lillian Blauvelt; holograph score in NYp-HMC; title page in French

125. *A Match;* text by C. A. Swinburne; dedicated to his wife; holograph score in NYp-HMC

126. *Morning Hymn;* text by C. Wesley; "To my dear Babetta";
     holograph score in NYp-HMC

s   127. *Summer's Rain and Winter's Snow;* text by R. W. Gilder;
     "Especially composed for Mr. Tomlin's Children's Cho-
     rus"; two holograph scores in NYp-HMC; both scores are
     for soprano and piano; second score carries dedication to
     Miss Denise [?] D. Anderson; cf. No. 192

s   128. *There's A River Goes Laughing All Day;* text by E. J. Cooley;
     "Especially composed for Mr. Tomlin's Children's Chorus";
     holograph score in NYp-HMC; cf. No. 193

Choral Music

Voicing assumes *a cappella* SATB chorus unless otherwise indicated following each of these titles. Text sources not identified are
unknown.

129. *Anthem;* text from Psalms 25 and 34; holograph score
     (dated 22 Feb 1879 at the beginning and April 2, 1879 at
     the end) in NYp-HMC

130. [*We sing the praise of Him who died*]; based on text of
     "Hymn 618" by T. Kelly; holograph score (dated 15
     April 1879) in NYp-HMC

131. *Motett;* text from Psalm 30; holograph score (dated 21
     November 1881) in NYp-HMC; not same as Nos. 137 or
     138

132. *I Love the Lord;* text from Psalms 116 and 106; holograph
     score (dated 10 January 1882) in NYp-HMC

133. *A Four-Voiced Double Fugue;* text from Psalm 9; holograph
     sketches (dated 27 January 1882) in NYp-HMC

134. *The Ship of State,* male chorus and piano or organ ad lib.;
     text by H. W. Longfellow; holograph score (dated Febru-
     ary 1887) and sketches in NYp-HMC; cf. No. 167

*p   135. *Ave Maria, Op. 4,* soprano and alto solos, female chorus,
     harp, organ, violin, cello, and string orchestra; NP/1888
     by Huss; timing 6:00; dedicated to the Rubinstein Club
     and William R. Chapman; cf. No. 140

p   136. *The Fountain,* female chorus; ST/1889 by Huss; text by
     J. R. Lowell

*p   137. *Holy! Holy! Holy!,* soprano solo, chorus, and orchestra;

also known as "Motette"; NP/1889 (June) by Huss; first version of No. 138; not same as No. 131; possibly the same as Nos. 139 or 143

*p   138. *Festival Sanctus,* soprano solo, chorus, and orchestra or organ; ST/1889 (October) by Huss; timing 8:30; dedicated to the Metropolitan Musical Society of New York and William R. Chapman, Director; published copy labeled "New Revised Edition"; opus 7 (worklist in Huss's hand in NYp-HC) or opus 9 (worklist in Huss's hand in NYp-HC); two holograph scores (one dated June 1889 whose title page has "sung in St. Bartholomew's under Richard Henry Warren?"), sketches (one titled "Motette"), and set of parts [some also with "Benedictus" as part of main title] in NYp-HMC; not the same as No. 131; revision of No. 137; may be the same as Nos. 139 or 143

   139. *Easter Theme,* chorus, organ, and orchestra; ST [no copy appears extant; the work and its publication known from autobiography in Huss's hand in NYp-HC]; possibly the same as another choral work but under a different title (possibly Nos. 137, 138, 142, or 143)

*p   140. *Ave Maria, Op. 4,* soprano and alto solos, female chorus, and orchestra; NV/1890; timing 5:15; dedicated to the Rubinstein Club and William R. Chapman; holograph orchestra score (copied by Otto Löbner) and parts, piano/vocal score, and sketches in NYp-HMC; both "Ave Maria" and "Save Me, O God" texts can be found in various of these items; cf. No. 135

   141. *The Ballade of the Song of the Syrens,* male chorus and orchestra; written by 29 January 1891 program; arrangement by Huss of his own song (cf. Nos. 10 and 375)

   142. *Christ Is Risen,* chorus, orchestra, and organ; written by 1893; dedicated to his wife; composed under pseudonym "Enharmonic"; four holograph scores (keyboard-vocal and full scores) and two sets of parts in NYp-HMC; one title page has "Easter Anthem"; one score has title "Easter Anthem 'Christ Is Risen' for chorus, orchestra and organ"; two scores refer to Ed. Schuberth & Co., in one case as publisher; may be the same as Nos. 139 or 143; not the same as No. 123

143. *Festival Anthem for Easter,* chorus and organ or orchestra; known from *Half Hours with the Best Composers* (1894); mentioned in promotional item in NYp-HCF; may be the same as Nos. 137, 138, 139 or 142; if a separate work, it is apparently lost

144. *The Song of the Winds,* soprano and alto solos, chorus, and orchestra; also known as "The Winds"; known from *Half Hours With the Best Composers* (1894); composed under pseudonym "Tempo Rubato"; holograph score in NYp-HMC

145. *"Song" from Milton's Masque of "Comus,"* vocal octet; also titled "Sabrina Fair"; text by Milton; holograph score (dated July 1899) in NYp-HMC

*p 146. *Adeste Fideles, Op. 14;* GS/1900; traditional text and tune; incomplete holograph score (dated 4 November 1899) in NYp-HMC; same opus number as No. 367

*p 147. *Pater Noster, Op. 15,* vocal sextet; GS/1900; timing 5:00; dedicated to Huss's father; holograph score (dated 25 August 1898 and with both Latin and English texts) in NYp-HMC; two holograph scores (one dated 29 January 1907, but last page has "full score was finished in 1907 but the number was composed and performed before? 1904—?") and parts of same work arranged for chorus and orchestra in NYp-HMC

*p 148. *Crossing the Bar,* chorus and keyboard; SU/1901; timing 2:15; text by Tennyson; published separately and in *Laurel Song Book;* recorded in arrangement by Richard Condie ("The Mormon Tabernacle Choir at the World's Fair," Columbia ML 6019/MS 6619 [1964])

s 149. *The Recessional,* chorus and orchestra, with organ ad lib.; SU/1901; timing 3:30; text by Kipling; published, as one of the *Laurel Octavo* series and in *Laurel Song Book,* for mixed chorus and keyboard; two holograph scores and parts in NYp-HMC (one score has note that orchestration was begun on 8 December 1903)

150. *The Flag,* male chorus; GS/1903; text by H. C. Potter; timing 2:45; dedicated to the Mendelssohn Glee Club and Arthur Mees; holograph score (with "A.D. 1887" on title page but "Copyright 1903 by G. Schirmer" on manuscript paper used for first page) and holograph

sketch (dated 11 September 1902 above pseudonym "poco meno mosso") in NYp-HMC

151. *Sunset,* female chorus and piano; SU/1904; timing 2:00; published separately and in *The Laurel Song Series;* text by J. P. Peabody; two holograph scores (one dated 15 June 1901, and one termed "Op. 19") in NYp-HMC; one score dedicated to Mrs. Edward Palmer Mason; two holograph scores and parts of arrangement (in different key) for female chorus and orchestra in NYp-HMC

152. *O the Blue Air;* SU/1907; copy unavailable for estimated timing; text by F. Manley

153. *Hymn for Christmas,* soprano solo, chorus, and organ; "composed for my darling Hildegard"; text ("While Shepherds Watched Their Flocks by Night") by N. Tate; holograph score (dated 24 December 1907) in NYp-HMC; different setting from Nos. 22, 98, 120 and 175

*p 154. *O Captain, My Captain,* male chorus, organ, and piano; GS/1909 by the Pittsburgh Male Chorus; copy unavailable for estimated timing; text by Whitman; composed under pseudonym "Passing Tone"

155. *Te Deum,* soprano, alto, tenor, bass solos, chorus, and organ; holograph score (dated 20 February 1911) in NYp-HMC along with holograph sketch (dated 14 February 1911)

*p 156. *The Fool's Prayer,* bass-baritone solo, male chorus, and piano; GS/1911; text by E. R. Sill; timing 2:30; dedicated to James Stephen Martin and the Pittsburgh Male Chorus; two holograph scores in NYp-HMC, one composed by "Free Suspension"; cf. No. 29

157. *For Whatsoever Is Born of God,* chorus and organ; text from John 20; two holograph scores (one dated 31 January [?] 1908) in NYp-HMC; one has subtitle "(Over Cometh the World)"; other has title "Who Is He That Overcometh the World?" and is marked "First Sunday After Easter"

158. *Te Deum,* solos, chorus, and organ; two holograph scores (one dated 14 February 1911 and the other 20 February 1911) in NYp-HMC; "For the Dedication of the Cathedral of St. John the Divine" on [?] "Easter 1911"

159. [Untitled choral work], [male?]; holograph score (dated

31 March and 15 April 1911) in NYp-HMC; for Rafael
Joseffy "For dinner of 'The Bohemians' "

*p 160. *My Luv' Is Like a Red, Red Rose,* male chorus; text by
R. Burns; holograph score in NYp-HMC; cf. No. 41

161. *How Sweet the Moonlight Sleeps, Op. 27,* soprano solo, female
chorus, and orchestra; also known as the "Nocturne"; text
by Shakespeare; for first performance on 24 April 1914,
Huss reduced the orchestration; this opus number also
published with No. 234; two holograph (labeled "Op.
25"; this opus number also with No. 233) and one
copyist's (dated 15 September 1913) scores and some
sketches in NYp-HMC; one score states the piano part is
an arrangement by Huss from an orchestra score; one
carries dedication to Arthur D. Woodruff and the Musical
Art Society of Orange, NJ; five holograph orchestra full
scores (one dedicated to Arthur Woodruff and the Musical
Art Society of Orange, NJ and labeled "Op. 25" and
dated 1913) and set of parts in NYp-HMC

162. *The Night Has a Thousand Eyes;* SB/1915; published in
Progressive Music Series, Book 4; timing 1:30; text by F. B.
Bourdillon; holograph score (dated 19 February 1913) in
NYp-HMC; manuscript has "For Burdett Silver School
Song Book"

163. *Music, When Soft Voices Die, Op. 28;* written around or after
1917; text by Shelley; holograph score in NYp-HMC;
score has "Sweet" crossed out and replaced by "Soft"; cf.
Nos. 42, 349, and 386

p 164. *Mankind's Own Song,* female chorus and orchestra; GS/
1918; timing 2:30; text by Lanier; one holograph piano-
vocal score and three holograph orchestral scores (one has
copyright date on title page [1917 by Huss]) and set of
parts in NYp-HMC; scores in two different keys; scores
have dedications to the Misses Masters and/or for the 40th
anniversary of their school; one score indicates text is from
" 'The Centennial Meditation of Columbia' from *Poems of
Sidney Lanier,* copyright 1884, 1891 by Mary Day Lanier,
pub. by Chas. Scribner's Sons"—"sixth line changed, by
permission, from 'A man's own song' to 'Mankind's own
song' "; another has "The Centennial Cantata/The Meditation of Columbia"

165. *Dedication Hymn,* female chorus and piano; text by M. Blatchford; dedicated to the Misses Masters; two holograph scores (one dated 15 April 1921) and sketches of piano-vocal score and one holograph score of arrangement for female chorus and orchestra (dated April 1921) in NYp-HMC; one score titled "A Hymn of Dedication"

p 166. *The Night Dance,* female chorus; GR/1921; text by T. Moore; two holograph scores and sketches (one dated 3 August 1911) of arrangement for soprano and alto solo, female chorus, and orchestra (one with "Intermezzo" as subtitle and dedicated to Dr. Arthur Woodruff) in NYp-HMC; arranged for female chorus and piano (holograph score signed "Covered Fifth" in NYp-HMC); cf. No. 30

167. *The Ship of State,* "junior" chorus (SAB) and orchestra; text by Longfellow; two holograph scores (one dated 30 October 1926; the other is a piano-vocal score) in NYp-HMC; composed under pseudonym "Diminished Seventh"; cf. No. 134

168. *Invictus,* male chorus and piano; text by W. E. Henley; holograph score (dated 3 and 30 November 1927; probably beginning and ending dates for the composition) in NYp-HMC

169. *I Dare Not Ask A Kiss,* female chorus and piano; CF/1928; timing 1:00; text by R. Herrick; dedicated to his wife; three holograph scores (all with descriptor "Canzonet"; one without "Electra" ["Electra"] as subtitle and two with it crossed out) in NYp-HMC; one score has markings for copyist referring to "Master School (Dobbs Ferry)," "Mr. Salmond (Bklyn Choral Soc)," and "Victor Harris"; cf. No. 74

170. [*Psalm 23*], female chorus, keyboard; holograph score (dated 21 December 1928) in NYp-HMC

171. *Bless the Lord, O My Soul,* solo vocal quartet and organ; text from Psalm 103; dedicated to his wife; composed under pseudonym "Organ Point"; holograph score (dated 28 January 1929) and sketches in NYp-HMC

172. *Crown Him with Many Crowns,* ad lib. vocal solos, chorus, and organ; two holograph scores (one dated 22 November 1931) in NYp-HMC; one score labeled "Anthem" for the "1st Sunday after Easter"

173. *Lord, Make My Heart a Place Where Angels Sing,* chorus and piano; GS/1935; timing 4:30; text by J. Keble; dedicated to the Reverend and Mrs. Felix G. Robinson and the Mountain Choir Festival; holograph score in NYp-HMC; also holograph score of arrangement for chorus and orchestra with same dedication in NYp-HMC

*p   174. *Winged Messengers of Peace,* chorus and piano; GS/1937; timing 8:45; text by A. Feddé; dedicated to the "Mothers of the World"; holograph vocal and two holograph orchestra (dated 1936) scores and parts (marked "Introduction especially for Choir Festival at Mt. Lake Park," 18 July 1937) in NYp-HMC; arranged for male chorus and piano (two holograph scores, dated 4 September 1936) in NYp-HMC; copyist's orchestra score in NYp-HMC

175. *Hymn for Christmas,* soprano solo, chorus, and piano; text ("While Shepherds Watched Their Flocks by Night") by N. Tate; holograph score (dated December 1937) in NYp-HMC; different from Nos. 22, 98, 120, and 153

p   176. *The Lord Is My Shepherd,* female chorus and keyboard; GS/1938; text from Psalm 23; dedicated to the Hunter College Choir; holograph score for soprano duet with keyboard (dated April 1939) in NYp-HMC; holograph score (dated April 1939) of arrangement for female chorus and string orchestra in NYp-HMC; cf. No. 363

p   177. *The Mystery of Night,* female chorus and organ; GS/1940; text by E. Dobbins; published score dedicated to the City Federation Choral, but manuscript score "composed for and dedicated to [Mrs.] Kate Fassler Chase"; holograph score (dated February 1939) and part (for organ or cabinet organ) in NYp-HMC

178. *The Right Will Win,* chorus and piano; GS/1943; timing 2:00; text by Huss; cf. No. 114

179. *The Ride of Paul Revere,* chorus and orchestra; text by Longfellow; holograph score (dated 27 January 1928) and sketch (dated 3 January 1928) of setting for chorus and keyboard in NYp-HMC; this score has title "Midnight Ride of Paul Revere" and was composed "by chord of the 9th"; two holograph scores (both composed by "A Lover of Peace"; one title page has "orchestration finished" 22

November 1945; first page dated 4 August 1945) of
setting for chorus and orchestra and sketch (composed by
"Chacun à son gout") of setting for baritone, chorus, and
orchestra in NYp-HMC; two holograph scores of arrangement (one entitled "Paul Revere's Ride" and labeled
"cantata") for mixed junior chorus and baritone solo ad
lib. and orchestra, with the orchestra arranged for piano
by Huss in NYp-HMC

180. *A Grace for Christmas;* text by J. F. Cooke; holograph score
(dated December 1950) in NYp-HMC

UNDATABLE CHORAL WORKS
(IN ALPHABETICAL ORDER)

181. *God Be Merciful,* chorus and keyboard; text from Psalm
67; holograph score (with title "Deus misereatur") in
NYp-HMC

182. *God is Love,* chorus and organ; text by J. Browning;
composed by "Deceptive Cadence"; holograph score in
NYp-HMC

183. *Hymn in Cantata Style,* solo quartet, chorus, and piano;
text by T. Moore; composed under pseudonym "Laborare
est Orare"; holograph score in NYp-HMC

184. *Hymn of Freedom,* chorus and keyboard; text by M. P.
King; composed by "Enharmonic Change"; holograph
score and sketch in NYp-HMC

185. *Jesus Christ, Our Strong Salvation;* GR/[no date given in
source]; text written by or music edited for publication by
[Emily?] Dickinson; known from *Choral Music in Print*

186. *Make a Joyful Noise Unto God, All Ye Lands;* text from Psalm
66; score dedicated to "Our Vocal Society"; holograph score
(also titled "Anthem") and sketch in NYp-HMC

187. *New America,* chorus and organ; text by [?] E. Markham
("Freedom we children all Long heard thy Mother call
. . ."); holograph text in NYp-HMC; has motto from
T. Roosevelt ("Brotherhood Is the American Ideal")

188. *O Beautiful for Spacious Skies,* chorus and piano; text by
K. L. Bates; composed by "Augmented 4th"; holograph
score in NYp-HMC

189. *Psalm 84,* chorus and organ; by "Sing unto the Lord"; holograph score (piano score with text written into it—no actual choral parts) in NYp-HMC; score has organ prelude and interlude ad lib.; different setting from No. 190

190. *Psalm 84,* chorus and organ; composed by "Cross Relation"; holograph score (piano score with text written into it—no actual choral parts) in NYp-HMC; different setting from No. 189

191. *The Song of the Winds,* chorus, solos, and orchestra; composed by "Tempo Rubato"; vocal-keyboard score with orchestration indications and marked "accompaniment arranged for piano"

192. *Summer's Rain and Winter's Snow,* "children's" chorus; cf. No. 127

193. *There's a River Goes Laughing All the Day,* "children's" chorus; cf. No. 128

194. *Worship—Hymn,* soprano and alto [children's voices] and piano; text by Whittier; "Especially composed for Mr. Tomlin's Children's Chorus"; two holograph scores (one incomplete) in NYp-HMC

Piano Music

195. *Lullaby;* holograph score (dated 13 and 19 June 1877) in NYp-HMC

196. *Wedding Fantasia;* "dedicated to my dear Father and Mother/July 1877/on their 25th Wedding Day"; two holograph scores (one dated 11 August, 28 July, and 10 September 1877; other dated only 1877) in NYp-HMC

p 197. *Ballade in F;* GS/1885; timing 4:30; dedicated to Mrs. Colonel May; piece is Op. 1, but this is not on score; worklist in Huss's hand in NYp-HC lists this as Op. 2

198. *Valse Characteristique;* written by 27 February 1889; if not a secondary title, the work is apparently lost

*p 199. *Drei Bagatellen für das Pianoforte;* also known as "Three Pieces for Piano," Op. 5; SM/1889; timing of set 5:45

    #1   *Étude Mélodique;* timing 2:45; dedicated to R. L. Cutting, Jr.

#2 *Albumblatt;* timing 1:30; dedicated to Mrs. Colonel May

#3 *Pastorale;* timing 1:30; dedicated to "Dottie" Webb

*p 200. [*Two Piano Pieces*]; SM/1891; timing of set 3:30; may be Op. 7 (this designation may only apply to #2)

#1 "Prelude Appassionata"; also known as "Othello" or "Otello"; timing 1:45; dedicated to Adele aus der Ohe

#2 "The Rivulet" Etude; also known as "The Rivulet Arabesque"; timing 1:45

201. *Valse;* in A-flat Major; holograph score (9 May 1891) in NYp-HMC

202. *Romance for Piano;* "Being a paraphrase of the slow movement of his concerto played in Boston last night"; NY/1894; timing 1:30; paraphrase presumably by Huss; cf. No. 372

*p 203. *Three Intermezzi;* MI/1894; published in *Half Hours with the Best Composers;* timing 1:30/1:30/2:30 (5:30 total); #2 subtitled *Le Crepuscule* ("The Twilight"); manuscript score of set at Boston Public Library

204. *Impromptu;* in A Major; composed by "Enharmonic"; holograph score (dated 22 May 1896) in NYp-HMC; later in score referred to as a "prelude"

205. *Cleopatra's Death;* written by 30 August 1897 program; transcription (presumably by Huss) of Huss's work for soprano and orchestra; apparently lost; cf. No. 377

206. *Home They Brought Her Warrior Dead;* transcription (presumably by Huss) of No. 12; written by 24 August 1898 program; apparently lost

207. *Birthday Prelude;* "to my dear father on his 70th birthday Sept 25 '98"; holograph score in NYp-HMC

s 208. *The Summer Sketch Book,* Op. 13; subtitled "Six Piano Pieces for Young Players"; GS/1899; set title page reads "A Summer Sketch Book"; timing of set 8:45

#1 "A May-Morning"; timing 0:30; dedicated to Edith

#2 "An Evening Song"; timing 1:30; dedicated to Ethel

#3 "Valse Petite"; timing 2:00; dedicated to George; not same as No. 288

#4 "Alla Zingaresa" ("Gipsy Dance"); timing 1:15; dedicated to Paul

#5 "A Summer Sunset"; timing 1:30; dedicated to Bessie

#6 "Alla Tarantella"; timing 2:00; dedicated to Helen

209. *Wedding Prelude;* in A Major; dedicated to Louise Shephard; holograph score (dated 26 November 1899) in NYp-HMC

210. *Wedding Prelude;* in E-flat Major; dedicated to Miss Gretchen von Bicesen [?]; holograph score (dated 27 November 1899) in NYp-HMC

211. [Untitled piano work]; holograph score (dated 5 January 1900) in NYp-HMC

212. *Prelude Easter Morn;* holograph score (dated 16 April 1900) in NYp-HMC

213. *Pastorale for Christmas;* "to my dear Father and Mother"; holograph score (dated 22 December 1900) in NYp-HMC

*p 214. *Quatre Préludes en forme d'Études,* Op. 17; GS/1901; timing of set 8:45

#1 in D-flat; timing 2:00; dedicated to Madame de Levenoff

#2 in D; timing 2:30; dedicated to Ella A. Wrigley

#3 in E; timing 2:15; "Pour la main droite *ad lib.*"; dedicated to Miss M. Wood

#4 in A-flat; timing 2:00; dedicated to Jane Carlyle Wilson

*p 215. *Menuet et Gavotte Capricieuse,* Op. 18; GS/1901; timing of set 6:00

#1 in C; timing 4:00; dedicated to L. Therese Wilcox

#2 in G minor; timing 2:00; dedicated to Mrs. Elford Gould

216. *Man's Ego Remains the Same Thro' Changing Scenes of Life;* holograph score (dated 6 February 1902) in NYp-HMC

217. [Untitled piano work]; dedicated to Miss Alethea Crawford; holograph score (dated 28 March 1902) in NYp-HMC

* 218. *Preludes in A-flat Major and G minor;* paraphrase of Chopin's Op. 28 by Huss; written by 14 May 1903 program; apparently lost

*p 219. *Three Pieces for Pianoforte,* Op. 20; GS/1904; timing of set
11:30
#1 "Valse"; in A; timing 7:30; written by 1903;
dedicated to William H. Sherwood
#2 "Nocturne"; in D; timing 2:00; dedicated to "My
Father and Mother"
#3 "Gavotte"; in F; timing 2:00; written by 1903;
dedicated to William H. Barber

*p 220. *La Nuit,* Op. 21; "Poem for the Piano"; GS/1904; timing
3:00; written by 1903; dedicated to Mildred Barnes;
orchestrated by Huss in 1939 (No. 393)

221. *Sarabande in D;* written by 20 April 1904 program; may
be the same as another work under another title

s 222. *Condensed Piano Technics;* "Original Analytical Exercises in
Double Notes, Scale- & Arpeggio-forms and Trills";
GS/1904; written with Huss's father

223. *Petite Prelude;* in G Major; holograph score (dated 15
September 1906) in NYp-HMC

224. *Dedication;* arrangement of Schumann's Op. 25 by Huss;
written by 17 February 1909 program; apparently lost

225. *Dance of the Seven Veils;* transcription from Strauss's *Salome*
by Huss; written by 18 August 1909 program; apparently
lost

226. *En Bateau;* transcription from Debussy by Huss; written
by 18 August 1909 program; apparently lost

227. *Wedding Prelude;* in D Major; dedicated to Miss Annie
Fisk; holograph score (dated 5 April 191 [*sic*]) in NYp-
HMC

*p 228. *Seven Sketches for Piano,* Op. 32; CF/1925 for #5 and #6,
others 1927; timing of set 12:45
#1 "The Optimist" Prelude; timing 1:45; dedicated to
Katherine
#2 "Petite Humoresque"; timing 1:45; dedicated to
"My Pupil Edmund Nasadoski"
#3 "Menuet à l'Antique"; timing 3:00; dedicated to
"My Dear Pupil Katherine Morris"; holograph
scores (dated 4 February 1911 and 13 December
1919) in NYp-HMC
#4 "Pensée Fugitive"; timing 2:00; dedicated to Mrs.
E. B. Sexton; holograph sketch (dated 29 December

1923) of this, with original title of "Momens Musicale" [*sic*] and dedicated to Mrs. E. D. Layton [?], in NYp-HMC

#5   "Christmas Prelude"; timing 1:45; dedicated to "My Dear Pupil Katherine Elizabeth Clark Morris"

#6   "Mazurka Capricieuse"; timing 1:30; dedicated to Mrs. E. B. Sexton

#7   " 'The Joy of Autumn,' Concert Prelude"; timing 1:00; dedicated to "My Dear Pupil Katherine Elizabeth Clark Morris"

229. [Untitled piano work]; dedicated to Gustav Heuback [?] ("Herzlichen Glückwunsch zu deinen Geburtstag"); holograph score (dated 15 September 1911) in NYp-HMC

*p   230. *Six Pieces for the Pianoforte,* Op. 23; GS/1912; timing of set 11:45; either #2 or #3 called "Prelude" in programs of 26 October and 22 November 1938

#1   "Étude Romantique"; also known as "Étude Erotik"; timing 3:00; dedicated to Paderewski

#2   "Intermezzo"; in B-flat; "Brahmsianer"; timing 0:45; dedicated to Joseffy

#3   "Intermezzo"; in G; "Brahmsianer"; timing 0:45; dedicated to Joseffy

#4   "Impromptu"; timing 2:00; dedicated to Pugno; may originally have been meant to be in Op. 25 (cf. No. 233)

#5   "Albumleaf"; timing 1:15; dedicated to Emilie Frances Bauer

#6   "Polonaise brillante"; also known as "Polonaise de Concert" and "Concert Caprice en Forme de Polonaise"; timing 4:00; dedicated to Mrs. Elford Gould

231. *Theme and Variations en forme de* [*sic*] *Preludes;* holograph score of theme and 5 variations (last one dated January 1913) in NYp-HMC

*p   232. *Three Pieces for Piano,* Op. 26; GS/1917; timing of set 9:00; this opus number also associated with No. 345

#1   "Menuet Rococo"; timing 2:45; dedicated to Ossip Gabrilowitsch; described by Huss as being in the Lydian mode in "New Etude Played at Huss Concert," the *Sun,* 17 April 1917

#2   "On the Lake" Étude; also known by French title

"Sur le Lac"; timing 3:45; dedicated to Leopold Godowsky

#3 "The Brooklet" Étude; also known by French title "Le Ruisselet"; timing 2:30; dedicated to Rudolph Ganz; holograph score (dated 4 August 1913) in NYp-HMC

*p 233. *Sans Souci,* Op. 25, #2; "Morceau characteristique pour piano"; GS/1915; timing 1:30; dedicated to Katherine Goodson; this opus number also with No. 161; cf. No. 230

*p 234. *{Two Pieces} For the Piano,* Op. 27; DI/1917; timing for set 8:00; same opus number published with No. 161

#1 "Menuet Mignon"; also spelled "Mignonne"; timing 2:45; dedicated to Mrs. Denny Brereton; holograph score (dated 3 March 1915) in NYp-HMC

#2 "Valse Intime"; also known as "Valse Arabesque"; timing 5:15; dedicated to Harold Bauer; holograph score of a "Variant of 'Valse Arabesque' " in NYp-HMC

235. *Berceuse Slave;* written by 1916; holograph score with two covers in NYp-HMC; one cover has (in Huss's hand) "No date—Zimbalist played (violin)/Carnegie Hall prgr 1916/publ by Schirmer"; also titled "Slavic Cradle Song"; same music as No. 348

236. *Little Prelude;* dedicated to Katherine [Morris] Hall; holograph score (dated 26 May 1917 and December 1928) in NYp-HMC

237. *Intermezzo;* "From the Orient"; written by 20 February 1918 program; may be from 1894 set; if not, apparently lost

238. *Petite Valse;* in A-flat; holograph score (dated 20 December 1918) in NYp-HMC

s 239. [Untitled set of three piano works], Op. 29; AP/1919; published in the *Progressive Series of Piano Lessons;* timing of set 6:30; this opus number also associated with No. 343

#1 "The Two Comrades"; timing 2:00; dedicated to Philip

#2 "A Walk in Autumn"; timing 2:30; dedicated to Laurie

#3 "Dolly's Cradle Song"; timing 2:00; dedicated to Rosamond

s   240. *Three Bagatelles,* Op. 30; AP/1919; published in the
       Progressive Series of Piano Lessons; timing of set 7:15; all
       dedicated to Katherine Elizabeth Clark Morris
       #1   "Prelude"; timing 2:00
       #2   "In Arcady"; timing 3:30
       #3   "Orientale"; timing 1:45; holograph score for an
             "Etude Orientale" (dated 19 December 1917) is in
             NYp-HMC
    241. *Intermezzo "La Misericordia";* written by 3 March 1919;
       may be from 1894 set; if not, apparently lost
    242. *Cinq Petites Momens Musicales* [*sic*]; subtitled "5 Etudes
       Melodique sans octaves"; holograph score (dated 5 June
       1920) of Nos. 1 and 2 only are in NYp-HMC
    243. *Humoresque;* holograph score (dated 5 June 1920) in
       NYp-HMC
    244. *The Shepherdess;* dedicated to his wife; holograph score
       (dated 15 July 1920) in NYp-HMC
    245. *Wedding March;* in F Major; dedicated to Miss Charlotte
       Eaton; holograph score (dated 16 September 1920) in
       NYp-HMC
*s 246. *Happy Days;* subtitled "Nine Sketches for Piano"; CF/
       1923; timing of set 14:30
       #1   "The Fairy Princess"; timing 2:30; dedicated to
             Margaret M.; a "Valse of the Fair Princess," subti-
             tled "Petite Valse" (dated 1 November 1920) is in
             NYp-HMC
       #2   "March of the Boy Scouts"; timing 1:30; dedicated
             to the Boy Scouts of America; holograph score
             (dated 17 November and inscribed "No. 2") in
             NYp-HMC
       #3   "The Peter Pan Baby"; subtitled "Cradle Song";
             timing 1:30; dedicated to Frances B.; a "Cradle
             Song of the Peter Pan Baby" (dated 19 November
             1920) is in NYp-HMC
       #4   "The Old Duchess at the Court Ball"; timing 2:15;
             dedicated to Mary W[oodbury]; a "The Old Duke
             and Duchess at the Court Ball" (dated 17 Novem-
             ber 1920) is in NYp-HMC
       #5   "Cherry Blossoms"; timing 1:00; dedicated to

Lilian Loewe; holograph score (inscribed "named by Miss Pauline Jennings") in NYp-HMC

#6 "The Sicilian Brigands"; subtitled "Tarantelle"; timing 1:45; dedicated to Mary S.; two holograph scores (one titled "Tarentella of the Sicilian Brigands on the Eve of War" and the other "Sicilian Sailor's Song") in NYp-HMC

#7 "The Cloud on the Hill Top"; timing 1:30; dedicated to Audrey

#8 "The Skaters"; timing 0:45; dedicated to Peggy; two holograph scores (one dated 17 November) in NYp-HMC

#9 "Lake Como by Moonlight"; subtitled "Barcarolle"; timing 1:45; dedicated to Jane C. Cathcart; holograph score titled "Barcarolle/Lake Como by Moonlight" in NYp-HMC; cf. No. 87

247. *Xmas Prelude;* in E-flat Major; holograph score (dated December 1920) in NYp-HMC; for Katherine Morris

248. *Wedding March;* in E Major; "to my dear pupil Florence Walker [?]"; holograph score (dated 21 August 1921) in NYp-HMC

249. *The Devine Parlons;* subtitled "Minuet Langoureuse"; holograph score (dated 12 October 1921) in NYp-HMC

250. *Wedding March;* in D Major; holograph score (dated 9 December 1921) in NYp-HMC

251. *Prelude;* to Katherine Morris; holograph score (dated 19 December 1921) in NYp-HMC

252. *Sonata in D minor;* [author's note: Huss evidently toyed with the idea of writing a piano sonata over several years, sketching movements and contemplating various titles, all the while performing versions of movements on recitals; this entry attempts to pull the evidence together.]; holograph sketches (dated 19 January 1922), especially of movement I, in NYp-HMC; movements I and II (one of which was subtitled "Intermezzo") written by 6 April 1922 program; partial score and holograph score of movement I as part of *Sonata Invictus* (also known as "Life's Conflicts" and with subtitle "Poem for Piano") in NYp-HMC; "Life's Conflicts" may have appeared

intially as a single-movement piano work that later became the first movement of a projected sonata; one sketch for for the second theme of movement II in NYp-HMC; movement III may never have been completed but was planned (cf. No. 314); cf. Nos. 316, 319, 389, and 391

253. *Prelude* _____ [obscure]; subtitled "And He Shall Be Called 'The Prince of Peace' "; to Mr. and Mrs. Sexton; holograph score (dated Xmas 1924) in NYp-HMC

254. *Prelude;* in F Major; "to my dear pupil Katherine Morris Hall [?]"; holograph score (dated December 1924) in NYp-HMC

255. *Wedding March;* in C Major; to Kathy Fielding; holograph scores (one dated 15 September 1925, and the other dated 16 September 1925) in NYp-HMC; later score titled "Wedding March for Kathy Fielding" for organ

256. *Berceuse;* to John Hudson Hale; holograph score (dated 21 December 1926) in NYp-HMC

257. *Happy Days,* 2nd Series
> [#1]"3rd Grand Valse"; subtitled "Field Flowers"; holograph score (dated 16 April 1928) in NYp-HMC
> [#2]"Rolling Hoopes" [?]; holograph score (dated September 1938) in NYp-HMC
> [#3]"The Little Optimistic Bird"; holograph score in NYp-HMC
> [#4]"It's Fun to Be Alive"; holograph score (dated September 1938) in NYp-HMC
> [#5]"Joie de Vivre"; holograph score in NYp-HMC
> [#6]"Tobogganing"; holograph score in NYp-HMC
> [#7]"The Trout Brook"; dedicated to Anne Ross [?]; holograph score (dated September 1938) in NYp-HMC
> [#8]"The Little Red Automobile"; holograph score (dated September 1938) in NYp-HMC
> [#9]"Playing Indians"; holograph score (dated September 1938) in NYp-HMC
> [#10]"Sunshine [?] in the Hand"; dedicated to dear Nelle; holograph score in NYp-HMC
> [#11]"The Old Chapel at Turlegell" [?]; dedicated to dear Marion; holograph score in NYp-HMC

258. *Etude Mignonne;* holograph score (dated 31 May 1928) in NYp-HMC

259. *Easter Prelude;* "Christ is risen from the dead and is become the first fruits of them that slept" (reference to I Corinthians 15:20) underlies the first line of music; to Mrs. L. R. Morris; holograph score (dated March 1929) in NYp-HMC; cf. No. 285

260. *Lorelei;* to Eleanor; holograph score of transcription and sketch by Huss (both dated May 1929) in NYp-HMC

261. *The Doll's Lullaby;* "for Carl Fischer"; holograph score (dated 17 May 1929) in NYp-HMC

262. *Petite Valse at the Court of King Lilliput;* subtitled "Children's Prelude [?]"; holograph score (dated 15 September 1930) in NYp-HMC; score has reference to "Bergmesure" [pseudonym?]

263. *A Xmas Prelude;* to Mr. Howard Bayne; holograph score (dated December 1930) in NYp-HMC

264. *Petite Minuet;* "to my dear Katherine"; holograph score (dated December 1930) in NYp-HMC

265. *Xmas Prelude;* to Mrs. L. R. Morris; holograph score (dated Xmas 1930) in NYp-HMC

266. *Xmas Prelude;* in E-flat Major; "to my dear friend E. Marion Sexton"; holograph score (dated 1932) in NYp-HMC

267. [Untitled piano work]; in C Major; holograph score (dated 21 October 1932) in NYp-HMC

268. *Xmas Prelude;* in G Major; "to dear Katherine Morris Hall"; holograph score (dated December 1932) in NYp-HMC

269. *A Xmas Meditation/The Holy Night;* to Mrs. L. R. Morris; holograph score (dated December 1932) in NYp-HMC

270. *Petite Valse Exotic;* holograph score (dated 10 February 1933) in NYp-HMC

271. [Untitled piano work]; "to my dear friend Marion Sexton on her birthday"; holograph score (dated 2 June 1933) in NYp-HMC

272. *Prelude;* "to my dear pupil Betty Bayne"; holograph score (dated 27 June 1933) in NYp-HMC

273. *Thanksgiving Prelude;* "Composed for and dedicated to our dear, generous, greatly gifted friend Dr. Max Bloom-

field"; holograph score (dated November 1933) in NYp-HMC

274. *A New Year's Prelude;* to Mrs. L. R. Morris; holograph score (dated December 1933) in NYp-HMC

275. *Wedding March;* in A Major; "to my dear pupil Agnes Cooke"; holograph score (dated 20 September 1934) in NYp-HMC

276. *Prelude for Xmas;* "to my dear friend E. Marion Sexton"; holograph score (dated 22 December 1934) in NYp-HMC

277. *Xmas Pastorale;* subtitled "While Shepherds Watched Their Flocks by Night"; to Mrs. L. R. Morris; holograph score (dated 24 December 1934) in NYp-HMC

278. *A Note of Introspection;* also titled "A Moment of Introspection"; "to my dear pupil and friend May [?] Schuffeln [?]"; holograph score (dated 25 June 1935) in NYp-HMC; may be the same as No. 284

279. *Valse/The Sunshine Faery;* holograph score (dated July 1935) in NYp-HMC

280. *Etude Melodique 3;* subtitled "(Kaleidoscope?)" [?]; holograph score (dated 29 July 1935) in NYp-HMC

281. *Prelude "Life's Kaleidoscope";* sometimes subtitled "Miniature"; "to my dear and gifted pupil Jeanette Wiedman" [*sic*]; holograph score (dated August 1935) in NYp-HMC; first page has "Motto from Percy Byshes [*sic?*] Shelley 'Life like a many coloured dome of glass stains the white radiance of eternity' "

282. *Wedding March;* in F Major; "to my dear pupil Anne Cotte"; holograph score (dated 12 September 1935) in NYp-HMC

283. *March of the 3 Wise Men;* to Katherine Hall; holograph score (dated 22 December 1935) in NYp-HMC

284. *Un Moment de Tendresse;* written by 12 March 1936 program; may be the same as No. 278; apparently lost

285. *Easter Prelude/Now Is Christ Risen from the Dead and Is Become the First Fruits of Them That Sleep;* in B-flat Major; "to my dear friend Marion"; holograph score (dated April 1936) in NYp-HMC; cf. No. 259

286. *Thought for Xmas;* to Mrs. Morris; holograph score (dated 18 December 1936) in NYp-HMC

287. *A Thought for Xmas;* to Marion Sexton; holograph score (dated Xmas 1936) in NYp-HMC

288. *Valse Petite for Piano;* TP/1937; timing 2:00; holograph score with variant rhythms in NYp-HMC; not the same as the work of the same title in No. 208

289. *The New Year's Sunshine March;* dedications read "to my dear cousin Elsa and John" and "to dear people who have all their lives made sunshine for others"; holograph score (dated 1 January 1938) in NYp-HMC

290. *The Good Fairy Valse;* DI/1938; timing 2:30; "Composed for and dedicated to Mrs. Vincent H. Ober, President of The National Federation of Music Clubs, as a tribute to her wonderful work for the Junior Clubs"

291. *An Xmas Wish;* to Katherine M. Hall; holograph score (dated December 1938) in NYp-HMC; comments on score include "arrange this for organ?" and "also String quartet?"

292. *A Prayer for Victory and Peace;* "to dear Marion"; holograph score (dated June 1940) in NYp-HMC

293. *A Christmas Thought;* holograph score (dated 18 December 1940) in NYp-HMC

294. [Untitled piano work]; to "dear Dr. and Mrs. Mason with gratitude and beautiful memories of the many many times we have enjoyed the sunshine of your gracious hospitality. May New York City still keep its attractiveness so we may often have the pleasure of seeing Dr. and Mrs. Mason many times each winter when Maine altho' always beautiful may be a _____ [obscure]." [signed by Huss and wife] April 1942; holograph score in NYp-HMC; similar to a Christmas greeting (cf. Nos. 408, 409, and 410)

295. [Untitled piano work]; "To my darling little girl forever!"; holograph score (dated 15 June 1942) in NYp-HMC

296. [Untitled piano work]; to "dear Mrs. Sally on her 80th birthday"; holograph score (dated 18 November 1942) in NYp-HMC

297. *Lullaby;* to Mrs. Morris; holograph score (dated December 1942) in NYp-HMC; inscribed "Mirnalous [?] for Xmas"

298. *Prelude for Xmas;* in E-flat Major; dedications "to Marion"

and "to Katherine Hall" (both dedications given as well as "Not to be published with dedication"); holograph score (dated December 1944) in NYp-HMC

299. *Wedding Prelude;* holograph score (dated December 1944) in possession of dedicatee ("To My Dear Peggy"), Margaret M. Meachem

300. *Wedding Prelude;* in B-flat Major; "to Sidney and Louise [Homer?] on their 50th Wedding Anniversary"; holograph score (dated 12 December 194[4?]) in NYp-HMC

301. *Wedding Prelude;* in C Major; "to my dear Peggy Meacham née Ramsay"; holograph score (dated 6–7 December 1945) in NYp-HMC

302. *Xmas Prelude;* in G Major; "to dear Katherine"; holograph score (dated 22 December 1945) in NYp-HMC

303. *Wedding Prelude;* in D Major; "to Herbert A. B."; holograph score (dated November 1946) in NYp-HMC

304. *Prelude for Easter;* dedicated to his wife; holograph score (dated April 1947) in NYp-HMC

305. *Easter Prelude;* in D-flat Major; "to Mrs. R. L. Morris"; holograph score (dated April 1947) in NYp-HMC

306. *Easter;* in D Major; dedicated to his wife; holograph score (dated 4 April 1947) in NYp-HMC

307. *Sunset in Central Park;* "for Mary Cavpoto" [?]; holograph score (dated 6 July 1947) in NYp-HMC

308. *Wedding Prelude for Piano;* holograph score (dated October 1947) in possession of dedicatee, Mary Woodbury

309. [Untitled piano work]; in D Major; inscribed "Kath. Hall"; holograph score (dated February [?] 1948) in NYp-HMC

310. [Untitled piano work]; a march in D Major; "to Dewey"; holograph score (dated July 1948) in NYp-HMC

311. *Italian Folk Song;* arrangement by Huss of piece by Tchaikovsky; inscribed "3rd grade," "For music ____ [circle?]," and "Hershberg Prel"; second score is for piano duet; two holograph scores (dated November 1948) in NYp-HMC; cf. No. 312

312. *Italian Folk Song for Piano Duet;* "After Tchaikovsky"; holograph score in NYp-HMC; cf. No. 311

313. *The Great Joy of Xmas;* holograph score (dated December 1948) in NYp-HMC

314. *Rhapsody for Piano "The Conflicts of Life";* dedicated to Isidor Philipp; two holograph scores and sketches (one dated 7 January 1950; the other only January 1950) in NYp-HMC—both in the sketchbook whose cover has "Finale of Invictus/Jan. 1950" and "Finale of Life's Conflicts 1950"; one sketch has "If God is for us what shall we fear?"; three-part work in progress in 1950; may be part of No. 252; if not identical with another work, apparently unfinished; cf. Nos. 316, 319, 389, and 391

315. *Easter Prelude;* dedicated to his wife; holograph score (dated Easter 1950) in NYp-HMC

316. *Rhapsodie "Life's Vicissitudes";* written by 21 June 1952 program; dedicated to Isidor Philipp; possibly a movement from No. 252; may be a portion of No. 314; unless identical with another work, apparently lost; cf. Nos. 319, 389, and 391

317. *Scherzino;* dedication reads "For my own Darling Little Girl Forever May She continue to bless the World for many years with messages of joy and gladness"; holograph score (dated 19 July 1952) in NYp-HMC

318. *Humoresque (Bagatelle);* dedication reads "For my own Darling Little Girl Forever Whose magic smile can walk a mile and brighten any dark and dismal day"; holograph score (dated 15 July 1953) in NYp-HMC

319. *This Mortal Life;* written by 23 June 1953 program; may be movement from No. 252; may be portion of No. 314; unless identical with another work, apparently lost; cf. Nos. 316, 389, and 391

UNDATABLE PIANO WORKS
(IN ALPHABETICAL ORDER)

320. *Album for E. M. Sexton;* holograph score in NYp-HMC

321. *A Birthday Prelude;* "to dear Elsa"; holograph score in NYp-HMC

322. *Chinese Melodies for Piano;* holograph score in NYp-HMC
     #1   "Guiding March"
     #2   "Funeral March"

#3   "Wedding March"; based on same melody as that
       used for all of No. 330
#4   "Wang Ja-niang"

323. *Fantasy for the Pianoforte on Old Acadian Contra-Dances;* also
     titled " 'Rhapsodietta' on Two Acadian Contradances";
     dances transcribed by George W. Cable; holograph score
     in NYp-HMC

324. *A l'Hongroise;* holograph score (dated May 20 [1896?
     1936? 1926?]) in NYp-HMC

325. *March of the Amazons;* holograph score in NYp-HMC

326. *March of the Puppets;* holograph score in NYp-HMC

327. *Musical Frolics for Pupil and Teacher;* holograph score in
     NYp-HMC

328. [Piano exercises and duets]; holograph scores in NYp-
     HMC; seven teaching pieces, four with titles ("Look out
     for the drip," "Some distance from Prussia," "Life is
     checkered," and "The Wig")

329. *Presto;* in B-flat; holograph score in NYp-HMC

330. *Three Paraphrases on an Ancient Chinese Wedding March;*
     holograph score in NYp-HMC; cf. No. 322
     #1   "Valse Lento"
     #2   "Berceuse"
     #3   "Wedding Procession"

331. *Valse lento;* holograph score in NYp-HMC; inscribed
     "(Vocal?)"

332. *Wedding Prelude;* in D Major; to Harriet Thompson;
     holograph score in NYp-HMC

333. *With a Xmas Thought;* "to Katherine Hall"; holograph
     score in NYp-HMC

334. *Xmas Prelude;* in D Major; holograph score in NYp-HMC

Chamber Music

The instrumentation, when not a part of the title, is given following
each of these titles.

335. *Quartet in E;* strings; written in 1878 (known from letter
     of 11 March 1879 from Huss to a Mr. Belkman in

NYp-HC); holograph sketches (dated in the 1870s) for a string quartet in NYp-HMC; apparently lost

336. *Fuge für Streich Quartett;* holograph score (dated München, September 1882) in NYp-HMC; on theme by Josef Rheinberger

*p 337. *Trio für Pianoforte, Violin und Violoncello {No. 1 in D minor, Op. 8};* dedicated to Josef Rheinberger; holograph scores (one dated 1887, and one dated 1900) and parts (one dated 1887) in NYp-HMC, along with sketches dated 12 May 1886; one sketch titled "Three mood sketches" and composed under pseudonym "Covered Fifth"; movement II (labeled variously in NYp-HMC materials "Larghetto," "Romance," and "Intermezzo/(Romanze)") arranged by Huss as No. 402; movement III labeled variously "Scherzo" and "Finale"

338. *Mazurka Caprice;* violin and piano; also titled "Hungarian Song and Dance"; holograph score and parts (incomplete), dated 1888, in NYp-HMC; arranged by Huss from "Hungarian Melody and Dance/Matus" given to him by Maud Powell

339. *Romanze für 'Cello und Piano;* written by 10 April 1889 program; two copies of solo part only to a cello "romance" (one dedicated to Mr. F. Bergner) in NYp-HMC

340. *Romanze à Capriccio and Polonaise;* violin and piano; written by 1889; probably a piano reduction of No. 383; apparently lost

341. *Legende-Pastorale;* oboe; being written or completed by June 1895 (known from 10 June 1895 letter from D. G. Mason to Huss in NYp-HC); possibly an arrangement from another work; apparently lost

*p 342. *Sonata for Violin and Piano,* Op. 19; GS/1903; timing 5:00/7:30/4:30 (total 17:00); dedicated to Franz Kneisel; two holograph scores (one dated 22 May 1896; the other "A.D. 1900") and sketches (part of movement II ["Scherzo"] and of "Scherzo") in NYp-HMC; no dedication on holograph materials; movement II also known as "A Northern Melody" and sold separately; revised by Huss by 1920 and reprinted in that year

343. *Quartet in E minor {No. 2, Op. 29};* strings; written at Ysaÿe's request and dedicated to him; this opus number

printed on No. 239; two movements orchestrated (cf. No. 381); apparently lost

*p   344. *Romance;* violin and piano; GS/1907; timing 3:00; dedicated to Maud Powell; also issued simultaneously for violoncello and piano; may have been orchestrated in 1901 by Frank Van der Stucken (cf. No. 380); manuscript apparently lost

345. *Quartet {No. 1} in G minor {Op. 26};* strings; written in 1908; this opus number printed with No. 232; apparently lost

346. *Sonata for Violoncello and Piano in C;* dedicated to Alwin Schroeder; written by 1910; probably Op. 24 but also known as Op. 20 and 30; apparently lost

347. *After Sorrow's Night,* Op. 28, No. 1; voice and instrumental ensemble; holograph scores (one dated 22 December 1911) and parts in NYp-HMC; cf. Nos. 42 and 350

*p   348. *Berceuse Slave;* violin and piano; subtitled "Slavic Cradle Song" and "Slavic Lullaby"; DI/1916; timing 3:00; dedicated to "My Friend Efrem Zimbalist"; three holograph scores (two dated July 1915) in NYp-HMC; same music as No. 235

349. *Music, When Soft Voices Die,* Op. 28, No. 2; voice and string quartet; dedicated to his wife; two holograph score (both dated 18 July 1915) and parts in NYp-HMC; on title page "Sweet" is crossed out and replaced by "Soft"; cf. Nos. 42, 163, and 386

350. *Four Intermezzi;* soprano and instrumental ensemble; scores bear dedications to Miss Carolyn Beebe and the New York Chamber Music Society; arrangements include settings for woodwinds, horn, piano, and strings and for string quartet and piano

   #1   "Before Sunrise"; two scores (one inscribed "Instrumentation Aug 8 1916") and parts in NYp-HMC; cf. No. 28

   #2   "It Was a Lover and His Lass"; four scores (different keys for the two different orchestrations) and parts in NYp-HMC; cf. Nos. 28 and 366

   #3   "The Birds Were Singing"; three scores and parts, one titled "A Song of Despair," in NYp-HMC; cf. Nos. 36 and 352

#4 "After Sorrow's Night"; score and parts set in NYp-HMC; cf. Nos. 42 and 347

351. *The Very Speech Love Learnt in Paradise;* "Song for High Voice and Piano With Violin Obbligato"; text by J. Thompson; holograph score (dated December 1916) and parts in NYp-HMC; cf. No. 50

352. *The Birds Were Singing;* arranged (presumably by Huss) for voice, piano, and string quartet by 1921; apparently lost; cf. Nos. 36 and 350

*p 353. *Quartet for Strings, Op. 31, in B minor;* GS/1921 (by Huss); published by GS for the Society for the Publication of American Music; edited for publication by Hugo Kortschak; timing 7:30/4:45/4:00/3:15 (total 19:30); dedicated to Elizabeth Sprague Coolidge; two manuscript scores (one dated 1918) and parts in Wc; two holograph scores (of movement II, "Scherzo," dated June 1918, and of "Largo") and sketch of "Finale" in NYp-HMC; there is also a holograph score (dated 25 February 1913 and labeled "recommenced May 29 1918") of a movement I from a B-Major quartet, as Op. 21, in NYp-HMC

354. *Sonata for Viola and Piano;* called "Sonata Rhapsodic" in 22 November 1938 program; holograph score (only movement I is complete; dated June 1919) and viola part (all three movements present) in NYp-HMC; may be Op. 34

355. [Quartet sketches]; strings; holograph score for "Introduction to Quartette" (dated 8 September 1920) in NYp-HMC; holograph sketch "For Finale of String Quartet" (dated 2 October 1921) in NYp-HMC; holograph score for "String Quartet" (labeled "sketch begun May 5 1920" and "Score begun June 3 1920") in NYp-HMC; holograph sketch of a (first?) movement in D minor in NYp-HMC; holograph score for "Finale of String Quartette" (dated 2 October 1921) in NYp-HMC

*p 356. *Trio for Piano, Violin and Violoncello,* No. 2, Op. 34; holograph scores (one dated July 1921 and one 26 September 1920), sketches (dated September 1920 and 23 July 1921) and parts in NYp-HMC

I. "1914–1918 Hatred-Mercy-Courage-Terror"; one sketch, dated 1 and 23 June 1921, entitled "1914–

1918 Hatred, Mercy, Courage, Selfishness, Self-sacrifice"

II. "The Devil's Carnival"; some titles on sketches include the motto "600% profit while millions starved"; one sketch has "Intermezzo" before "The Devil's Carnaval [*sic*]" but another has "Intermezzo/ The Devil's [?] Carnaval [*sic*]"; movement II later orchestrated by Huss and given the titles "In Memoriam 1914–1918" and "Elegy, Poem for Orchestra"; cf. No. 388

III. "Elegy, Marche funèbre"; one sketch has inscription "In Memoriam our boys who made the supreme sacrifice that wars might be no more"; another (dated July 13 1921) has this as movement II "Elegy. In Memoriam of those who gave their all and died that there might be no more war"

IV. "The Dawn of a Better Day"; one sketch has "Finale" before "The Dawn of a Better Day"; another has this as movement III

357. *The Corn Song;* two-part setting for voices and piano; holograph score (dated 31 December 1920) in NYp-HMC

*p 358. *Sonata for Violin and Piano in D minor,* No. 2, Op. 33; completed by 30 August 1926 program; holograph sketches of various movements and parts of movements (dated 26 March 1925, December 1925, 1925, and 28 March 1926) as well as piano score and 2 copies of solo violin part of "Legende" in NYp-HMC; two movements carry titles "Legende" and "Finale"; cf. No. 387

359. *In Love, If Love Be Love;* voice, viola obbligato, and piano; subtitled "Vivian's Song"; text by Tennyson; holograph score in NYp-HMC; cf. No. 69

360. *Pack, Clouds Away;* voice and string quartet; written by 6 April 1926 program; apparently lost, however score for arrangement for voice, strings, and piano in NYp-HMC; cf. No. 56

361. *Pan;* voice, violin, and piano; holograph score in NYp-HMC; cf. No. 70

362. *Quartet in C minor;* strings; known from *American Compos-*

ers/A Record of Works Written Between 1912 and 1932, 2nd ed.; apparently lost

363. *The Lord Is My Shepherd;* soprano, alto, and piano; GS/ 1938; cf. No. 176

364. *Finale for String Quartette;* incomplete holograph sketch (dated "1942?") in NYp-HMC

365. [Untitled chamber work], violin and piano; dedicated to Claude; holograph sketch (dated July 1945) in NYp-HMC

UNDATABLE CHAMBER WORKS
(IN ALPHABETICAL ORDER)

366. *It Was a Lover and His Lass;* voice and string quartet; holograph score and parts in NYp-HMC; cf. Nos. 28 and 350

367. *Nocturne,* Op. 14; piano, violin, and cello; arrangement by Huss of No. 422; same opus number as No. 146; known from worklist in Huss's hand in NYp-HC; apparently lost

368. *Now the Golden Morn Aloft;* soprano, contralto, and piano; text by T. Gray; manuscript score and parts in NYp-HMC

369. *Worship;* duet for soprano, alto, and piano; text by Whittier; holograph score in NYp-HMC

Orchestral Music

Works are assumed to be for standard later nineteenth-century orchestra except where noted.

370. *Wald-Idylle,* Op. 2; small orchestra; written by an 1884 program (exact date unknown); apparently lost

371. *Rhapsodie in C minor,* Op. 3; piano and orchestra; also known as "Fantasy" for piano and orchestra and "Symphonic Rhapsody" for piano and orchestra; written by 15 July 1885 program; copyist's score of "Symphonisches Fantasie Stück (Rhapsodie) für Clavier und Orchester" in NYp-HMC; holograph score of "Rhapsodie for Piano-

forte and Orchestra" in two-piano arrangement (by Huss) in NYp-HMC

*   372. *Concerto in B Major,* Op. 10; piano and orchestra in two-piano version arranged by Huss; dedicated to Adele aus der Ohe; GS/1898; may have been begun in 1888; movement II also known as "Romanza"; cf. Nos. 202 and 382

    373. *March;* written by 10 April 1891 program; may be an alternative title or reworking of another piece (cf. Nos. 374, 376, 379, or 394); apparently lost

    374. *Nuptial March No. 2;* written by 10 April 1891 program; may be an alternative title or reworking of another piece (cf. Nos. 373, 376, 379, or 394); apparently lost

    375. *The Ballad of the Song of the Syrens;* orchestrated version of song (cf. Nos. 10 and 141); holograph score for soprano and orchestra in NYp-HMC; written ca. 1891 (may be related to 29 January 1891 performance)

    376. *Festival March;* organ and orchestra; written by 24 January 1894 program; if this is the *Festival March* mentioned by Sigmund Spaeth's *Guide to Great Orchestral Music,* then it was written for an 1891 program honoring the fiftieth anniversary of the founding of the *New York Tribune;* apparently lost; may be an alternative title or reworking of another piece (cf. Nos. 373, 374, 379, or 394)

*p 377. *Cleopatra's Death;* soprano and orchestra; also known as "Dramatic Scene"; text by Shakespeare; holograph score (dated December 1892 at beginning and 19 January 1893 at end), holograph sketches (one labeled "To Mad. Clementine De Vere Sapio/Cleopatra's Death/August 16, 1892"), and three holograph piano-soprano scores (one with English text and a German translation by H. Behr ("Cleopatra's Death, dramatic fragment for Soprano and Orchestra"); one in version for mezzo and dated 1899; one labeled "aria") in NYp-HMC; cf. No. 205

    378. *All the World's a Stage;* bass and orchestra; orchestrated version of No. 16; two holograph orchestra scores (one dated 18 May 1898), five piano-vocal scores, and set of parts in NYp-HMC; one full score marked "Property of David Bispham," and one piano score signed by Bispham; some scores marked "Composed for and dedicated to Mr.

David Bispham"; several scores indicate that the closing cadenza was written by Bispham

379. *Festival March in E-flat;* known from 1901 biography in NYp-HC; may be an alternative title or reworking of another piece (cf. Nos. 373, 374, 376, or 394); may be orchestrated version of a piano work; apparently lost

380. *Romance;* violin and orchestra; written by 1901; probably orchestrated by Frank Van der Stucken if this is the piece referred to in a 13 August 1901 letter from Van der Stucken to Huss in NYp-HC; cf. No. 344; apparently lost

381. *Legend and Allegretto;* orchestrated version of two movements of No. 343; known from Sigmund Spaeth's *Guide to Great Orchestral Music;* apparently lost

*p 382. *Concerto in B Major,* Op. 10, in second edition, revised by Huss; piano and orchestra in two-piano version; dedicated to Adele aus der Ohe; GS/1910; timing 14:00/5:00/15:00 (34:00 total; Huss himself once estimated the timing at 29 or 30 minutes); two copyist's orchestra scores (neither with dedication) and one set of parts in NYp-HMC; cf. No. 372

383. *Romance et Polonaise pour violon avec l'accompagnement d'orchestre;* usually known as "Romanze and Polonaise," Op. 11, for violin and orchestra; also known as "Andante and Polonaise" for violin and orchestra and as *Romanze à Capriccio and Polonaise* for violin and orchestra; dedicated to Maud Powell; holograph scores (one dated 1889), piano-reduction scores (one marked "Composed for and dedicated to Miss Maud Powell"), solo violin part, and set of parts (written on a trombone part: "Republicque Francaise, Exposition universelle/1889/Touremo [?] du consero [?] dome [?] au Trocadéro le 12 [empty space] 1889/M. van de Stucken en un grand chef d'orchestra a gaus [?] toutes le qualité riuna [?] [signed] Ch. Laroste Opera Comique") in NYp-HMC; No. 340 is probably a piano reduction of this

384. *Concerto in D minor,* Op. 12; violin and orchestra; dedicated to Maud Powell; three holograph scores and set of parts and two holograph solo violin parts (one title page has dedication to Miss Maud Powell "1894—?," dates of 5 May 1889 and 1901–1904, and is marked "Performed,

Carnegie Hall 1904/Modest Altschuler, cond—?/Maud Powell, soloist") in NYp-HMC; holograph score of arrangement for violin and piano (dated 1889 and marked "commenced Aug. 89—Revised Sep. '91") in NYp-HMC; second movement of piano score has "Concerto composed ca. 1891–1894/played 1904 by M. Powell"; in one solo violin part, movement II is titled "Intermezzo"; in piano score movement III is subtitled "Saltarello" and labeled "June 3, '90"

385. *Fantasie;* piano and orchestra; dedicated to Raoul Pugno; worked on in 1911, but apparently never finished and now lost; known from "New Works by Huss," *Musical America,* 12 August 1911; NYp-HMC has extensive but incomplete sketches (dated October 1906) for a "Fantasy" for piano and orchestra on two systems (orchestra = piano score), but no mention of Pugno; NYp-HMC also has a sketch for an "Intermezzo" and two for a "Finale" (dated 3 December 1916 and 26 August 1919) of a concerto

386. *Music, When Soft Voices Die;* holograph score and parts of arrangement for soprano and string orchestra in NYp-HMC; labeled "Op. 28 No. 2"; cf. Nos. 42, 163, and 349

387. [*Two movements from the Sonata for Violin,* No. 2]; two movements of No. 358 were orchestrated, according to Sigmund Spaeth's *Guide to Great Orchestral Music;* apparently lost

388. *In Memoriam 1914–1918;* orchestrated version of movement II of Piano Trio No. 2 (cf. No. 356); also known as "Elegy: Poem for Orchestra," as "Elegie and Marche Funebre," and as "Funeral March and Elegy"; referred to in 3 August 1928 [?] letter from Van der Stucken to Huss in NYp-HC; apparently lost

389. *Life's Conflicts;* written by 1921; known from Huss entry in *Baker's Biographical Dictionary of Musicians,* 5th ed.; may be orchestrated version of Nos. 252, 314, 316, or 319; apparently lost; cf. 391

390. *Allegretto Giocoso;* strings; written by 1938; known from Huss entry in the *International Who is Who in Music,* 5th ed.; may be orchestrated version for strings of a piano work or may be a different title for another work

391. *Invictus;* written by 1939; known from Huss entry in the *International Who Is Who in Music,* 5th ed.; may be orchestrated version of Nos. 252, 314, 316, or 319; entitled *Invictus and Peace* in Sigmund Spaeth's *Guide to Great Orchestral Music;* apparently lost; cf. No. 389

392. *Concerto Rhapsodique;* violin and orchestra; only movement I completed; two holograph scores (one in a folder labeled "Violin Concerto No. 2, 'Concerto Rhapsodique,' 1940—movement I only"), both composed "By 'Tempo Primo' " in NYp-HMC; two holograph scores and solo part for arrangement for violin and piano in NYp-HMC; NYp-HMC also has piano-score sketches for a "Violin Concerto" (dated Sept 39, 22 February 1940, and 27 March 1940), variously labeled "Opus 36" and "Violin Concerto Rhapsodique," and having one movement titled "Romanza"

393. *La Nuit;* orchestrated version of No. 220; orchestrated by 1941 (known from 12 December 1941 letter in NYp-HC from F. H. Price of the Fleisher Collection to Huss returning his score); copyist's score in Fleisher Collection at the Free Library in Philadelphia; one page of a piano score with orchestration markings (dated 1942 and titled "La Nuit/Poem for Orchestra") in NYp-HMC

394. *Festival March in B;* written by 10 April 1948 program; may be an alternative title or reworking of another piece (cf. Nos. 373, 374, 376, or 379); apparently lost

Miscellaneous Music

395. Incomplete individual pages of sketches, sketchbooks (from 1869 to 1953) containing pages of exercises, chorale settings, and other student pieces, and sketches for individual sections in NYp-HMC

396. *How Sweet the Name of Jesus Sounds;* labeled "hymn" but nature of work and performing medium unknown; known from 11 March 1879 letter from Huss to Belkman in NYp-HC; dedicated to a Mr. Belkman

397. *Wedding March;* organ; written by 17 November 1885

performance; may be different title for another work; if not another work, apparently lost

398. *Nuptiale in F;* organ; written by 3 December 1885 program; may be different title for another work; if not another work, apparently lost

399. *Andante in C;* organ; written by 3 December 1885 program; may be different title for another work; if not another work, apparently lost

400. *Suite in D;* two pianos; written by 10 April 1889 program; only titles of two movements known ("Prelude" and "Minuet"); "Prelude" may be No. 411; "Minuet" may be No. 417; both movements apparently lost

401. *Wedding March No. 2 in E-flat;* organ; written by 16 January 1890 program; may be different title for another work; if not another work, apparently lost

402. *Romanze;* Mason and Hamlin Liszt Organ and piano; SM/1890; timing 1:45; arranged by Huss from movement II of No. 337

403. *Reverie;* Mason and Hamlin Liszt Organ and piano; may be another title for No. 404; if separate work, apparently lost; written by 23 January 1891 program

404. *Idyll Pastorale;* Mason and Hamlin Liszt Organ; SM/1891; may be another title for No. 403; apparently lost

405. *Alla Marcia;* organ; MI/1896; timing 2:45; in *Vox Organi,* Vol. II (edited by Dudley Buck); subtitled "Impromptu"; manuscript at Boston Public Library; reprinted in the *American Organist* by TP (1918)

406. *Offertoire Religieuse;* organ; MI/1896; timing 2:45; in *Vox Organi,* Vol. III (edited by Dudley Buck); dedicated to Dr. Gerrit Smith; manuscript at Boston Public Library

407. *Sakuntalá or the Fatal Ring;* incidental music for a play arranged by Huss from Goldmark's Overture to *Sakuntalá* and music from Wagner's *Tristan und Isolde, Parsifal, Lohengrin,* and *Das Rheingold;* written by 18 December 1899 program; apparently lost

408. *Glory to God in the Highest;* voice(s) (?) and piano; holographs reproduced on card stock and used as a Christmas or Christmas/New Year's greeting; various settings from 1915–1950 with copies in NYp-HC; origi-

nals of various Christmas greetings (1899 [?], 1899 [sent to (among others) M/M E. P. Mason, Miss E. F. Bauer; Mrs. _____ Finck], 1901 [five settings; sent to (among others) Miss M. Bauer, M/M E. P. Mason, M/M Finck, Miss E. F. Bauer, and F. Van der Stucken], 1903 [sent to (among others) Miss E. F. Bauer and Marion Bauer], 1915, 1918, 1920, 1921, 1922, 1923, 1924 [two settings], 1925, 1926 [?; to Mr. Epstean (?)], 1928, 1929, 1930, 1931, 1932, 1933 [for Marion Sexton], 1935, 1936 [two settings], 1938, 1941, 1942, 1943 [two settings], 1944 [two settings], 1945 [3], 1948, 1950, 1951, 1952, over 30 without year given [sent to (among others) Miss Wrigley, Miss M. Bauer [?], and Mr. _____ D. Mason]) in NYp-HMC; cf. Nos. 294, 409, and 410

409. *May the New Year;* voice(s) (?) and piano; holograph reproduced on card stock and used as a New Year's greeting; various settings from 1915–1950 with copies in NYp-HC; originals of various New Year's greetings (1903 [five settings; sent to H. E. Krehbiel, G. Schirmer, Miss P. Jennings, and others], 1906 [four settings; sent to Dr. William Mason, Nellie Orr, G. Schirmer, M/M A. Whiting, A. Foote, and others], 1907 [five settings; sent to M/M Herman Behr, W. Safonoff, Arthur Foote, Miss N. E. Orr, Gustav Schirmer, M/M E. R. Kroeger, Marion Bauer, M/M A. Whiting, Maud Powell, R. Pugno, M/M Denny Brereton, and others], 1909 [four settings; sent to E. F. Bauer, Maud Powell, Whiting, R. Schirmer, Gabrilowitsch, N. Orr, Pugno, R. Gilder, R. Ganz, Safonoff, Marion Bauer, and others], 1910 [four settings; sent to Schumann-Heink, Pauline Jennings, Whiting, A. Foote, R. Pugno, Maud Powell, H. E. Krehbiel, Rebecca Crawford, R. Schirmer, M. Bauer, Lillian Littlehales, A. Foote, Isaye (*sic*), and others], 1911, 1912 [four settings; sent to Rebecca Crawford, Maud Powell, Marion Bauer, E. F. Bauer, Joseffy, H. Irion, Rudolph Schirmer, Efrem Zimbalist, Krehbiel, Theo. Speiring, D. Mason, M/M Arthur Whiting, Alma Gluck, Boris Hambourg, Pauline Jennings, Harold Bauer, R. Ganz, Kneisel, and others, and one setting "To my darling Hildegard from your own

Henry Jan 1st 1912"], 1925 [for Mr. Epstean (?)], 1929 [for Mr. Epstein], 1944) in NYp-HMC; cf. Nos. 294, 408, and 410

410. [Christmas greetings]; voice(s) (?) and piano; holograph reproduced on card stock and used as greeting to Carl Tollefsen; 11 settings dated December 1914, December 1915, Xmas 1918, December 1921, 1926, and 6 undated in Tollefsen Collection, Southern Illinois University at Edwardsville; cf. Nos. 294, 408, and 409

411. *Carnival Prelude;* piano duo; written by 11 September 1908 program; may be from No. 400; apparently lost

412. *Moment Musical;* mentioned in publication agreement of 27 July 1914 with GS in NYp-HC but no performing medium specified; may be alternative title for another work; if not alternative title, apparently lost

413. *Wedding March;* organ; in D Major; holograph score (dated 19 April 1906) in NYp-HMC

414. *Wedding March;* organ; in D Major; "for Dorothy"; holograph score (dated 9 December 1921) in NYp-HMC; not same as No. 423

415. *Wedding March;* organ; dedications read "To Katherine Morris" and "For my dear pupil Katherine Morris"; two holograph scores (one dated December 1923 and the other 22 December 1923) in NYp-HMC

416. *The Cow Is in the Garden;* written on back of 21 July 1923 letter from Helen H. Fetter to Huss in NYp-HC; melody and text only, no harmony

417. *Minuet Rococo;* two pianos; written by 17 May 1934 program; may be from No. 400; apparently lost

418. *Festival March;* piano, four hands; written by 18 March 1938 program; "For the Sixtieth Anniversary of the Master's School"; apparently lost

419. [Easter greetings]; two originals of Easter greetings (dated 1940 ["To dear Marion Sexton"], 1942 ["To my Hildegard"], 1946) in NYp-HMC

420. [Prelude?]; organ; written by 21 June 1953 performance (unnamed work used as prelude for church service; may be a different title for another work); if not another work, apparently lost

UNDATABLE MISCELLANEOUS WORKS
(IN ALPHABETICAL ORDER)

421. *Glimmering Star;* known only from transcription by Neal Ramsay (*Seven Solos for Alto Saxophone and Piano,* SH/ 1978); timing 1:30; Ramsay is unable to recall his source for the original

422. *Nocturne;* piano and organ; known from No. 367; if not alternative title for another work, apparently lost

423. *Wedding March;* organ; in D Major; "for Dorothy"; holograph score in NYp-HMC; not same as No. 414

NOTES

I. The Student Years

1. This is an appropriate moment to discuss the question of pronunciation. In most of my dealings with people who know of Huss, the name seems to be said as if to rhyme with "fuss." However, Valeska Becker Appleberry recalls that her father Gustave (a good friend of Huss) always pronounced it as if to rhyme with "noose." Huss's great-grand-nephew Andrew Schuman says family members "have always pronounced it" as if to rhyme with Puss (in Boots) or Bonus. Fae Elaine Scott, in her genealogical study of a different group of Hus descendants in America (*The Christian Huss Family Tree*), writes that the name is pronounced with a phonetic long double *o* in Bohemian and that the name means "goose."

2. Andrew Schuman, Huss's great-grand-nephew, says, "None of my uncles/aunts/cousins have any interest in HHH's music—Winthrop Parkhurst was the only one who did, I think." This disinclination of Huss's family to promote him, in contrast to the tendency among other relatives of late musicians, may provide one small clue to Huss's failure to retain some presence in the musical world.

II. The Young Professional

1. Huss's friendship with Foote may date from this convention. Foote's *Autobiography* (1946) includes this comment: "I look back with gratitude to the great number of good friends I have fortunately had among musicians, such as Gabrilowitsch, . . . Emil Liebling, Ernest R. Kroeger, Huss, Arthur Whiting, Converse, Rivé-King, Adele aus der Ohe, Madame Zeisler, . . . Maud Powell."

2. This review is known from its quotation by Charles Darcourt in the *American Musician,* 3 August 1889, which was in turn quoted by Sumner Salter in the *Musical Quarterly,* January 1932.

3. Tchaikovsky recorded in his diary his memory of the rehearsal, which apparently also included one of his quartets: "The Quartet was played rather poorly and the Trio even worse, for the pianist (Mr. Huss, modest and cowardly) is quite inferior and can't even count." The diary is excerpted by Elkhonon Yoffe in *Tchaikovsky in America: The Composer's Visit in 1891.*

III. Relations with Other Musicians

1. Huss later wrote in a notebook, "To my keen regret no student had prepared a Paderewski composition."

2. A curious aspect of this recital is that one of the two extant programs has written upon it a detailed account (in an unknown hand) of the finances of such an enterprise in 1898. The performers spent a total of $32.25 on the printing of circulars (2000), tickets (400), programs (400), and placards (36), and on envelopes (500 plain and 1375 prestamped) and two-cent stamps (100). Other expenses included $1.50 for the cab used in distributing the placards, $50 for rental of the hall, and a $2 fee "for selling tickets at the door." Accompanist Waller's services cost $15 plus $2.50 for his cab fare. A total of $268 was received from the sale of tickets (the price per ticket is not known), leaving a net gain of $147 (about $2,598 in May 1994 dollars). Clearly Huss was sufficiently talented to be able to command respectable sums for his work as a performer.

3. I have assumed that Mary Mason is a part of this Mason family because she wrote from Boston and had musical interests. I have been unable to learn her exact connection, if any, to the family.

4. Whiting also included the following cryptic New Year's greeting for those living at the street number of the Huss residence: to "all at No 318 = E + a, s = T + 15 = OT − H + S + T."

5. The Mason and Hamlin Liszt Orchestral Cabinet Organ, a very

large reed organ, was first marketed in 1876. Liszt received at least two of the instruments for his own use in gratitude for his endorsement, and he arranged for the purchase of the instrument by others on occasion. Mason and Hamlin commissioned or encouraged a number of works for their various Cabinet Organs. Indeed, this 1891 program states that others writing or having written works for the instrument included Foote, Bruno Oscar Klein, Kroeger, Dulcken, Nevin, Weld, Dubois, and Gigout.

IV. The Mature Years

1. The presence of names like Zimbalist and Goodson—that is, of established artists—in lists of Huss students is somewhat puzzling since there appears to be no reason for these persons to have studied with Huss. For example, Zimbalist arrived in the United States as a fully formed musician, so it seems unlikely that he would have "studied" with anyone. On the other hand, it also seems unlikely that this claim would have been made repeatedly—all during Zimbalist's lifetime—without some basis. Moreover, Huss evidently was scrupulously accurate in any number of other situations, so the fabrication of such a claim would be considerably out of character. On the other hand, a meeting is not unlikely since Zimbalist presented Huss's *Berceuse Slave* in a recital at Carnegie Hall on 21 October 1916. Perhaps Huss gave him (and the others) short-term instruction in some specific topic (e.g., orchestration, the editing of some work, or the performance of Huss's own pieces). Confirmation of these claims has not been forthcoming.
2. Pugno wrote on 24 July 1910 to invite the couple to lunch. About this time, the Husses were supposed to play a recital in Paris, according to the *Musical Courier* of 20 July; whether this happened is not known.
3. A secretary for Kaiser Wilhelm II replied to Huss on 15 August 1910: "Auf das an Seine Majestät den Kaiser und König gerichtete Immediatgesuch von 8. d. Mts. habe ich Ihnen zu erwidern, dass sich während des Aufenthalts Ihrer Kaiserlichen

Majestäten in Wilhelmshöle keine Gelegenheit zur Vor-
führung amerikanischer Kompositionen finden wird" [On the
petition of the eighth of the month submitted to His Majesty
the Emperor and King, I have to report to you that during the
stay of Their Imperial Majesties in Wilhelmshöle no opportunity for performances of American compositions will be
found].

4. Reference to Huss and NFMC prizes appeared much later as
   well. The first known Huss performance in 1940 was the
   presentation of two works on a program of "prize-winning
   compositions sponsored by the National Federation of Music
   Clubs." This concert was offered to the National Association of
   American Composers and Conductors on 11 February at the
   Hotel des Artistes in New York City, and on this occasion Huss
   presented a *Poem for Piano,* and Emily Rossevelt sang his *Faery
   Song* (probably *Shed No Tear*). Though not yet documented,
   apparently both works had won prizes given by the NFMC; any
   prize won by the piano work is not known, but *Shed No Tear*
   would later win first prize in the 1948 contest sponsored by its
   publisher, the Composer's Press.

V. The Last Years and Beyond

1. The Huss iconography file at the New York Public Library
   contains several photographs of Huss and students seated about
   the lawn at Lake George, the students in casual clothing and
   Huss dressed as suggested in this letter.
2. On 4 April 1944 Carl Dies of the Bohemians wrote to extend
   an invitation to dinner with the club from the Board of
   Directors, saying, "We naturally want you to be present—it
   would not be [a] representative gathering of the Bohemians
   were you not there."

VI. Introduction to the Musical Works

1. It is possible to calculate a portion of Huss's income from
   royalties on publications, but gaps in the records make such a

calculation interesting rather than useful. For some of the works, the reader will be advised of information taken from the royalty reports by which publishers informed Huss as to the number of copies sold of works in their charge and the amount of royalty payment due based on some percentage of the price. Huss's usual royalty rate was 10 percent of the cover price, based on the extant letters of agreement and contracts.

CATALOG OF PUBLISHED WRITINGS

This bibliography contains titles of Huss's various published writings. Manuscript drafts of some of these items and of sundry unpublished writings may be found in NYp-HC.

"The Anarchic Element in Some Ultra-Modern Futurist Music," *Art World* II/2 (May 1917), 139–141.

"Artistic Piano Touch and How to Achieve It," *Etude* XXXII/12 (December 1914), 869.

"Beauty and the Child," *A.M.T.L. Bulletin* IV/1 (November 1950), 1, 4. Written with Cecile Hindman.

"Death Knell Sounded to Mechanical Routine in Piano Pedagogy," *Musical Courier* LXXVII/8 (22 August 1918), 29.

"Deeds Not Words!" *Etude* XXXIII/9 (September 1915), 669.

"Distinctiveness of American Music," *Music Trade Review* XXXIX/21 (19 November 1904), 4.

"Huss Points Out Piano Pitfalls Before New York State Teachers," *Musical America* XXIV/10 (8 July 1916), 17.

"Indispensable Aids to Efficient Piano Practice," *Musical Review* IV/2 (March 1935), 7.

"The Indispensable but Misunderstood Art of Reviewing," *Etude* XL/4 (April 1922), 240.

"Interesting Studies in Piano Touch," *Etude* XXXII/11 (November 1914), 787.

"International Copyright," *Musical Courier* XLI/9 (29 February 1888), 163.

"A Loyal Republican," *New York Herald Tribune,* 14 August 1952, 16.

"The Magical and Misunderstood Art of Reviewing," *Etude* LV/1 (January 1937), 11, 60.

"The Musical and Cultural Education of the Modern Pianist," *Etude* XXXV/1 (January 1917), 11.

"The New Era in Piano-Study," *Papers and Proceedings of the Music Teachers' National Association at Its Thirty-Sixth Annual Meeting.* Hartford: By the Association, 1915, 101–108.

"Pianistic Development: Intellectual, Emotional and Technical," *Musical Leader* XXXII/1 (6 July 1916), 7–8.

"Poison Ivy a Menace," *New York Times,* 17 July 1930, 20.

"The Problem of the Piano Pupil with Only One Hour's Daily Practice," *Papers and Proceedings of the Music Teachers' National Association at Its Thirty-Second Annual Meeting.* Hartford: By the Association, 1911, 132–135.

"Rheinberger as a Teacher," *Musical Courier* XVII/1 (4 July 1888), 18.

"What Henry Holden Huss Would Do About Prohibition," *Musical America* XXX/7 (14 June 1919), 22.

"What to Consider in Judging Music Contests," *Musical Observer* XXIV/5 (May 1925), 21, 30.

SELECTED BIBLIOGRAPHY

This bibliography contains complete titles of sources referred to in the text as well as representative other items drawn from a large body of Huss and Huss-related sources.

Books and Monographs

Aldrich, Richard. *Concert Life in New York, 1902–1923,* edited by Harold Johnson. Freeport, NY: Books for Libraries Press, 1971. (Originally published in 1941.)

—————. "Huss, Henry Holden," in *Grove's Dictionary of Music and Musicians,* 3rd edition, edited by H. C. Colles. New York: Macmillan, 1927, and its *American Supplement,* edited by Waldo Selden Pratt (1952). Also, the 5th edition, edited by Eric Blom (1954); *The New Grove Dictionary of Music and Musicians,* edited by Stanley Sadie (1980); and *The New Grove Dictionary of American Music,* edited by H. Wiley Hitchcock and Stanley Sadie (1986).

American Composers: A Record of Works Written Between 1912 and 1932, 2nd edition, edited by Claire Reis. New York: United States Section of the International Society for Contemporary Music, 1932.

Baker, Theodore. *A Biographical Dictionary of Musicians.* New York: Schirmer, 1900, and its 2nd (1905) through 7th editions (1984) and the various *American Supplements.*

Brower, Harriette Moore. *Piano Mastery,* second series. New York: Stokes, 1917.

Choral Music in Print, 2 vols., Thomas Nardone et al. Philadelphia: Musicdata, 1974.

Claghorn, Charles. "Huss, Henry Holden," in *Biographical Dictionary of American Music.* West Nyack, NY: Parker, 1973.

Elson, Louis C. *The History of American Music.* New York: Macmillan, 1925. (Revised from 1904 edition.)

Emery, Frederic B. *The Violin Concerto,* 2 vols. New York: Da Capo, 1969. (Reprint of 1928 edition.)

Famous Composers and Their Works, edited by John Knowles Paine, Theodore Thomas, and Karl Klauser. Boston: Millet, 1891.

Farwell, Arthur. *Songs and Music of Today.* Boston: Birchard, 1902.

Foote, Arthur. *An Autobiography.* New York: Da Capo, 1979. (Reprint of 1946 edition.)

"Giehrl, Joseph," in *Kurzgefasstes Tonkünstler-Lexikon,* 15th edition, edited by Wilhelm Altmann (Wilhelmshaven: Heinrichshofen, 1971).

Gillespie, John, and Anna Gillespie. *A Bibliography of Nineteenth-Century American Piano Music.* Westport, CT: Greenwood, 1984.

Half Hours with the Best Composers, edited by Karl Klauser. Boston: Millet, 1894.

Hess, Willy. *Verzeichnis der nicht in der Gesamtausgabe veröffentlichten Werke Ludwig van Beethovens.* Wiesbaden: Breitkopf und Härtel, 1957.

Hubbard, William L. *History of American Music,* vol. 8 of *The American History and Encyclopedia of Music,* edited by William L. Hubbard. Toledo: Irving Square, 1976. (Originally published in 1908.)

Hughes, Rupert. "Huss, Henry Holden," in *The Biographical Dictionary of Musicians,* revised and edited by Deems Taylor. New York: Blue Ribbon Books, 1940.

———. "Huss, Henry Holden," in *Music Lovers' Encyclopedia,* revised and edited by Deems Taylor and Russell Kerr. Garden City, NY: Garden City, 1950. (Originally published in 1903.)

Hughes, Rupert, and Arthur Elson. *American Composers.* Boston: Page, 1914.

A Hundred Years of Music in America, edited by W. S. B. Matthews. Chicago: Howe, 1889.

Huss, Henry Holden. "A Few Suggestions," in *Official Report of the Proceedings of the Twentieth Annual Convention of the New York State Music Teachers' Association.* By the Association, 1909, 58–60.

"Huss, Henry Holden," in *American Biographies.* Washington, DC: The Editorial Press Bureau, 1954, IV, 192–196.

"Huss, Henry Holden," in *Enciclopedia della Musica,* 4 vols., edited by Claudio Sartori. Milan: Ricordi, 1964.

"Huss, Henry Holden," in *Encyclopedie van de Muziek,* 2 vols., edited by L. M. G. Arntzenius et al. Amsterdam: Elsevier, 1956.

"Huss, Henry Holden," in *The Encyclopedia of American Music,* edited by Edward Jablonski. Garden City, NY: Doubleday, 1981.

"Huss, Henry Holden," in *Frank-Altmann Kurzgefasstes Tonkünstler-Lexikon,* 3 vols., 15th edition, edited by Helmut Rösner et al. Wilhelmshaven: Heinrichshofen, 1974. Huss's name appears in Bund 1 (reprint of 1936 edition) and Bund 1 of Part 2 (supplemental material since 1937).

"Huss, Henry Holden," in the *International Who Is Who in Music,* 5th edition, edited by J. Mize. Chicago: Sterling, 1951.

"Huss, Henry Holden," in *La Musica,* 4 vols., edited by Guido M. Gatti. Turin: Unione Tipographico-Editrice, 1968.

"Huss, Henry Holden," in *The National Cyclopedia of American Biography,* no editor given. New York: White, 1900. Also, 1924 edition, edited by Ainsworth R. Spofford et al.

"Huss, Henry Holden," in *Who's Who in America,* edited by John W. Leonard. Chicago: Marquis, 1899. Also in 2nd (1901) through 20th (1940) editions.

"Huss, Henry Holden," in *Who Was Who in America,* no editor given. Chicago: Marquis, 1960 (ongoing series).

The International Cyclopedia of Music and Musicians, 9th edition, edited by

Robert Sabin. New York: Dodd, Mead, 1964. Also, the 5th edition, edited by Nicolas Slonimsky (1952).

Kinkeldey, Otto. "Huss, Henry Holden," in *A Dictionary of Modern Music and Musicians,* edited by Hugh Allen et al. New York: Dutton, 1924.

Krehbiel, Henry E. *Afro-American Folksongs: A Study in Racial and National Music,* 4th edition. Portland, ME: Longwood, 1976. (Originally published in 1914.)

Mason, Daniel Gregory. *Music in My Time.* Freeport, NY: Books for Libraries Press, 1970. (Originally published in 1938.)

———. *Tune In, America.* Freeport, NY: Books for Libraries Press, 1969. (Originally published in 1931.)

Modern Music and Musicians, 7 vols., edited by Louis C. Elson. New York: University Society, 1918.

"Music in America," edited by Daniel Gregory Mason, vol. 4 of *The Art of Music,* edited by Arthur Farwell and W. Dermot Darby. New York: The National Society of Music, 1915.

Parkhurst, Winthrop, and L. J. de Bekker. "Huss (Henry Holden)," in *The Encyclopedia of Music and Musicians.* New York: Crown, 1937.

Perkins, Henry Southwick. *A History of the Music Teachers' National Association.* By the Association, 1893.

Pratt, Waldo Selden. "Huss, Henry Holden," in *The New Encyclopedia of Music and Musicians.* New York: Macmillan, 1924.

Riemann, Hugo. *Musik-Lexikon,* 5th edition. Leipzig: Max Hesse, 1900. Also, *Hugo Riemanns Musik Lexikon,* 2 vols., 11th edition, edited by Alfred Einstein (1929), and *Riemann Musik Lexikon,* 5 vols., 12th edition, edited by Wilibald Gurlitt. Mainz: Schotts Söhne, 1959.

Ritter, Frederic. *Music in America,* new edition. New York: Charles Scribner's Sons, 1890.

Scott, Fae Elaine. *The Christian Huss Family Tree.* Angola, IN: For the author, 1972.

Shepherd, Arthur. "Huss, Henry Holden," in Walter W. Cobbett *Cyclopedic Survey of Chamber Music,* 2nd edition, 3 vols., edited by Colin Mason. London: Oxford, 1963, I, 585.

Smith, Thayer Adams, and Dorothy May Parkhurst Smith. *The Smith-Parkhurst Story.* Los Angeles: Transamerican Press, 1967.

Spaeth, Sigmund. *A Guide to Great Orchestral Music.* New York: Random House, 1943.

Upton, William Treat. *Art-Song in America.* Boston: Ditson, 1930.

Yoffe, Elkhonon. *Tchaikovsky in America: The Composer's Visit in 1891,* translated by Lidya Yoffe. New York: Oxford University Press, 1986.

Author's Personal Correspondence and Interviews

Baker, Jo Ann. Telephone interview on 19 September 1986.

Beswick, Mrs. Richard. Letter of 18 September 1986.

Buckell, Betty. Letter of 25 October 1986.

Henderson, Charles N. [American Guild of Organists]. Letter of 11 June 1986.

Meachem, Margaret M. Letters of 21 March and 3 April 1987. Also, a letter from her to Paul Traver of 3 March 1986, given to me by him.

Schuman, Andrew [Great-grand-nephew of Huss]. Letters of 30 April, 15 May, 21 June, 5 October, and 22 October 1985; 11 May, 23 May, 5 August, and 13 August 1986; 30 September, 10 October, 28 November, and 19 December 1987; and 4 January 1988.

Truesdale, Lillian. Letter of 19 September 1986.

Woodbury, Mary [Mrs. Alfred Sylvan]. Telephone interview of 24 October 1986 and letter of 3 November 1986.

Periodicals

A.M.T.L. BULLETIN

"In Memoriam," VII/1 (November 1953), 2.

AGE-HERALD {BIRMINGHAM, AL}

Dalrymple, Dolly. "Noted Pianist and Composer Mr. Henry Holden Huss Pays Flying Visit to Birmingham," 28 January 1911, 7.

AMERICAN ART JOURNAL

"First Night with American Composers," XLVIII/5 (19 November 1887), 68–69.

AMERICAN MUSICIAN

Gori, Americo. "Concert of the Rubinstein Club," [April 1889] (otherwise unidentified item in NYp-HCF).

Kelley, Edgar S. "Henry Holden Huss' Concerto," [April 1889] (otherwise unidentified item in NYp-HCF).

AMERICAN ORGANIST

"Obituary Notices," XXXVI/10 (October 1953), 350.

BILLBOARD

"Huss, Henry H.," in "The Final Curtain," LXV/40 (3 October 1953), 54.

BOSTON DAILY ADVERTISER

Elson, Louis C. "The Symphony," 31 December 1894, 4.

BOSTON EVENING TRANSCRIPT

R.R.G. "Music and Drama," 16 November 1903, 13.

"Theatres and Concerts," 31 December 1894, 6.

BOSTON GLOBE

"Music and Musicians," 30 December 1894, 23.

BROOKLYN EAGLE

Affelder, Paul. "Chamber Society Debut; Stokowski Conducts," 27 October
    1952, 6.

"Huss Concert at Academy," 14 February 1913, 7.

"Mr. and Mrs. Huss' Recital," 23 April 1907, 7.

CINCINNATI ENQUIRER

"Discussion," 23 June 1899, 7.

CINCINNATI VOLKSFREUND

"M.T.N.A.," 23 June 1899, 2.

CONCERT-GOER

"Henry Holden Huss and David Bispham," in "Major Events," old No. 234/new No. 16 (1 June 1898), 1.

"Kneisel Quartet Concert," old 377/new 158 (16 November 1901), 3.

DETROIT FREE PRESS

Tarney, Charlotte M. "Composer-Pianist Charms Audience," 12 April 1920, 9.

DETROIT JOURNAL

Holmes, Ralph F. "Orchestra Plays All American Program, Henry Huss, Soloist," 12 April 1920 (otherwise unidentified item in NYp-HCF).

DETROIT NEWS

Cline, Leonard Lanson. "Detroit Orchestra in All-American Program," 12 April 1920, 8.

EMPIRE RECORD

"Henry Holden Huss—Composer," 4 (labeled "Feb '34" but otherwise unidentified item in NYp-HCF).

ENQUIRER [CINCINNATI]

"Heard at Symphony Concert," 23 June 1899, 7.

ETUDE

Huneker, James. "M.T.N.A.," V/8 (August 1887), 106.

"If I Had to Begin All Over Again," XXXIV/12 (December 1916), 847–848.

EVENING MAIL [N.Y.C.]

Bauer, Emilie Frances. "Alwin Schroeder in Huss Sonata," [1 February 1910] (otherwise unidentified article in NYp-HCF).

————. "Toscanini in Role of Symphony Conductor," 14 April 1913 (otherwise unidentified item in NYp-HCF).

————. "Wife and Husband Win Applause at Recital," 11 December 1913 (otherwise unidentified item in NYp-HCF).

EVENING POST [N.Y.C.]

"Another American Concert," in "Music and Drama," 3 April 1906, 7.

"Music and Drama," 24 December 1900, 7.

"Ysaÿe's Last Recital," 14 April 1913, 9.

EVENING STAR [WASHINGTON, DC]

De Sayn, Elena. "Garzia Wins Ovation with Symphony," 16 March 1942, B-18.

"The Social World," 23 January 1904, I, 5.

HOBBIES

Walsh, Jim. "The Tollefsen Trio," Part III, LXXXIII/9 (November 1978), 35–36, 58.

————. "The Tollefsen Trio," Part IV, LXXXIII/10 (December 1978), 35–36.

INDIANAPOLIS JOURNAL

Matthews, W. S. B. "America's Music Makers," 6 July 1887, 4–5.

INDIANAPOLIS NEWS

Staff, Charles. "Gates Meant for Concerto by Huss," 13 March 1972, 10.

INDIANAPOLIS SENTINEL

"Feasting upon Music," 6 July 1887, 4–5.

LEDGER [PHILADELPHIA]

"The Kosman Quartette," 12 February 1903.

"Manuscript Music Society/New Work by Huss Performed by Hahn Quartet," 19 November 1908, 4.

MENTOR

Henderson, W. J. "American Composers," V/24 (1 February 1918), *Department of Music,* 1–11.

MESSENGER

"Senate and Council, 1903," IV/5 (June 1903), 226.

MUNSEY'S MAGAZINE

Hughes, Rupert. "American Composers," XI/2 (May 1894), 157–165.

MUSIC

"Editorial Bric-a-brac," XX/6 (November 1901), 422–429.

"Henry Holden Huss: Compositions," in "Reviews and Notices," XXI/2 (January 1902), 181–182.

MUSIC TRADE REVIEW

"An American Pianist and Composer," XXXII/1 (5 January 1901), 1.

MUSICAL ADVANCE

"Huss Joint Recital," I/16 (January 1914), 16–17.

MUSICAL AMERICA

"Artistic Concert by the Huss Family," XIV/21 (30 September 1911), 31.

"Concert Tour in South," XIII/16 (25 February 1911), 19.

E.C.S. "Coveted Prize for Henry Holden Huss," XI/12 (29 January 1910), 2.

F.L.C.B. "Mr. and Mrs. Huss Score with St. Paul Orchestra," XVII/6 (14 December 1912), 31.

"First Program at New Music School," XI/2 (20 November 1909), 4.

H.F.P. "American Work on Last Ysaÿe Program," XVII/24 (19 April 1913), 34.

————. "Mr. and Mrs. Huss Prove Versatility," XXV/25 (21 April 1917), 19.

"Hobbies and Antipathies of Henry Holden Huss," XXIV/11 (15 July 1916), 29.

"The Huss Cello Sonata," XIII/18 (11 March 1911), 9.

"Huss Sonata Has Another Hearing," XI/20 (26 March 1910), 21.

"Improvises on 'Bispham,' " XXV/23 (7 April 1917), 49.

Jennings, Pauline. "Henry Holden Huss' Contribution to American Song Literature," XXVI/20 (15 September 1917), 24.

K[ramer], A. W[alter]. "Elimination of 'Dry Studies' as an Efficacious Teaching Method," XVIII/3 (24 May 1913), 13.

————. "An Evening of Huss Compositions," XVII/13 (1 February 1913), 25.

————. "Federation of Musical Clubs Makes Eventful Pilgrimage to Shrine of MacDowell for Its 11th Biennial," XXX/11 (12 July 1919), 1, 3–5.

————. "Henry Holden Huss and Mrs. Huss, April 6," in "Week's Round of Concerts and Recitals in New York," XXXV/25 (15 April 1922), 45.

————. "Henry Holden Huss's Piano Concerto," XIV/11 (22 July 1911), 27.

————. "Henry Krehbiel's New Book on 'Afro-American Folk Songs,' " XIX/18 (7 March 1914), 40.

————. "Huss Concert for War Relief Funds," XXIV/3 (20 May 1916), 36.

————. "Is the Sonata Form Obsolete?" XVI/4 (1 June 1912), 9.

————. "New Music—Vocal and Instrumental," XVI/5 (8 June 1912), 28.

————. "New Music—Vocal and Instrumental," XXVII/3 (17 November 1917), 40.

————. "Nikisch Weeps at Farewell Banquet," XVI/1 (11 May 1912), 1, 3.

"Mr. and Mrs. Huss in Successful Recitals," XI/7 (25 December 1909), 34.

"New Music—Vocal and Instrumental," XIV/13 (5 August 1911), 20.

"New Music—Vocal and Instrumental," XXV/19 (10 March 1917), 36.

"New Music—Vocal and Instrumental," XXV/22 (31 March 1917), 36.

"New Works By Huss," XIV/14 (12 August 1911), 17.

"Opens Brooklyn Season," XX/25 (24 October 1914), 25.

P.J. "Notable Playing of Huss Pupils," XXVI/7 (16 June 1917), 31.

"Personalities," XXVIII/4 (25 May 1918), 26.

R.M.K. "Henry Holden Huss Plays Own Tone-Poem," XXXV/7 (10 December 1921), 53.

Stanley, May. "Artist Couples Uphold Feminist Belief," XXXIV/4 (27 May 1916), 3.

MUSICAL COURIER

"The American Composers' Concert," XX/4 (2 April 1890), 304.

"Another Engagement for Mr. and Mrs. Henry Holden Huss," LXXII/23 (8 June 1916), 31.

Arens, F[ranz] X[avier]. "The American Composer Abroad," XXII/19 (13 May 1891), 489.

"Composers in New York," XX/15 (9 April 1890), 325.

"Concert by Huss Pupils," LXII/19 (10 May 1911), 34.

"Henry Holden Huss Compositions," LXXX/14 (1 April 1920), 35.

"Henry Holden Huss Publishes His Well Known Shakespeare Soliloquy," XCVIII/7 (14 February 1924), 14.

"Henry Holden Huss to Appear with the Seidl Society," XXXV/24 (15 December 1897), 35.

"Huss' Activities," LXIX/12 (23 September 1914), 10.

"The Huss Concert," XVIII/16 (17 April 1889), 305.

"Huss Concert in London," LXI/14 (5 October 1910), 13.

"Huss Evening of Music," LXVI/20 (14 May 1913), 13.

"Huss-Hartmann Matinee," LXXVI/9 (28 February 1918), 16.

"Huss-Hoffmann Recital," XLIX/24 (14 December 1904), 15.

"Huss Honored on 90th Birthday," CXLVI/1 (July 1952), 8.

"Huss Musicale at Burritt Studios," LXIV/16 (17 April 1912), 47.

"Huss Musicale at Steinway Hall," XC/14 (2 April 1925), 20.

"Huss November Concert Tour," LXV/24 (11 December 1912), 19.

"Huss, 'One of the Best of American Composers,'" LXXVI/12 (21 March 1918), 40.

"Huss Recital in Newburgh a Great Success," LXXII/10 (9 March 1916), 57.

"Huss Tour Successful in South and West," LXIII/23 (6 December 1911), 9.

"The Last Philharmonic Concert," XXXVI/14 (6 April 1898), 36.

"London," LXI/3 (20 July 1910), 12.

[Maas, Louis], "Boston Correspondence," XIII/19 (10 November 1886), 294.

"Mr. and Mrs. Henry Holden Huss Present Impressive Program at Brooklyn Recital," LXXII/16 (20 April 1916), 24.

"Mr. and Mrs. Huss Applauded in Atlantic City Recitals," LXXVII/11 (12 September 1918), 47.

"Mr. and Mrs. Huss Give Successful Recital," LXXVIII/16 (17 April 1919), 36.

"New York State Music Teachers' Association," XLV/2 (9 July 1902), 20–26.

"Raconteur," XXVIII/25 (20 June 1894), 8–9.

Untitled item, XXIII/2 (8 July 1891), 29.

"Ysaÿe Plays Huss Sonata," LXVI/18 (30 April 1913), 32.

MUSICAL LEADER

"American Guild of Organists," 4 (labeled "Dec 19——01" but otherwise unidentified in NYp-HCF).

Bauer, Emilie Frances. "A Tireless Fight for the American Composer," in "Music in New York," XX/18 (3 November 1910), 12.

"Mr. and Mrs. Paderewksi Patrons of the Huss Artist Pupils' Charity Concert," XXXI/17 (27 April 1916), 526.

"New Holden Huss 'Nocturne,' " XXVII/13 (26 March 1914), 443.

"Now for the American Pianist-Composer," XXXVII/15 (10 April 1919), 369.

"Paderewski Applauds Huss Pupils," XXXIII/24 (14 June 1917), 825.

"Ruth Kemper's Sonata Recital," L/21 (19 November 1925), 455.

MUSICAL LEADER AND CONCERT GOER

Bauer, Emilie Frances. "The American and His Place in Music," VI/2 (9 July 1903), 9.

―――. "American in Today's Music," VI/4 (23 July 1903), 14–15.

―――. "The Boston Symphony Orchestra in Brooklyn," in "Music in New York," VI/25 (17 December 1903), 3.

―――. "The Huss Concerto in Boston," in "Music in New York," VI/21 (19 November 1903), 3.

―――. "The Huss-MacDowell Fund Concert," XIII/20 (16 May 1907), 6–7.

―――. "The Misses Crawford Picture Recitals," in "Music in New York," VI/24 (10 December 1903), 4.

―――. "Music in New York," XI/15 (12 April 1906), 3.

―――. "Some New Works by Huss," in "Music in New York," VII/20 (19 May 1904), 4.

―――. "What Mr. Finck Says of Mr. Huss," in "Music in New York," VII/20 (19 May 1904), 4.

French, Florence. "Illinois Music Teachers' Association," V/26 (25 June 1903), 8, 9, 12.

"Henry Holden Huss," VII/3 (21 January 1904), 5.

"Henry Holden Huss' Recital," in "Music Teachers National Association," VI/2 (9 July 1903), 6–7.

"Huss Concerto in Paris," VIII/25 (22 December 1904), 6.

"MacDowell and the American Composer," VII/8 (25 February 1904), 12.

"Mr. and Mrs. Henry Holden Huss," XVI/19 (5 November 1908), 13.

"Mostly About People," VII/5 (4 February 1904), 4.

Seeligson, Edouard. "Around New York Studios," V/8 (19 February 1903), 7.

"Winona State Music Teachers' Association," IX/24 (15 June 1905), 19–20.

MUSICAL MONITOR

"Henry Holden Huss," VIII/10 (July 1919), 536.

Murray, W. B. "Eleventh Biennial Convention of the National Federation of Musical Clubs," VIII/11 (August 1919), 573–576.

MUSICAL MONITOR AND WORLD

"Huss Manuscripts for the National Library of Congress," III/8 (April 1914), 236–237.

"Two American Artists Offer Joint Program of Unique Value," in "Among American Musical Artists," III/7 (March 1914), 206–207.

MUSICAL OBSERVER

Antrim, Doron K. "Famous Pianists Tell How Success Is Won," XXIII/9 (September 1924), 22–24, 55.

————. "What Are the Requirements of the Music Teaching Profession?" XXIV/3 (March 1925), 17, 25.

"Henry Holden Huss, Optimist," XXII/12 (December 1923), 35.

Kramer, A. Walter. "A Plea for the Preservation of Ideals in Elementary Piano Teaching," XI/1 (September 1914), 9–10.

MUSICAL QUARTERLY

Salter, Sumner. "Early Encouragements to American Composers," XVIII/1 (January 1932), 76–105.

Sonneck, O. G. "The American Composer and the American Music Publisher," IX/1 (January 1923), 122–144.

MUSICIAN

Anderton, Margaret. "How to Study/How to Teach," XXXVII/12 (December 1932), 10–11.

Brower, Harriette. "Pure Technic Versus Piece Technic," XXIX/8 (August 1924), 25–26.

"Chamber Music Dedicates New Steinway Hall," XXX/12 (December 1925), 41.

Hodgson, Leslie. "What to Put on an All-American Piano Program," XXX/6 (June 1925), 13–14.

Jennings, Pauline. "A Modern Romanticist," XXXII/11 (November 1927), 15, 33–34.

Wood, Myron Clemens. "The Cornerstone of Piano Technic!" XLI/7 (August 1936), 123–124.

NEW JERSEY MUSIC

"Native of Newark," II/10 (June 1947), 5–6.

NEW YORK AMERICAN

Bennett, Grena. "Ukranian Music Offered in Carnegie Hall Concert," 1 June 1936, I, 9.

"Mr. and Mrs. Huss in Joint Recital," 11 December 1913, 8.

NEW YORK HERALD

"Hearts Beat to Love and Music," 24 January 1904, 4.

NEW YORK HERALD-TRIBUNE

"Soloists at Town Hall," 12 April 1948, 13.

NEW YORK POST

McElroy, Peter J. "49 Yrs. of Making Beautiful Music Together," 15 June 1952, 6.

NEW YORK TIMES

[Aldrich, Richard]. "Huss Joint Recital," 11 December 1913, 11.

"American Sonata at Ysaÿe Farewell," 14 April 1913, 9.

"Forum Program Given," 23 November 1938, 25.

"Henry H. Huss, 91, Composer, Pianist," 19 September 1953, 15.

"Henry Holden Huss's Music," 18 April 1906, 11.

"Honor Huss and Sowerby," 20 March 1921, VI, 5.

"The Kaltenborn Quartet," 4 January 1899, 6.

"The Kneisel Quartet," 13 November 1901, 9.

"The Manuscript Society," in "Amusements," 26 March 1892, 4.

"Music by Americans," in "Record of Amusements," 16 November 1887, 5.

"The Philharmonic Society," 22 December 1900, 5.

"Steinway Hall," 12 April 1889, 4.

"Three Appear in Recital," 10 November 1925, 23.

NEW YORK TRIBUNE

"Hear Ysaÿe at His Best," 14 April 1913, 7.

K[rehbiel], H[enry] K. "Compositions by Mr. Huss," in "Music," 18 April 1906, 7.

———. "Mr. Huss's New Concerto," 30 December 1894, 7.

———. "Musical Autographs," 27 February 1898, *Illustrated Supplement,* 20.

———. "Native Works Produced," 6 July 1889, 7.

———. "A New Beethoven Song," 6 March 1898, *Illustrated Supplement,* 4–5.

"Mr. Huss's Concert," 11 April 1889, 6.

"Musical Matters," 29 November 1896, II, 7.

"Musical Nation," 16 December 1900, II, 14.

"Musical Notes," 10 November 1901, II, 12.

NEW YORKER ECHO

"Echoklänge aus Kunstkreisen," 25 June 1904, 11.

NEW YORK WORLD-TELEGRAM

L.B. "Huss, Veteran Composer, in Conservative Program," 4 June 1936, 22.

NEWARK DAILY ADVERTISER

"Newarkers at Huss Concert," 26 April 1904, 3.

NOTES

Lowens, Irving et al. "The American Recordings Project/Progress Report of the Committee," XVII/2 (March 1960), 213–220.

OUTLOOK

Mason, Daniel Gregory. "Some American Composers," LXX/11 (15 March 1902), 674–678.

PACIFIC COAST MUSICAL REVIEW

Housman, Rosalie. "Recognition of the American Composer," XXXIX/5 (30 October 1920), 20, 22, 26.

PHILADELPHIA INQUIRER

"Concert of the Kosman Quartet," 12 February 1903, 8.

"The Musical Season," 10 December 1903, 6.

PIANIST AND ORGANIST

Huss, Henry Holden. "A Few Observations on Modern Orchestration," III/5 (May 1897), 119–120.

PITTSBURGH DISPATCH

Cadman, Charles Wakefield. "Huss Prize-Winner in Annual Contest for Setting of Poem," 21 January 1910, 3.

"Enjoyed New Pianist," 11 January 1902, 6.

PITTSBURGH GAZETTE TIMES

"Huss Wins Coveted Male Chorus Prize," 21 January 1910 (otherwise unidentified item in NYp-HCF).

PITTSBURGH POST

G.S. "Orchestra Was Encored," 11 January 1902, 6.

J.M. "Male Chorus Prize Won By New York Musician," 21 January 1910, 6.

PRESS [SHEBOYGAN, WI]

"Musicians of Note, Well Known Here, to Broadcast," 3 April 1926, 12.

RECORD [PHILADELPHIA]

"An American Composers' Concert," 12 February 1903.

REPUBLICAN [GARRETT COUNTY, MD]

"Features of Mt. Choir Festival Are Announced," 13 June 1935, 1.

"Johnstown Choir Takes First Prize at Festival," 27 June 1935, 1, 8.

SAINT PAUL PIONEER-PRESS

"At the Auditorium: Third 'Pop' Concert," 25 November 1912, 4.

SUN {N.Y.C.}

"More American Music/Henry Holden Huss Gives a Concert of Original Compositions," 18 April 1906, 7.

"New Etude Played at Huss Concert," 17 April 1917, 6.

"Third Philharmonic Concert," 22 December 1900 (otherwise unidentified article sent in 2 June 1986 letter from the Masters School).

SUNDAY CALL {NEWARK, NJ}

"Henry Holden Huss, a Newark Musician," 29 August 1909, 9 (otherwise unidentified item in the NYp-HCF)

SUNDAY HERALD {BOSTON}

"The Symphony Concert," 30 December 1894, 3.

TEMPO

Huss, Henry Holden. "A New Era in Piano Study," I/5 (May 1934), 12–13.

THEATRE

Gilman, Lawrence. "Some Vital Figures in American Music," XI/21 (November 1902), 26–28.

THE TIMES {LONDON}

"Steinway Hall," 9 July 1910, 12.

VIOLIN WORLD

"The American Neglect of the Violin," 70 (this page, labeled "10-15-1911," is from a larger article otherwise unidentified in NYp-HCF).

WASHINGTON POST

Brown, Ray C. B. "Garziglia Performs Ably as Substitute for Kindler," 16 March 1942, 7.

"Guests of First Lady," 23 January 1904, 7.

WORLD [N.Y.C.]

"$12,000 Raised by Paderewski for Poland's Relief," 24 October 1915, IV, 1.

INDEX

ABOUT THE AUTHOR

GARY A. GREENE (B.S., University of Indianapolis; M.M., Butler University; Ph.D., University of Maryland) is Assistant Professor of Music at Northeast Louisiana University in Monroe and is the Principal Horn of the Monroe Symphony Orchestra. He has taught in public and private schools in Indiana and Illinois and at Danville (Illinois) Area Community College. Immediately prior to coming to Louisiana, he was the Reference Specialist for the American Symphony Orchestra League, Washington, D.C. Though his primary interest is in American music, Dr. Greene has published and spoken on a number of musical topics. He also serves on the editorial board for the *Horn Call Annual* of the International Horn Society.